Praise for *The Stat*

"In Russia, no author has proved detective fiction's literary worthiness as definitively as Boris Akunin . . . An intelligent and entertaining detective novel that is simultaneously an excursion into Russian history and culture."   —*Los Angeles Review of Books*

"A welcome revival of Russia's premier detective, Erast Fandorin . . . Evocative of our own age of political turmoil, this exploration of how terror worked back in the 1890s stars men and women pushed by conviction and ambition to wage war on the tsarist system or to support it to the death. Readers of Sam Eastland's 'Inspector Pekkala" series set just a few decades later in Russian history will embrace Fandorin as a similarly honorable hero. Let's hope for more US editions of works by an author who is popular worldwide."   —*Library Journal*

"This rousing historical mystery, fluidly translated from the Russian by Bromfield, continues to draw its appeal from the Holmes-like Fandorin and from the author's antic stylistic flourishes."   —*Booklist*

"Akunin's descriptions of characters' appearances and temperaments, as well as the time period, call to mind Conan Doyle's Sherlock Holmes adventures. Narrative sleights of hand and copious red herrings will keep readers guessing until the end."
—*Publishers Weekly*

"Through every twist and turn, both Akunin and his hero maintain an imperturbable decorum that makes this the most ceremonious tale of terrorism and counterterrorism you're ever likely to read."   —*Kirkus Reviews*

THE
STATE
COUNSELLOR

THE
STATE
COUNSELLOR

A Fandorin Mystery

BORIS AKUNIN

**Translated from the Russian
by Andrew Bromfield**

The Mysterious Press
New York

Published simultaneously in Canada
Printed in the United States of America

First published in Great Britain in 2008
by Weidenfeld & Nicolson.

First published in Russian as *Statskii sovietnik* by
Zakharov Publishers, Moscow, Russia and Edizioni Frassinelli, Milan, Italy.

First Grove Atlantic hardcover edition: July 2017
First Grove Atlantic paperback edition: February 2019

Library of Congress Cataloguing-in-Publication data available for this title.

ISBN 978-0-8021-2782-2
eISBN 978-0-8021-8908-0

The Mysterious Press
an imprint of Grove Atlantic
154 West 14th Street
New York, NY 10011

Distributed by Publishers Group West

groveatlantic.com

19 20 21 22   10 9 8 7 6 5 4 3 2 1

Prologue

The windows on the left were blank, sightless wall eyes, crusted with ice and wet snow. The panes of glass jangled dolefully as the wind hurled the soft, sticky flakes against them and swayed the heavy carcass of the carriage to and fro in an obstinate effort to shove the train off the slippery rails and send it tumbling over and over, like a long black sausage, across the broad white plain – over the frozen river, over the dead fields, and on towards the blurred streak of dark forest at the distant junction of earth and sky.

A wide expanse of this mournful landscape could be examined through the remarkably clear-sighted windows on the right, but what point was there in looking out at it? Nothing but snow, nothing but the wild whistling of the wind, the low, murky sky – darkness, cold and death.

On the inside, however, the ministerial saloon carriage was warm and welcoming: a cosy gloom, tinged with blue from the silk lampshade, logs crackling behind the bronze door of the stove, a teaspoon tinkling rhythmically in a glass. The small but excellently equipped study – with a conference table, leather armchairs and a map of the Empire on the wall – was hurtling along at a speed of fifty versts an hour through the raging blizzard and the dead light of the inclement winter dawn.

An old man with a virile and imperious face was dozing in one of the armchairs, with a warm Scottish rug pulled right up to his chin. Even in sleep the grey brows were knitted sternly, the corners of the mouth were set in world-weary folds, and from time to time the wrinkled eyelids fluttered nervously. The circle of light cast by the lamp swayed this way and that, repeatedly plucking out of the darkness a sturdy hand set on the mahogany armrest and glinting brightly in the diamond ring set on one finger.

On the table, directly below the lamp, there was a pile of newspapers. Lying on top was the illegal Zurich publication *The People's Will*, the very latest issue from only two days before. On the open page an article had been circled in angry red pencil:

Hiding the Butcher from Vengeance

Our editors have been informed by a highly reliable source that Adjutant General Khrapov, who last Thursday was removed from the positions of Deputy Minister of the Interior and commander of the Special Corps of Gendarmes, will shortly be appointed Governor General of Siberia and will depart to take up his new post immediately.

The motives underlying this move are only too clear. The Tsar wishes to save Khrapov from the people's revenge by hiding his vicious guard dog away for a while in a place as far removed as possible from the two capitals. But the sentence that our party has pronounced on this bloody satrap remains in force. By issuing the monstrous command to subject the political prisoner Polina Ivantsova to a savage flogging, Khrapov has set himself outside the laws of humanity. He cannot be allowed to live. The butcher has twice succeeded in evading his avengers, but nonetheless he is doomed.

From the same source we have learned that Khrapov has already been promised the portfolio of Minister of the Interior. The appointment to Siberia is a temporary measure intended to place Khrapov beyond the reach of the chastening sword of the people's wrath. The tsar's *oprichniks* anticipate being able to locate and eliminate our Combat Group, which has been instructed to carry the butcher's sentence into effect. And then, when the danger has passed, the minion Khrapov will make a triumphant return to St Petersburg and assume

2

unlimited powers.

This shall not be! The wasted lives of our comrades cry out for retribution.

Unable to bear her shame, Ivantsova hanged herself in her cell. She was only seventeen years old.

The twenty-three-year-old student Skokova fired at the satrap, missed and was hanged.

One of our comrades from the Combat Group, whose name must remain secret, was killed by a splinter from his own bomb, and Khrapov survived yet again.

But never you mind, Your Excellency, no matter how much a string might twist and turn, it cannot go on for ever. Our Combat Group will seek you out even in Siberia.

A pleasant journey to you!

The locomotive gave a long, quavering howl, followed by several short blasts on its whistle: Whoo-ooo-ooo-ooo! Whoo! Whoo! Whoo!

The sleeper's lips trembled restlessly and a low, dull moan escaped from between them. The eyes opened, darting in bewilderment to the left – towards the white windows – and then to the right – towards the black ones; gradually their gaze cleared, acquiring intelligence and focus. The stern old man threw off the rug to reveal a velvet jacket, a white shirt and a black tie. Working his dry lips, he reached out and rang a small hand bell.

A moment later the door leading from the study into the reception room opened. A smart young lieutenant colonel in a blue gendarme uniform with white aiguillettes came dashing in, adjusting his sword belt.

'Good morning, Your Excellency!'

'Have we passed Tver?' the General asked in a thick voice, ignoring the greeting.

'Yes indeed, Ivan Fyodorovich. We're approaching Klin.'

'What do you mean, Klin?' the seated man asked, growing angry. 'Already? Why didn't you wake me earlier? Did you oversleep?'

The officer rubbed his creased cheek. 'Certainly not, sir. I saw *you* had fallen asleep. And I thought, *Let Ivan Fyodorovich get a bit of a rest.* It's all right, you'll have enough time to get washed and dressed and drink tea. There's a whole hour to go to Moscow.'

The train slowed down, preparing to brake. Occasional lights began flitting past outside the windows and then widely spaced lamp posts and snow-covered roofs came into view.

The General yawned. 'All right, have them put the samovar on. I just can't seem to wake up somehow.'

The gendarme saluted and went out, closing the door soundlessly behind him.

In the reception room there was a bright light burning and the air smelled of liqueur and cigar smoke. Sitting at the writing desk with his head propped in his hands was another officer – bright blond hair, light eyebrows and long eyelashes that made his pink face resemble a piglet's. He stretched, cracking his joints, and asked the Lieutenant Colonel: 'Well, how are things in there?'

'He wants tea. I'll see to it.'

'A-ha,' the albino drawled and glanced out of the window. 'What's this – Klin? Sit down, Michel, I'll tell them about the samovar. I'll get out for a moment and stretch my legs. And at the same time I'll check to make sure those devils aren't dozing.'

He stood up, pulled down his uniform jacket and walked out, spurs jangling, into the third room of this remarkable carriage. The conditions here were basic: chairs along the walls, pegs for hanging outer clothing, a little table in the corner with tea things and a samovar. Two sturdy men wearing identical three-piece camlet suits and sporting identically curled moustaches (one of which was sandy-coloured and the other ginger), sitting motionless facing each other; another two men sleeping on chairs set together.

When the white-haired officer appeared, the two men who were sitting jumped to their feet, but he put one finger to his lips, as if to say: *Let the others sleep,* then pointed to the samovar and whispered: 'Tea for His Excellency. Phew, it's stuffy in here. I'm going out for a breath of air.'

4

In the small vestibule two gendarmes stood smartly to attention. The vestibule was not heated, and the sentries were wearing their greatcoats, caps and hoods.

'Are you off duty soon?' the officer asked, pulling on a pair of white gloves and peering out at the station platform as it slowly drifted closer.

'Only just come on, Your Honour!' the watch leader barked. 'Now it's all the way to Moscow for us.'

'All right, all right.'

The albino pushed the heavy door and a breath of fresh wind, damp snow and fuel oil blew into the carriage.

'Eight o'clock, and the sky's only just turning grey,' the officer sighed, speaking to no one in particular, and lowered one foot on to the top step.

The train had not yet stopped, its brakes were still screeching and grinding, but already there were two figures hurrying along the platform towards the saloon carriage: a short man carrying a lantern and a tall, slim man in a top hat and a loose, sporty mackintosh with a cape.

'There, that's the special!' cried the first man (the stationmaster, to judge from his peaked cap), turning to his companion.

The other man stopped in front of the open door, holding his top hat down on his head, and asked the officer: 'Are you M-Modzalevsky? – His Excellency's adjutant?'

Unlike the railway official, the man with the stammer did not shout, and yet his calm, clear voice was distinctly audible above the howling of the blizzard.

'No, I'm the head of his guard,' the white-haired man replied, trying to make out the fop's face.

It was a remarkable face: the features were subtle but severe, the moustache was neatly trimmed, the forehead dissected by a resolute vertical crease,

'Aha, Staff Captain v-von Seidlitz – excellent,' the stranger said with a nod of satisfaction, and immediately introduced himself. 'Fandorin, Deputy for Special Assignments to His Excellency the Governor General of M-Moscow. I expect you have heard of me.'

'Yes, Mr State Counsellor, we were informed by encrypted message that you would be responsible for Ivan Fyodorovich's safety in Moscow. But I had assumed you would meet us at the station there. Come up, come up, the snow's blowing in.'

The State Counsellor nodded farewell to the stationmaster and tripped lightly up the steep steps into the carriage, slamming the door shut behind him and reducing the sounds from outside to a hollow, rumbling echo.

'You have already entered the p-province of Moscow,' he explained, removing his top hat and shaking the snow off its crown. This revealed that his hair was black, but his temples, despite his young years, were completely grey. 'My jurisdiction, s-so to speak, starts here. We shall be stuck here at Klin for at least t-two hours – they're clearing snow off the line up ahead. We shall have time enough to agree everything and allocate responsibilities. But f-first I need to see His Excellency, introduce myself and c-convey an urgent message. Where can I leave my coat?'

'This way, please, into the guardroom. There's a coat rack in there.'

Von Seidlitz showed the State Counsellor through into the first room, where the security guards in civilian dress were on duty. Then, after Fandorin had removed his mackintosh and put his soaking-wet top hat down on a chair, he showed him into the second room.

'Michel, this is State Counsellor Fandorin,' the head of the guard explained to the Lieutenant Colonel. 'We were told about him. He has an urgent communication for Ivan Fyodorovich.'

Michel stood up. 'His Excellency's adjutant, Modzalevsky. May I see your documents, please?'

'N-Naturally.' The official took a folded sheet of paper out of his pocket and handed it to the adjutant.

'He is Fandorin,' the head of the guard affirmed. 'His verbal portrait was given in the message, I remember it very clearly.'

Modzalevsky carefully examined the seal and the photograph and returned the paper to its owner. 'Very good, Mr State Counsellor. I'll announce you.'

A minute later the State Counsellor was admitted into the kingdom of soft carpets, blue light and mahogany furnishings.

'Hello, Mr Fandorin,' the General growled amiably. He had already changed his velvet jacket for a military frock coat. 'Erast Petrovich, isn't it?'

'Yes ind-deed, Your Excellency.'

'So you decided to engage your charge out on the route of approach? I commend your diligence, although I consider all this fuss entirely unnecessary. Firstly, I left St Petersburg in secret; secondly, I am not even slightly afraid of our revolutionary gentlemen; and thirdly, we are all of us in God's hands. If the Lord has spared Khrapov thus far, he must need the old war dog for something.' The General, evidently this self-same Khrapov, crossed himself devoutly.

'I have an extremely urgent and absolutely c-confidential message for Your Excellency,' the State Counsellor said impassively, with a glance at the adjutant. 'I beg your pardon, L-Lieutenant Colonel, but those are the instructions I was g-given.'

'Off you go, Misha,' said the new Governor General of Siberia, the man whom the newspaper from abroad had called a butcher and a satrap. 'Is the samovar ready? As soon as we finish talking business, I'll call you and we'll have some tea.' When the door closed behind his adjutant, he asked: 'Well, what have you got for me that's so mysterious? A telegram from the sovereign? Let's have it.'

The functionary moved close to the seated man, slipping one hand into the pocket of his beaver jacket, but then his eyes fell on the illegal newspaper with the article circled in red. The General caught the glance and his face darkened.

'The nihilist gentlemen continue to flatter me with their attention. A "butcher" they call me! I suppose you have also read all sorts of rubbish about me, Erast Petrovich. Don't believe the slanderous lies of vicious tongues; they turn everything back to front! She wasn't flogged by brutal jailers in my presence, that's pure slander!' His Excellency had clearly found the unfortunate incident of Ivantsova's suicide by hanging very disturbing, and it was still bothering him. 'I'm an honest soldier, I have two

7

George medals – for Sebastopol and the second battle of Plevna!' he exclaimed heatedly. 'I was trying to save that girl from a penal sentence, the young fool! What if I did speak to her in a familiar fashion? I was only being fatherly! I have a granddaughter her age! And she slapped my face – me, an old man, an adjutant general – in front of my guards, in front of the prisoners. According to the law, the tramp should have got ten years for that! But I gave orders for her just to be whipped, and not to let the business get out – not to flog her half to death, as they wrote in the newspapers afterwards; just to give her ten lashes, and to go easy on her as well! And it wasn't the jailers who whipped her, it was a female warder. How could I know that crazy Ivantsova would lay hands on herself? She's not even blue-blooded, just an ordinary bourgeois girl – why all this nonsensical delicacy?' The General gestured angrily. 'Now I'll have her blood on my hands for ever. And afterwards another stupid fool tried to shoot me. I wrote to the sovereign, asking him not to have her hanged, but His Majesty was adamant. He wrote on my request in his own hand: "For those who raise the sword against my faithful servants there will be no mercy."' Moved by this memory, Khrapov began blinking and an old man's tear glinted briefly in his eye. 'Hunting me down like a wolf. I was only acting for the best . . . I don't understand it, for the life of me, I don't!'

The Governor General spread his hands in regretful despair, but the man with the black hair and grey temples snapped back, without a trace of a stammer: 'How could *you* ever understand the meaning of honour and human dignity? But that's all right: even if you don't understand, it will be a lesson to the other dogs.'

Ivan Fyodorovich gaped at this amazing official and tried to get up out of the chair, but the other man had already removed his hand from his pocket, and the object in it was not a telegram but a short dagger. The hand plunged the dagger straight to the General's heart. Khrapov's eyebrows crept upwards and his mouth dropped open, but no sound escaped from it. The Governor General's fingers clutched at the State Counsellor's hand, locking on to it, and the diamond ring flashed again in the lamplight. Then his head slumped backwards lifelessly and a thin trickle of scarlet blood ran down his chin.

The killer unclasped the dead man's fingers from his hand with fastidious disgust. Then he tore off his false moustache and rubbed his grey temples, which turned as black as the rest of his hair.

With a glance round at the closed door, the resolute man of action walked over to one of the blind windows overlooking the railway tracks, but the frame was frozen solid and absolutely refused to budge. The strange State Counsellor, however, was not disconcerted. He took hold of the curved handle with both hands and heaved. The veins stood out on his forehead, his clenched teeth ground together and – wonder of wonders! – the window frame squeaked and started moving downwards. A chilly blast flung powdery snow into the strong man's face and set the curtains flapping in delight. In a single agile movement the killer threw himself through the open frame and melted away into the grey morning twilight.

The scene in the study was transformed: overjoyed at this sudden opportunity, the wind started driving important documents across the carpet, tugging at the fringe of the tablecloth, tousling the grey hair on the General's head.

The blue lampshade began swaying impetuously and the patch of light began dodging about on the dead man's chest, revealing two letters carved into the ivory handle of the dagger driven in right up to the hilt: CG.

CHAPTER I

in which Fandorin finds himself under arrest

The day got off to a bad start. Erast Petrovich Fandorin rose at the crack of dawn because at half past eight he had to be at the Nikolaevsky Station. He and his Japanese valet performed their usual comprehensive gymnastics routine, he drank green tea and was already shaving while performing his breathing exercises at the same time, when the telephone rang. It turned out that the State Counsellor need not have risen at such an ungodly hour after all: the express train from St Petersburg was expected to arrive two hours late because of snowdrifts on the railway line.

Since all the necessary instructions for ensuring the safety of the important visitor from the capital had been issued the previous day, Erast Petrovich could not immediately think of any way to occupy his unexpected leisure time. He thought of going to the station early, but decided against it. Why set his sub-ordinates' nerves on edge unnecessarily? He could be quite certain that Colonel Sverchinsky, the acting head of the Provincial Office of Gendarmes, had carried out his instructions to the letter: platform one, at which the express train would arrive, was surrounded by agents in civilian clothes, there was an armoured carriage waiting right beside the platform, and the escort had been selected with meticulous care. It should really be quite enough to arrive at the station fifteen minutes ahead of time – and that merely for the sake of good order rather than to expose any oversights.

The task he had been set by His Excellency Prince Vladimir Andreevich Dolgorukoi was a highly responsible one, but not difficult: meet a VIP, accompany him to breakfast with the prince, after that escort him to the securely guarded residence on the Sparrow Hills to take a rest, and in the evening take the newly appointed Governor General of Siberia to the Chelyabinsk train, on to which the ministerial carriage would already have been coupled. That was really all there was to it.

There was only one point of difficulty, which had been tormenting Erast Petrovich since the previous day: should he shake the hand of Adjutant General Khrapov, who had sullied his own name with a base or, at the very least, unforgivably stupid act?

From the point of view of his position and career, of course, he ought to disregard his own feelings, especially since those who should know were predicting a rapid return to the highest echelons of power for the former gendarme commander. Fandorin, however, decided not to decline the handshake for a quite different reason – a guest is a guest, and it is not permissible to insult him. It would be sufficient to maintain a cool attitude and an emphatically official tone.

This decision was correct, indeed indisputably so, but nonetheless it had left the State Counsellor with an uneasy feeling: perhaps careerist considerations had played some part in it after all?

That was why Erast Petrovich was not at all upset by this unexpected delay – he now had extra time to resolve his complex moral dilemma.

Fandorin ordered his valet Masa to brew some strong coffee, settled into an armchair and began weighing up all the pros and cons again, involuntarily clenching and unclenching his right hand as he did so.

But before long his musings were interrupted by another ring, this time at the door. He heard the sound of voices in the hallway – at first quiet, and then loud. Someone was attempting to force his way through into the study, but Masa was keeping him out, making hissing and spluttering sounds eloquently expressive of the former Japanese subject's bellicose state of mind.

'Who's there, Masa?' Erast Petrovich shouted, walking out of the study into the drawing room.

There he saw that he had unexpected visitors: the head of Moscow's Department of Security, Lieutenant Colonel of Gendarmes Burlyaev, accompanied by two gentlemen in check coats, evidently plain-clothes agents. Masa was holding his arms out wide, blocking the three men's way: he was clearly intending to move from words to action in the immediate future.

'My apologies, Mr Fandorin,' said Burlyaev, doffing his cap and running one hand through his stiff salt-and-pepper French crop. 'It's some kind of misunderstanding, but I have here a telegram from the Police Department' – he waved a piece of paper through the air – 'informing me that Adjutant General Khrapov has been murdered, and that ... er, er ... you killed him ... and that you must be placed under arrest immediately. They've completely lost their minds, but orders are orders ... You'd better calm your Japanese down, I've heard about the spry way he fights with his feet.'

The first thing Erast Petrovich felt was an absurd sense of relief at the realisation that the problem of the handshake had been resolved of its own accord, and it was only afterwards that the full, nightmarish force of what he had heard struck him.

Fandorin was only cleared of suspicion after the delayed express finally arrived. Before the train had even stopped moving, the white-haired Staff Captain leapt out of the ministerial carriage on to the platform and set off along it at a furious pace, spewing out curses with his face contorted in rage, towards the spot where the arrested State Counsellor was standing surrounded by police agents. But when he was only a few steps away, the Staff Captain slowed to a walk and then came to a complete halt. He fluttered his white eyelashes and punched himself hard on the thigh.

'It's not him. Like him, but not him! And not even really like him! Just the moustache, and the grey temples – no other similarity at all!' the officer muttered in bewilderment. 'Who's this you've brought? Where's Fandorin?'

'I assure you, M-Mr von Seidlitz, that I am Fandorin,' the State Counsellor said with exaggerated gentleness, as if he were speaking to someone who was mentally ill, and turned to Burlyaev, who had flushed a deep crimson. 'Pyotr Ivanovich, please tell your men that they can let go of my elbows now. Staff Captain, where are Lieutenant Colonel Modzalevsky and your men from the guard? I need to question them all and record their testimony.'

'Question them? Record their testimony?' Seidlitz cried in a hoarse voice, raising his clenched fists to the heavens. 'What damned testimony! Don't you understand? He's dead, dead! My God, it's the end of everything, everything! I have to run, get the gendarmes and the police moving! If I don't find that masquerading blackguard, that—' He choked and starting hiccupping convulsively. 'But I *will* find him, I *will*! I'll exonerate myself! I'll move heaven and earth! Otherwise there'll be nothing for it but to blow my brains out!'

'Very well,' Erast Petrovich said in the same placid tone. 'I think I'll question the Staff Captain a little later when he recovers his composure. But let us make a start with the others now. Tell them to clear the stationmaster's office for us. I request Mr Sverchinsky and Mr Burlyaev to be present at the interrogation. And afterwards I shall go and report to His Excellency.'

The head porter of the train, who had been maintaining a respectful distance, asked timidly: 'Your Honour, what are we to do with the body? Such an important person . . . Where should we take him?'

'What do you mean, where?' the State Counsellor asked in surprise. 'The morgue carriage will be here any minute; send him for a post-mortem.'

'. . . And then the adjutant Modzalevsky, who was the first to recover his wits, ran to the Klin passenger terminal and sent off a coded telegram to the Police Department.' Fandorin's lengthy report was nearing its end. 'The top hat, mackintosh and dagger have been sent to the laboratory for analysis. Khrapov is in the morgue. Seidlitz has been given a sedative injection.'

Silence fell in the room, broken only by the ticking of the clock and the quivering of the windowpanes under the pressure of the stormy February wind. The Governor General of the ancient capital of Russia, Prince Vladimir Andreevich Dolgorukoi, worked his wrinkled lips intently, tugged on his long, dyed moustache and scratched himself behind the ear, causing his chestnut wig to slip slightly to one side. Erast Petrovich had not often had occasion to see the all-powerful master of Russia's old capital in a state of such hopeless bewilderment.

'There's no way the St Petersburg camarilla will ever forgive me for this,' His Excellency said mournfully. 'It won't bother them that their damned Khrapov never even reached Moscow. Klin is part of Moscow province too ... Well then, Erast Petrovich, I suppose this is the end?'

The State Counsellor merely sighed in reply.

Dolgorukoi turned to the liveried servant standing at the door with a silver tray in his hands. The tray held several little bottles and phials and a small bowl of eucalyptus cough pastilles. The servant's name was Frol Grigorievich Vedishchev, and he held the modest position of valet, but the prince had no more devoted and experienced adviser than this wizened old man with his bald cranium, massive sideburns and gold-rimmed spectacles with thick lenses.

There was no one else in the study apart from these three.

'Well, Frolushka,' Dolgorukoi asked, his voice trembling, 'are we for the scrap heap then? Dismissed in dishonour. Scandal and disgrace ...'

'Vladimir Andreevich,' the valet whined miserably, 'to hell with the sovereign's service. You've served long and well, thank God, and you're past eighty now ... Don't go tormenting yourself over this. The Tsar might not honour you, but the people of Moscow will remember you with a kind word. It's no small thing, after all: twenty-five years you've been looking after them, barely even sleeping at night. Let's go to Nice, to the sunshine. We'll sit on the porch and reminisce about the old days, why, at our age ...'

The prince smiled sadly: 'I couldn't, Frol, you know that. I'll die without any work to do, I'll pine away in six months. It's Moscow that supports me, that's the only reason I'm still hale and hearty. I wouldn't mind if there were good cause, but they'll just throw me out for nothing at all. Everything in my city is in perfect order. It's unjust . . .' The tray of bottles began rattling in Vedishchev's hands and tears streamed down his cheeks.

'God is merciful, little father; perhaps this will pass over. Look at all the other things that have happened, but with God's help we survived. Erast Petrovich will find us the villain who killed the General, and the sovereign will mellow.'

'He won't mel-low,' Dolgorukoi muttered dejectedly. 'This is a matter of state security. When the sovereign power feels threatened, it has no pity on anyone. Everyone has to feel terrified, and especially its own – so that they will keep their eyes peeled and fear the authorities even more than the killers. It's my jurisdiction, so I'm answerable. There's only one thing I ask of God: to let me find the criminal quickly, using my own resources. At least then I won't leave in disgrace. I've served with dignity and my end will be dignified.' He cast a hopeful glance at his deputy for special assignments. 'Well, Erast Petrovich, will you be able to find this "CG" for me?'

Fandorin paused before replying in a quiet, uncertain voice. 'Vladimir Andreevich, you know me, I do not like to make empty promises. We cannot even be certain that after committing this atrocity the murderer made for Moscow and not St Petersburg . . . After all, the Combat Group's activities are directed from St Petersburg.'

'Yes, yes, that's true,' the prince said, nodding sadly. 'Really, what am I thinking of? The combined forces of the entire Corps of Gendarmes and the Police Department have failed to catch these villains, and here I am appealing to you. Russia is a big country, the villain could have gone anywhere . . . Do please forgive me. When he is drowning a man will clutch at any straw. And then, you have already rescued me from so many absolutely hopeless situations . . .'

Somewhat piqued at being compared to a straw, the State Counsellor cleared his throat and said in a mysterious tone: 'But nonetheless. . .'

'What "nonetheless"?' Vedishchev asked with a start, putting down the tray. He rapidly wiped his tear-stained face with a large handkerchief and ambled closer to Fandorin. 'You mean you have some kind of clue?'

'But nonetheless I can try,' Fandorin said thoughtfully. 'Indeed, I must. I was actually going to request Your Excellency to grant me the appropriate authority. By using my name, the killer has thrown down the gauntlet to me – not to mention those moments of extreme discomfort for which I was obliged to him this morning. Furthermore, I believe that when the criminal left Klin he *did* make his way towards Moscow. It takes only one hour to get here by train from the scene of the crime, too short a time for us even to gather our wits. But it is nine hours back to St Petersburg in the opposite direction; in other words, he would still be travelling even as we speak. And in the meantime the investigation has begun, the search was already started at eleven o'clock, all the stations have been sealed and the railway gendarmes are checking the passengers on all trains within a distance of three hundred versts. No, he could not possibly have headed for St Petersburg.'

'But maybe he didn't go by rail at all?' the valet asked doubtfully. 'Maybe he got on a horse and trudged off to some place like Zamukhransk, to sit it out until the hue and cry die down?'

'Zamukhransk would be no g-good for sitting it out. In a place like that, everyone is in open view. The easiest place to hide is in a large city, where no one knows anyone else, and there is already a conspiratorial network of revolutionaries.'

The Governor General glanced quizzically at Erast Petrovich and clicked open the lid of his snuffbox, a gesture indicating his transition from a mood of despair to a state of intense thoughtfulness.

The State Counsellor waited while Prince Dolgorukoi charged both of his nostrils and gave vent to a thunderously loud sneeze. After Vedishchev had blotted his sovereign lord's eyes and nose with the same handkerchief that he had just used to wipe away his own tears, the prince asked: 'But how are you going to look for him, if he is here, in Moscow? This is a city of a million people. I can't even put the police and the gendarmes under your authority; the most I can do is oblige them to cooperate. You know yourself, my dear fellow, that the upper levels have been shuffling my request for you to be appointed head police-master from desk to desk for more than two months now. Just look at the chaotic state our police work is in.'

The chaos to which His Excellency was referring had developed in the old capital city following the dismissal of the previous head police-master, after it was discovered that he had taken the meaning of the words 'discretionary secret funds' rather too literally. A protracted bureaucratic intrigue was under way in St Petersburg: a court faction hostile to Prince Dolgorukoi absolutely refused to hand over a key appointment to one of the prince's creatures, but at the same time these implacable foes lacked the strength to impose their own placeman on the Governor General. And in the meantime the immense city had been left to carry on without its principal defender and guardian of law and order. In principle, the role of the head police-master was to lead and coordinate the activities of the Municipal Police and the Provincial Office of Gendarmes and the Department of Security, but the present state of affairs was an absolute shambles: Lieutenant Colonel Burlyaev of the Department of Security and Colonel Sverchinsky of the Office of Gendarmes wrote complaints about each other, and both of them complained of brazen obstruction by high-handed police superintendents.

'Yes, the situation at present is not propitious for joint operations,' Fandorin admitted, 'but in this p-particular case the disunity of the investigative agencies might just, perhaps, be to our advantage ...' Erast Petrovich puckered up his smooth forehead and his hand seemed to move of its own accord to draw out of his pocket the jade rosary beads that assisted the State Counsellor in focusing his thoughts.

The two old men, Prince Dolgorukoi and Vedishchev, well used to Fandorin's ways, waited with bated breath, their faces set in identical expressions, like little children at the circus who know for certain that the conjuror's top hat is empty and at the same time have no doubt that the sly trickster is about to pull a rabbit or a pigeon out of it.

The State Counsellor pulled out his rabbit. 'Allow me to ask exactly why the criminal's plan succeeded so brilliantly,' Erast Petrovich began, and then paused as if he were really expecting a reply. 'The answer is very simple: he possessed detailed information concerning matters that very few people should have known about. That is one. The arrangements for the protection of Adjutant General Khrapov on his journey across Moscow province were only determined the day before yesterday, with the involvement of a very limited number of people. That is two. One of them, who knew the plan in its minutest details, betrayed that plan to the revolutionaries – either consciously or unconsciously. That is three. All we have to do is find this individual, and through him we shall find the Combat Group and the killer himself.'

'How do you mean, "unconsciously"?' the Governor General asked with a frown. 'Consciously, now – that's clear enough. Even in the state service there are turncoats. Some sell the nihilists secrets for money, some because the devil prompts them to do it. But when they're unconscious? You mean when they're drunk?'

'More likely out of carelessness,' Fandorin replied. 'The way it usually happens is that some official blurts out a secret to someone close to him who has connections with the terrorists – a son, a daughter, a lover. But that will merely add one more link to the chain.'

'Well then,' said the prince, reaching for his snuff again, 'the day before yesterday at the secret meeting concerning Ivan Fyodorovich's arrival (may the old sinner rest in peace), the only people present, apart from myself and you, were Sverchinsky and Burlyaev. Not even the police were involved – on instructions from Petersburg. So do we have to regard the heads of the Office of Gendarmes and the Department of Security as suspects? That seems rather outlandish. A ... aa ... choo!'

'Bless you,' Vedishchev put in, and began wiping His Excellency's nose again.

'Yes, even them,' Erast Petrovich declared decisively. 'And in addition, we need to find out who else in the Office and the

Department was privy to all the details. I assume that can only be three or four people at most, no more.'

Frol Grigorievich gasped. 'Good Lord, why that's mere child's play to you! Vladimir Andreevich, for goodness' sake don't go into mourning yet. If this is the end of your career, then you'll leave the service with full honours, in style. They'll see you off waving and cheering, not with a boot up the backside! Erast Petrovich will have this Judas sorted out for us in a jiffy. "That is one, that is two, that is three," he'll say – and all done and dusted!'

'It's not as simple as that,' said the State Counsellor, with a shake of his head. 'Yes, the Office of Gendarmes is the first place where there could have been a leak. And the Department of Security is the second. But unfortunately there is a third possibility, which I shall not be able to investigate. The plan that we agreed for the protection of Khrapov was sent to St Petersburg for confirmation by coded telegram. It included information about me, as the person responsible for our visitor's safety – with an abstract of my service record, a verbal description, intelligence profile and so forth; in short, everything that is normally required in such cases. Seidlitz had no doubts about the false Fandorin, because the impersonator had been informed in minute detail about my appearance and even my st-stammer ... If the source of the leak is in St Petersburg, it is unlikely that I shall be able to do anything. My writ doesn't run there, as they say ... But even so the chances are two out of three that the trail begins in Moscow. And the killer is most likely hiding somewhere here. We have to look for him.'

From the Governor General's house the State Counsellor went directly to the Office of Gendarmes on Malaya Nikitskaya Street. As he rode in the prince's blue-velvet-upholstered carriage, he wondered what approach he ought to take with Colonel Sverchinsky. Of course, the hypothesis that Sverchinsky, a long-standing confidant of the prince and Vedishchev, could be involved with revolutionaries required a certain liveliness of the imagination, but the good Lord had endowed the State

Counsellor plentifully with that particular quality, and in the course of a life rich in adventures he had come across surprises more bizarre than that.

And so, what could be said about Colonel Stanislav Sverchinsky of the Special Corps of Gendarmes?

He was secretive, cunning and ambitious, but at the same time very cautious – he preferred to stay in the background. A meticulous career man. He knew how to bide his time and wait for his chance, and this time it seemed to have come: as yet he was only acting head of the Office of Gendarmes, but in all likelihood he would be confirmed in that post, and then the most mouth-watering career prospects would be open to him. Of course, it was well known in both Moscow and St Petersburg that Sverchinsky was Prince Dolgorukoi's man. If Vladimir Andreevich were to leave the old capital city for the sunny scrap heap of Nice, the colonel might never be confirmed in his coveted appointment. And so, as far as Stanislav Filippovich Sverchinsky's career prospects were concerned, the death of General Khrapov was a distressing, perhaps even fatal, event. At least, that was how matters appeared at first glance.

The journey from Tverskaya Street to Malaya Nikitskaya Street was no distance at all and were it not for the cold wind driving the slanting snow, Fandorin would have preferred to go on foot: walking was better for thinking. Here was the turn off the boulevard already. The carriage drove past the cast-iron railings of the mansion of Baron Evert-Kolokoltsev, where Fandorin lived in the outhouse, and two hundred paces further on the familiar yellowish-white building with a striped sentry box at the entrance emerged from the white shroud of the blizzard.

Fandorin climbed out, held down the top hat that was straining to take flight, and ran up the slippery steps. In the vestibule a familiar sergeant saluted the State Counsellor smartly and reported without waiting to be asked: 'In his office. He's expecting you. Your coat and hat, if you please, Your Honour. I'll take them to the cloakroom.'

Erast Petrovich thanked him absent-mindedly and looked

round the familiar interior as if he were seeing it for the first time.

A corridor with a row of identical oilcloth-upholstered doors, drab pale-blue walls with perfunctory white skirting, and – at the far end – the gymnastics hall. Could state treason really be lurking here, within these walls?

The departmental adjutant on duty in the reception room was Lieutenant Smolyaninov, a ruddy-faced young man with lively black eyes and a dashingly curled moustache.

'Good health to you, Erast Petrovich,' he said, greeting the habitual visitor. 'Terrible weather, eh?'

'Yes, yes,' said the State Counsellor, nodding. 'May I go in?' And he walked straight into the office without any further ado, as an old colleague and, perhaps – in the near future – an immediate superior.

'Well, what news of happenings in higher places?' asked Sverchinsky, rising to greet him. 'What does Vladimir Andreevich say? What are we to do, what measures are we to take? I confess I'm at a loss.' He lowered his voice to a terrible whisper and asked: 'What do you think – will they dismiss him?'

'To some extent that will depend on the two of us.'

Fandorin lowered himself into an armchair, the Colonel sat down facing him, and the conversation immediately turned to business.

'Stanislav Filippovich, I shall be frank with you. We have a t-traitor among us, either here, in the Office of Gendarmes, or in the Department of Security.'

'A traitor?' The Colonel shook his head violently, inflicting serious damage on the ideal parting that divided his smoothly slicked hairstyle into two symmetrical halves. 'Here?'

'Yes, a traitor or a blabbermouth, which in the given case is the same thing.' The State Counsellor expounded his reasoning to the Colonel.

Sverchinsky listened, twirling the ends of his moustache in agitation. Having heard Fandorin out, he set his hand on his heart and said with feeling: 'I entirely agree with you! Your reasoning is absolutely just and convincing. But I ask you please to exempt my office from suspicion. Our assignment in the matter of General Khrapov's arrival was extremely simple – to provide a uniformed escort. I didn't even take any special measures, simply ordered a mounted half-platoon to be made ready, and that was all. And I assure you, my esteemed Erast Petrovich, that in the entire Office only two men were aware of all the details: myself and Lieutenant Smolyaninov. I had to explain everything to him, as the adjutant. But you know him yourself; he's a responsible young man, bright and very high-minded, not the kind to fall down on the job. And I dare to hope that I am known to you as a man not given to gossiping.'

Erast Petrovich inclined his head diplomatically: 'That is precisely why I came to you in the first instance and am keeping nothing back from you.'

'I assure you, it must be the Petersburg crew or those types from Gnezdikovsky!' the Colonel said, opening his handsome, velvety eyes wide – by 'those types from Gnezdikovsky' he meant the Department of Security, located on Bolshoi Gnezdikovsky Lane. 'I can't say anything about Petersburg, I'm not in possession of adequate information; but Lieutenant Colonel Burlyaev has plenty of riff-raff among his helpers – former nihilists and all sorts of shady characters. That's the place you need to sound out. Of course, I wouldn't dream of accusing Pyotr Ivanovich himself, God forbid, but his agents were responsible for the secret security arrangements, so there must have been some kind of briefing and an explanation – to a pretty large group of highly dubious individuals. Very imprudent. And another thing . . .' Sverchinsky hesitated, as if unsure whether or not to continue.

'What?' asked Fandorin, looking him straight in the eye. 'Is there some other possible explanation that I have overlooked? Tell me, Stanislav Filippovich, tell me. We are speaking frankly here.'

'Well, there are also the secret agents, whom we refer to in our department as "collaborators" – that is, the members of revolutionary groups who collaborate with the police.'

'Agents provocateurs?' the State Counsellor enquired with a frown.

'No, not necessarily provocateurs. Sometimes simply inform-ants. Our work would be quite impossible without them.'

'How could your spies know the detailed arrangements for the reception of a secret visitor, right down to the description of my appearance?' asked Erast Petrovich, knitting the black arrowheads of his eyebrows in a frown. 'I can't see why they should.'

The Colonel was clearly in some difficulty. He blushed slightly, twisted one side of his moustache into an even tighter curl and lowered his voice confidentially.

'There are different kinds of agents. And the way the author-ised officers handle them varies too. Sometimes it's a matter of entirely private . . . mmm . . . I would even say, intimate, contact. Well, you understand.'

'No,' said Fandorin with a shudder, looking at the other man in some fright. 'I do not understand and I do not wish to. Do you mean to tell me that for the good of the cause employees of the Office of Gendarmes and the Department of Security enter into sodomitical relations with their agents?'

'Ah, why necessarily sodomitical!' Sverchinsky exclaimed, throwing his hands up. 'The collaborators include quite a large number of women, as a general rule quite young and good-looking. And you know what a free attitude our modern revolutionary youth and their associates have towards matters of sex.'

'Yes, yes,' said the State Counsellor in a rather embarrassed tone. 'I have heard about it. I really do not have a very clear idea of the activities of the secret police. And I have not previously had any dealings with revolutionaries – mostly murderers, swindlers and foreign spies. However, Stanislav Filippovich, you are clearly pointing me in the direction of one of the Department's officers. Who is it? Which of them, in your view, has suspicious connections?'

The Colonel maintained his expression of moral torment for about half a minute and then, as if he had come to a difficult decision, he whispered: 'Erast Petrovich, my dear fellow, to some extent, of course, this is private business, but knowing you as I do to be a highly scrupulous and broadminded individual, I feel that I have no right to conceal the facts, especially since this is a matter of exceptional importance, in the face of which all personal considerations pale into insignificance, no matter—' At this point, having lost the thread of his tangled grammar, Sverchinsky broke off and began speaking more simply. 'I am in possession of information indicating that Lieutenant Colonel Burlyaev maintains an acquaintance with a certain Diana – of course, that is her agent's alias – a very mysterious individual who collaborates with the authorities without reward, out of ideological considerations, and therefore sets her own terms. For instance, we do not know her real name or where she lives – only the address of the secret apartment that the Department rents for her. From what we know, she is a young woman, or married lady, from a very good family. She has extremely wide and extremely useful contacts among the revolutionary circles of Moscow and St Petersburg, and she renders the police truly invaluable service . . .'

'Is she Burlyaev's mistress, and could he have revealed secrets to her?' the State Counsellor asked impatiently, interrupting Sverchinksy. 'Is that what you are hinting at?'

Stanislav Filippovich unbuttoned his stiff collar and moved closer. 'I . . . I am not certain that she is his mistress, but I think it possible. Very possible, in fact. And if she is, Burlyaev could easily have told her things that he shouldn't have. You understand, double agents, especially of this complexion, are not very predictable. Today they collaborate with us, tomorrow they reverse direction and . . .'

'Very well, I'll bear it in mind.'

Erast Petrovich began thinking about something and suddenly changed the subject: 'I assume Frol Grigorievich has telephoned and asked you to offer me every possible assistance.'

Sverchinsky pressed his hands to his chest, as if to say: *Everything that I can possibly do.*

'Then I tell you what. For this investigation I shall require a smart assistant who can also act as my liaison officer. Will you lend me your Smolyaninov?'

The State Counsellor had not spent very long in the yellowish-white building, probably no more than half an hour; but when he came back out into the street, the city was unrecognisable. The wind had wearied of driving white dust through the crooked streets and the snow had settled in loose heaps on the roofs and roadways. In some magical manner, the sky, so recently completely obscured, had now cleared, and the low, grainy ceiling was gone, replaced by a joyous, soaring vault of blue, crowned, just as it should be, by a small circle of gold that glittered like a shiny new imperial. Church domes looking like New Year's tree toys had sprung up out of nowhere above the roofs of the buildings, the freshly fallen snow sparkled with all the colours of the rainbow, and Moscow had performed her favourite trick of changing from a frog into a princess so lovely that the sight of her took your very breath away.

Erast Petrovich looked around and even came to a halt, almost blinded by the bright radiance.

'How beautiful!' exclaimed Lieutenant Smolyaninov and then, suddenly ashamed of his excessive enthusiasm, felt it necessary to add: 'Really, what remarkable metamorphoses . . . Where are we going now, Mr State Counsellor?'

'To the Department of Security. This weather really is glorious. L-Let's walk there.'

Fandorin sent the carriage back to the Governor General's stables, and five minutes later the deputy for special assignments and his ruddy-cheeked companion were striding down Tverskaya Street, which was already full of people strolling along, half-crazed by this sudden amnesty that nature had granted them, although the yard-keepers had barely even begun clearing the alleyways of snow.

Every now and then Erast Petrovich caught people glancing at him – sometimes in fright, sometimes in sympathy, sometimes with simple curiosity – and it was a while before he realised the reason. Ah yes, it was the fine young fellow in the blue gendarme's greatcoat, with a gun-holster and a sword, walking to one side and slightly behind him. A stranger could easily assume that the respectable-looking gentleman in the fur cloak and suede top hat was under armed escort. Two engineering students whom Fandorin did not know at all nodded as they walked towards him and gave his 'escort' a look of hatred and contempt. Erast Petrovich glanced round at the Lieutenant, but he was smiling as serenely as ever and seemed not to have noticed the young men's hostility.

'Smolyaninov, you are obviously going to spend several days with me. Don't wear your uniform; it may interfere with our work. Wear civilian clothes. And by the way, I've been wanting to ask you for a long time ... How did you come to be in the gendarmes corps? Your father's a privy counsellor, is he not? You could have served in the g-guards.'

Lieutenant Smolyaninov took the question as an invitation to reduce the respectful distance that he had been maintaining. In a single bound he overtook the State Counsellor and walked on shoulder to shoulder with him. 'What's so good about being in the guards?' he responded readily. 'Nothing but parades and drunken revels: it's boring. But serving in the gendarmes is pure pleasure. Secret missions, tailing dangerous criminals, sometimes even gunfights. Last year an anarchist holed up in a dacha at Novogireevo, do you remember? He held us off for three whole hours, wounded two of our men. He almost winged me too; the bullet whizzed by just past my cheek. Another half-inch, and it would have left a scar.'

The final words were spoken with obvious regret for an opportunity lost.

'But are you not distressed by the ... the hostile attitude taken by society towards blue uniforms, especially among your own contemporaries?' Erast Petrovich looked at his companion with keen curiosity, but Smolyaninov's expression remained as untroubled as ever.

'I take no notice of it, because I serve Russia and my conscience is clear. And the prejudice against members of the gendarmes corps will evaporate when everyone realises how much we do to protect the state and victims of violence. I'm sure you know that the emblem assigned to the corps by the Emperor Nikolai Pavlovich is a white handkerchief for wiping away the tears of the unfortunate and the suffering.'

Such simple-hearted fervour made the State Counsellor look again at the Lieutenant, who began speaking with even greater passion: 'People think our branch of service is scandalous because they know so little about it. But in actual fact, it is far from easy to become a gendarme officer. Firstly, they only take hereditary nobles, because we are the principal defenders of the throne. Secondly, they select the most deserving and well educated of the army officers, only those who have graduated from college with at least a first-class diploma. There mustn't be a single blot on your service record, and God forbid that you should have any debts. A gendarme's hands must be clean. Do you know what difficult exams I had to take? It was terrible. I got top marks for my essay on the subject "Russia in the twentieth century", but I still had to wait almost a year for a place on the training course, and after the course I waited another four months for a vacancy. Although it's true, Papa did get me a place in the Moscow office . . .' Smolyaninov need not have added that, and Erast Petrovich appreciated the young man's candour.

'Well, and what future awaits Russia in the twentieth century?' Fandorin asked, glancing sideways at this defender of the throne with obvious fellow-feeling.

'A very great one! We only need to reorientate the mood of the educated section of society, redirect their energies from destruction to creation, and we must also educate the unenlightened section of society and gradually nurture its self-respect and dignity. That's the most important thing! If we don't do that, then the trials in store for Russia are truly appalling . . .'

However, Erast Petrovich never discovered exactly what trials were in store for Russia, since they had already turned on to Bolshoi Gnezdikovsky Lane, and ahead of them they could see the unremarkable, two-storey green building that housed the Moscow Department of Security, or 'Okhranka'.

*

Anyone unfamiliar with the tangled branches of the tree of Russian statehood would have found it hard to understand what the difference was between the Department of Security and the Provincial Office of Gendarmes. Strictly speaking, the former was supposedly responsible for the detection of political criminals and the latter for their investigation and interrogation, but since in secret police work detection and investigation are often inseparable, both agencies performed the same job – they strove to eradicate the revolutionary plague by any and every means possible, regardless of the provisions of the law. Both the gendarmes and the *okhranniks* were serious people, tried and tested many times over, privy to the deepest of secrets, although the Office of Gendarmes was subordinated to the senior command of the Special Corps of Gendarmes, and the Department of Security, or Okhranka, was subordinated to the Police Department. The confusion was further exacerbated by the fact that senior officers of the Okhranka were often officially listed as serving in the Gendarmes Corps, and the provincial offices of gendarmes often included in their staff civilian officials from the Police Department. Evidently at some time in the past someone wise and experienced, with a none-too-flattering opinion of human nature, had decided that a single eye was insufficient for observing and overseeing the restive Empire. After all, the Lord himself had decreed that man should have not one eye but two. Two eyes were more practical for spotting sedition, and they reduced the risk of a single eye developing too high an opinion of itself. Therefore, by ancient tradition the relations between the two branches of the secret police were founded on jealousy and hostility, which were not only tolerated from on high but actually encouraged.

In Moscow the eternal enmity between gendarmes and *okhranniks* was mitigated to a certain extent by unified management – both sides were subordinated to the head police-master of the city – but under this arrangement the inhabitants of the green house were at a certain advantage: since they possessed a larger network of agents, they were better informed than their blue-uniformed colleagues about the life and moods of the great city, and for the top brass, better informed meant more valuable. The relative superiority of the Okhranka was evident even in the Department's location: in the immediate vicinity of the residence of the head police-master, with only a short walk across a closed yard from one back entrance to the other, whereas from Malaya Nikitskaya Street to the police-master's home was a brisk walk of at least a quarter of an hour.

However, the prolonged absence of a supreme police commander in Moscow had disrupted the fragile equilibrium between Malaya Nikitskaya Street and Gnezdikovsky Lane, a fact of which Erast Petrovich was well aware. Therefore Sverchinsky's insinuations concerning Lieutenant Colonel Burlyaev and his subordinates had to be regarded with a certain degree of circumspection.

Fandorin pushed open the plain door and found himself in a dark entrance hall with a low, cracked ceiling. Without slowing his stride, the State Counsellor nodded to an individual in civilian clothes (who bowed respectfully in reply, without speaking) and set off up the old winding stairs to the first floor. Smolyaninov clattered after him, holding his sword still.

Upstairs the ambience was quite different: a broad, brightly lit corridor with a carpet runner on the floor, the brisk tapping of typewriters from behind leather-upholstered doors, tasteful prints with views of old Moscow hanging on the walls.

The gendarme lieutenant, evidently in hostile territory for the first time, gazed around with undisguised curiosity.

'You sit here for a while,' said Erast Petrovich, pointing to a row of chairs, and walked into the commander's office.

'Glad to see you looking so well!' the Lieutenant Colonel declared, jumping up from behind the desk and hastening to shake his visitor's hand with exaggerated vivacity, although they had parted only some two hours previously and the State Counsellor had not given the slightest reason for any apprehension concerning his state of health.

Fandorin interpreted Burlyaev's nervousness as an indication of the Lieutenant Colonel's embarrassment over the recent arrest. However, all the appropriate apologies had been made in exaggeratedly verbose style at the railway station, and so the State Counsellor did not return to the annoying incident, regarding the matter as already closed, but went straight to the main point.

'Pyotr Ivanovich, yesterday you reported to me on the measures proposed for ensuring s-security during Adjutant General Khrapov's visit. I approved your proposals. As far as I recall, you allocated twelve agents to cover the General's arrival at the station, another four dressed as porters to accompany him in the street, and two brigades of seven men to patrol the environs of the mansion on the Sparrow Hills.'

'Precisely so,' Burlyaev confirmed cautiously, anticipating a trick.

'Were your agents informed of the name of the individual who w-was arriving?'

'Only the leaders of each brigade – four men in total, all highly reliable.'

'I see.' The State Counsellor crossed one leg over the other, set his top hat and gloves down on a nearby chair and enquired casually, 'I hope you did not forget to inform these four men that overall command of the security operation had been entrusted to me?'

The Lieutenant Colonel shrugged and spread his hands. 'Why no, I didn't do that, Erast Petrovich. I didn't think it necessary. Should I have done? My apologies.'

'Well then, apart from you no one in the entire department knew that I had been charged with receiving the General?' asked Fandorin, suddenly leaning forward.

'Only my closest aides knew that – Collegiate Assessor Mylnikov and my senior operations officer, Zubtsov – no one else. In our organisation it's not customary to gossip. Mylnikov, as you know, is in charge of the plain-clothes section, it could not have been kept from him. And Sergei Vitalievich Zubtsov is the most competent man I have; he was the one who invented the COM scenario. It's his professional pride and joy, you might say.'

'I beg your pardon, what scenario was that?' Erast Petrovich asked in surprise.

'COM – Category One Meeting. That's our professional terminology. We conduct secret surveillance according to categories, depending on the number of agents involved. "Category Two Shadowing", "Category Three Arrest", and so forth. "Category One Meeting" is when we need to ensure the safety of an individual of the first rank. For instance, two weeks ago the heir to the Austrian throne, the Archduke Franz Ferdinand, arrived in Moscow. Thirty agents were involved then too: twelve at the station, four in droshkies and two teams of seven around the residence. But the "Supreme Category" is only used for His Imperial Majesty. All sixty agents work on that, and the Flying Squad comes down from St Petersburg as well. That's not counting the court security guards, the gendarmes and so forth.'

'I know Mylnikov,' Fandorin said in a thoughtful voice. 'Evstratii Pavlovich, I believe his name is? I've seen him in action; he's very adroit. Didn't he serve his way up from the ranks?'

'Yes, he rose from being a simple constable. Not well educated, but sharp and tenacious, very quick on the uptake. The agents all idolise him, and he looks out for them too. Worth his weight in gold; I'm delighted with him.'

'Gold?' Fandorin queried doubtfully. 'I've heard it s-said that Mylnikov is light-fingered. He lives beyond his means and supposedly there was even an internal investigation into the expenditure of official funds?'

Burlyaev lowered his voice confidentially.

'Erast Petrovich, Mylnikov has total control of substantial funds to provide financial incentives for the agents. How he disposes of that money is none of my concern. I require first-class service from his section, and that's what Evstratii Pavlovich provides. What more can I ask?'

The Governor General's assistant for special assignments pondered this opinion and was clearly unable to think of any objections to it.

'Very well. Then what sort of man is Zubtsov? I hardly know him at all. That is, I've seen him, of course, but never worked with him. Do I remember aright that he is a former revolutionary?'

'Indeed he is,' the boss of the Okhranka replied with obvious relish. 'That's a story I'm very proud of. I arrested Sergei Vitalievich myself, when he was still a student. He cost me a fair deal of trouble – at first he just scowled and wouldn't say a word. I had him in my punishment cell, on bread and water, and I yelled at him and threatened him with hard labour. But the way I finally got him was not through fear, but through persuasion. Looking at the lad, I could see he had very nimble wits, and people like that, by the very way their brains work, aren't naturally inclined to terror and other violent tactics. The bomb and the revolver are for the stupid ones, who don't have enough imagination to realise you can't butt your way through a brick wall. But I noticed that my Sergei Vitalievich liked to discuss parliamentarianism, an alliance of right-thinking patriots and so forth. Conducting his interrogations was a sheer pleasure – would you believe that sometimes we sat up in the holding cell until morning? He used to make critical comments about his comrades in the revolutionary group; I could see he understood how limited they were, that they were doomed, and he was looking for a way out: he wanted to correct social injustice, but without blowing the country to pieces with dynamite. I really liked that. I managed to get his case closed. Naturally, his comrades suspected he had betrayed them and they turned their backs on him. He was offended – his conscience was clear as far as they were concerned. You could say I was the only friend he had left. We used to meet to talk about this and that, and I told him what I could about my work, about the various difficulties and snags. And what do you think? Sergei Vitalievich started giving me advice – on the best way to talk to young people, how to tell a propagandist from a terrorist, which pieces of revolutionary literature I should read, and so forth. Extremely valuable advice it was too. One day over a glass of cognac I said to him: "Sergei Vitalievich, my dear fellow, I've grown quite fond of you over all these months, and it pains me to see the way you're torn between two truths. I understand that our nihilists have their own truth, only now there's no way back to them for you. But I tell you what," I said, "you join our truth and, by God, you'll find it's more profound. I can see you're a genuine patriot of the Russian land; you couldn't care less for all their Internationals. Well, I'm just as much a patriot as you are. Let's help Russia together." And what do you think? Sergei Vitalievich thought about it for a day or two, wrote a letter to his former friends – you know, saying our ways have parted, and so on – and then put in an application to be taken on to serve under my command. Now he's my right hand, and he'll go a long way yet, you'll see. And by the way, he's a passionate admirer of yours. He's simply in love with you, on my word of honour. Talks of nothing all the time except your great feats of deduction. Sometimes it makes me feel quite jealous.'

The Lieutenant Colonel laughed, apparently very pleased at having shown himself in a positive light and also having paid his future superior a smart compliment.

Fandorin, however, followed his usual habit and suddenly started talking about something else: 'Ivan Petrovich, are you familiar with a certain lady by the name of Diana?'

Burlyaev stopped laughing and his face turned to stone, shedding some of its usual expression of coarse, soldierly forthrightness – his glance was suddenly sharp and cautious.

'May I enquire, Mr State Counsellor, why you are interested in that lady?'

'You may,' Fandorin replied dispassionately. 'I am seeking the source from which information about our plan reached the t-terrorists. So far I have managed to establish that outside the Police Department the details were known only to you, Mylnikov, Zubtsov, Sverchinsky and his adjutant. Colonel Sverchinsky thinks it possible that the collaborator with the c-conspiratorial alias of Diana could have been informed of the security measures. You are acquainted with her, are you not?'

Burlyaev replied with sudden rancour: 'I am. She's a splendid collaborator, no doubt about it, but Sverchinsky's hints are misplaced. A clear case of the pot calling the kettle black! If anyone could have let something slip to her, then it's him. She can twist him round her little finger!'

'What, you mean Stanislav Filippovich is her lover?' the State Counsellor asked in astonishment, barely managing to swallow the words 'as well'.

'The devil only knows,' the Lieutenant Colonel growled in the same furious tone. 'It's very possible!'

The bewildered State Counsellor took a moment to gather his thoughts. 'And is she so very attractive, this Diana?'

'I really don't know! I've never seen her face.'

Pyotr Ivanovich emphasised the final word, which lent the entire phrase a distinct air of ambiguity. The Lieutenant Colonel evidently felt this himself, because he found it necessary to explain: 'You see, Diana doesn't show her face to any of our people. All the meetings take place at the secret apartment, in semi-darkness, and she wears a veil as well.'

'But that's quite unheard of!'

'She plays the romantic heroine,' Burlyaev said with a scowl. 'I'm sure Sverchinsky hasn't seen her face either. The other parts of her body – very probably; but our Diana conceals her face like a Turkish odalisque. That was a strict condition of her collaboration. She threatens to stop providing us with any help if there is even the slightest attempt to discover her real identity. There was a special instruction from the Police Department not to make any such attempts. Let her play the mysterious heroine, they said, just as long as she provides information.'

Erast Petrovich mentally compared the manner in which Burlyaev and Sverchinsky spoke about the mysterious collaborator and discovered distinct elements of similarity in the words and intonations of the two staff officers. Apparently the rivalry between the Office and the Department was not limited to the field of police work.

'I'll tell you what, Pyotr Ivanovich,' Fandorin said with a perfectly serious expression: 'you have intrigued me with this mysterious Diana of yours. Contact her and say I wish to see her immediately.'

CHAPTER 2

The man of steel rests

Seven hundred and eighty-two, seven hundred and eighty-three, seven hundred and eighty-four . . .

The lean, muscular man with the stony face, calm grey eyes and resolute vertical crease in the centre of his forehead lay on the parquet floor, counting the beats of his own heart. The count proceeded automatically, without involving his thoughts or hindering them in any way. When the man was lying down, each heartbeat was precisely one second – that had been verified many times. The old habit, acquired during imprisonment at hard labour, of listening to the workings of his internal motor while he rested had become such an integral part of the man's very existence that sometimes he would wake in the middle of the night with a four-figure number in his mind and realise that he hadn't stopped counting even in his sleep.

There was a point to this arithmetic: it trained and disciplined his heart, heightened his endurance, strengthened his will and – most importantly – allowed him to relax his muscles and restore his strength in the space of only fifteen minutes (nine hundred heartbeats) just as well as he could have done in three hours of sound sleep. Once the man had had to go without sleep for a long time, when the common convicts in the Akatuisk penal prison had decided to kill him. Too afraid to come near him during the day, they had waited for darkness to come, and the same scene had been played out over and over again for many nights in a row.

The practice of lying on a hard surface had remained with him since the days of his early youth, when Green (that was what his comrades called him – no one knew his real name) had

35

worked hard to develop his self-discipline and wean himself of everything that he regarded as 'luxury', including in this category any habits that were harmful or simply unnecessary for survival.

He could hear muted voices behind the closed door: the members of the Combat Group were excitedly discussing the details of the successful operation. Sometimes Bullfinch got carried away and raised his voice, and then the other two hissed at him. They thought Green was asleep. But he wasn't sleeping. He was resting, counting the beats of his heart and thinking about the old man who had grabbed hold of his wrist just before he died. He could still feel the touch of those dry, hot fingers on his skin. It prevented him from feeling any satisfaction in the neat execution of the operation – and the grey-eyed man had no other pleasures apart from the feeling of duty fulfilled.

Green knew the English meaning of his alias, but he experienced his own colour differently. Everything in the world had a colour, every object and concept, every person – that was something Green had felt since he was a little child; it was one of the special things about him. For instance, the word 'earth' was a clay-brown colour, the word 'apple' was bright pink even for a green winter apple, 'empire' was maroon, 'father' was a dense purple and 'mother' was crimson. Even the letters of the alphabet had their own coloration: 'A' was scarlet, 'B' was bright lemon-yellow, 'C' was pale yellow. Green made no attempt to analyse why for him the sound and meaning of a thing, a phenomenon or a person had these particular colours and no others – he simply took note of this information, and the information rarely misled him. The fact was that every colour also had its own secret meaning on a scale that was an integral, fundamental element of Green's soul. Blue was doubt and unreliability, white was joy, red was sadness, and that made the Russian flag a strange combination: it had joy and sadness, both of them strangely equivocal. If the glow given off by a new acquaintance was blue, Green didn't exactly regard him with overt mistrust, but he watched a person like that closely and assessed him with particular caution. And there was another thing: people were the only items in the whole of existence capable of changing their colour over time – as a result of their own actions, the company they kept and their age.

Green himself had once been sky-blue: soft, warm, amorphous. Later, when he decided to change himself, the sky-blue had faded and been gradually supplanted by an austere, limpid ashgrey. In time the once dominant light-blue tones had receded somewhere deep inside, reduced to secondary tints, and Green had become bright grey, like Damask steel – just as hard, supple, cold and resistant to rust.

The transformation had begun at the age of sixteen. Before that Green had been an ordinary grammar-school pupil – he used to paint landscapes in watercolour, recite poetry by Nekrasov and Lermontov, fall in love. But, of course, even then he had been different from his classmates – if only because they were all Russian and he was not. They didn't persecute him in the classroom, or bait him with being a 'Yid', because they could sense the future man of steel's intensity of feeling and calm, imperturbable strength; but he had no friends and he could not have had. The other pupils skipped lessons, talked back to the teachers and copied from cribs, but Green was obliged to earn top marks in every subject and conduct himself in the most exemplary fashion, because otherwise he would have been expelled, and that would have been too much for his father to bear.

The sky-blue youth would have gone on to graduate from the grammar school, then become a university student and after that a doctor, or perhaps – who could tell? – an artist, if the Governor General Chirkov had not suddenly taken it into his head that there were too many Jews in the city and given instructions for all the pharmacists, dentists and tradesmen who did not possess a permit to reside outside the pale to be sent back to their home towns. Green's father was a pharmacist, and so the family found itself back in the small southern town that Grinberg senior had left many years before in order to acquire a clean, respectable profession.

Green's natural response to such malicious, stupid injustice was one of genuine bewilderment, which passed through the stages of acute physical suffering and seething fury before it culminated in a craving for retaliation.

There was a lot of malicious, stupid injustice around. The juvenile Green had agonised over it earlier, but so far he had managed to pretend that he had more important things to do: justify his father's hopes, learn a useful trade, search within himself and grasp the reason why he had appeared in the world. But now that the inexorable locomotive of malicious stupidity had come hurtling down the rails straight at Green, puffing out menacing steam and tossing him aside down the embankment, it was impossible to resist the inner voice that demanded action.

All that year Green was left to his own devices. He was supposedly preparing to sit the final grammar-school examinations as an external student. And he did read a great deal: Gibbon, Locke, Mill, Guizot. He wanted to understand why people tormented each other, where injustice came from and what was the best way of putting it right. There was no direct answer to be found in the books, but with a little bit of serious thought, it could be read between the lines.

If society was not to become overgrown with scum like a stagnant pond, it needed the periodical shaking-up known as revolution. The advanced nations were those that had passed through this painful but necessary process – and the earlier the better. A class that had been on top for too long became necrotic, like callused skin, the pores of the country became blocked and, as society gradually smothered, life lost its meaning and rule became arbitrary. The state fell into dilapidation, like a house that has not been repaired for a long time, and once the process of disintegration had gone too far, there was no longer any point in propping and patching up the rotten structure. It had to be burned down, and a sturdy new house with bright windows built on the site of the fire.

But conflagrations did not simply happen of their own accord. There had to be people willing to take on the role of the match that would be consumed in starting the great fire. The mere thought of such a fate took Green's breath away. He was willing to be a match and to be consumed, but he realised that his assent alone was not enough. Also required were a will of steel, Herculean strength and irreproachable moral purity.

He had been born with a strong will; all he needed to do was develop it. So he devised an entire course of exercises for overcoming his own weaknesses – his main enemies. To conquer his fear of heights he spent hours at night walking backwards and forwards along the parapet of the railway bridge, forcing himself to keep his eyes fixed on the black, oily water below. To conquer his squeamishness he caught vipers in the forest and stared intently into their repulsive, hissing mouths while their spotted, springy whiplash bodies coiled furiously round his naked arm. To conquer his shyness he travelled to the fair at the district town and sang to the accompaniment of a barrel organ, and his listeners rolled around in laughter, because the sullen little Jewish half-wit had no voice and no ear.

Herculean strength was harder to obtain. Nature had given Green robust health, but made him ungainly and narrow-boned. For week after week, month after month, he spent ten, twelve or fourteen hours a day developing his physical strength. He followed his own method, dividing the muscles into those that were necessary and those that were not, and wasting no time on the unnecessary ones. He began by training his fingers and continued until he could bend a five-kopeck piece or even a three-kopeck piece between his thumb and forefinger. Then he turned his attention to his fists, pounding an inch-thick plank until his knuckles were broken and bloody, smearing the abrasions with iodine and then pounding again, until his fists were covered with calluses and the wood broke at his very first blow. In order to develop his shoulders, he took a job at a flour mill, carrying sacks that weighed four *poods*. He developed his stomach and waist with French gymnastics and his legs by riding a bicycle up hills and carrying it down them.

It was moral purity that gave him the greatest difficulty. Green quickly succeeded in renouncing intemperate eating habits and excessive domestic comfort, even though his mother cried when he toughened his will by fasting or went off to sleep on the sheet-metal roof on a rainy October night. But he was simply unable to deny his physiological needs. Fasting didn't help, nor did a hundred pull-ups on his patented English exercise bar. One day he decided to fight fire with fire and induce in himself an aversion to sexual activity. He went to the district town and hired the most repulsive slut at the station. It didn't work – in fact it only made things worse; and he was left with nothing but his willpower to rely on.

Green spent a year and four months whittling himself into a match. He still hadn't decided where he would find the box against which he was destined to be struck before being consumed in flame, but he already knew that blood would have to be spilled and he prepared himself thoroughly. He practised shooting at a target until he never missed. He learned to grab a knife out of his belt with lightning speed and throw it to hit a small melon at twelve paces. He pored over chemistry textbooks and manufactured an explosive mixture to his own formula.

He followed the activities of the resolute members of the People's Will party with trepidation as they pursued their unprecedented hunt of the Tsar himself. But somehow the Tsar evaded them: the autocrat was protected by a mysterious power that miraculously saved his life over and over again.

Green waited. He had begun to suspect what this mysterious power might be, but was still afraid to believe in such incredible good fortune. Could history really have chosen him, Grigory Grinberg, as its instrument? After all, he was still no more than a boy, only one of hundreds or even thousands of youngsters who dreamed, just as he did, of a brief life as a blazing match.

His wait came to an end one day in March when the surface of the long-frozen river waters cracked and buckled and the ice began to move.

Green had been mistaken. History had not chosen him, but another boy a few years older. He threw a bomb that shattered the Emperor's legs and his own chest. When he came to for a moment just before dying and was asked his name, he replied, 'I don't know,' then he was gone. His contemporaries showered curses on him, but he had earned the eternal gratitude of posterity.

Fate had enticed Green and duped him, but she did not abandon him. She did not release him from her iron embrace, but picked him up and dragged him, confused and numb with disappointment, along a circuitous route towards his goal.

The pogrom began when the pharmacist's son was away from the little town. Consumed by an insatiable, jealous curiosity, he had gone to Kiev to find out the details of the regicide – the newspaper reports had been vague, for the most part emphasising the effusive outpourings of loyal subjects.

On Sunday morning the alarm bell sounded in the Orthodox quarter on the other side of the river, where the goys lived. The community had sent their tavern-keeper, Mitrii Kuzmich, to Belotserkovsk on a special errand and he had returned, bringing confirmation that the rumours were true: the Emperor-Tsar had been killed by Yids – which meant you could give the sheenies a good beating with no fear of the consequences.

The crowd set off across the railway bridge that divided the little town into two parts, Orthodox and Jewish. They walked in a calm, orderly fashion, carrying church banners and singing. When they were met by representatives of the other community – the rabbi, the director of the Jewish college and the market warden – they did nothing to them, but they did not listen to them either. They simply pushed them aside and spread out through the quiet, narrow streets where the closed shutters stared at them blindly. They spent a long time wondering where to start, waiting for the impulse they needed to unlock the doors of their souls.

The tavern-keeper himself set things moving: he stove in the door of a tavern that had opened the previous year and ruined his trade. The crashing and clattering dispelled the people's lethargy, and put them in the right mood.

Everything happened just the way it was supposed to: they fired the synagogue, rummaged through the little houses, broke a few men's ribs, dragged a few around by their sidelocks and in the evening, when the barrels of wine hidden in the tavern's cellar were discovered, some of the lads even got their hands on the Yids' young wenches.

It was still light as they made their way back, bearing off their bales of plunder and drunks. Before they dispersed, the whole community decided not to work the next day, because it was a sin to work when the people were grieving so badly, but to go across the river again.

When Green came back that evening the little town was unrecognisable: broken doors, feathers and fluff drifting in the air, a smell of smoke and from the windows the sound of women wailing and children crying.

His parents had survived by sitting it out in the stone cellar, but the house was in an appalling state: the anti-Semites had smashed more than they had taken, and they had dealt most viciously of all with the books – in their furious zeal they had torn the pages out of all five hundred volumes.

Green found the sight of his father's white face and trembling lips unbearable. His father told him that the pharmacy had been ransacked in the morning, because there was medical alcohol there. But that was not the most terrible thing. They had smashed in the old *tsaddik* Belkin's head, and he had died, and because the cobbler's wife Gesa refused to give them her daughter, they had chopped away half of her face with an axe. The next day the mob would come again. The people had collected together nine hundred and fifty roubles and taken the money to the district police officer and the police officer had taken it, saying he would go to fetch a troop of armed men, and left, but he would not be back before the following morning, so they would have to endure yet more suffering.

As Green listened, he blanched in his terrible mortification. Was this what fate had been preparing him for? – not a blinding flash erupting from beneath the wheels of a gilded carriage with a thunderclap that would echo round the world, but a senseless death under the cudgels of a drunken rabble? – In a remote backwater, for the sake of wretched people in whom he felt no interest, with whom he had nothing in common? He couldn't even understand their hideous dialect properly, because he had always spoken Russian at home. Their customs seemed savage and absurd to him, and he himself was a stranger to them, the half-crazy son of a Jew who hadn't wanted to live like a Jew (and what, I ask you, had come of that?).

But the stupidity and malice of the world demanded retaliation, and Green knew that he had no choice.

In the morning the bell sounded again in the goys' quarter and a dense crowd, more numerous than the previous day's, set off from the marketplace towards the bridge. They weren't singing today. After the wine from the tavern and the neat alcohol from the pharmacy, they were bleary-eyed, but still brisk and determined. Many of them were dragging along trolleys and wheelbarrows. Walking at the front with an icon in his hands was the man of the moment, Mitrii Kuzmich, wearing a red shirt and a new knee-length coat of good-quality cloth.

Stepping on to the bridge, the crowd stretched out into a grey ribbon. On the river below porous ice floes drifted downstream, another unstoppable mass of grey.

Standing in the middle of the rails at the far end of the bridge was a tall young Yid with the collar of his coat turned up. He had his hands in his pockets and the sullen wind was tousling the black hair on his hatless head.

The men at the front drew closer and the young Yid took his right hand out of his pocket without saying a word. The hand was holding a heavy, black revolver.

The men at the front stopped, but those at the back could not see the revolver; they pressed forward, and the crowd kept moving at the same speed.

Then the dark-haired man fired over their heads. The report boomed hollowly in the clear morning air and the river took it up eagerly, echoing it over and over again: Cra-ack! Cra-ack! Cra-ack!

The crowd stopped.

The dark-haired man still did not speak – his face was serious and still. The black circle of the revolver's muzzle moved lower, staring straight into the eyes of those standing at the front.

Egorsha the carpenter, an unruly and dissolute man, worked furiously with his elbows as he squeezed his way through the crowd. He had spent the whole previous day lying in a drunken stupor and had not gone to beat the Yids, so now he was burning up with impatience.

'Come on, come on,' said Egorsha, laughing and pushing up the sleeve of his tattered coat. 'Don't you worry; he won't fire; he won't dare.'

The revolver immediately replied to Egorsha's words with a loud crack and blue smoke.

The carpenter gasped, clutching at his wounded shoulder and squatting down on his haunches, and the black barrel barked another four times at regular intervals.

Now there were no more bullets in the cylinder, and Green took a home-made bomb out of his left pocket. But he did not need to throw it because Mitrii Kuzmich, wounded in the knee, began howling so terribly – 'Oh, oh, they've killed me, they've killed me, good Orthodox believers!' – that the crowd shuddered and pressed back and then set off at a run, with men trampling each other, back across the bridge into the Orthodox quarter.

As he watched the backs of the fleeing men, Green felt for the first time that there was very little sky-blue left in him. His dominant colour was steel-grey now.

At twilight the district police officer arrived with a platoon of mounted police and was surprised to see that all was quiet in the little town. He spoke with the Jews first and then took the pharmacist's son away to jail.

Grigory Grinberg became Green at the age of twenty, after one of his repeated escapes. He had walked one and a half thousand versts and then, just outside Tobolsk, been caught in a stupid police raid on tramps. He had had to give some kind of name, and that was what he called himself – not in memory of his old surname, but in honour of Ignatii Grinevitsky, who had killed the Tsar.

At the one thousand eight hundredth heartbeat he felt that his strength was fully restored and got lightly to his feet, without touching the floor with his hands. He had a lot of time. It was evening now; there was the whole night ahead.

He did not know how long he would have to spend in Moscow.

Probably about two weeks at least. Until they took the plain-clothes police agents off the turnpikes and the railway stations. Green was not concerned for himself; he had plenty of patience. Eight months of solitary confinement was good training for that. But the lads in the group were young and hot-headed; it would be hard for them.

He walked out of the bedroom into the drawing room, where the other three were sitting.

'Why aren't you sleeping?' asked Bullfinch, the very youngest of all, flustered. 'It's my fault, isn't it? I was talking too loud.'

All the members of the group were on familiar terms, regardless of their age or services to the revolution. What point was there in formality if tomorrow, or next week, or next month you might all go to your death together? Of all the people in the world Green only spoke like that to these three: Bullfinch, Emelya and Rahmet. There had been others before, but they were all dead.

Bullfinch was looking fresh, which was natural enough – they hadn't taken the boy on the operation, although he had begged them to, even weeping in his rage. The other two looked cheerful but tired, which was also only natural.

The operation had gone off more easily than expected. The blizzard had helped, but the greatest help of all had been the snowdrift on this side of Klin, a genuine gift of fate. Rahmet and Emelya had been waiting with a sleigh three versts from the station. According to the plan Green had been supposed to throw himself out of a window while the train was moving, and he could have been hurt. Then they would have picked him up. Or the guards could have spotted him as he jumped and opened fire. The sleigh would have come in handy in that case too.

Things had turned out better than that. Green had simply run along the track, entirely unharmed. He hadn't even got cold – running the three versts had warmed him up.

They had driven round the water meadows of the Sestra river, where workmen were clearing the line. At the next station they had stolen an old abandoned handcar and ridden it all the way to Sortirovochnaya Station in Moscow. Of course, pumping the rusty lever for fifty-something versts in the wind and driving snow had not been easy. It was hardly surprising that the lads had exhausted themselves: they weren't made of steel. First Rahmet had weakened, and then the doughty Emelya. Green had had to work the handle on his own for the entire second half of the journey.

'You're like the dragon Gorynich, you're Greenich!' Emelya said, shaking his flaxen-haired head in admiration. 'You crawled into your cave for half an hour, cast off your old scales, grew back the heads that had been cut off and now you're as good as new. Look at me, a big strapping hulk, but I haven't got my breath back yet, my tongue's still hanging out.'

Emelya was a good soldier. Strong, without any prissy intelligentsia pretensions. A wonderful, calming dark-brown colour. He had chosen his own alias, in honour of Emelya Pugachev; before that he had been known as Nikifor Tyunin. He was an armoury artisan, a genuine proletarian. Broad-shouldered and pie-faced, with a childish little nose and genial round eyes. It wasn't often that the oppressed class threw up steadfast, class-conscious warriors, but when one of these strapping heroes did appear, you could put your life in his hands with complete confidence. Green had personally selected Emelya from five candidates sent by the party. That was after Sable had failed when he flung his bomb at Khrapov, and a vacancy had appeared in the Combat Group. Green had tested the novice's strength of nerve and quickness of wit and been satisfied.

Emelya had really shown what he was worth during the operation in Ekaterinburg. When the Governor's droshky had driven up to the undistinguished townhouse on Mikhelson Street at the time indicated in the letter (and even, as promised, with no escort), Green had walked up to the fat man who was laboriously climbing out of the carriage and shot him twice at point-blank range. But when he ran through a passage to the next street, where Emelya was waiting disguised as a cab driver, they'd had a stroke of bad luck: at that very moment a police officer and two constables just happened to be walking past the false cabby. The policemen had heard the shots in the distance, and now here was a man running out of the yard – straight into their arms. Green had already thrown his revolver away. He felled one of them with a blow to the chin, but the other two clung to his arms and the one on the ground started blowing his whistle. Things were looking really bad, but the novice Emelya hadn't lost his head. He climbed down from his coachbox without hurrying and hit one constable on the back of the head with his massive fist so hard that he instantly went limp, and Green dealt with the other one himself. They had driven off like the wind, to the trilling of the police whistle.

It warmed his heart to look at Emelya. *The people won't carry on just lounging their lives away for ever*, he thought. *The ones with keen wits and active consciences have already started waking up. And that means the sacrifices are not in vain and the blood – ours and theirs – is not spilt for nothing.*

'So that's what sleeping on the floor and absorbing the juices of the earth does for you,' Rahmet said with a smile, tossing a picturesque lock of hair back off his forehead.

'I'd just started composing a poem about you, Green.'
And he declaimed:

> Once there was a Green of iron
> With a talent to rely on,
> Scorning sheets and feather bed,
> On bare boards he laid his head.

'There's another version too.' Rahmet raised his hand to stop Bullfinch laughing and continued:

> Once there was a poor knight errant,
> Green the Fearless was his name,
> With a very useful talent –
> He slept on floors to earn his fame.

His comrades laughed in unison and Green thought to himself: *That's a verse from Pushkin he rewrote; I suppose it's funny.* He knew that he didn't understand when something was funny, but that didn't matter, it wasn't important. And he mentally corrected the verse: I'm not iron, I'm steel.

He couldn't help himself – this thrill-seeking adventurer Rahmet simply wasn't to his liking, although he had to admit that he did a lot of good for the cause. Green had chosen him the previous autumn, when he needed a partner for a foreign operation – he couldn't take Emelya to Paris.

He had arranged for Rahmet to escape from the prison carriage as he was being driven away from the courthouse after sentencing. At the time all the newspapers were full of the story: the Uhlan cornet Seleznyov had interceded with his commanding officer for one of his men and in response to the colonel's crude insults had challenged him to a duel. And when his affronter had refused to accept the challenge, he had shot him dead in front of the entire regiment.

What Green had especially liked about this gallant story was the fact that a junior officer had not been afraid to ruin his entire life for the sake of a simple man. There was a promising recklessness in that, and Green had even imagined a certain kinship of souls – a familiar fury in response to base stupidity.

However, Nikolai Seleznyov's motivation had turned out to be something quite different. On close acquaintance, his colour proved to be an alarming cornflower-blue. 'I'm terribly inquisitive; I like new experiences,' Rahmet used to repeat frequently. What drove the fugitive cornet on through life was curiosity, a pointless and useless feeling that forced him to try first one dish and then another – the spicier and hotter the better. Green realised that he had not shot the colonel out of a sense of justice, but because the entire regiment was watching with bated breath, waiting to see what would happen. And he had joined the revolutionaries out of a craving for adventures. He had enjoyed the shooting during his escape, and he had enjoyed the trip to Paris even more.

Green had no illusions left about Rahmet's motives. He had chosen his alias in honour of the hero of Chernyshevsky's 'What is to be Done?', but he was a different sort of creature altogether. As long as he still found terrorist operations interesting, he would stay. Once his curiosity was satisfied, he'd be off, and never be seen again.

Green's secret concern in dealing with Rahmet was to extract the maximum benefit for the cause from this vacuous individual. The idea he had in mind was to send him on one of those important missions from which no one returns. Let him throw himself, a living bomb, under the hooves of the team pulling the carriage of a minister or a provincial governor. Rahmet wouldn't be afraid of certain death – that was one trick life hadn't shown him yet. If the operation at Klin had been a failure, Rahmet's mission would have been to blow up Khrapov this evening at the Yaroslavl Station, just before he left for Siberia. Well, Khrapov was dead already, but there would be others; autocracy kept plenty of other vicious guard dogs. The important thing was not to miss the moment when boredom appeared in Rahmet's eyes.

This was the only reason why Green had kept him in the group after what had happened with Shverubovich in December.

The order had come from the party to execute the traitor who had betrayed the comrades in Riga and sent them to the gallows. Green didn't like that kind of work, so he had not objected when Rahmet volunteered to do it.

Instead of simply shooting Shverubovich, Rahmet had chosen to be more inventive and splash sulphuric acid into his face. He had said it was to put a fright into any other stoolpigeons, but in reality he had simply wanted to see what it looked like when a living man's eyes poured out of their sockets and his lips and nose fell off. Ever since then Green had been unable to look at Rahmet without a feeling of revulsion, but he put up with him for the good of the cause.

'You should go to bed,' he said in a quiet voice. 'I know it's only ten. But you should sleep. It's an early start tomorrow. We're changing apartments.'

He glanced round at the white door of the study where the owner of this apartment, Semyon Lvovich Aronson, a private lecturer at the Higher Technical College, was sitting. They had planned to stay at a different address in Moscow, but there had been a surprise waiting for them. The female courier who met the group at the agreed spot had warned them that they couldn't go to the meeting place – it had just been discovered that the engineer Larionov, who owned the apartment, was an agent of the Okhranka.

The courier had a strange alias: Needle. Green, still reeling after pumping the handcar, had told her: 'You Muscovites do poor work. An agent at a meeting place could destroy the entire Combat Group.'

He had said it without malice, simply stating a fact, but Needle had taken offence.

Green didn't know much about her. He thought she came from a rich family. A dry, gangling, ageing young lady. Bloodless, pursed lips; dull, colourless hair arranged in a tight bun at the back of her head – there were plenty like that in the revolution.

'If we did poor work, we wouldn't have exposed Larionov,' Needle had retorted. 'Tell me, Green, do you absolutely need an apartment with a telephone? It's not that easy.'

'I know, but there must be a telephone – for emergency contact, an alarm signal, warning,' he explained, promising himself to make do in future with only his own resources, without help from the party.

'Then we'll have to assign you to one of the reserve addresses, with one of the sympathisers. Moscow's not St Petersburg; not many people have their own telephones here.'

That was how the group had come to be billeted at the private lecturer's place. Needle had said he was more of a liberal than a revolutionary, and he didn't approve of terrorist methods. That was all right: he was an honest man with progressive views and he wouldn't refuse to help; but there was no point in telling him any details.

Having taken Green and his people to a fine apartment house on Ostozhenka Street (a spacious apartment on the very top floor, and that was valuable, because there was access to the roof), before she left the courier had briskly and succinctly explained the elementary rules of the clandestine operation to their jittery host.

'Your building is the tallest in this part of the city, and that is convenient. From my mezzanine floor I can see your windows through binoculars. If everything is calm, do not close the curtains in the drawing room. Two closed curtains mean disaster. One closed curtain is the alarm signal. I'll telephone you and ask for Professor Brandt. You will reply: "You are mistaken, this is a different number" – and in that case I shall come immediately; or if you say: "You are mistaken, this is private lecturer Aronson's number" – I shall send a combat squad to assist you. Will you remember that?'

Aronson nodded, pale-faced, and when Needle left he muttered that the 'comrades' could use the apartment as they saw fit, that he had given the servants time off, and if he was needed, he would be in his study. And in half a day he hadn't peeped out of there even once. He was a real 'sympathiser' all right. *No, we can't stay here for two weeks*, Green had decided immediately. *Tomorrow we have to find a new place.*

'What's the point in sleeping?' Rahmet asked with a shrug. 'Of course, you gentlemen do as you wish, but I'd rather pay a visit to that Judas Larionov – before he realises he's been discovered. Twenty-eight Povarskaya Street, isn't it? Not so far away.'

'That's right!' Bullfinch agreed enthusiastically. 'I'd like to go along. It would be even better if I went on my own, because you've already done your job for the day. I can manage, honest I can! He'll open the door, and I'll ask: "Are you engineer Larionov?" That's so as not to kill an innocent man by mistake. And then I'll say: "Take this, you traitor." I'll shoot him in the heart – three times to make sure – and run for it. A piece of cake.'

Rahmet threw his head back and laughed loudly. 'A piece of cake, of course it is! You shoot him – go on, just try. When I let von Bock have it point-blank on the parade ground, his eyes leapt out of their sockets, I swear to God! Two little red balls. I dreamed about it for ages. Used to wake up at night in a cold sweat. A piece of cake . . .'

And what about Shverubovich with his face melting, Green thought, *do you dream about him?*

'It's all right; if it's for the cause, I can do it,' Bullfinch declared manfully, turning pale and then immediately flushing bright red. He had got his nickname from the constant high colour of his cheeks and the light-coloured fluff that covered them. 'The bastard betrayed his own, didn't he?'

Green had known Bullfinch for a long time, a lot longer than the others. He was a special boy, bred from precious stock – the son of a hanged regicide and a female member of the People's Will party, who had died in a prison cell while on hunger strike; the child of unmarried parents, not christened in church, raised by comrades of his mother and father; the first free citizen of the future free Russia; with no garbage in his head, no filth polluting his soul. Some day boys like that would be quite ordinary, but for now he was one of a kind, the invaluable product of a painful process of evolution, and so Green had really not wanted to take Bullfinch into the group.

But how could he not have taken him? Three years earlier, when Green had escaped from the state prison and was making his way home the long way round the world – through China, Japan and America – he had been detained for a while in Switzerland. Just hanging about with nothing to do, waiting for the escort to guide him across the border. Bullfinch had only just been sent there from Russia, where his guardians had been arrested yet again, and there was no one in Zurich to take care of the little lad. They had asked Green, and he had agreed because at that time there was nothing else he could do to help the party. The escort was delayed and then disappeared completely. Before they managed to arrange a new one, a whole year had gone by.

For some reason Green didn't find the boy a burden – quite the opposite, in fact; perhaps because for the first time in a long time he was obliged to concern himself not with the whole of mankind but with one single individual. And not even an adult, but a raw young boy.

One day, after a long, serious conversation, Green made his

young ward a promise: when Bullfinch grew up, Green would let him work with him, no matter what he might happen to be doing at the time. The Combat Group had not even been thought of then, or Green would never have promised such a thing.

Then he had come back home to Russia and set to work. He often remembered the boy, but of course he completely forgot about his promise. And then, just two months ago, in Peter, they had brought Bullfinch to him in a clandestine apartment. *Here, comrade Green, meet our young reinforcements from the emigration.* Bullfinch had gazed at him with adoration in his eyes and started talking about the promise almost from the very first moment. There was nothing Green could do about it – he didn't know how to go back on his word.

He had taken care of the boy and kept him away from the action, but things couldn't go on like that for ever. And after all, Bullfinch was grown up now – eighteen years old. The same age Green had been on that railway bridge.

Not just yet, he had told himself the previous night, as he prepared for the operation. Next time. And he had ordered Bullfinch to leave for Moscow – supposedly to check on their contacts.

Bullfinch was a delicate peach colour. What kind of warrior would he make? Though it did sometimes happen that people like that turned out to be genuine heroes. He ought to arrange a baptism of fire for the boy, but the execution of a traitor was not the right place to start.

'Nobody's going anywhere,' Green said with authority. 'Everybody sleep. I'll take first watch. Rahmet's on in two hours. I'll wake him.'

'E-eh,' said the former cornet with a smile. 'You're a fine man in every way, Green, only boring. Terror's not the right business for you. You ought to be a bookkeeper in a bank.' But he didn't argue, he knew there was no point.

They drew lots. Rahmet got the bed to sleep on, Emelya got the divan and Bullfinch got the folded blanket.

For fifteen minutes he heard talking and laughter from behind the door, and then everything was quiet. After that their host looked out of the study, his gold pince-nez glinting in the semi-darkness, and muttered uncertainly: 'Good evening.'

Green nodded, but the private lecturer didn't go away.

Green felt that he had to show some consideration. After all, this was inconvenient for the man, and risky. They gave you penal servitude for harbouring terrorists. He said politely: 'I know we've incommoded you, Semyon Lvovich. Be patient – we'll leave tomorrow.'

Aronson hesitated, as if there were something he was afraid to ask, and Green guessed that he wanted to talk. After all, he was a cultured man, a member of the intelligentsia. Once he got started, he wouldn't stop until morning.

Oh no. Firstly, it was not a good idea to strike up a speculative conversation with an unproven individual, and secondly, he had something serious to think over.

'I'm in your way here,' he said, getting up decisively. 'I'll sit in the kitchen for a while.'

He sat down on a hard chair beside a curtained entrance (he had already checked it: it was the servant girl's box room). He started thinking about 'TG'. For perhaps the thousandth time in the last few months.

It had all started in September, a few days after Sable blew himself up – he had thrown a bomb at Khrapov as the General was coming out of a church, but the device had struck the kerb of the pavement and all the shrapnel had been thrown back at the bomber.

That was when the first letter had come.

No, it hadn't come; it had been found – on the dining table in the apartment where the Combat Group was quartered at the time, a place to which only very few people had access.

It wasn't really a group – that was just a name, because after Sable's death Green was the only active warrior left. The helpers and the couriers didn't count.

The Combat Group had been formed after Green returned to Russia illegally. He had spent a long time assessing where he could be most useful, where he should apply the match so that the blaze would flare up as fiercely as possible. He had transported leaflets, helped to set up an underground printing works, guarded the party congress. All this was necessary, but he had not forged himself into a man of steel in order to do work that anyone could manage.

His goal had gradually taken clear shape. It was the same as before: terror. After the destruction of the People's Will party the level of militant revolutionary activity had dwindled away to almost nothing. The police was no longer what it had been in the seventies. There were spies and agent provocateurs everywhere. In the whole of the last decade there had only been a couple of successful terrorist operations and a dozen failures. What good was that?

If there was no struggle against tyranny, revolutions did not happen – that was axiomatic. Tsarism would not be overthrown by leaflets and educational groups. Terror was as necessary as air, as a mouthful of water in the desert.

After carefully thinking everything through, Green had begun to act. He had a word with Melnikov, a member of the Central Committee whom he trusted completely, and was granted qualified approval. He would carry out the first operation entirely at his own risk. If it was successful, the party would announce the establishment of a Combat Group and provide financial and organisational support. If it failed, he had been acting alone.

That was logical. In any case acting alone was safer – you certainly wouldn't betray yourself to the Okhranka. Green also set one condition: Melnikov was to be the only member of the Central Committee who knew about him; all contacts had to go through him. If Green required helpers, he would choose them himself.

The first mission he was given was to carry out the sentence that had been pronounced a long time ago on Privy Counsellor Yakimovich. Yakimovich was a murderer and a villain. Three years earlier he had sent five students to the scaffold for planning to kill the Tsar. It had been a dirty case, based from the beginning on entrapment by the police and Yakimovich himself, who was not yet a privy counsellor, but only a modest assistant public prosecutor.

Green had killed him during his Sunday walk in the park – simply, without any fancy business: just walked up and stabbed him through the heart with a dagger, with the letters 'CG' carved into its handle. Before the people around him realised what had happened, he had already left the park – at a quick walk, not a run – and driven away in an ordinary cab.

This terrorist act, the first to be carried out after a long hiatus, had really shaken up public opinion. Everyone had started talking about the mysterious organisation with the mysterious name, and when the party announced what the letters meant and declared that revolutionary war had been renewed, a half-forgotten nervous tremor had run through the country – the tremor without which any social upheavals were unthinkable.

Now Green had everything necessary for serious work: equipment, money, people. He found the people himself or selected them from candidates proposed by the party. He made it a rule that there should be no more than three or four people in the group. For terror that was quite enough.

Big operations were planned, but the next assassination attempt – on the butcher Khrapov – had ended in failure. Not total failure, because a revolver bearing the letters 'CG' had been found on the dead bomber, and that had produced an impression. But even so, the group's reputation had been damaged. There could not be any more flops.

And that had been the situation when Green discovered the sheet of paper with the neatly typed lines of words, lying folded in two on the table. He had burned the paper, but he remembered what was written on it word for word.

Better not touch Khrapov for the time being; he is too well guarded now. When there is a chance to reach him, I shall inform you. Meanwhile, I can tell you that Bogdanov, the Governor of Ekaterinburg, visits house number ten on Mikhelson Street in secret at eight o'clock in the evening on Thursdays. Alone, with no guards. Next Thursday he is certain to be there. Burn this letter and those that follow as soon as you have read them.

TG

The first thought that had occurred to him was that the party was overdoing its conspiratorial methods. Why the melodramatic touch of leaving the letter like that? And what did 'TG' mean?

He asked Melnikov. No, the party Central Committee had not sent the note.

Was it a gendarme trap? It didn't look like one. Why beat about the bush like that? Why lure him to Ekaterinburg? If the police knew his clandestine apartment, they would have arrested him right there.

It had to be a third option. Someone wanted to help the Combat Group while remaining in the shadows.

After some hesitation, Green had decided to risk it. Of course, Governor Bogdanov was no major VIP, but the year before he had been condemned to death by the party for his vicious suppression of peasant riots in the Streletsk district. It wasn't a top priority mission, but why not? Green needed a success.

And he had got one. The operation went off wonderfully well, if you disregarded the scuffle with the police. Green left a sheet of paper at the scene – the party's death sentence, signed with the initials 'CG'.

Then, at the very beginning of winter, a second letter had appeared: he found it in the pocket of his own coat. He was at a wedding – not a genuine wedding, of course, but a fictitious one. Two party members had wed for the sake of the cause, and at the same time an opportunity had been provided to meet legally and discuss a few urgent matters. There had not been any letter in his coat when he took it off. But when he put his hand in the pocket as he was leaving, there was the sheet of paper.

The lieutenant general of gendarmes, Selivanov, who is well known to you, is inspecting the foreign agents of the Department of Security incognito. At half past two in the

afternoon on 13 December he will go to a clandestine
apartment at 24 rue Annamite in Paris.

TG

And once again everything had happened exactly as the
unknown TG had promised: taking the cunning fox Selivanov
had been almost child's play, in fact – something they could
never have dreamed of in St Petersburg. They waited for the
gendarme in the entrance, Green grabbed him by the elbows,
and Rahmet stuck the dagger into him. The Combat Group
became the sensation of Europe.

Green had found the third letter on the floor in the entrance
hall earlier this year, when the four of them were living on
Vasilievsky Island in St Petersburg. This time the writer had
directed his attention to Colonel Pozharsky, an artful rogue who
was one of the new crop of gendarmes. The previous autumn
Pozharsky had destroyed the Warsaw branch of the party, and
he had just arrested an anarchist sailors' organisation in Kronstadt that had been planning to blow up the royal yacht. As a
reward he had received a high post in the Police Department
and an aide-de-camp's monogram for saving the imperial family.
The note had read as follows:

The search for the CG has been entrusted to the new deputy
director for political affairs at the Police Department, Count
Pozharsky. He is a dangerous opponent who will cause you
a lot of trouble. On Wednesday evening between nine and
ten he has a meeting with an important agent on Aptekarsky
Island near the Kerbel company dacha. A convenient
moment: do not let it slip.

TG

They *had* let the moment slip, even though it really was
convenient. Pozharsky had demonstrated quite supernatural
agility, returning fire as he melted away into the darkness. His
companion had proved less nimble and Rahmet had caught him
with a bullet in the back as he was running off.

Even so, the operation had proved useful and caused a sensation, because Green had recognised the man who was killed as Stasov, a member of the party's Central Committee and an old veteran of the Schlisselburg Fortress who had only just returned illegally to Russia from Switzerland. Who could have imagined that the police had people like that among their informers?

The latest message from TG, the fourth and most valuable, had appeared yesterday morning. It was hot in the house, and they had left the small upper window open for the night. In the morning Emelya had found the letter wrapped round a stone on the floor beside the window. He had read it and gone running to wake Green.

And now it is Khrapov's turn. He is leaving for Siberia today by the eleven o'clock express, in a ministerial carriage. I have managed to discover the following: Khrapov will make a stop in Moscow. The person responsible for his security while in Moscow is State Counsellor Fandorin, Prince Dolgorukoi's Deputy for Special Assignments. Description: 35 years old, slim build, tall, black hair, narrow moustache, grey temples, stammers in conversation. Extreme security measures have been planned in St Petersburg and Moscow. It is only possible to get close to Khrapov between these points. Think of something. There will be four agents in the carriage, and a duty guard of gendarmes in both lobbies (the front lobby is blind, with no access to the saloon). The head of Khrapov's guard is Staff Captain von Seidlitz: 32 years of age, very light hair, tall, solidly built. Khrapov's adjutant is Lieutenant Colonel Modzalevsky: 39 years of age, stout, medium height, dark-brown hair, small sideburns.

TG

Green had put together a daring but perfectly feasible plan and made all the necessary preparations. The group had left for Klin on the three o'clock passenger train.

Once again TG's information had proved to be impeccable. Everything went without a hitch. It was the Combat Group's greatest triumph so far. It might have seemed that now he could afford to relax and congratulate himself on a job well done. The match had not been extinguished, it was still burning, and meanwhile the fire it had kindled was blazing ever more furiously.

But his enjoyment was marred by the mystery. Green could not abide mystery. Where there was mystery, there was unpredictability, and that was dangerous.

He had to work out who TG was – understand what kind of man he was and what he was after.

He had only one possible explanation.

One of his helpers, or even a member of the actual Combat Group, had someone in the secret police from whom he received confidential information that he passed on anonymously to Green. It was clear why he did not make himself known. That was to maintain secrecy; he did not wish to increase the number of people who knew his secret (Green himself always behaved in the same way). Or he was shielding his informant, bound by his word of honour – that sort of thing happened.

But what if it was entrapment?

No, that was out of the question. The blows that the group had struck against the machinery of state with the assistance of TG were too substantial. No tactical expediency could possibly justify an entrapment operation on that level. And most importantly of all: not once in all these past months had they been under surveillance. Green had an especially keen nose for that.

Two abbreviations: CG and TG. The first stood for an organisation. Did the second stand for a name? Why had there been any need for a signature at all?

That was what he must do when he got back to Peter: draw up a list of everyone who had had access to the places where the notes had been left. If he included only those who could have reached all four places, the list was a short one. Only a few people in addition to the members of the group. He had to identify who it was and engage them in candid conversation. One to one, with proper guarantees of confidentiality.

But it was a quarter past twelve already. His two hours were up. It was time to wake Rahmet.

Green walked through the drawing room into the dark bedroom. He heard Bullfinch's regular snuffling, Emelya's gentle snoring.

'Rahmet, get up,' Green whispered, leaning down over the bed and reaching out his hand.

There was nothing there. He squatted down and felt around on the floor: there were no boots.

Rahmet, the cornflower-blue man, was gone. He had either set out in search of adventures or simply run off.

CHAPTER 3

in which the costs of dual subordination are demonstrated

'How much l-longer will we be subjected to scrutiny?' Erast Petrovich asked drearily, glancing round at Burlyaev.

About five minutes had passed since the State Counsellor and the Lieutenant Colonel (who had changed his blue uniform for civilian clothes) first entered the gate of the modest townhouse on Arbat Street and rang the bell. At first the curtain in the window of the attic storey had swayed in very promising fashion, but since then nothing had happened.

'I warned you,' the head of the Okhranka said in a low voice: 'a capricious character. Without me here she wouldn't open the door to a stranger at all.' He threw his head back and shouted – not for the first time: 'Diana, it's me, open up! And the gentleman I telephoned you about is with me!'

No reply.

Fandorin already knew that this little townhouse, rented through an intermediary, was one of the Department of Security's clandestine meeting places, and it had been placed entirely at the disposal of the highly valued collaborator. Meetings with her always took place here and nowhere else, and always by prior arrangement, for which purpose a telephone had been specially installed in the house.

'Madam!' said Erast Petrovich, raising his voice, 'you will f-freeze us! This is quite simply impolite! Do you wish to take a better look at me? Then you should have said so straight away.'

He took off his top hat, raised his face, swung round to present his left profile, then his right and – oh, wonder of wonders! – a small window frame opened slightly, white fingers were thrust out through it and a bronze key fell at his very feet.

'Ooph,' said the Lieutenant Colonel, bending down. 'Let me do it. There's a trick to the lock . . .'

They took off their coats in the empty hallway. Pyotr Ivanovich seemed strangely agitated. He combed his hair in the mirror and set off first up the creaking stairs to the mezzanine.

At the top of the stairs there was a short corridor with two doors. The Lieutenant Colonel knocked briefly on the door on the left and entered without waiting for an answer.

Strangely enough, it was almost completely dark in the room. Erast Petrovich's nostrils caught the scent of musk oil, and on looking round he saw that the curtains were tightly closed and there was no lamp in the room. It seemed to be a study. At least, there was the dark form of something like a secretaire over by the wall, and the grey silhouette of a desk in the corner. It was a few moments before the State Counsellor spotted the slim female figure with the disproportionately large head that was standing motionless beside the window. Fandorin took two steps forward and realised that his hostess was wearing a hat with a veil.

'Please be seated, gentlemen,' the woman said in a voice hushed to a sibilant whisper, gesturing elegantly to a pair of armchairs. 'Good morning, Pyotr Ivanovich. What is so very urgent? And who is your companion?'

'This is Mr Fandorin, Count Dolgorukoi's Deputy for Special Assignments,' Burlyaev replied, also in a whisper. 'He is conducting the investigation into the murder of Adjutant General Khrapov. Perhaps you have already heard?'

Diana nodded and waited until her guests were seated, then also sat down – on a divan standing against the opposite wall.

'How could you have heard? There's been n-nothing in the newspapers about it yet.'

The words were pronounced in a perfectly normal voice, but by contrast with the whisper that had preceded them, they sounded very loud.

'News travels fast,' the collaborator murmured mockingly. 'We revolutionaries have our own telegraph wires.'

'But more p-precisely? Where could you have heard?' said the State Counsellor, ignoring her frivolous tone.

'Diana, this is very important,' Burlyaev rumbled in his deep bass, as if he were trying to smooth over the abruptness of the question. 'You can't possibly imagine just how important—'

'Why not? – I understand.' The woman leaned back. 'For Khrapov you could all be thrown out of your cosy little jobs. Is that not so, Erast Petrovich?'

There was no denying that the low, hushed voice was provocatively sensuous, thought Fandorin – like the scent of musk, and the casually graceful movements of the slim hand idly toying with the earring in her ear. He was beginning to understand why this Messalina roused such intense passions in the Office of Gendarmes and the Department of Security.

'How do you know my first name and patronymic?' he asked, leaning forward slightly. 'Has somebody already told you about me?'

He thought Diana must have smiled – her whisper became even more insinuating.

'On more than one occasion. There are many people in Moscow who take an interest in you, Monsieur Fandorin. You are a fascinating character.'

'And has anybody spoken to you about the State Counsellor just recently?' Burlyaev put in. 'Yesterday, for instance? Have you had any visitors here?'

Erast Fandorin glanced sideways in displeasure at this intrusive assistance, and Diana laughed soundlessly.

'I have many visitors, Pierre. Have any of them spoken to me about Monsieur Fandorin? I can't really recall ...'

She won't say, Erast Petrovich realised, taking mental note of that 'Pierre'. This was a waste of time.

He introduced a hint of metal into his voice. 'You have not answered my first question. From whom exactly did you learn that General Khrapov had been killed?'

Diana rose abruptly to her feet and the tone of her whisper changed from caressing to piercing, like the hiss of an enraged snake. 'I am not on your payroll and I am not obliged to report to you! You forget yourself! Or perhaps they have not explained to you who I am? Very well, I shall answer your question, but that will be the end of the conversation. And do not come here any more. Do you hear, Pyotr Ivanovich – let me never see this gentleman here again!'

The Lieutenant Colonel stroked his short-cropped hair in bewilderment, clearly not knowing whose side to take, but Fandorin replied imperturbably.

'Very well, we will go. But I am waiting for an answer.'

The woman moved towards the window, so that the grey rectangle framed her shapely silhouette.

'The killing of Khrapov is an open secret. Every revolutionary group in Moscow already knows about it and is rejoicing. This evening there will be a party to celebrate the occasion. I have been invited, but I shall not go. You, however, could call in. If you are lucky you might pick up a few illegal activists. The gathering is at the apartment of engineer Larionov. Twenty-eight Povarskaya Street.'

'Why didn't you ask her directly about Sverchinsky?' the Lieutenant Colonel exclaimed angrily as they rode back to the Department in the sleigh. 'I suspect that he visited her yesterday and he could easily have given something away. You saw for yourself what kind of character she is. She toys with men like a cat with mice.'

'Yes,' Fandorin replied absent-mindedly, nodding. 'A lady of some character. But never mind her. What we have to do is put this Larionov's apartment under surveillance. Assign the most experienced agents, let them follow each of the guests home and establish their identity. And then we'll run through all of their contacts, right along the chain. And when we come across the person who was the first to find out about Khrapov, from there it will only be a short step to the Combat Group.'

Burlyaev responded patronisingly: 'There's no need to do any of that. Larionov's one of our agents. We set up the apartment specially – to maintain our surveillance of discontents and dubious individuals. It was Zubtsov's idea, the clever chap. All sorts of riff-raff with revolutionary connections get together at Larionov's place – to abuse the authorities, to sing forbidden songs and, of course, for a drink and a bite to eat. Larionov keeps a good table; our secret fund pays for it. We take note of the blabbermouths and open a file on each one of them. As soon as we can nab them for something serious, we already have the full collected works on the little darlings.'

'But that's entrapment!' Erast Petrovich protested with a frown. 'First you engender nihilists, and then you arrest them.'

Burlyaev set his hand to his chest in a gesture of respect. 'Begging your pardon, Mr Fandorin, you are, of course, a well-known authority in the field of criminal investigation, but you have little understanding of our trade in the line of security.'

'Well then, there is no need to have Larionov's guests shadowed?'

'There is not.'

'Then what d-do you suggest?'

'No need to suggest anything; everything's clear enough as it is. When I get back now, I'll instruct Evstratii Pavlovich to put together an arrest operation. A single broad sweep – we'll pull in all the little darlings at once, then I'll give them the full works. One thing you're right about is that the thread leads from one of them to the Combat Group.'

'Arrest? On what grounds?'

'On the grounds, dear Erast Petrovich, that, as Diana so rightly remarked, in a day or two you and I will be flung out on our backsides. There's no time to waste on tailing people. We need results.'

Fandorin felt it necessary to adopt an official tone. 'Do not forget, Mr Lieutenant Colonel, that you have been instructed to follow my directions. I will not permit any arrests without due grounds.'

Burlyaev, however, did not buckle under pressure. 'Correct, I have been so instructed. By the Governor General. But in the line of investigation I am subordinated to the Police Department, not the Governor's office and so I must politely beg your pardon. If you wish to be present at the arrest – by all means; only do not interfere. If you prefer to stay out of it – that's up to you.'

Erast Petrovich said nothing. He knitted his brows and his

eyes glinted menacingly, but no thunderbolt or peal of lightning followed.

After a pause the State Counsellor said coolly: 'Very well. I shall not interfere, but I shall be present.'

At eight o'clock that evening all the preparations for the operation were complete

The building on Povarskaya Street had been surrounded since half past six. The first ring of the cordon, the closest, consisted of five agents: one of them, in a white apron, was scraping up the snow outside the very doors of the single-storey house that bore the number twenty-eight; three, the shortest and puniest, were pretending to be juveniles, building a snow castle in the yard; another two were repairing a gas lamp on the corner of Ss. Boris and Gleb Lane. The second ring, consisting of eleven agents, had a radius of a hundred paces: three 'cabbies', a 'police constable', an 'organ-grinder', two 'drunks' and four 'yard-keepers'.

At five minutes past eight Burlyaev and Fandorin rode down Povarskaya Street on a sleigh. Sitting on the driving box, half-turned towards them, was the undercover agents' commander, Mylnikov, pointing out how things had been set up.

'Excellent, Evstratii Pavlovich,' the Lieutenant Colonel said, approving the arrangements with a triumphant glance at the State Counsellor, who so far had not said a single word. 'Well now, Mr Fandorin, do my men know how to do their job or not?'

Erast Petrovich said nothing. The sleigh turned on to Skaryatinsky Lane, drove on a little further and stopped.

'How many of the little darlings are there?' asked Burlyaev.

'In all, not counting Larionov and his cook, there are eight individuals,' Mylnikov began explaining in a pleasant north Russian accent. He was a plump gentleman who looked about forty years old, with a light-brown beard and long hair cut pudding-basin style. 'At six o'clock, when we started setting up the cordon, by your leave, Pyotr Ivanovich, I sent in one of my men, supposedly with a registered letter. The cook whispered to him that there were three outsiders. And then another five showed up – all of them individuals known to us, and the list has already been drawn up: six individuals of the male sex and two of the female. My man told the cook to stay in her room and not stick her head out. I took a look in through the window from the next roof – the nihilists are enjoying themselves, drinking wine; they've already started singing. A real revolutionary Shrovetide it is.'

Mylnikov giggled briefly, to make quite sure no doubt could remain that these final words were a joke.

'I think, Pyotr Ivanovich, that now's the time to take them. Or else they'll take a drop too much; they might even offer resistance if they get their Dutch courage up. Or some early bird will make for the door and we'll have to divide our forces. We'd have to take him real careful like, some ways off, so as not to stir up the rest of them.'

'Perhaps you haven't brought in enough men, Evstratii Pavlovich. After all, there are eight of them,' the Lieutenant Colonel said doubtfully. 'I told you it would be a good idea to take some police constables from the station and put a third circle round the yards and the crossroads.'

'No need for that, Pyotr Ivanovich,' Mylnikov purred, unconcerned. 'My men are trained wolfhounds, and this lot, begging your pardon, are only small fry, minnows – young ladies and little students.'

Burlyaev rubbed his nose with his glove (as evening approached it had started to get frosty). 'Never mind; if the small fry already know about Khrapov, that means one of them is well in with a big fish. Godspeed, Evstratii Pavlovich; get to work.'

The sleigh drove along Povarskaya Street again, but this time the false cabby had hung a lantern on the horses' shaft, and at this signal the second ring moved in closer. At precisely eight thirty Mylnikov put four fingers in his mouth and whistled, and that very instant the seven agents broke into the house.

The top men – Burlyaev, Mylnikov and Fandorin – entered immediately behind them. The others formed a new cordon and stood under the windows.

In the entrance hall Erast Petrovich peeped out from behind the Lieutenant Colonel's back and saw a spacious drawing room, a number of young people sitting at a table and a young lady at a piano.

'Don't get up, or I'll put a bullet through your bonce!' Mylnikov thundered in a terrible voice quite unlike his previous one and struck a student who had jumped up off his chair on the forehead with the handle of his revolver. Instantly turning pale, the student sat back down and a scarlet stream sprang from his split eyebrow. The other guests at the party stared at the blood, spellbound, and not one of them said a word. The agents quickly took up positions round the table, holding their guns at the ready.

'Two, four, six, eight,' Mylnikov said quickly, counting the heads. 'Eremeev, Zykov, check the rooms, quick! There should be another one!' As the agents went out, he shouted at their backs: 'And don't forget the privy!'

'Well now, well now, what's the meaning of all this?' the man with spectacles and a goatee beard sitting at the head of the table – evidently the host – exclaimed in a trembling voice. 'This is my name-day celebration! I am engineer Larionov of the Tryokhgorny cement factory! This is absolutely outrageous!'

He smashed his fist down on the table and stood up, but the agent standing behind him seized his throat in a grip of iron, reducing Larionov's voice to a feeble wheeze.

Mylnikov said imposingly: 'I'll give you a name day. If anyone else so much as twitches, it's a bullet in the belly, straight off. I have my orders: if there's any resistance, shoot without warning. Sit down!' he barked at the engineer, who was pale from pain and fear, and the man plumped down on to his chair.

Eremeev and Zykov came in from the corridor, leading a man who was doubled over with his hands forced up behind his back. They tossed him into an empty seat.

Burlyaev cleared his throat and stepped forward. Evidently it was his turn now. 'Hmm, Mr Collegiate Assessor, that's going a bit too far. You need to see who it is you're dealing with. We appear to have been misled. These people are not bombers;

they're a perfectly decent group. And then' – he lowered his voice, but it could still be heard – 'I told you to manage the arrest tactfully. Why go hitting people on the head with revolvers and twisting their arms? That really is too bad.'

Evstratii Pavlovich frowned in annoyance and muttered: 'As you wish, Mr Lieutenant Colonel, but I'd like to have a little talk with these bastards after my own fashion. You'll only spoil everything with all this liberalism of yours. Just give them to me for half an hour and they'll sing like nightingales, I give you my word of honour as a gentleman on that.'

'Oh no,' Pyotr Ivanovich hissed. 'Spare me your methods, please. I'll find out everything I need to know for myself. Mr Larionov, what have you got behind that door over there – a study? You don't mind if I use it to have a chat with your guests, one at a time, do you? Please do excuse me, gentlemen, but this is a bit of an emergency.' The Lieutenant Colonel ran his glance over the detainees. 'This morning Adjutant General Khrapov was murdered. The same Khrapov . . . Ah, but I see you're not surprised? Well, we'll have a little chat about that too. If you have no objections.'

'"If you have no objections" – Oh, my God!' Mylnikov exclaimed, grinding his teeth as he dashed out into the corridor in a fury, knocking over a chair on the way.

Erast Petrovich gave a doleful sigh – the entire manoeuvre was far too transparent; but it seemed to produce the required effect on the detainees. At least, all of them were gazing in stupefaction at the door through which Evstratii Pavlovich had made his exit.

But no, not all of them. One slim young lady who was sitting by the piano, off to one side of the main developments, did not appear to be stupefied at all. Her black eyes were blazing with indignation, the pretty, dark features of her face contorted into a mask of hatred. The young woman curled up her scarlet lips in a furious, silent whisper, reached out one slim hand to the handbag lying on the piano and pulled out a small, elegant revolver.

The intrepid young miss grasped the gun tightly with both

hands, aiming it straight at the back of the Lieutenant Colonel of gendarmes. From a standing start, Erast Petrovich vaulted almost halfway across the drawing room in a single prodigious leap, lashing his cane down on the gun barrel before his feet even touched the floor.

The toy with the mother-of-pearl handle struck the floor and fired – not really all that loudly, but Burlyaev flung himself violently to one side and all the agents swung their gun barrels round towards the reckless young woman. They would undoubtedly have riddled her with bullets if not for Erast Petrovich, whose tremendous jump had terminated just in front of the piano, so that the malefactress was hidden behind the State Counsellor's back.

'Ah, so that's the way!' exclaimed the Lieutenant Colonel, still recovering from the shock. 'So that's the way! You bitch! I'll kill you where you stand!' And he pulled a large revolver out of his pocket.

Mylnikov came running in from the corridor at the noise and shouted: 'Pyotr Ivanovich! Stop! We need her alive! Take her, lads!'

The agents lowered their guns and two of them dashed over to the young lady and seized her by the arms.

Burlyaev unceremoniously shoved the State Counsellor aside and stood in front of the black-haired terrorist, towering over her by almost a full head.

'Who are you?' he gasped out, struggling to recover his breath. 'What's your name?'

'I shall not reply to impolite questions,' the nihilist replied jauntily, looking up at the gendarme.

Mylnikov came over. 'Would you please tell me your name?' he asked patiently. 'And your title. Do let us know who you are.'

'Esfir Litvinova, daughter of a full state counsellor,' the detainee replied with equal politeness.

'The banker Litvinov's daughter,' Evstratii Pavlovich explained to his superior in a low voice. 'Under investigation. But not previously known to be involved in anything like this.'

'I don't care if her father's Rothschild himself!' Burlyaev

hissed, wiping the sweat off his forehead. 'You'll get hard labour for this, you scum. Where they won't feed you any of your Yiddish kosher delicacies.'

Erast Petrovich knitted his brows, preparing to intercede for the young mademoiselle's honour, but apparently his intercession was not required.

The banker's daughter propped her hands on her hips and screeched contemptuously at the Lieutenant Colonel: 'You bastard! You animal! How would you like a slap in the face, like Khrapov?'

Burlyaev began rapidly turning scarlet. When he reached a genuine beetroot colour, he roared: 'Evstratii Pavlovich, put the detainees in the sleighs and take them to the remand cells.'

'Wait, Mr Mylnikov,' said the State Counsellor, raising one finger. 'I will not allow you to take anyone away. I came here especially to see whether the provisions of the law would be observed during the operation. Unfortunately, you have disregarded them. On what grounds have these people been detained? They have not committed any overt offence, and so there can be no question of detaining them for the actual commission of a crime. If you intend to make an arrest on grounds of suspicion, you require specific sanction. Mr Burlyaev recently told me that in the matter of investigation the Department of Security is not subordinated to the municipal authorities. That is correct. But the making of arrests falls within the jurisdiction of the Governor General. And as His Excellency's plenipotentiary representative I order you to release your prisoners immediately.'

Fandorin turned towards the detainees, who were listening to his dispassionate and authoritative speech in dumbfounded amazement.

'You are free to go, ladies and gentlemen. On behalf of Count Dolgorukoi I apologise to you for the wrongful actions of Lieutenant Colonel Burlyaev and his subordinates.'

'This is unheard of!' Pyotr Ivanovich roared, the colour of his face now resembling not so much a beetroot as an aubergine. 'Whose side are you on?'

'I am on the side of the l-law. And you?' Fandorin enquired.

Burlyaev threw his arms up as if he were lost for words and demonstratively turned his back on the State Counsellor.

'Take Litvinova and let's go,' he ordered his agents and shook his fist at the seated guests. 'You just watch out, you cattle! I know every one of you!'

'You will have to release Miss Litvinova too,' Erast Petrovich said in a soft voice.

'But she fired at me!' said the Lieutenant Colonel, swinging round again and fixing the Governor's Deputy for Special Assignments with an incredulous stare. 'At an officer of the law! Engaged in the performance of his duty!'

'She did not fire at you. That is one. As for you being an officer of the law, she was not necessarily aware of that – since you did not introduce yourself and you are not in uniform. That is t-two. And as for the performance of your duty, it would be better not to mention that. You did not even announce that an arrest was taking place. That is three. You broke down the door and burst in, shouting and waving guns about. In the place of these gentlemen, I should have taken you for bandits and if I had had a revolver I should have fired first and asked questions later. You could have taken Mr Burlyaev for a b-bandit, could you not?' Erast Petrovich asked the young lady, who was regarding him with an extremely strange look.

'Why, is he not a bandit?' Esfir Litvinova responded immediately, assuming an expression of great amazement. 'Who are you all, anyway? Are you from the Department of Security? Then why didn't you say so straight away?'

'Right, I shan't let it go at this, Mr Fandorin,' Burlyaev said menacingly. 'We'll see whose department is the more powerful. Let's go, damn it!'

This final remark was addressed to the agents, who put their guns away and filed towards the door in disciplined fashion.

Mylnikov brought up the rear of the procession. In the doorway he looked round, smiled as he wagged a monitory finger at the young people, bowed politely to the State Counsellor and went out.

For about half a minute the only sound in the drawing room

was the ticking of the clock on the wall. Then the student with the split eyebrow jumped to his feet and dashed headlong for the door. Without bothering to take their leave, the others followed him out no less rapidly.

After another half-minute there were only three people left in the room: Fandorin, Larionov and the fiery young lady.

The banker's daughter stared hard at Erast Petrovich with her bold, lively eyes, and those full lips that seemed almost out of place on the thin face curved into a caustic grin.

'So that was your little drama, was it?' Mademoiselle Litvinova enquired, shaking her short-cropped head in feigned admiration. 'Original. And superbly played – as good as Korsh's Theatre. What should come next according to your scenario? The grateful maiden falls on the chest of her handsome saviour, sprinkling his starched shirt with her tears, and vows eternal devotion? And then she informs against all her comrades, right?'

Erast Petrovich noticed something quite astonishing: the short haircut, far from spoiling the young lady, actually suited her boyish face very well.

'Surely you didn't really intend to fire, did you?' he asked. 'Stupid. With a t-trinket like that' – he pointed with his cane to the little revolver lying on the floor – 'you wouldn't have killed Burlyaev anyway, but they would certainly have torn you to pieces on the spot. And in addition—'

'I'm not afraid!' the effusive damsel interrupted him. 'What if they would have torn me to pieces? This bestial despotism must be given no quarter!'

'And in addition,' Fandorin continued, paying no heed to her impassioned retort, 'you would have doomed your friends. Your soirée would have been declared a gathering of terrorists and they would all have been sent off to penal servitude.'

Mademoiselle Litvinova was taken aback, but only for an instant. 'My, how very humane!' she exclaimed. 'But I don't believe in noble musketeers from the gendarmerie. The polished and polite ones like you are even worse than the outright bloodsuckers like that red-faced brute. You're a hundred times more dangerous! Do you at least understand, Mr Handsome, that none of you will escape retribution?'

The young lady stepped forward belligerently, and Erast Petrovich was obliged to retreat as a slim finger with a sharp nail sliced through the air just in front of his nose.

'Butchers! *Oprichniks!* You won't be able to hide from the people's vengeance behind the bayonets of your bodyguards!'

'I'm not hiding at all,' the State Counsellor replied resentfully. 'I don't have any bodyguards and my address is listed in all the address books. You can check for yourself: Erast Petrovich Fandorin, Deputy for Special Assignments to the Governor General.'

'Aha, *that* Fandorin!' the young woman said with an excited glance at Larionov, as if she were calling on him to witness this astounding discovery. 'Haroun al-Rashid! The slave of the lamp!'

'What lamp?' Erast Petrovich asked in surprise.

'You know what I mean. The mighty genie who stands guard over the old sultan, Dolgorukoi. So that, Ivan Ignatievich, was why he threatened the police agents with the Governor,' she said, turning to the engineer once again. 'But I wonder just what kind of high-up it is who doesn't give a fig for the Okhranka? I rather thought, Mr Genie, that you despised political detective work.'

She transfixed Erast Petrovich with a final, lethal, withering glance, nodded in farewell to her host and set off majestically towards the door.

'Wait,' Fandorin called to her.

'What else do you want from me?' the young lady asked, bending her elegant neck into a proud curve. 'Have you decided to arrest me after all?'

'You have forgotten your gun.' The State Counsellor picked up the revolver and held it out to her, handle first.

Esfir took the gun with her finger and thumb, as if she disdained to touch the official's hand, and walked out of the room.

Fandorin waited until the front door slammed shut, then turned to the engineer and said in a low voice: 'Mr Larionov, I am aware of your relationship with the Department of Security.'

The engineer shuddered as if he had been struck. An expression of melancholy despair appeared on his yellowish face with the puffy bags under the eyes. 'Yes,' he said with a nod, wearily lowering himself on to a chair. 'What do you want to know? Ask.'

'I do not make use of the services of secret informers,' Erast Petrovich replied coolly. 'I regard it as odious to spy on one's comrades. The name for what you do here is entrapment. You make new acquaintances among the romantically inclined youth, you encourage talk against the government, and then you report on your achievements to the Okhranka. Aren't you ashamed of yourself? After all, you're a n-nobleman, I've read your file.'

Larionov laughed unpleasantly and took a *papyrosa* out of a pack with trembling fingers.

'Ashamed? You try talking about pangs of conscience with Mr Sergei Vitalievich Zubtsov. And about entrapment too. That's a word Mr Zubtsov doesn't like at all. He calls it "public sanitation". Says it's better to mark down potentially dangerous parties at an early stage and sift them out. If they don't meet at my place, under Sergei Vitalievich's watchful eye, they'll only meet somewhere else. And there's no knowing what ideas they'll come up with there, or what they might get up to. But here they're all in open view. The moment anyone stops making idle conversation and turns to serious talk, they grab the poor fellow straight away. Peace and quiet for the state, promotion for Mr Zubtsov and sleepless nights for the Judas Larionov ...' The engineer covered his face with his hands and stopped speaking. To judge from the heaving of his shoulders, he was struggling against his tears. Erast Petrovich sat down facing him and sighed. 'What on earth made you do it? It's loathsome.'

'Of course it's loathsome,' Larionov replied, speaking through his hands in a dull, muffled voice. 'As a student I used to dream of social justice too. I pasted up leaflets in the university. That was what I was doing when they took me.'

He took his hands away and Fandorin saw that his eyes were

moist and gleaming. The engineer struck a match and drew in the smoke of his *papyrosa* convulsively.

'Sergei Vitalievich is a humane individual. "You, Ivan Ignatievich," he said, "have an old mother, in poor health. If they throw you out of university – and that's the least that you're looking at – she'll never survive it. Well, and if it's exile or, God forbid, prison, you'll send her to her grave, no doubt about it. For what, Ivan Ignatievich? For the sake of chimerical fantasies!" And then he went on explaining about public sanitation, only in more detail, with more fine phrases. Telling me he wasn't inviting me to be an informer, but a rescuer of children. "There they are, the silly, pure-hearted creatures, running around among the flowers, and they don't see the steep precipice down at the end of the meadow. Why don't you stand on the edge of that precipice and help me save the children from falling?" Sergei Vitalievich is a great talker and, above all, he believes what he says himself. Well, I believed it too' – the engineer smiled bitterly – 'or, to be more honest, I made myself believe it. My mother really wouldn't have survived the blow . . . Well, anyway, I graduated from university, and Mr Zubtsov found me a good job. Only it turned out that I wasn't a rescuer at all, just a perfectly ordinary collaborator. As they say, it's not possible to be half-pregnant. I even get a salary, fifty-five roubles. Plus fifty roubles expenses, payable on account.' His smile widened even further, becoming a mocking grin. 'All in all, life simply couldn't be better. Except that I can't sleep at night.' He gave a chilly shudder. 'I nod off for a moment and then I wake with a start – I hear a knock and I think they've come for me – one side or the other. And I carry on shuddering like that all night long. Knock-knock. Knock-knock.'

At that very moment the door-knocker clattered loudly. Larionov shuddered and laughed nervously. 'Someone's come late. Missed all the fun. Mr Fandorin, you hide behind that door there for the time being. No point in your being seen. You can explain your business afterwards. I'll get rid of them quickly.'

Erast Petrovich walked through into the next room. He tried not to eavesdrop, but the caller's voice was loud and clear.

'. . . And they didn't tell you we were going to stay with you? Strange.'

'Nobody gave me any message!' Larionov replied and then, speaking louder than necessary, he asked, 'Are you really in the Combat Group? You mustn't stay here! They're looking for you everywhere! I've just had the police round!'

Forgetting his scruples, Fandorin stole quietly up to the door and opened it a crack.

The young man standing in front of the engineer was wearing a short winter coat and an English cap, with a long strand of light-coloured hair dangling out from under it. The late visitor was holding his hands in his pockets and there were sparks of mischief glinting in his eyes.

'Are you alone here?' the visitor asked.

'There's the cook. She's sleeping in the boxroom. But you really mustn't stay here.'

'So the police came, took a sniff around and went away again?' The blond-haired man laughed. 'Well, isn't that just miraculous?

> 'In Bryansk the cats on Railway Street
> Caught a sparrow they could eat.
> They licked a lot and licked a lot,
> But didn't eat a single jot.'

The jolly young man moved so that his back was towards the State Counsellor, while Larionov was obliged to stand facing the door.

The intriguing guest made a movement of his hand that Fandorin couldn't see and the engineer suddenly gasped and staggered back.

'What's wrong, Iscariot – afraid?' the caller enquired in the same flippant tone as ever.

Sensing that something was wrong, Erast Petrovich jerked the door open, but just at that moment there was the sound of a shot.

Larionov howled and doubled over; the shooter glanced round at the sudden clatter behind him and raised his hand. It was holding a compact, burnished-steel Bulldog. Fandorin dived under the shot and hurled himself at the young man's feet, but the caller leapt back nimbly, striking his back against the door jamb, and tumbled out into the hallway.

Fandorin sat up over the wounded man and saw he was in a bad way: the engineer's face was rapidly turning a ghastly shade of blue.

'I can't feel my legs,' Larionov whispered, gazing into Erast Petrovich's eyes in fright. 'It doesn't hurt at all, I just want to sleep . . .'

'I've got to catch him,' Fandorin said rapidly. 'I'll be quick, then I'll get a doctor straight away.'

He darted out into the street and looked to the right – nobody there; he looked to the left – there it was, a fleeting shadow moving rapidly in the direction of Kudrinskaya Street.

As the State Counsellor ran, two thoughts came into his mind. The first was that Larionov wouldn't need a doctor. To judge from the symptoms, his spine was broken. Soon, very soon, the poor engineer would start making up for all his sleepless nights. The second thought was more practical. It was no great trick to overtake the killer, but then how would he deal with an armed man when he himself had no gun? The State Counsellor had not expected this to be a day of risky undertakings and his trusty Herstahl-Baillard (seven shots, the latest model) had been left at home. How useful it would have been just at this moment!

Erast Petrovich was running quickly, and the distance between him and the shadow was rapidly shortening. That, however, was no cause for rejoicing. At the corner of Ss. Boris and Gleb Street the killer glanced back. With a sharp crack, his gun spat a tongue of flame at the pursuer and Fandorin felt a hot wind fan his cheek.

Suddenly two more swift shadows sprang straight out of the wall of the nearest house and fused with the first, forming a nebulous, squirming tangle.

'Ah, you lousy scum, kick me, would you!' someone shouted in an angry voice.

By the time Erast Petrovich got close, the commotion was already over.

The jovial young man was lying face down with his arms twisted behind his back, swearing breathlessly. A solidly built man was sitting on him and grunting as he twisted his elbows even higher. Another man was holding Fandorin's fallen quarry by the hair, forcing his head back and up.

On looking more closely, the State Counsellor saw that the unexpected assistance had been provided by two of the police agents on duty that evening.

'You see, Erast Petrovich, even the Okhranka can come in useful sometimes,' an amiable voice said out of the darkness.

There proved to be a gateway close by, and standing in it was none other than Evstratii Pavlovich Mylnikov in person.

'Why are you here?' the State Counsellor asked, and then answered his own question. 'You stayed to follow me.'

'Not so much you, Your Honour – you're an individual far above suspicion; more the general course of events.' The head of the plain-clothes squad came out from the shadows on to the illuminated pavement. 'We were particularly curious to see whether you would go off anywhere with that fiery young hussy. My belief is that you decided to win her over with the carrot rather than the stick. And quite right too. The foolhardy ones like that only turn vicious under direct pressure and insults. You have to avoid rubbing them up the wrong way, stroke them with the fur, stroke them, and as soon as they roll over – go for their soft underbelly!'

Evstratii Pavlovich laughed and held up one palm in a conciliatory gesture, as if to say: *Don't bother to deny it, I wasn't born yesterday*.

'When I saw the young lady leave alone, I almost sent my dunderheads after her, and then I thought no, I'll wait a bit. His Honour is a man of the world, with a keen nose. If he's staying back, he has something in mind. And sure enough – soon this character turns up.' Mylnikov nodded at the arrested man, who was howling in pain and cursing. 'So it turns out I was right after all. Who is he?'

'Apparently a member of the Combat Group,' Erast Petrovich replied, feeling indebted to this obnoxious but far from stupid collegiate assessor.

Evstratii Pavlovich whistled and slapped himself on the thigh: 'Good old Mylnikov! He knew which horse to back, all right. When you write your report, don't forget this humble servant of God. Hey, lads, call for a sleigh! Give over twisting his arms, or he won't be able to write a confession.'

One of the agents ran for the sleigh and the other clicked a pair of handcuffs on to the recumbent man's wrists.

'You can go whistle for your confession,' the prisoner hissed.

It was well after midnight before Erast Petrovich reached the Department of Security. First he had had to attend to Larionov, who was bleeding to death. When he got back to the apartment, Fandorin found the engineer already unconscious. By the time the carriage he summoned by telephone from the Hospital of the Society of Fraternal Love finally arrived, there was no longer any point in taking the wounded man away. It had been a pointless waste of time. And the State Counsellor had had to make his own way to Bolshoi Gnezdikovsky Lane on foot – at that hour of the night he hadn't met a single cab.

The quiet side street was completely dark, only the windows of the familiar two-storey building were aglow with cheerful light. The Department of Security had no time for sleeping tonight.

Once inside, Erast Petrovich witnessed a curious scene. Mylnikov was concluding his analysis of the evening's operation. All sixteen agents were lined up against the wall of the long corridor and the collegiate assessor was prowling softly along the ranks like some huge cat, admonishing them in a calm, measured voice, like a teacher in front of his class.

'Let me repeat that again, so that you blockheads will finally remember it. When detaining a group of political suspects, proceed as follows. First – stun them. Break in, making a din, yelling and banging and crashing, so you set their knees knocking. Even a brave man freezes when he's taken by surprise.

Second – immobilise them. Make sure every single detainee is rooted to the spot and can't even move a finger, let alone open their mouths. Third – search them for weapons. Did you do that? Ah? You, Guskov, it's you I'm asking; you were the senior man at the raid.' Mylnikov stopped in front of a middle-aged plain-clothes man with red slime streaming out of his flattened nose.

'Evstratii Pavlovich, Your Honour,' Guskov boomed. 'They was only small fry, snot-nosed kids, that was obvious straight off. Got a seasoned eye, I have.'

'I'll give you another one in that eye of yours,' the collegiate assessor said amicably. 'Don't even try to think, you numskull. Just do it right. And the fourth thing – keep a close watch on all the detainees all the time. But you sloppy dunces go and let a young lady take a pop-gun out of her reticule and none of you even see it. Right, then . . .' Mylnikov clasped his hands behind his back and swayed back on his heels.

The agents waited for his verdict with baited breath.

'Only Shiryaev and Zhulko will receive gratuities. Fifteen roubles each, from me personally, for the arrest of a dangerous terrorist. And that goes in the official orders. As for you, Guskov, it's a ten-rouble fine. And one month's demotion from senior agent to the ranks. I reckon as that's fair, don't you?'

'I'm sorry, Your Honour,' said the punished man, hanging his head. 'Only don't take me off operations work. I'll make it up to you, I swear to God.'

'All right, I believe you.'

Mylnikov turned towards Erast Petrovich and pretended to have only just noticed him.

'Delightful of you to drop in, Mr Fandorin. Pyotr Ivanovich and Zubtsov have been chatting with our friend for the best part of an hour and getting nowhere.'

'He refuses to talk?' the State Counsellor asked as he followed Mylnikov up the narrow winding stairs.

'On the contrary. He's a cocky one. I listened for a bit and then left. Nothing's going to come of it anyway. After what happened today Pyotr Ivanovich's nerves are a bit jittery. And then he's a bit vexed it was you and me as nabbed such a big fish,' Evstratii Pavlovich added in conspiratorial tones, half-turning round as he spoke.

They were conducting the interrogation in the boss's office. Fandorin's jovial acquaintance was sitting on a chair in the middle of the spacious room. It was a special chair, massive, with straps on the two front legs and the armrests. The prisoner's arms and legs were strapped down so tight that he could only move his head. The commanding officer of the Department of Security was standing on one side of him, and standing on the other was a lean gentleman of rather agreeable appearance who looked about twenty-seven, with a narrow English moustache.

Burlyaev scowled as he nodded to Fandorin and complained: 'A hardened villain. I've been flogging away for an hour now, and all for nothing. He won't even tell us his name.'

'What meaning has my name for thee?' the impudent prisoner asked the Lieutenant Colonel in a soulful voice. 'My darling, it will perish in a doleful murmur.'

Paying no attention to this insolent remark, the Lieutenant Colonel introduced the other man: 'Sergei Vitalievich Zubtsov. I told you about him.'

The lean man bowed respectfully and smiled at Erast Petrovich in an extremely affable manner.

'Delighted to make your acquaintance, Mr Fandorin. And even more delighted to be working with you.'

'Aha,' the prisoner exclaimed in delight. 'Fandorin! That's right; now I see the grey temples. Didn't spot them before, I was in too much of a hurry. Why are you just standing there, gentlemen? Seize him, he killed that old ass Khrapov!' He laughed, delighted with his own joke.

'With your permission, I'll proceed,' Zubtsov said to both of his superiors and turned to face the criminal. 'All right, we know you're a member of the Combat Group and you were involved in the assassination of General Khrapov. You have just implicitly admitted that you were in possession of a description of the State Counsellor's appearance. We also know that your accomplices are in Moscow at present. Even if the prosecution is unable to prove your involvement in the assassination, you are still facing the severest possible penalty. You killed a man and offered armed resistance to representatives of the law. That is quite enough to send you to the gallows.'

Unable to restrain himself, Burlyaev interrupted: 'Do you realise, you scum, that you're going to dangle at the end of a rope? It's a terrible way to die, I've seen it more than once. First the man starts croaking and thrashing about. Sometimes for as long as fifteen minutes – it all depends how the knot's tied. Then his tongue flops out of his gullet, his eyes pop out of his skull and all the filth drains out of his belly. Remember the Bible, about Judas? "And falling headlong he burst asunder in the midst and all his bowels gushed out."'

Zubtsov cast a reproachful glance at Burlyaev: he evidently felt that these were the wrong tactics.

The prisoner responded lightheartedly to the threatening words: 'So what, I'll croak a bit and then stop. I'll be beyond caring then, but afterwards you'll have to clean up my shit. That's what your job is, fat-face.'

The Lieutenant Colonel struck the defiant man a sharp, crunching blow in the mouth.

'Pyotr Ivanovich!' Zubtsov exclaimed in protest, even taking the liberty of seizing his superior by the arm. 'This is absolutely impermissible. You are bringing the authorities into disrepute!'

Burlyaev turned his head in fury and was clearly about to put the insolent subordinate in his place, but at that point Erast Petrovich struck his cane against the floor and said in a commanding voice: 'Stop this!'

The Lieutenant Colonel pulled his arm free, breathing heavily. The terrorist spat a thick gob of blood out on to the floor, together with his two front teeth, then stared at the Lieutenant Colonel with a gleam in his blue eyes and a gap-toothed smile.

'I beg your pardon, Mr Fandorin,' Burlyaev growled reluctantly. 'I got carried away. You can see for yourself what a fine hero we have here. What would you have me do with someone like this?'

'What is your opinion, Sergei Vitalievich?' the State Counsellor asked the likeable young man.

Zubtsov rubbed the bridge of his nose in embarrassment, but he replied immediately, with no hesitation. 'I think we are wasting our time here. I would postpone the interrogation.'

'Qu-Quite right. And what we should also do, Mr Lieutenant Colonel, is the following. Immediately draw up a verbal portrait of the prisoner and carry out a thorough Bertillonage, complete in every detail. And then send the description and the results of the anthropometric measurements to the Police Department by telegram. They might possibly have a file on this man there. And be so good as to make haste. The message must reach St Petersburg no later than an hour from now.'

Once again – how many times was it now in the last twenty-four hours – Fandorin walked along Tverskaya Boulevard, which was entirely deserted at this dead hour of night. The long day that seemed so reluctant to end had brought a bit of everything – raging blizzards, quiet snowfalls, and sudden, bright interludes of sunshine; but the night was filled with a calm solemnity: the soft light of the gas lamps, the white silhouettes of the trees that seemed to be draped with muslin, the gentle, gliding fall of the snowflakes.

The State Counsellor himself did not really understand why he had declined the official state sleigh until he felt the fresh, untrampled snow on the pathway crunching crisply beneath his feet. He needed to rid himself of a painful, nagging sense of defilement: if he didn't, he would not be able to sleep in any case.

Erast Petrovich strode unhurriedly between the melancholy elms, striving to comprehend why any business connected with politics always had such a rotten smell about it. This seemed like a normal enough investigation, simply one that was more important than the others. And the objective was a worthy one: to protect public peace and the interests of the state. So why this feeling of contamination?

Clean up dirt, and you're bound to get dirty – it was a

sentiment Fandorin had heard often enough, especially from practitioners of law enforcement. However, he had concluded long ago that only people who lacked any talent for this subtle trade reasoned in that way. Those who were lazy, who sought simple means to resolve complex problems, never became genuine professionals. A good yard-keeper's apron was always snow-white, because he didn't scrape up the dirt with his hands, down on all fours – he had a broom, a spade and a shovel, and he knew how to use them. In all his dealings with heartless killers, ruthless swindlers and bloodthirsty monsters, Erast Petrovich had never experienced such keen revulsion as today.

Why? What was wrong?

He could not find the answer.

He turned on to Malaya Nikitskaya Street, where there were even fewer street lamps than on the boulevard. The pavement began here and the steel tip of his cane repeatedly clacked against the flagstones as it pierced the thin layer of snow.

At the wicket gate, scarcely visible among the fancy lacework of the estate gates, the State Counsellor froze as he sensed, rather than saw, a slight movement off to one side of him. He swung round sharply, his left hand grabbing the shaft of his cane (there was a sword with a thirty-inch blade inside it), but then immediately relaxed his taut muscles.

There *was* someone standing in the shadow of the railings, but this individual was clearly a member of the weaker sex.

'Who are you?' Erast Petrovich asked, peering intently into the gloom.

The slight figure moved closer. First he saw the fur collar of the winter coat and the sable semicircle of the hood, then the immense eyes set in the triangular face glittered as they suddenly caught the light of a distant street lamp.

'Miss Litvinova?' Fandorin asked in surprise. 'What are you doing here? And at such a late hour!'

The young lady from Larionov's apartment moved very close to him. She was holding her hands in a thick fur muff. Her eyes glowed with a truly unearthly radiance.

'You scoundrel!' the ecstatic maiden proclaimed in a voice

that rang with hatred. 'I've been standing here for two hours! I'm frozen through!'

'Why am I a scoundrel?' Erast Petrovich protested. 'I had no idea that you were waiting . . .'

'That's not why! Don't pretend to be a dunce! You understand perfectly well! You're a scoundrel! I've got your measure! You deliberately tried to hoodwink me! Making yourself out to be an angel! Oh, I can see right through you! You really are a thousand times worse than all the Khrapovs and Burlyaevs! You have to be eliminated without mercy!'

So saying, the reckless young lady drew her hand out of the muff, and there glinting in it was the familiar revolver that the State Counsellor had so imprudently returned to its owner.

Erast Petrovich waited to see if a shot would follow, but when he saw that the hand in the fluffy glove was trembling and the gun was swaying erratically, he took a quick step forward, grabbed hold of Mademoiselle Litvinova's slim wrist and turned the barrel aside.

'Are you quite determined to shoot a servant of the law today?' Fandorin asked in a quiet voice, gazing into the young lady's face, which was very close now.

'I hate you! You *oprichnik*!' she whispered and struck him on the chest with her free fist.

He was obliged to drop his cane and grasp the girl's other hand too.

'Police spy!'

As Erast Petrovich examined her more closely, he noticed two things. First, framed in fur that was dusted with snowflakes, in the pale light of the gas lamps, the stars and the moon, Mademoiselle Litvinova's face was quite stunningly beautiful. And second, her eyes seemed to be blazing altogether too brightly for mere hatred.

He leant down with a sigh, put his arms round her shoulders and kissed her firmly on the lips – in defiance of all the laws of physics, they were warm.

'Gendarme!' the nihilist protested languidly, pulling away from him. But then she instantly put both arms round his neck and pulled him towards her. The hard edge of the revolver jabbed into the back of Fandorin's head.

'How did you find me?' he asked, gasping for air.

'And you're a fool too!' Esfir declared. 'You told me yourself it was in all the address books . . .'

She pulled him to her again, with a fierce, sharp movement, and the toy revolver fired up into the sky, deafening Erast Petrovich's right ear and startling into flight the jackdaws sitting on a nearby poplar tree.

CHAPTER 4

Money is needed

All the necessary measures had been taken.

They had waited for Rahmet for precisely one hour before moving on to the reserve meeting place. And a wretched place it was: a little railway lineman's house close to the Vindava Station. It wasn't just that it was dirty, cramped and cold, but there was only one small room, with bedbugs and, of course, no telephone. The only advantage was an open view in all directions.

While it was still dark, Green had sent Bullfinch to leave a note in the 'post box' for Needle: 'Rahmet has disappeared. We need another address. Ten o'clock, same place.'

It would have been more convenient to telephone the courier while they were still at Aronson's place, but the cautious Needle had not left them any number or address. A house with a mezzanine, from which she could see the private lecturer's apartment through binoculars – that was all Green knew about where she lived. Not enough. No way to find it.

The role of the 'post box' for emergency communications was played by an old coach house in a side street close to Prechistenky Boulevard – there was a convenient crevice between its beams, wide enough to thrust your hand into as you walked by.

Before they left, Green had told the private lecturer to remember the system of signals. If their comrade came back, to speak to him as if he were a stranger: *I've never seen you before, and I don't know what you're talking about.* Rahmet was no fool; he would understand. He knew about the post box. If he wanted to explain himself, he would find a way.

From nine o'clock Green took up his observation post beside the Sukharev Tower, where he had met Needle the day before. The place and the time were convenient, there were crowds of people pouring into the market.

He had made his way across a courtyard and in through a back entrance to the position he had spied out the day before – a small, inconspicuous attic with a little window, half boarded up, that looked straight out on to the square. Intently, without allowing himself to be distracted, he studied everyone hanging around anywhere nearby. The hawkers were genuine. So was the organ-grinder. The customers kept changing; not one of them lingered for very long without a good reason.

That meant it was all clear.

Needle appeared at a quarter to ten. First she walked past in one direction, then she came back again. She was checking too. That was right. He could go down.

'Bad news,' the courier said instead of greeting him. Her thin, severe face looked pale and she seemed upset. 'I'll start at the beginning.'

They walked along Sretenka Street side by side. Green listened without saying anything.

'First. Yesterday evening the police raided Larionov's apartment. They didn't arrest anyone. But afterwards there was a shooting. Larionov was killed.'

That was Rahmet, he did that, Green thought, and he felt relief and rage at the same time. Just let him come back and Green would have to give him a lesson in discipline.

'Second?' he asked.

Needle just shook her head. 'You're too quick with your reprisals. We needed to investigate first.'

'What's second?' Green asked again.

'We haven't been able to find out where your Rahmet has got to. As soon as I find out something, I'll let you know. Third. There's no way we can send you out of the city soon. We were going to use a wagon on a goods train, but the railway gendarmes are checking all the seals at twelve versts and sixty versts outside Moscow.'

'Never mind that. There's even worse news, I can see. Tell me.'

She took hold of his elbow and led him off the crowded street into a quiet lane. 'An urgent message from the Centre. A courier brought it on the morning train. Yesterday at dawn, at the same time as you executed Khrapov, the Police Department Flying Squad smashed up the secret apartment on Liteiny Prospect.'

Green frowned. The security arrangements for the clandestine apartment on Liteiny Prospect were excellent, and the party funds were kept in a secret hiding place there – all the funds remaining from the January expropriation, when they had hit the office of the Petropolis Credit and Loan Society.

'Did they find it?' he asked curtly.

'Yes. They took all the money. Three hundred and fifty thousand. It's a terrible blow for the party. I've been instructed to tell you that you're our only hope. In eleven days' time we have to make the final payment for the printing works in Zurich. A hundred and seventy-five thousand French francs. Otherwise the equipment will be repossessed. We need thirteen thousand pounds sterling to buy arms and freight a schooner in Bristol. Forty thousand roubles have been promised to a warder at the Odessa Central Prison to arrange for the escape of our comrades. And more money's needed for the usual outgoings ... Without the funds, the party's activities will be completely paralysed. You must give your reply immediately – under the present circumstances, is your Combat Group capable of obtaining the sum required?'

Green did not answer immediately: he was weighing things up.

'Do they know who betrayed us?'

'No. All they know is that the operation was led in person by Colonel Pozharsky, the deputy director of the Police Department.'

In that case, Green had no right to refuse. He had let Pozharsky get away on Aptekarsky Island; now he would have to make amends for his blunder.

However, under present conditions carrying out an expropriation was extremely risky.

First, there was the uncertainty about Rahmet. What if he had been arrested? It was hard to know how he would react under interrogation. He was unpredictable.

Second, he didn't have enough men. In effect, he only had Emelya.

Third, all the police forces of the city must have been thrown into the search for the CG. The city was swarming with gendarmes, agents and plain-clothes men.

No, the risk was unacceptable. It was no good.

As if she had been listening to his thoughts, Needle said: 'If you need people, I have them. Our Moscow combat squad. They don't have much experience – so far all they've done is guard meetings; but they're brave lads and they have guns. And if we tell them this is for the Combat Group, they'll go through hell and high water. And take me with you. I'm a good shot. I can make bombs.'

For the first time Green took a proper look into those serious eyes that seemed to be dusted with ash, and he saw that Needle's colour was like his own – grey and cold. *What was it that dried you up?* he thought. *Or were you born that way?*

Out loud he said: 'No need for hell and high water. At least, not yet. I'll tell you later. Now, a new apartment. If we can't have a telephone, all right. Only there must be a second exit. Seven this evening, same place. And be very careful with Rahmet if he turns up. I'm going to check him.'

He'd had an idea about where to get the money. Without any shooting.

It was worth a try.

Green let his cabby go outside the gates of the Lobastov plant then, as usual, waited for a minute in case another sleigh came round the corner with a police agent in it, and only when he was sure he wasn't being followed did he turn and walk into the factory grounds.

As he walked to the main office past the workshops, past the snow-covered flower beds and the elegant church, he gazed around curiously.

Lobastov managed his business in capital fashion. Even in the very best American factories you wouldn't often see such good order.

The workers Green encountered on his way were striding along with a purposeful air that was not Russian somehow, and he didn't spot a single face puffy and swollen from drink, even though it was Monday and still the morning. He'd been told that at the Lobastov plant the mere smell of drink would get you sacked on the spot and put straight out of the gates. But then the pay here was twice what it was at other plants, you got free company accommodation and almost two weeks of holiday on half-pay.

What they said about the holiday was probably a fairy tale, but Green knew for a certain fact that the working day at Timofei Grigorievich Lobastov's enterprises was nine and a half hours, and eight hours on Saturdays.

If all the capitalists were like Lobastov, there'd be no reason left for kindling any conflagration – Green was suddenly struck by this surprising idea when he saw the sturdy brick building with the sign 'Factory Hospital'. But it was a stupid idea, because in the whole of Russia there was only one Lobastov.

In the factory-office reception room Green wrote a short note and asked for it to be handed to the owner. Lobastov received his visitor straight away.

'Good morning, Mr Green.'

The short, solidly built man with a plain peasant face on which the carefully tended goatee beard looked entirely out of place came out from behind his broad desk and shook his visitor firmly by the hand.

'To what do I owe this honour?' he asked, screwing up his lively, dark eyes inquisitively. 'It must be something urgent, I suppose? Could it perhaps be connected with yesterday's mishap on Liteiny Prospect?'

Green knew that Timofei Grigorievich had his own people in the most unexpected places, but even so he was astonished that the industrialist could be so exceptionally well informed.

He asked: 'Do you really have someone in the Police Department on your payroll?' and then immediately frowned, as if he were withdrawing the inappropriate question.

Lobastov wouldn't answer in any case. He was a meticulous man, with that dense ochre colour that comes from great internal strength and unshakeable self-belief.

'It is written: "Cast thy bread upon the waters for thou shalt find it after many days,"' the factory owner said with a cunning smile, lowering his round head as if he were going to butt – the forehead was heavy and bullish. 'How much did they relieve you of?'

'Three hundred and fifty.'

Lobastov whistled and stuck his thumbs into the pockets of his waistcoat. The smile disappeared from his face.

'Goodbye, Mr Green,' he said crisply. 'I'm a man of my word. You are not. I do not wish to have any more dealings with your organisation. I paid my last contribution in January, absolutely on the nail – fifteen thousand – and I asked not to be bothered again until July. My purse is deep, but not bottomless. Three hundred and fifty thousand! Why not ask for more?'

Green paid no heed to the insult. That was just emotion. 'I only answered your question,' he said in a calm voice. 'We have urgent payments to make. Some people are waiting, others simply won't. We must have forty thousand. Otherwise it's the gallows. They don't forgive that sort of thing.'

'Don't you try to frighten me,' the factory owner snapped. '"They don't forgive"! Do you think I give you money out of fear? Or that I'm buying indulgences against the possibility of your victory?'

Green didn't say anything, because that was exactly what he thought.

'Oh no! I'm not afraid of anything or anybody!' Timofei Grigorievich's face began flushing crimson in anger and one cheek started twitching. 'God forbid that you should ever win! And you never will win. I suppose you imagined you were using Lobastov? Like hell you were! It's me who's been using you. And if I speak frankly with you, it's because you're a pragmatist, without any emotional histrionics. You and I are berries from the same field. Although we taste rather different. Ha-ha!' Lobastov gave a short, dry laugh, exposing a set of yellowish teeth.

What have berries got to do with anything? Green thought; *why speak in jokes if you can speak seriously?*

'Then why do you help?' he asked, and then corrected himself: 'Why did you help?'

'Because I realised our idiotic stuffed shirts needed a good scare, a few spokes stuck in their wheels, so they wouldn't stop intelligent people hauling the country out of the mire. The stupid asses need to be taught a lesson. They need their noses rubbed in the dung. So you go and rub them in it. To make them get it through those thick heads of theirs that Russia either goes with me, Lobastov, or goes to hell with you. There's no third choice on offer.'

'You're investing your money,' Green said with a nod, 'that's clear enough. I've read about it in books. In America they call it lobbying. We don't have a parliament, so you use terrorists to put pressure on the government. So will you give me forty thousand?'

Lobastov's face turned to stone, leaving the nervous tic agitating his cheek. 'I will not. You're an intelligent man, Mr Green. My budget for "lobbying", as you call it, is thirty thousand a year. And not a single kopeck more. If you like, take the fifteen thousand for the second half of the year now.'

Green thought for a moment and said: 'Fifteen, no. We need forty. Goodbye.' He turned and walked towards the door.

His host came after him and showed him out. Could he possibly have changed his mind? Hardly. He wasn't that kind. Then why had he come after Green?

'Was Khrapov your work?' Timofei Grigorievich whispered in his ear.

So that was why.

Green walked down the stairs in silence. On his way back through the factory grounds, he thought about what to do next.

There was only one answer: it would have to be an expropriation.

It was actually no bad thing that the police were preoccupied with the search. That meant there would be fewer men assigned to the usual requirements. For instance, to guarding money.

He could take some men from Needle.

But he still couldn't manage without a specialist. He'd have to send a telegram to Julie and get her to bring that Ace of hers.

Once outside the control post, Green stopped behind a lamp post and waited for a while.

He was right. An inconspicuous individual who looked like a shop assistant came hurrying out of the gates, turning his head this way and that and, when he spotted Green, pretended to be waiting for a horse-tram.

Lobastov was cautious. And curious.

That was all right. It wasn't hard to get rid of a tail.

Green walked a little way along the street, turned into a gateway and stopped. When the shop assistant slipped in after him, he punched him hard on the forehead. Let him have a lie-down for ten minutes.

The strength of the party lay in the fact that it was helped by all sorts of different people, some of them quite unexpected. Julie was precisely one such rare bird. The party ascetics took a dim view, but Green liked her.

Her colour was emerald: light and festive. Always gay and full of the joys of life, stylishly dressed, scented with heavenly fragrances, she set Green's metallic heart ringing in a strange way, simultaneously alarming and pleasurable. The very name 'Julie' was vibrant and sunny, like the word 'life'. If Green's fate had been different, he would probably have fallen in love with a woman just like that.

It wasn't done for members of the party to talk much about their past, but everyone knew Julie's story – she made no secret of her biography.

She had lost her parents when she was a teenager and been made a ward of a relative, a certain high-ranking official of advanced years. On the threshold of old age the old fool had run riot, as Julie put it: he squandered the inheritance entrusted to him, debauched his young ward and shortly thereafter a stroke left him paralysed. Young Julie had been left without a kopeck in her pocket and without a roof over her head, but with substantial carnal experience. The only career that lay open to her was that of a professional woman, and in this field Julie had demonstrated quite exceptional talent. For a few years she had lived as a kept woman, moving from one rich mentor to another. Then Julie had grown weary of 'fat old men' and set up her own business. Now she chose her own lovers, as a rule not fat, and certainly not old, and she didn't take money from them but earned her own income from her 'agency'.

The women Julie employed in her agency were her friends – some of them kept women like herself, and some perfectly respectable ladies in search of additional income or adventures. The firm had rapidly become popular among the capital's pleasure-seekers, because Julie's female friends were all first-class beauties who enjoyed a laugh and were keen on love-making, and confidentiality was maintained meticulously.

But the women had no secrets from each other, and especially from their merry madam, and since their clients included important civil servants and generals, and even highly placed police officers, Julie received a constant stream of the most various kinds of information, some of which was extremely important for the party.

What no one in the organisation knew was why this frivolous creature had started helping the revolutionary cause. But Green found nothing surprising in that. Julie was just as much a victim of a villainous social system as an oppressed peasant woman, a beggar woman or some downtrodden mill hand. She fought injustice with the means available to her, and she was far more useful than some of the chatterboxes in the Central Committee.

Apart from providing highly valuable information, she could find a convenient apartment for Green's group in just a few hours, more than once she had helped them with money, and sometimes she had put them in touch with the right people, because she had the most extensive contacts at all levels of society.

She was the one who had brought them Ace. An interesting character, no less colourful in his own way than Julie herself.

The son of an archpriest who was the preceptor of one of St Petersburg's main cathedrals, Tikhon Bogoyavlensky was an apple who had rolled a very long way from the paternal tree. Expelled from his family for blaspheming, from his grammar school for fighting and from his secondary college for stealing, he had become an authoritative bandit, a specialist in hold-ups. He worked with audacious flare and imagination, and he had never, even once, fallen into the hands of the police.

When the party needed big money last December, Julie had blushed slightly as she said: 'Greeny, I know you'll think badly of me, but just recently I got to know a very nice young man. I think he could be useful to you.'

Green already knew that in Julie's lexicon the words 'get to know' had a special meaning, and he had no illusions concerning the epithet 'nice' – that was what she called all her transient lovers. But he also knew that when Julie said something, she meant it.

In just two days Ace had selected a target, worked out a plan and assigned the various roles, and the expropriation had gone off like clockwork. The two sides had parted entirely satisfied with each other: the party had replenished its coffers and the specialist had received his share of the expropriated funds – a quarter.

At midday Green sent off two telegrams: '*Order accepted. Will be filled very shortly. G.*' That one went to the central post office in Peter, poste restante. The second went to Julie's address: '*There is work in Moscow for a priest's son. Terms as in December. He will select the site. Expect you tomorrow, nine o'clock train. Will meet. G.*'

Once again Needle omitted to greet him. She clearly regarded the conventions as superfluous, just as Green did.

'Rahmet has turned up. A note in the post box. Here.'

Green opened the small sheet of paper and read: '*Looking for my friends. Will be in the Suzdal tea rooms on Maroseika Street from six to nine. Rahmet.*'

'A convenient spot,' said Needle: 'a student meeting place. Outsiders are obvious immediately, so the police agents don't stick their noses in. He's chosen it deliberately so we can check he's not being tailed.'

'What about tails near the post box?'

She knitted her sparse eyebrows angrily: 'You're too high and mighty altogether. Just because you're in the Combat Group, that doesn't give you the right to regard everyone else as fools. Of course I checked. I never even approach the box until I'm certain everything's all right. Will you go to see Rahmet?'

Green didn't answer, because he hadn't decided yet. 'And the apartment?'

'We have one. There's even a telephone. It belongs to the attorney Zimin. He's at a trial in Warsaw at the moment, and his son, Arsenii Zimin, is one of our combat squad. He's reliable.'

'Good. How many men?'

'Listen, why do you talk in that strange way? The words just drop out, like lead weights. Is it meant to impress people? What does that mean – "how many men"? What men? Where?'

He knew the way he spoke wasn't right, but it was the only way the words came. The thoughts in his head were precise and clear, their meaning was absolutely obvious. But when they emerged in the form of phrases, the superfluous husk simply fell away of its own accord and only the essential idea was left. Probably sometimes rather more fell away than ought to.

'In the squad,' he added patiently.

'Six that I can vouch for. First Arsenii – he's a university student. Then Nail, a foundryman from—'

Green interrupted: 'Later. You can tell me and show me. Is there a back entrance? Where to?'

She wrinkled up her forehead, then realised what he meant. 'You mean at the Suzdal? Yes, there is. You can get away through the connecting yards at the back in the direction of Khitrovka.'

'I'll meet him myself. Decide there and then. Your men must

be in the room. Two, better three. Strong ones. If Rahmet and I leave via Maroseika Street, OK. If I leave alone the back way, it's a signal. Then he must be killed. Will they manage? He's quick on his feet. If not, I'll do it.'

Needle said hastily: 'No-no, they'll manage. They've done it before. A police spy once, and then a provocateur. I'll explain to them. Can I?'

'You must. They have to know. Since we're doing an ex together.'

'So there's going to be an ex?' she asked, brightening up. 'Really. You are an unusual man after all. I . . . I'm proud to be helping you. Don't worry, I'll do everything properly.'

Green hadn't expected to hear that, so he found it agreeable. He searched for something equally pleasant to say to her and came up with: 'I'm not worried. Not at all.'

Green only walked into the tea rooms at five minutes to nine in order to give Rahmet time to feel uneasy and grasp his situation.

The establishment proved to be rather poor, but clean: a large room with a low vaulted ceiling, tables covered with simple linen tablecloths, a counter with a samovar and brightly painted wooden trays with heaps of spice cakes, apples and bread rings.

The young men there – most of them wearing student blouses – were drinking tea, smoking tobacco and reading newspapers. Those who had come in groups were arguing and laughing; some were even trying to sing in chorus. But Green didn't see any bottles on the tables.

Rahmet was sitting at a small table by the window reading *New Word*. He glanced briefly at Green and turned over a page.

There were no signs of anything suspicious, either in the room or on the street outside. The back door was over there, to the left of the counter. There were two lads sitting without speaking in the corner by the large double-decker teapot. From the descriptions they had to be Nail and Marat, from the combat squad. The first was tall and muscular, with straight hair down to his shoulders. The second was broad-shouldered and snub-nosed, in spectacles.

Green strolled across to the table without hurrying and sat down facing Rahmet. He didn't say anything. Rahmet could do the talking.

'Hello,' Rahmet said in a low voice, putting down the newspaper and looking up at Green with his blue eyes. 'Thank you for coming . . .'

He pronounced the words strangely, with a lisp: 'sank you'. *Because his front teeth are missing*, Green noted. He had dark circles under his eyes and a scratch on his neck, but his glance was still the same: bold, without the slightest trace of guilt.

But what he said was: 'It's all my fault, of course. I didn't listen to you. But I've paid the price for that, even paid over the odds . . . I was beginning to think no one would come. I tell you what, Green, you listen to me and then decide. All right?'

All this was superfluous. Green was waiting.

'Well then.' Rahmet smiled in embarrassment as he brushed back his forelock, which had thinned noticeably since the previous day, and started his story.

'So what did I think I was doing? I thought I'd just slip out for an hour, finish off that rat and slip back in on the sly. Go to bed and start snoring. You'd come to wake me up, and I'd bat my eyelids and yawn as if I'd been asleep all the time. And the next day, when the news about Larionov broke, I'd confess . . . What an impression that would make . . . Well, I made my impression all right.

'Anyway, I ran smack into an ambush on Povarskaya Street. But I'd already done for Larionov. Put a slug in the bastard's bladder – so he wouldn't die straight away but have plenty of time to think about his filthy treachery. But the son of a bitch had gendarmes in the next room. Mr Fandorin himself, your twin brother. Well, I broke out on to the street, but they already had the place sealed off. The rotten dogs jumped me and tied me up – just look what they did to my hair.

'They took me to Bolshaya Gnezdikovskaya Street, to the Okhranka. First the boss interrogated me, Lieutenant Colonel Burlyaev. Then Fandorin arrived as well. They played good cop and bad cop with me. It was Burlyaev who thinned out my teeth.

See – pretty, isn't it? But that doesn't matter. I'll survive – I'll have gold ones put in. Or iron ones. I'll be an iron man, like you. Anyway, they worked on me a bit without getting anywhere, and then they got tired and sent me off to spend the night in a cell. They have special ones there at the Okhranka. Pretty decent they are, too. A mattress, curtains. Only the bastards cuffed my hands behind my back, so I couldn't do all that much sleeping.

'This morning they didn't touch me at all. The warden fed me breakfast with a spoon, like a little baby. But instead of lunch they dragged me off upstairs again. And goodness gracious me, who did I find there but my old friend Colonel Pozharsky! The same man who put a bullet through my cap on Aptekarsky Island. He'd come down urgently from Petersburg specially to see me.

'*There's no way he can recognise me*, I thought. It was dark that time on Aptekarsky. But the moment he saw me he grinned from ear to ear ... "Bah," he said, "Mr Seleznyov in person, the fearless hero of terror!" He'd found my old file, the one about von Bock, from my verbal description.

'*Now he's going to threaten me with hanging*, I thought, *like Burlyaev*. But no, this one was craftier than that. "Nikolai Iosifovich," he says, "you're like manna from heaven to us. The minister's trampling all over me and the director because of Khrapov. In fact, he's in even worse trouble – the Emperor's threatening to remove him from his post if he doesn't find the perpetrators immediately. But who's going to look for them, the minister? No, your humble servant Pozharsky. I had no idea at all where to begin. And then you go and fall straight into our hands. I could just kiss you." What do you think of that line? And it got worse. "I've already written a little article for the newspapers," he says. "It's called 'The end of the Combat Group'. And then under that, in smaller print, 'A triumph for our valiant police'. About the capture of the extremely dangerous terrorist N.S., who has provided extensive and frank testimony, from which it is clear that he is a member of the notorious Combat Group that has just treacherously murdered Adjutant General Khrapov." I have to confess, Green, I blundered there.

When I shot Larionov, I said: "Take that, you traitor, from the Combat Group." I didn't know Fandorin was listening behind the door . . .

'All right. So, I sit there, listening to Pozharsky. I realise he's trying to frighten me: "You may not be afraid of dying," he says, "but the idea of disgrace will scare you all right." *Hang on, you foxy gendarme*, I think. *You're cunning, but I'm even more cunning*. I bite my lip and start twitching my eyebrow, as if I'm getting nervous. He's pleased with that and he piles on the pressure. "You know, Mr Seleznyov," he says, "for making our day like this, we're not even going to hang you. To hell with Larionov. Just between ourselves, he was a real little shit. For von Bock, of course, we'll give you hard labour, there's no way round that. What a great time you'll have out in the camps when all your comrades turn their backs on you as a traitor. You'll put the noose round your own neck." So then I fall into hysterics, and I yell at him a bit and start foaming at the mouth – I know how to do that. And I started moping, as if I'd lost heart. Pozharsky carries on for a while, and then he throws me the bait. "There is another way," he says. "You give us your accomplices in the Combat Group and we'll give you a passport in any name you like. And then the whole world's your oyster. Europe, if you like, even America, or the island of Madagascar." Well, I twisted and turned this way and that and finally swallowed the bait.

'I wrote a statement, agreeing to collaborate. I'm telling you about that straight away, so I won't have it hanging over me later. But to hell with that. The worst thing is that I had to tell them about who's in the group – their aliases, what they look like. Hang on, Green, don't go flashing your eyes like that. I had to make them believe me. How could I know – they might have had something on us already. If they'd checked and seen I was lying, I'd have been a goner. But as it was, Pozharsky took a look at some piece of paper and he was satisfied.

'I left the Okhranka a useful man, a servant of the throne, a collaborator with the alias Gvidon. They gave me a hundred and fifty roubles, my first salary. And nothing much to do: find you and let Pozharsky and Fandorin know where you are. They put tails on me, of course, but I lost them on the way through Khitrovka. You know yourself, it's easy to disappear there.

'So that's my entire Odyssey for you. Now you decide what to do with me. Bury me in the ground if you like, I won't kick up a fuss. Let those two sitting over there in the corner take me out in the yard and finish me off straight away. Or if you like, Rahmet will leave this life in style, the way he lived it. I'll strap a bomb to my belly, go to Gnezdnikovsky Lane and blow the entire Okhranka to kingdom come, together with all the Pozharskys, Fandorins and Burlyaevs. Do you want me to?

'Or consider something else. Maybe it's not such a bad thing that I'm Gvidon now? There could be advantages in that too . . .

'You decide – you're the one with all the brains. It's all the same to me whether I'm lying under the ground or walking around on top of it.'

One thing was clear: turned comrades didn't behave like this. Rahmet's glance was clear and bold, even insolent. And his colour was still the same, cornflower-blue; the treacherous blue tones were no denser than before. And was it really possible that they could have broken Rahmet in a single day? He would never have given in so quickly. Out of sheer stubbornness.

There was still a risk, of course. But it was better to trust a traitor than to spurn a comrade. It was more dangerous, but in the long run it was worth it. Green had quarrelled with party members who held a different point of view.

He stood up and spoke for the first time: 'Let's go. There's work to be done.'

CHAPTER 5

in which Fandorin suffers from wounded vanity

Esfir Litvinova's awakening in the house on Malaya Nikitskaya Street was truly nightmarish. When a quiet rustling roused her from sleep, at first all she saw was the dark bedroom, with the diffident light of morning peeking through the curtains. Then she saw the impossibly handsome dark-haired man lying beside her with his eyebrows raised dolefully in his sleep, and for a moment she smiled. Then, catching a faint movement with the corner of her eye, she turned her head – and squealed in horror.

There, creeping towards the bed on tiptoe, was a fearsome creature with a face as round as a pancake and ferocious narrow slits for eyes, dressed in a white shroud.

At the sound of her squeal the creature froze and bent over double. As it straightened up it said: 'Goo' morin'.'

'A-a-a,' Esfir heard her own voice reply, trembling in shock. She turned towards Fandorin and grabbed his shoulder so that he would wake up and then wake her as quickly as possible in order to free her from this evil apparition.

But Erast Petrovich was apparently already awake.

'Morning, Masa, morning. I'll be right there,' he said and explained: 'This is my valet, Masa. He's Japanese. Yesterday he hid – that's why you didn't see him. He's c-come now because he and I always do our g-gymnastic exercises in the morning, and it's already very late, eleven o'clock. The exercises will take forty-five minutes. I'm going to get up now,' he warned her, apparently expecting Esfir to avert her eyes delicately.

Esfir didn't. On the contrary, she sat up a little and propped her cheek on one arm bent at the elbow in order to give herself a better view.

The State Counsellor hesitated for a moment, then emerged from under the blankets and got dressed very quickly in the same kind of white overalls as his Japanese valet.

On calmer consideration, she could clearly see that it wasn't a shroud at all, but a loose white jacket, with pants in the same style. It looked rather like underwear, except that the material was denser and there were no ties on the trouser legs.

Master and servant walked out through the door and a moment later Esfir heard an appalling crash from the next room (which she thought was the drawing room). She jumped up, looking round for something to throw on quickly, but couldn't see anything. Fandorin's clothes were lying neatly on a chair, but Esfir's dress and other elements of her attire were scattered about chaotically on the floor. As a progressive young woman, she despised the corset, but even the other items of harness – brassiere, drawers and stockings – took too long to put on, and she was simply dying to see what those two were doing in there.

She opened the massive wardrobe, rummaged about and took out a man's dressing gown with velvet trimming and tassels. It was almost a perfect fit, except that it trailed along the floor a little bit.

Esfir cast a quick glance at the mirror and ran one hand through her short-cropped black hair. She didn't look too bad at all – which was surprising really, since she hadn't had very much sleep. A short hairstyle was a wonderful thing. Not only was it progressive, it made life so much simpler.

The goings-on in the drawing room were as follows (Esfir had half-opened the door, slipped in without making a sound and stood by the wall): Fandorin and the Japanese were fighting, uttering wild yells as they flung their feet through the air at each other. Once the master landed a resounding kick on his half-pint servant's chest and the poor fellow was sent flying back against the wall; but he didn't pass out, just gave an angry squawk and threw himself at his assailant yet again.

Fandorin shouted something unintelligible and the fighting stopped. The valet lay down on the floor, the State Counsellor took hold of his belt with one hand and his neck with the other and began lifting him up to chest height and lowering him down again without any visible effort. The Japanese hung there calmly, as straight as a ramrod.

'Not only an *oprichnik*, but a loony as well,' Esfir declared out loud, expressing her opinion of what she had seen. She went off to perform her toilette.

Breakfast brought the necessary explanations, for which there had been too little time during the night.

'What happened changes nothing in principle,' Esfir declared sternly. 'I'm not made of wood, and of course you are rather attractive in your own way. But you and I are still on opposite sides of the barricades. If it's of any interest, I'm risking my reputation by getting involved with you. When my friends find out—'

'Perhaps they don't n-necessarily have to know about it?' Erast Petrovich interrupted her cautiously, holding a piece of omelette suspended halfway to his mouth. 'After all, it is your own personal business.'

'Oh no, I'm not having any secret assignations with an *oprichnik*. I don't want them to think I'm an informer! And don't you dare address me in such a formal tone.'

'All right,' Fandorin agreed meekly. 'I understand about the barricades. But you won't shoot at me again, will you?'

Esfir spread jam (excellent raspberry jam, from Sanders) on a bread roll – she had a simply ferocious appetite today.

'We'll see about that.' And she went on with her mouth full: 'I'll come here to see you. But don't you come to my place. You'll frighten off all my friends. And then, dear Papchen and Mamchen will imagine that I've picked up a desirable fiancé.'

They were unable to clarify the situation completely because just at that moment the telephone rang. As he listened to his invisible interlocutor, Fandorin frowned in concern.

'Very well, Stanislav Filippovich. Call round in five minutes. I'll b-be ready.'

He apologised, saying it was urgent business, and went to put on his frock coat.

Five minutes later a sleigh with two gendarmes in blue

greatcoats (Esfir saw them through the window) stopped at the gates. One gendarme remained seated. The other, an erect and dashing figure, came running towards the outhouse, holding down his sword.

When Esfir peeped out into the hallway, the dashing young gendarme was standing beside Fandorin, who was putting on his coat. The pretty boy officer, with an idiotic curled moustache and features ruddy from the frost, bowed and gave her a keen, curious glance. Esfir nodded coolly in farewell to Fandorin and turned away.

'... with quite incredible speed,' Sverchinsky exclaimed excitedly. He was concluding his story as they rode along. 'I know about yesterday's arrest and your part in it. My congratulations. But for Pozharsky himself to arrive from St Petersburg on the twelve o'clock train! The deputy director of the Police Department, in charge of all political investigations! A man on his way to the top! He's been made an aide-de-camp. Anyway, he must have set out as soon as he got the telegram from the Department of Security. See what importance they attach to this investigation at the very highest level!'

'How did you f-find out that he had arrived?'

'What do you mean?' Stanislav Filippovich asked resentfully. 'I have twenty men on duty at each main station. Do you think they don't know Pozharsky? They were watching him when he took a cab and told the driver to go to Gnezdnikovsky Lane. They telephoned me and I telephoned you straight away. He wants to steal your laurels, absolutely no doubt about it. See what a rush he was in to get here!'

Erast Petrovich shook his head sceptically. In the first place, he had seen brighter stars from the capital than this one and, in the second place, to judge from the prisoner's behaviour of the previous day, the aide-de camp was hardly likely to win any easy laurels there.

The journey from Malaya Nikitskaya Street to Bolshoi Gnezdnikovsky Lane was much shorter than from the Niko-laevsky Station, and so they arrived ahead of their exalted visitor.

They even beat Burlyaev there, since the Lieutenant Colonel still hadn't heard about his superior's arrival from St Petersburg.

However, no sooner did the five of them – Erast Petrovich, Burlyaev, Sverchinsky, Zubtsov and Smolyaninov – sit down to determine their general position, than the Deputy Director of Police put in an appearance.

A tall, slim gentleman, still by no means old, walked into the room. An astrakhan peaked cap, an English coat, a tan briefcase in his hand. But it was the face that immediately attracted and held their attention: an elongated skull, narrowed at the temples, a hawk-like nose, a receding chin, light-coloured hair, lively black eyes. Not a handsome face, perhaps even ugly, but it possessed the rare quality of initially provoking dislike and then improving greatly on protracted examination.

They all examined the new arrival at length. Sverchinsky, Burlyaev, Smolyaninov and Zubtsov jumped to their feet. As the man of senior state rank, Erast Petrovich remained seated.

The man with the interesting face halted in the doorway, pausing to return the Muscovites' curious gaze, and then suddenly spoke in a loud, solemn voice: 'The official who has arrived from St Petersburg on special instructions himself requires your presence in his room immediately.' Then he laughed at the reference to Gogol, and corrected himself. 'Or, rather, he is glad to see you and requires only one thing: a cup of strong coffee. You know, gentlemen, I am quite unable to sleep in a train. The shaking of the carriage sets my brain fidgeting inside my head and prevents the thought process from closing down. You, of course, are Mr Fandorin' – the visitor bowed lightly to the State Counsellor. 'I've heard a lot about you. Glad to be working together. You are Sverchinsky. You are Burlyaev. And you?' he asked, glancing inquiringly at Smolyaninov and Zubtsov.

They introduced themselves, and the new arrival looked at Zubtsov with especial interest.

'Yes, of course, Sergei Vitalievich, I know. I've read your reports. Competent.'

Zubtsov turned pink.

'Judging from the considerate attention that you have

accorded my person, you have agents at the station and I was recognised. Nonetheless, I hope you will give a warm welcome to Prince Gleb Georgievich Pozharsky. For three hundred years the eldest sons of our clan have all been either Gleb or Georgii – in honour of our patron saints, Gleb of Murom and George the Victorious. A tradition hallowed by the centuries, so to speak. So, the minister has personally instructed me to head the investigation into the case of the murder of Adjutant General Khrapov. From us, gentlemen, rapid results are expected. Exceptional zeal will be required, *and especially from you.*' Pozharsky pronounced these final words with significant emphasis and paused for the Muscovites to take his meaning. 'Time, gentlemen – time is precious. Fortunately last night, when your telegram arrived, I was in my office. I packed this little briefcase here and grabbed my suitcase – I always keep one ready in case I need to leave at short notice – and caught the train. Now I'll take ten minutes to drink coffee and at the same time listen to your ideas. Then we'll have a talk with the prisoner.'

Erast Petrovich had not seen an interrogation like this one before.

'Why's he sitting there all trussed up, as if he was in the electric chair?' Prince Pozharsky exclaimed in surprise when they entered the interrogation room. 'Have you heard about the latest American invention? They connect electrodes here and here' – he jabbed a finger at the seated man's wrist and the back of his head – 'and switch on the current. Simple and effective.'

'Would you be trying to frighten me?' the bound man asked with an insolent smile that exposed the gap in his teeth. 'Don't bother. I'm not afraid of torture.'

'Oh, come now,' Pozharsky exclaimed in surprise. 'What torture? This is Russia, not China. Do tell them to untie him, Pyotr Ivanovich. This Asiatic barbarity really is too much.'

'He's a violent individual,' Burlyaev warned him. 'He could attack you.'

The prince shrugged: 'There are six of us, all exceptionally well built. Let him attack.'

While the straps were being unfastened, the man from St Petersburg examined the captured terrorist with keen interest. Then suddenly he spoke with intense feeling: 'My God, Nikolai Iosifovich, you have no idea just how glad I am to see you. Let me introduce you, gentlemen. You see before you Nikolai Seleznyov, a fearless hero of the revolution. The very man who shot Colonel von Bock last summer, and then escaped from a prison carriage with guns blazing and bombs exploding all around. I recognised him immediately from your description. So I grabbed the file and set off. For such a dear friend six hundred versts is no distance.'

It would be hard to say on whom this announcement produced the greatest effect – the dumbfounded Muscovites or the prisoner, who froze with an extremely stupid expression on his face: his lips extended in a smile, but his eyebrows already raised in surprise.

'And I am Colonel Pozharsky, deputy director of the Police Department. You, Nikolai Iosifovich, are a member of the Combat Group these days, which means we have already met, on Aptekarsky Island. A quite unforgettable encounter.'

Maintaining his energetic tempo, he continued: 'And you, my darling, have been sent to me by God himself. I was almost thinking of retiring, but now you've turned up. I could just kiss you.' He even made a move towards the prisoner as if he were about to embrace him, and the fearless terrorist involuntarily shrank back into his chair.

'On my way here in the train, I composed a little article,' the dashing aide-de-camp told Rahmet in a confidential tone, extracting a piece of paper covered in writing from his briefcase. 'It is entitled "The End of the Combat Group is Nigh". With a subheading: "A triumph for the Police Department". Listen to this: "The fiendish murder of the fondly remembered Ivan Fyodorovich Khrapov has not gone unavenged for long. The martyr's body has not yet been committed to the ground, but the investigative agencies of Moscow have already arrested the extremely dangerous terrorist N.S., who has provided detailed testimony concerning the activities of the Combat Group of which he is a member." The style's a little bit untidy, but never mind, the editor will fix that. I won't read any more – you get the gist.'

The prisoner, whose name was apparently Nikolai Iosifovich Seleznyov, chuckled: 'It's clear enough. So you're threatening to compromise me in the eyes of my comrades?'

'And for you that will be more terrible than the gallows,' the prince assured him. 'In the jails and labour camps, not a single political prisoner will offer you his hand. Why should the state take an unnecessary sin on its soul by executing you? You'll put the noose round your own neck.'

'Oh no I won't. They'll believe me before you. My comrades know all about the Okhranka's little tricks.'

Pozharsky did not try to deny that. 'Of course, who's going to believe that the immaculate hero of terror broke down and told all? It's psychologically unconvincing, I realise that. Only is he . . . Oh, Lord, where are they . . .?' He rummaged in his tan briefcase and drew out a pile of small rectangular cards. 'There now. I gave myself a fright – thought I must have left them behind on my desk. Only, as I was saying, is he really so immaculate? I know you have very strict morals in your party. You'd do better to join the anarchists, Nikolai Iosifovich; their morals are a bit more – you know, lively. Especially with your curious nature. Just take a look at these photographs, gentlemen. Taken through a secret aperture in one of the most depraved establishments on the Ligovka. It's our Nikolai Iosifovich here – there he is at the back. And he's with Lubochka, an eleven-year-old child. That is, of course, a child in terms of her age and physique, but in terms of experience and habit, very far indeed from a child. But if you don't know her personal history, it looks quite iniquitous. Here, Pyotr Ivanovich, take a look at this one. You can see Nikolai Iosifovich quite clearly here.'

The policemen crowded round Pozharsky, examining the photographs with keen interest.

'Look, Erast Petrovich, it's disgusting!' Smolyaninov exclaimed indignantly, holding out one of the photographs to Fandorin.

Fandorin glanced at it briefly and said nothing.

The prisoner sat there pale-faced, biting his lips.

'You take a good look too,' said the prince, beckoning him with his finger. 'You'll find it interesting as well. Sergei Vitalievich, my dear fellow, give them to him. It doesn't matter if he tears them up, we'll print more. When these photos are taken into account, Mr Seleznyov's psychological profile acquires a quite different emphasis. I understand, you know, Nikolai Iosifovich,' he said, turning back to the terrorist, who was gaping in stupefaction at one of the photographs; 'it's not that you're an out-and-out pervert, you simply felt curious. A dangerous quality, excessive curiosity.'

Pozharsky suddenly walked up to the terrorist, grasped his shoulders firmly in both hands and started speaking in a slow, regular rhythm, as if he were hammering in nails: 'You, Seleznyov, will not get a heroic trial with all the pretty ladies in the courtroom swooning over you. Your own comrades will spit at you as treacherous scum who has besmirched the bright countenance of the revolution.'

The prisoner gazed up, spellbound, as Pozharsky went on.

'And now let me outline another possibility to you.' The prince removed his hands from Seleznyov's shoulders, pulled up a chair and sat down, crossing one leg elegantly over the other. 'You are a brave man, vivacious and high-spirited. What do you find so interesting in hobnobbing with these miserable would-be martyrs, your tedious comrades in the revolutionary struggle? They're like bees who need to bunch together in a swarm and live according to the rules; but you're a loner, you do things your own way, you have your own laws. Admit it, in the depths of your heart you really despise them. They're alien to you. You enjoy playing cops and robbers, risking your life, leading the police a merry dance. Well, I'll give you a chance to play a game far more amusing and much riskier than revolution. Right now you're just a puppet in the hands of the party theoreticians, who drink their coffee with cream in Geneva and Zurich and other such places, while fools like you water the pavements of Russia with your blood. But I'm offering you the opportunity to become the puppet-master and pull the strings of the entire pack of them. And I assure you, you would find it delightful.'

'I'll be pulling their strings, and you'll be pulling mine?' Seleznyov asked in a hoarse voice.

'I can't see anyone ever pulling your strings.' Pozharsky laughed. 'On the contrary, I shall be totally and completely dependent on you. I'm staking a lot on you – going for broke, in fact. If you make a mess of things, my career's over. You see, Seleznyov, I'm being absolutely frank with you. By the way, what's your revolutionary alias?'

'Rahmet.'

'Well, for me you will be . . . let's say, Gvidon.'

'Why Gvidon?' Seleznyov asked with a puzzled frown, as if he were totally confused by the pace of events.

'Because you will come flying to me in the realm of the glorious Tsar Saltan from your island of Buyan, sometimes as a mosquito, sometimes as a fly, sometimes as a bumblebee.'

Erast Petrovich suddenly realised that the process of recruitment was already complete. The word 'yes' had not yet been spoken, but some invisible boundary line had been crossed. And after that everything happened very quickly, in the space of just a few minutes.

At first Rahmet answered his virtuoso interrogator's questions absent-mindedly, as if they concerned insignificant matters and not the membership of the Combat Group (it turned out that there were only four of them: the leader with the alias Green, Emelya, Bullfinch and Rahmet himself). Then he provided a clear and vivid psychological portrait of each of them. What he said about the leader, for instance, was: 'He's like Frankenstein's monster in the English novel, half man, half machine. Every time he speaks or moves, you can literally hear the gearwheels creaking. Green sees everything in black and white, nothing puts him off.'

Rahmet gave the address of the clandestine apartment just as willingly, offering no resistance at all, and he dashed off his agreement to cooperate on a voluntary basis as blithely as if it were a billet-doux. His expression as he did so was anything but frightened or even ashamed; it seemed more thoughtful, the expression of a man who has unexpectedly discovered wide new horizons and not yet had time to take in the stunning view now extending before his eyes.

'Off you go, Gvidon,' said Pozharsky, shaking him firmly by the hand. 'Your job is to find Green and hand him over to us. A difficult task, but you're up to it. And don't be afraid that we'll let you down. You're our most important man now; we're putting all our trust in you. Contacts as we agreed. Go with God. And if you don't believe in God, a fair wind to your sails.'

The moment the door closed behind the former terrorist Rahmet and the new collaborator Gvidon, Burlyaev said confidently: 'He'll make a run for it. Why don't you have us put a couple of good agents on his tail?'

'Under no circumstances,' said the prince, shaking his head and yawning. 'In the first place, the tails might be noticed, and we'll get him killed. And in the second place, let us not insult our little mosquito by not trusting him. I know his kind. Fear won't make him collaborate, but he'll put his heart into it, all his inspiration and imagination – until the keen edge of new sensations is blunted. The important thing here, gentlemen, is not to miss the moment that is bound to come, when our Gvidon realises it would be a greater thrill to commit double treason, that is, to pull the strings of both dolls, police and revolution, to make himself the head puppet-master. That's when our waltz with Nikolai Iosifovich will come to an end. We just have to hear that moment when the music stops playing.'

'How true that is!' Zubtsov exclaimed passionately, gazing at the psychologist from the capital with unfeigned admiration. 'I've thought about that a great deal myself, only I used a different name for it. Managing a collaborator, gentlemen, is like entering into a secret liaison with a married lady. You have to cherish her, love her sincerely and take constant care not to compromise her, not to destroy her family happiness. And when the feeling is exhausted, you have to part as friends and give her a nice present in farewell. There should be no bitterness, no mutual resentment.'

Pozharsky listened attentively to the young man's excited exclamations and commented: 'Romantically put, but essentially correct.'

'May I also say something?' Smolyaninov put in, blushing. 'Colonel, you were very cunning in the way you recruited this Rahmet, of course, but it seems to me unbecoming for the defenders of the state to employ dishonest methods.' At this point he started speaking quickly, obviously concerned that he might be interrupted. 'Actually, I've been wanting to speak out frankly for a long time ... The way we work isn't right, gentlemen. This Rahmet has shot the commander of a regiment, escaped from arrest, killed one of our people and committed God only knows how many other terrible crimes, but we let him go. He should be put in prison, but we wish to profit from his viciousness, and you even shake his hand. Of course, I understand that we shall solve the case more quickly that way, but do we want speed, if that is the price to be paid? We are supposed to maintain justice and morality, but we deprave society even more than the nihilists do. It is not good. Well, gentlemen?'

The Lieutenant looked round at both of his superiors, but Sverchinsky merely shook his head reproachfully in reply and while Fandorin's expression was sympathetic, he said nothing.

'Young man, where on earth did you get the idea that the state is justice and morality?' Pozharsky asked, laughing good-naturedly. 'Fine justice indeed! My ancestors and yours, the bandits, stole all their wealth from their fellow countrymen and passed it on by inheritance to us, so that we could dress elegantly and listen to Schubert. In my own case, admittedly, there was no inheritance, but that's a specific instance. Have you read Proudhon? Property is theft. And you and I are guards set to protect the stolen booty. So don't go filling your head with foolish illusions. Better try to understand this, if you really must have a moral justification. Our state is unjust and immoral. But better a state like that than rebellion, bloodshed and chaos. Slowly and unwillingly, society becomes just a little bit more moral, a little bit more decent. It takes centuries. And revolution will throw it back to the times of Ivan the Terrible. There still won't be any justice, new bandits will simply appear, and again they'll have everything and the others will have nothing. And what I said about guards is actually too poetic. You and I, Lieutenant, are night-soil men. We clean out the backhouse privies, to prevent the shit sluicing out into the street. And if you don't wish to get dirty, then take off that smart blue uniform and look for another profession. I'm not threatening you, just giving you some well-meant advice.'

The deputy director of police confirmed the sincerity of his final words with a gentle smile.

Lieutenant Colonel Burlyaev waited for the end of this abstract discussion and asked briskly: 'Your Excellency, then shall I give instructions for private lecturer Aronson's apartment to be surrounded?'

'No. Any tracks there are long since cold. Leave Aronson alone – or we risk giving Gvidon away. And what can the private lecturer give us? He's chicken feed, a "sympathiser". Will he tell us what the real fighters look like? We already know that. I'm more interested in this Needle, the party courier. That's the one we need to find, and then—'

Breaking off in mid-sentence, the prince suddenly leapt to his feet. In two rapid strides he was at the door and jerked it open. The gendarme officer caught in the doorway froze. He had very light hair and a face as pink as a piglet's, which turned even pinker as they watched. Erast Petrovich recognised the officer as Staff Captain Seidlitz, erstwhile protector of Khrapov, the general who was now lying in the autopsy room and had no more need of his guard.

'I – I came to see Mr Burlyaev. To ask if he'd found any clues that would lead to the murderers . . . I heard a whisper that there was an arrest last night . . . You're Prince Pozharsky, aren't you? I'm—'

'I know who you are,' the aide-de-camp interrupted sharply. 'You are a man who failed in an assignment of the utmost importance. You, Seidlitz, are a criminal, and you will be tried by a court of law. I forbid you to leave Moscow until specifically instructed to do so. What are you doing here anyway? Were you eavesdropping at the door?'

For the third time in the short period since his arrival the visitor from St Petersburg underwent a total metamorphosis. Benign with his colleagues and assertive with Rahmet, now he was sharp to the point of rudeness with this offender.

'I won't allow this!' Seidlitz burst out, almost crying. 'I'm a gendarme officer. Let them try me, but you have no right to talk to me like that! I know what I did was unforgivable. But I swear I will atone for it!'

'You'll atone for it in a penal battalion,' the prince interrupted him, and slammed the door unceremoniously.

When Pozharsky turned round, there was not a trace of anger in his face – only intense concentration and excitement. 'That's all, gentlemen; now to work,' he said, rubbing his hands. 'Let us assign roles. You, Pyotr Ivanovich, are responsible for intelligence work. Feel out all the revolutionary groups, all your contacts. If you can't find Green, then at least bring me Mademoiselle Needle. And one more job for your agents: sit on Seidlitz's tail, and his men's too. After the tongue-lashing I just gave him, that Ostsee blockhead will stop at nothing to save his own skin. He will demonstrate truly miraculous zeal. And he won't be any too particular about his methods either. Let him pull the chestnuts out of the fire, but we'll be the ones who eat them. Now for you, Stanislav Filippovich. Distribute the descriptions of the criminals to your men at the railway stations and turnpikes. You're responsible for making sure that Green doesn't leave the Moscow city limits. And I' – the prince smiled radiantly – 'will work with Gvidon. After all, that's only fair, since I recruited him. Now I'm going to the Loskutnaya Hotel, to take a good room and catch up on my sleep. Sergei Vitalievich, I ask you to stay by the telephone at all times in case a message comes in from Gvidon. Let me know immediately. Everything will be just fine, gentlemen, you'll see. As the Gallic gentlemen say, we shall not let our noses droop.'

★

They rode back in the sleigh in absolute silence. Smolyaninov looked as if he would have liked to express an opinion, but he didn't dare. Sverchinsky twirled the end of his pampered moustache. But Fandorin seemed unusually lethargic and subdued.

And in all honesty, he had good reason.

Set against the brilliant glow of the celebrity from the national capital, the flattering aura surrounding the State Counsellor had dimmed substantially. From being an individual of the first magnitude, whose every word, and even silence, commanded the respectful attention of those around him, Erast Petrovich had suddenly been transformed into a dispensable and even rather comical character. Who was he now? The investigation had been taken over by an experienced, brilliant specialist who would clearly manage the case better than the Moscow governor's Deputy for Special Assignments. The success of the search would also be facilitated by the fact that the aforementioned specialist was obviously not hampered by excessive scruples. However, Fandorin immediately relented of that thought as unworthy and prompted by his own wounded vanity.

The main cause of his discomfiture lay elsewhere – the State Counsellor honestly admitted that to himself. For the first time in his life, destiny had brought him face to face with a man who possessed greater talents as a detective. Well, perhaps not for the first time, but the second. A long, long time ago, at the very beginning of his career, Erast Petrovich had encountered another such talent, only he did not much like to recall that story from the dim and distant past.

But then, he couldn't withdraw from the investigation either, could he? That would be giving way to his pride and betraying his beneficent mentor Prince Dolgorukoi, who was relying on his deputy for support and even salvation.

When they reached the Office of Gendarmes they walked into Sverchinsky's office, still without speaking. Here it turned out that on the way the Colonel had also been thinking about the Governor General.

'Disaster, Erast Petrovich,' Stanislav Filippovich said, without any of his usual ambivalence, after they had settled into the armchairs and lit their cigars. 'Did you notice that he didn't even bother to present himself to Vladimir Andreevich? That's it. The old man's finished. The question's already been decided up at the top. It's obvious.'

Smolyaninov sighed regretfully and Fandorin shook his head sadly. 'This will be a terrible blow for the prince. He may be advanced in years, but he is still p-perfectly sound in body and mind. And he was good for the city.'

'To hell with your city,' the Colonel said sharply. 'The important thing is that working under Dolgorukoi was good for us. And things will go badly without him. Naturally, I shan't be confirmed as head of the Office. And it will be the end of your free and easy life, too. The new Governor General will have his own trusted associates.'

'No d-doubt. But what's to be done about it?'

The cautious Stanislav Filippovich was a completely changed man. 'What else? Make Pozharsky look stupid.'

'You're suggesting that we find the terrorist before C-Colonel Pozharsky does,' the State Counsellor stated rather than asked.

'Exactly. But that's not enough. This little prince is too smart by half; he has to be neutralised.'

Erast Petrovich almost choked on his cigar smoke. 'Good Lord, Stanislav F-Filippovich!'

'Not killed, of course. That's the last thing we need. But there are better ways.' Sverchinsky's voice became pensive. 'For instance, make this jumping jack look ridiculous. Turn him into a figure of fun. Erast Petrovich, my dear fellow, we have to show that we, Dolgorukoi's men, are worth more than this popinjay from the capital.'

'I have not actually withdrawn from the investigation,' the State Counsellor remarked. 'In his distribution of "roles", Pozharsky left me with nothing to do. But I am not accustomed to sitting around doing nothing.'

'Well, that's excellent.' The Colonel jumped to his feet and began striding energetically round the room, turning something over in his mind. 'Well then, you will apply the analytical talent that has saved us all more than once. And I shall take steps to make the little prince a general laughing stock.' Then Stanislav Filippovich went on to mutter something incomprehensible under his breath. 'The Loskutnaya, Loskutnaya ... I've got that, what's his name? ... the one in charge of the corridor attendants ... Terpugov? Sychugov? Damn it, it doesn't matter ... And Coco, yes, definitely Coco ... Just the job ...'

'Erast Petrovich, can I come with you?' Lieutenant Smolyaninov asked in a whisper.

'I'm afraid that I have now been reduced to the status of a private individual,' Fandorin replied in an equally low voice and then, seeing the Lieutenant's fresh features stretch into a long face of disappointment, he tried to console him. 'It's a great pity. You would have b-been very useful to me. But never mind, we are still both working on the same job.'

From the Office of Gendarmes to the State Counsellor's home was no more than five minutes' walk at a leisurely pace, but that was quite long enough for him to identify his niche in the investigation – a narrow one, alas, and not very promising.

Fandorin reasoned as follows.

Pozharsky had chosen the shortest route to the Combat Group – through Rahmet-Gvidon.

The Okhranka would creep up on the militants via roundabout paths, working its way along the chains of revolutionaries.

The gendarmes were ready to snap up the terrorists if they attempted to leave Moscow.

There was also Seidlitz, who would go at things like a bull in a china shop and employ methods that the State Counsellor didn't even want to think about. And he would have Mylnikov's agents on his tail.

So the Combat Group and its leader, Mr Green, were besieged from all sides. There was nowhere for them to go ... and there didn't seem to be any space left for a private investigator with a rather vague mandate to become involved in the case either.

There were already so many investigators around, he could easily be trampled underfoot.

But there were three motives insistently prompting Erast Petrovich to take urgent and decisive action.

He felt sorry for the old Prince Dolgorukoi. That was one.

He could not swallow the insult he had suffered at the hands of Green, who had dared to mask himself as State Counsellor Fandorin for his audacious crime. That was two.

And three. Yes, yes, three: his wounded vanity. *We shall see, Your St Petersburg Excellency, who is worth what and what they are capable of.*

After this concise formulation of his motivation, Fandorin's brain began functioning more clearly and precisely.

Let all his colleagues search for the infamous Combat Group. He would see how soon they managed to find it. But he was going to search for the traitor in the ranks of the upholders of law and order. That was probably more important than catching terrorists, even the very dangerous ones. And who could tell if this path might not actually prove to be the shortest to the Combat Group?

This final thought, however, smacked only too distinctly of self-deception.

CHAPTER 6

The expropriation

Of course, Green didn't go out on to the platform to the trains. He took a seat in the cafe in the waiting room for those expecting new arrivals, ordered tea with lemon and began observing the platform through the window.

It was interesting. He had never seen so many police spies in a single spot, even during the Emperor's outings. Almost a third of the people seeing passengers on their way consisted of inquisitive gentlemen with roving eyes and rubber necks. It was clear that the police agents were especially interested in men of a slim build with black hair. Not one of these managed to reach his train unchecked – all dark-haired male individuals were taken politely by the elbows and led away to one side, towards the door with the sign that said 'Duty Stationmaster'. Evidently there must be someone behind the door who had seen Green in Klin.

The dark-haired gentlemen were released again almost immediately, and hurried back on to the platform, glancing round indignantly. But blonds and even redheads were not immune – they were also taken for checking. So the police had at least enough imagination to suspect that their wanted man might have dyed his hair.

However, they had lacked the imagination to picture Khrapov's killer turning up among the people who were meeting new arrivals, not seeing off departing passengers. The hall in which Green had taken up his post was peaceful and deserted. No police spies, and not a single blue uniform.

This was precisely what Green had been counting on when he set out to meet the nine o'clock express on which Ace was due to arrive. It was a risk, of course, but he preferred to handle all business contacts with the specialist himself.

The train arrived precisely on schedule, presenting Green with a surprise. Even before he saw Ace, Green spotted Julie in the stream of newcomers. It would have been hard not to notice those purple ostrich feathers swaying above the wide-brimmed fur hat. Julie stood out from the crowd like a bird of paradise in a flock of black-and-grey crows. She was followed by porters lugging along suitcases and hatboxes, and walking beside her with a light, dancing step was a handsome young man with his hands stuck in his pockets: a close-fitting coat with a beaver collar, an American hat, a black strip of neatly shaved moustache. Mr Ace, the expropriation specialist, in person.

Green waited for the glamorous couple to walk out on to the square and approach the cab stop, then followed them at a leisurely pace.

Walking up from behind, he asked: 'Julie, what are you doing here?'

Ace swung round sharply without taking his hands out of his pockets. Recognising Green, he nodded briefly.

But Julie had never been notable for her reserve. Her fresh, pretty face lit up in a happy smile. 'Greeny, darling, hello!' she exclaimed, throwing herself on Green's neck and planting a resounding kiss on his cheek. 'I'm so glad to see you!' And she added in a whisper: 'I'm so proud of you, and I was so worried about you. You know you're our greatest hero now, don't you?'

Ace twisted up his lips scornfully and said: 'Didn't want to bring her. Told her it was a business trip, not a pleasure party. But there's no talking sense to her.'

It was true. Julie was hard to argue with. When she really wanted something, she swooped like some exotic whirlwind, smothering you with her perfume, overwhelming you with a torrent of words, demanding, laughing, imploring and threatening all at the same time, and her mischievous dark-blue eyes glittered and sparkled with devilment. At an exhibition in Paris Green had seen a portrait of an actress by the fashionable artist

Renoir. It could have been a picture of Julie – it looked exactly like her.

It would have been better for the job, kept matters simpler, if Ace had come alone. Nonetheless, Green was glad to see her. But this feeling was not right, so he knitted his brows and said, more sternly than necessary: 'You shouldn't have. At least don't get in the way.'

'When have I ever got in the way?' she asked, pouting prettily. 'I'll be as quiet as a teeny-weeny little mouse. You won't see me or hear me. Where are we going now? To an apartment or a hotel? I need to take a bath and tidy myself up. I'm sure I look a real fright.'

A fright was the last thing she looked like, as she knew perfectly well, so Green turned away and beckoned to a cabby.

'The Hotel Bristol.'

'Why not? – of course we can. Today if you like. If you can find me ten likely young blades,' Ace drawled lazily as he polished a manicured nail.

This affected air of laziness was evidently the apotheosis of bandit chic.

'Today?' Green asked suspiciously. 'Are you sure?'

The specialist shrugged impassively: 'Ace never makes idle promises. We'll net half a million, at least.'

'Where? How?'

The bandit smiled and Green suddenly understood what Julie had seen in this flashy young buck: the broad smile revealed Ace's white teeth and lent his features an expression of boyish, harum-scarum devilment.

'I'll tell you where later. And how after that. First I have to take a sniff around. I've got two rich targets in Moscow covered: the treasury of the military district and the forwarding office of the state financial instruments depository. I have to choose. We can take either of them, if we're not afraid of spilling a bit of blood. There are plenty of guards, but that's no real problem.'

'But can't you do it without bloodshed?' Julie asked.

She had already changed into a scarlet silk robe and let her hair down, but had not yet reached the bathroom. She had spurned the room booked for Ace by Green and the suitcases had been carried from the sleigh to a de luxe apartment on the *piano nobile*. That was her business. It was beyond Green's understanding what people found so enjoyable about luxury, but he felt no moral condemnation for this weakness.

'Better steal apples if you don't like blood,' Ace said dismissively, getting to his feet. 'My share's one third. We'll go this evening. If the job's at the treasury – at half past five. If there's a delivery from the depository today, at five. Tell your men to gather at the meeting place. They'll need revolvers and bombs. And a sleigh – a light one, American-style. Smear the runners with pork fat. And a horse, of course – one that flies like a swallow. You be here. I'll be back in about three hours.'

When Ace left and Julie went to take her bath, Green twirled the handle of the Erickson telephone on the wall and asked the hotel telephonist to give him subscriber number 38-34. After the untidy evacuation from Ostozhenka Street he had made Needle tell him her number – contact via the post box was too slow for the present circumstances.

When he heard a woman's voice in the earpiece he said: 'It's me.'

'Hello, Mr Sievers,' Needle replied, using the agreed code name.

'The goods will be despatched today. It's a large delivery; all your employees will be required. They should go to the shop immediately and wait there. And they should bring their tools, the full set. We'll be needing a sleigh too. Fast and light.'

'That's all clear. I'll give instructions straight away.' Needle's voice trembled with excitement. 'Mr Sievers, please, I'd like to ask you ... Can I not be involved? I would be a great help to you.'

Green said nothing and looked out of the window, feeling annoyed. He had to refuse in a way that would not offend her.

'I don't think that's necessary,' he said at last. 'We have plenty of men, and you will be more useful if—'

He didn't finish, because at that moment two hot, naked arms gently wound themselves round his neck from behind. One unfastened a button and slid in under his shirt, the other stroked his cheek. He felt a warm breath tickling the back of his neck, then it was scorched by the touch of tender lips.

'I can't hear you,' the shrill voice squeaked in his ear. 'Mr Sievers, I can't hear you any more!'

The hand that had crept under the shirt began playing tricks that made Green catch his breath.

'. . . If you stay by the telephone . . .' he said, forcing the words out with an effort.

'But I asked you specially! I told you that I possess all the requisite skills!' the earpiece persisted.

But in his other ear a low, chesty voice crooned: 'Greeny, darling. Come on . . .'

'You . . . Carry out your instructions,' Green mumbled into the mouthpiece and hung up.

Turning round, he saw a hot pink glow, and suddenly there was a fine crack in his secure steel shell. The crack spread rapidly, widening to release a torrent of something long ago locked away deep inside and forgotten, something that paralysed his mind and will.

The briefing began at half past two.

The barrister who owned the apartment where they gathered was presently in Warsaw, conducting the defence of a hussar who had shot an empty-headed actress out of scorned love. They were a large group – eleven men and one woman. One man spoke and the others listened – so attentively that the famous professor of history, Klyuchevsky himself, would have envied the orator.

The listeners were seated around him on chairs arranged along three walls of the barrister's study. Pinned to the fourth wall was a sheet of heavy paper, on which the instructor was drawing squares, circles and arrows in charcoal.

Green was already aware of the plan of action – Ace had told him about it on the way from the hotel – and so he was watching the listeners rather than the diagram. The arrangements were sensible and simple, but whether they would work depended entirely on those carrying them into effect, most of whom had never taken part in an ex and never even heard the whistle of bullets.

He could rely on Emelya, Rahmet and Ace himself. Bullfinch would do his best, but he was a greenhorn who had never smelled gunpowder. Green had no idea at all what sort of stuff the six lads from the Moscow combat squad were made of.

Green had seen two of them in the tea rooms on Maroseika Street: Nail, a worker from the Guzhonov plant, and Marat, a medical student. All they had managed to do there was give themselves away by staring too hard at Rahmet in their eagerness. The other four – Arsenii, Beaver, Schwartz and Nobel (the last two, both chemistry students, had chosen their aliases in honour of the inventors of gunpowder and dynamite) – looked scarcely more than boys. But they would be up against experienced guards. He hoped the guards wouldn't mow down the entire junior school.

Julie was sitting in the corner, with her eyebrows knitted in studious concentration. There was no reason at all for her to be there. As he looked at her, Green felt himself blushing, something that hadn't happened to him for more than ten years. With an effort of will, he drove the scorching memories of what had happened that day deeper, for analysis at some later time. His self-esteem and the strength of his protective shell had suffered substantial damage, but he was sure it could all be restored. He just had to think of a way. Not now. Later.

He cast a glance at Ace – not of guilt, but of appraisal. How would the specialist react if he knew? Obviously, the operation would be wrecked, since in the terms of criminal morality Ace had suffered a deadly insult. That was the main danger, Green told himself; but, glancing at Julie again, he suddenly had doubts: was it really? No, the main danger, of course, lay in her.

She had broken his steely will and iron discipline with ease. She was life itself, and everyone knew that life was stronger than any rules or dogmas. Grass grew through asphalt, water wore holes in rocks, a woman could soften the hardest of hearts. Especially a woman like that.

It had been a mistake to let Julie into the revolutionary movement. Mirthful pink playmates like that, who held out the promise of joyful oblivion, were not for the crusaders of the revolution. The travelling companions for them were steely-grey Amazons. Like Needle.

She was the one who ought to be sitting there, not Julie, who only distracted the men from the job with her bright plumage. But Needle had taken offence. She had brought the men to the apartment and left without waiting for Green. It was his fault again – he had spoken clumsily to her on the telephone.

'Well, why have you all pleated up your foreheads like accordions?' Ace laughed, wiping his dirty fingers on his black trousers of expensive English wool. 'Don't get the sulks, revolution! A hold-up needs gumption, not sour faces. You have to go at it cheerily, with your spirits up. And if anyone swallows a lead pellet, it means his time was up. Dying young is as sweet as honey. When you're old and sick it's frightening, but for one of us it's just like downing a glass of vodka on a frosty day: it stings, but not for long. You gulls don't even have to do much; Green and me will see to all the important stuff. And then it goes like this . . .' – he turned to speak directly to Green. 'We sling the loot into the sleigh and scram, we go to the India Inn, where Julietta will be waiting for us. It's a trading place, a market; nobody will be surprised to see sacks there. While I'm driving the horse, you have to cover the official seals with plain sackcloth, no one will ever twig it's not bay leaves we're carrying, but six hundred grand. Once we're inside, we divvy up. Like we agreed: two for me, four for you. And then adieu, until we meet again, but not too soon. Ace will be on the spree for a long time with that kind of loot.' He winked at Julie. 'We'll go to Warsaw, then on to Paris and from there – anywhere you like.'

Julie smiled tenderly and affectionately at him, then smiled at Green in exactly the same way. It was incredible, but Green could not read even a hint of guilt or embarrassment in her eyes.

'Now leave,' he said, getting to his feet. 'First Ace and Julie.

Then Nail and Marat. Then Schwartz, Beaver and Nobel.'

He gave them his final instructions as he saw them off in the hallway, trying to speak clearly, without swallowing his words.

'Throw the beam across at ten minutes to, no sooner and no later. Or the yard-keepers might roll it away ... Fire without breaking cover. Stick one hand out and blaze away. You don't need to shoot them, just deafen them and keep them busy ... The most important thing is that none of you should catch a bullet. There'll be no time to carry away any wounded. And we can't leave anyone behind. Anyone who's wounded and can't walk has to shoot himself. Do as Rahmet and Emelya tell you.'

When the last three had left, Green locked the door and was about to go back into the study when he suddenly noticed the corner of something white sticking out of the pocket of his black coat that was hanging on the hallstand.

Immediately realising what it was, he froze on the spot and instructed his heart not to falter in its rhythm. He took out the sheet of paper, lifted it up very close to his eyes (it was dark in the hallway) and read:

The city is sealed off by gendarmes. You must not show
yourself at the railway stations and turnpikes. The blockade
is under the command of Colonel Sverchinsky. Tonight he
will be at the Nikolaevsky Station, in the duty
stationmaster's office. Try to exploit this and strike to create
a diversion.

<u>And most important of all: beware of Rahmet, he is a
traitor.</u>

TG

Noting in passing that this note was not typed on an Underwood, like the previous ones, but on a Remington, Green began rubbing his forehead to make his brain work faster.

'Green, what are you doing out there?' he heard Emelya's voice call. 'Come here!'

'One moment!' he shouted back. 'I'll just go to the lavatory.'

In the water closet he leaned against the marble wall and

began counting off the points to consider, starting with the least important.

Where had the letter come from? When had it arrived? When Green went to the station he was wearing Rahmet's short coat, not his own black one – he had taken a bomb with him just in case, and Rahmet's coat had handy pockets. The black coat had been hanging on the hallstand all day long. That narrowed the circle somewhat. Everyone who was in St Petersburg could be excluded. And so could the Moscow lads – provided, of course, that TG was a single person, and not two or more. Perhaps this 'G' stood for 'group' too? Terrorist Group? Meaningless. All right, he'd think about it later.

Sverchinsky. It was an excellent idea – if not for the ex. Kill a high-ranking gendarme officer and at the same time divide the police's attention. A diversionary strike was just what was required. After all, the important thing was not to escape from Moscow themselves, but to get the money through. Time was short. But would they have enough men for both operations? That would only be clear after the ex.

And then he came to the most difficult thing in the note: the part underlined in blue pencil.

Rahmet, a traitor? Was that possible?

Yes, Green told himself. It was.

That would explain the glint of challenge and triumph in Rahmet's eyes. He hadn't been broken by the gendarmes, he was working his way into a new role. Mephistopheles, Dick Turpin or whoever he imagined himself to be.

But what if TG's information was wrong? TG had never been wrong before, but this was a matter of a comrade's life.

Since the day before, Green had made sure that Rahmet didn't leave the apartment. Today he had ordered Emelya to keep a close eye on the former Uhlan to see if he started acting suspiciously after his nocturnal escapade.

The plan had been to give Rahmet the riskiest job at the expropriation. What could be better than action for showing if a man was honest or not? But as things stood now, he couldn't take Rahmet to the ex.

Having reached his decision, Green pressed the copper knob of the flush mechanism, that latest innovation of sanitary technology, and walked out of the lavatory.

Rahmet, Emelya, Bullfinch and Arsenii, the son of the apartment's absent owner, were standing in front of the charcoal diagram.

'Aha, at last,' said Bullfinch, his eyes aglow with excitement as he turned to Green. 'We're worried about whether you and Ace can manage. After all, there are only two of you, and there's an entire gang of us.'

'It's far too risky,' said Rahmet, supporting the boy. 'And then, aren't you trusting this Rocambole from a priest's family a bit too far? What if he does a flit with the money? Let me go with you, and Emelya can throw the bomb.'

'No, I'll throw the bomb!' Bullfinch exclaimed. 'Emelya has to give the lads their orders.'

Is it the danger he's afraid of, or something else? Green thought, about Rahmet. In a dry voice that brooked no objections, he said: 'Ace and I will manage, just the two of us. Emelya will throw the bomb. Once it's thrown, run round the corner. Don't wait for it to explode. Just yell first, so everyone knows you've thrown it. Get down behind the wall and tell them when to shoot. And Rahmet's not going to the expropriation.'

'What do you mean by that?' Rahmet exclaimed furiously.

'You can't go,' Green explained. 'It's your own fault. They're looking for you. All the police agents have your description. You'll only get us killed. Stay here, by the telephone.'

They moved off at a quarter past four – a little earlier than they were supposed to.

Outside in the yard, Green looked back.

Rahmet was standing at the window. He saw Green looking and waved.

They walked out of the gateway into the lane.

'Damn,' said Green. 'Forgot my cleaning rod. Got to have it – what if a cartridge gets stuck?'

Crimson-faced with excitement, Bullfinch chirped up: 'Let

me run and get it. Where did you leave it? On the locker, right?'
And he turned to dash off; but Emelya grabbed hold of his collar.

'Stop, you little hothead! You can't go back. This is your first
operation – it's a bad sign.'

'Wait in the sleigh, I'll just be a moment,' Green said and
turned back.

He didn't walk straight out into the yard; first he glanced out
cautiously from the gateway. There was no one standing at the
window.

He ran quickly across the yard and up the stairs to the *piano
nobile*. The door had been specially oiled and it didn't squeak.

Leaving his boots on the staircase, he walked into the apartment without making a sound. He crept stealthily past the dining
room and heard Rahmet's voice from the study, where the telephone was.

'Yes, yes, twelve, seventy-four. And quickly, please, miss, this
is an urgent matter ... Security? Is that the Department of
Security? I need—'

Green cleared his throat.

Rahmet dropped the mouthpiece and spun round.

For a moment his face looked odd – without any expression
at all. Green realised Rahmet didn't know if the fatal words had
been overheard and didn't know what part he ought to play –
comrade or traitor. So that was what Rahmet's real face looked
like. Blank. Like a classroom blackboard that has been cleaned
with a dry rag, leaving dusty white smears.

But the face was only blank for a second. Rahmet realised that
he had been found out, the corners of his mouth extended into
a mocking leer and his eyes narrowed contemptuously.

'What is it, Greeny – don't trust your comrade-in-arms then?
Well, well, I never expected that from an old softy like you. Why
are you standing to attention like a little tin soldier?'

Green stood there stock-still with his arms at his sides and
didn't even move a muscle when the cornflower-blue man
snatched a Bulldog revolver out of his pocket.

'What are you doing here on your own?' Rahmet lisped,
'– without Emelya or little Bullfinch? Or did you come to prick

my conscience? The trouble is, Greeny old boy, I don't have a conscience. You know that. A pity, but now I'll have to eliminate you. Handing you in alive would have been far more impressive. What are you gawping at? I hate you, you blockhead.'

There was only one thing Green still had to find out – whether Rahmet had been collaborating with the Okhranka for a long time or had only been recruited yesterday.

He asked him: 'How long?'

'Let's say from the very beginning. You lifeless, long-faced bastards have made me feel sick for ages. And especially you, you thick-headed dolt! Yesterday I met a man far more interesting than you.'

'What does "TG" mean?' Green asked, just in case.

'Eh?' Rahmet said in surprise. 'What's that you say?'

There were no more questions, and Green didn't waste any more time. He flung the knife that was clutched in his right hand and dropped to the floor, to avoid being winged by a shot.

But there was no shot.

The Bulldog fell on the carpet as Rahmet clutched with both hands at the handle protruding from the left side of his chest. He lowered his head, gazing in amazement at the incongruous object, and tore it out of the wound. Blood flooded the entire front of his shirt; Rahmet stared round the room with blank, unseeing eyes and collapsed on to his face . . .

'Let's go,' said Green, taking a running jump into the sleigh, flopping into his seat and then slipping the small chest under it. The chest held everything they needed: detonators, false documents, spare guns. 'The rod fell under a chair. Barely managed to find it. Together as far as Khludovsky Lane. You get out there, I go on to meet Ace. And one more thing: don't come back here. After the ex, go to the lineman's place. And Arsenii too.'

Ace was already strolling along the pavement dressed as an undistinguished commercial traveller in a beaver-skin peaked cap, short coat, checked trousers and foppish white-felt boots. Green was dressed, as they had agreed, like a shop assistant.

'Where the hell have you been?' the specialist shouted at

Green, getting into his role. 'Tether the horse over there and get yourself over here.'

When Green came close, the bandit winked and said in a low voice: 'Well, you and I make a right pair. When I was still a young 'un I used to like fleecing geese like us. If only you could see Julietta – you'd never recognise her. I dolled her up like a real common little lady, so they wouldn't gape at her in the India. What a ruckus – a real scandal! Didn't want to make herself look ugly, no way she didn't.'

Green turned away in order not to waste time on idle conversation. He surveyed their position and decided it was ideal. The specialist knew his job all right.

Narrow Nemetskaya Street, along which the carriage would arrive, ran in a straight line all the way from Kukuisky Bridge. They'd be able to see the convoy from a distance, and there'd be plenty of time to take a good look and get ready.

Lying across the road just in front of the crossroads was a long timber beam of exactly the right thickness – a man on horseback would ride by without any trouble, but a sleigh would have to stop. Fifty paces further back on the right there was a gap between the buildings: Somovsky Cul-de-Sac. The gunmen should be there already, waiting in ambush behind the stone wall of the churchyard. A head appeared round the corner: Emelya, taking a look.

Ace's plan was a good one – sound and simple: there was no reason to expect any complications.

It wasn't quite getting dark yet, but the light at the edges of the sky was already dimming slightly, turning a murky grey. In half an hour the twilight would thicken, but by then the operation would already be over, and darkness would be very handy for the disengagement.

'It's five o'clock,' Ace announced, clicking shut the lid of an expensive watch on a thick platinum chain. 'They're just leaving the despatch room. We'll see them in about five minutes.'

He was taut and collected, his eyes sparkling merrily. Fate had played a cruel joke on the archpriest by planting a wolf cub like that in his family. Green was suddenly struck by an interesting theoretical question: what was to be done with characters like Ace in a free, harmonious society? Nature would still carry on producing a certain proportion of them, wouldn't she? And innate natural traits couldn't always be corrected by nurture.

There would still be dangerous professions, he thought; people with an adventurous bent would still be needed. That was where Ace and his kind would come in useful: for exploring the depths of the sea, conquering impregnable mountain peaks, testing flying machines. And later, after about another fifty years, there would be other planets to explore. There would be plenty of work for everyone.

'Clear off!' Ace shouted at a yard-keeper who was grunting as he struggled to roll the beam aside. 'That's ours; the cart'll be back in a minute to pick it up. Ah, these people, always looking for something they can pick up without paying for it.'

Faced with this furious assault, the yard-keeper withdrew behind his iron gates, leaving the street completely deserted.

'The money's coming; our little darlings are on their way,' Ace drawled in an unctuous voice. 'You get across to the other side. And don't go too early. Take your lead from me.'

At first all they could see was a long, dark blob; then they could make out individual figures – everything was exactly as Ace had said it would be.

At the front – two mounted guards with carbines over their shoulders.

Behind them – the despatch office's financial instruments carriage: a large enclosed sleigh, with a driver and two other men, a constable and a delivery agent.

Riding beside the carriage – more armed guards, two on the right, two on the left. And bringing up the rear of the convoy was a sleigh, which they couldn't make out clearly from where they were standing. It ought to be carrying another four guards with carbines.

Emelya came out from round the corner and leaned against the wall, watching the procession as it passed by. He was holding a small package: the bomb.

Green stroked the fluted handle of his Colt with his finger as he waited for the front riders to notice the beam and come to a halt. The clock above the pharmacy showed nine minutes past five.

The horses stepped indifferently over the barrier and ran on, but the driver of the carriage roared out 'Whoah!' and pulled hard on his reins.

'Where are you going?' the constable yelled, half-rising to his feet. 'Can't you see that beam? Dismount and drag it out of the way. And you give a hand too,' he added, nudging the driver.

Once he saw the convoy had halted, Emelya began strolling slowly towards the final sleigh from behind, like a curious onlooker.

When the two guards and the driver bent over and grabbed hold of the beam, Emelya took a short run, hurled his bundle and shouted in daredevil style: 'Hey-up!' He had to shout so that the guards would realise who had thrown the bomb. That was crucial for the plan.

Before the bundle had even touched the ground or the guards had realised what this strange object flying towards them was, Emelya had already spun round and set off back towards the corner.

The boom wasn't particularly loud, because the bomb was only half as powerful as an ordinary one. The power to kill wasn't needed here; this was only a demonstration. A powerful blast would have stunned the guards, or concussed them, but right now they had to have their wits about them and be quick on their feet.

'A bomber!' the constable yelled, looking back over the top of the carriage. 'There he goes – ducked round the corner!'

So far everything was going according to plan. The four men sitting in the sleigh (not one of them had been hurt by the blast) jumped out one after another and went dashing after Emelya. The other four, who were still sitting in their saddles, swung their horses round and set off whistling and hallooing in the same direction.

The only armed men left near the carriage were the two who had dismounted, now caught with the beam clutched in their hands, and the constable. The driver and the delivery agent didn't count.

Just a second after the pursuers turned into the cul-de-sac, a sharp crackle of revolver shots came from round the corner. The guards would be too busy to think about the carriage now. They would be stunned by the gunfire and their own fear; they would just lie down and start blazing away.

Now it was up to Ace and Green.

They stepped into the roadway almost simultaneously, each from his own side of the street. Ace shot one guard twice in the back and Green struck the other on the back of his head with the butt of his revolver – with Green's strength that was enough. The beam dropped on to the trampled snow with a dull thud and rolled away a little distance. The driver squatted down on his haunches, covered his ears with his hands and started howling quietly.

Green waved his revolver at the constable and the delivery agent, who were sitting on the coach-box, transfixed. 'Get down. Look lively.'

The agent pulled his head right down into his shoulders and jumped down clumsily, but the constable couldn't make up his mind whether to surrender or carry out his duty: he raised one hand as if he were surrendering, but fumbled blindly at his holster with the other.

'Don't play the fool,' said Green. 'I'll shoot you.'

The constable flung his second hand up in the air, but Ace fired anyway. The bullet hit the constable in the middle of his face, transforming his nose into a blackish-red hole, and the constable collapsed backwards with a strange sob, slapping his arms against the ground.

Ace grabbed hold of the delivery agent's coat collar and dragged him to the back of the carriage: 'Open it, serviceman, if you want to live!'

'I can't, I haven't got a key,' the agent whispered through lips white from terror.

Ace shot him in the forehead, stepped over his body and smashed the sealed lock with another two bullets.

There were six sacks inside, just as they had been told there would be. Green hastily scratched the letters 'CG' on the carriage door with the handle of his Colt. Let them know.

While they were carrying the loot to the sleigh, he asked as he ran: 'Why did you have to kill him? And the other one had surrendered too.'

'No one stays alive if he can identify Ace,' the specialist hissed through clenched teeth, tossing another sack over his shoulder.

The driver, who was still squatting down, heard what he said and made a run for it, hunched over.

Ace dropped his load and fired after him, but missed, and before he could fire again Green knocked the gun out of his hand.

'What are you doing?' The bandit clutched at his bruised wrist. 'He'll bring the police!'

'It doesn't matter. The job's done. Give the signal.'

Ace swore and whistled piercingly three times, and the shooting in the cul-de-sac was immediately cut by half – the whistle was the sign that the gunmen could stop firing.

The horse set off at a gallop with its studded hooves clattering and the light sleigh, not at all encumbered by its paper load, slid off weightlessly along the icy roadway.

Green looked back.

A few dark, shapeless heaps on the ground. Orphaned horses nuzzling at them. The empty carriage with its doors ajar. The clock above the pharmacy. Twelve minutes after five.

That meant the expropriation had taken less than three minutes.

The India Inn stood on a dingy depressing square beside the Spice Market. A long, single-storey building – not much to look at, but it had a good stable and its own goods warehouse. This was where merchants stayed when they came to Moscow for cinnamon, vanilla, cloves and cardamoms. The entire area around the Spice Market was impregnated with exotic aromas that set your head spinning, and if you closed your eyes to blot out the snowdrifts stained yellow by horses' urine and the lopsided little houses of this artisans' quarter, you could easily imagine that you really were in India, with sumptuous palm trees waving overhead, elephants swaying gracefully as they strolled past, and a sky that was the colour it ought to be: an unfathomable, dense blue, instead of the grey and white of Moscow.

Ace's calculations were right yet again. When Green walked into the hotel carrying two heavy sacks, nobody gave him a second glance. A man carrying samples of his wares – nothing out of the ordinary there. How could anyone possibly guess that what the dark-haired shop assistant was carrying in his sacks was not spices for trading but two hundred thousand roubles' worth of brand-new banknotes – while they were driving from Nemetskaya Street, Green had covered the sealing-wax eagles and dangling lead seals with plain, ordinary sackcloth.

Julie looked strange in a cheap *drap-de-dame* dress, with her hair set in a simple bun at the back of her head. She flung herself on his neck, scorching his cheek with her hot breath, and murmured: 'Thank God, you're alive . . . I was so worried, I was really shaking . . . That's the money, right? So everything's all right, is it? What about our men? Are they all safe and well? Where's Ace?'

Green had had time to prepare himself, so he bore the rapid, ticklish kisses without a shudder. Apparently that was perfectly possible.

'On guard,' he replied calmly. 'Now we'll bring in two more each, and that's it.'

When they brought in the remaining four sacks, Julie rushed to kiss Ace in exactly the same way, and Green was finally convinced that the danger had passed. He wouldn't be caught out again; his willpower would withstand even this test.

'Do you want to count it?' he asked. 'If not, choose any two. We'll take four to the sleigh and I'll go.'

'No, no!' Julie exclaimed. She kissed her lover on the lips once again and dashed over to the window sill. 'I knew everything would be all right. Look, I've got a bottle of Cliquot cooling outside. We have to raise a glass.'

Ace walked over to the sacks lying on the floor. He swung his foot and kicked them one at a time, as if he were checking how tightly they were packed. Then he turned slightly and swung his foot, with the same springy movement, but three times as hard, straight into Green's crotch.

For an instant the sudden pain made everything go dark. Green doubled over and another crushing blow landed on the back of his head. He saw the floorboards right in front of his eyes. He must have fallen.

He knew how to handle pain, even pain as sharp as this. He had to take three convulsive breaths in, forcing the breath back out each time, and disconnect the zone of pain from his physical awareness. Once he used to spend a lot of time practising with fire (burning the palm of his hand, the inside of his elbow, the back of his knee) and he had completely mastered this difficult art.

But the blows were still raining down – on his ribs, his shoulders, his head.

'I'll kill you, you louse,' Ace kept repeating. 'I'll trample you into manure! Trying to make a gull out of me!'

There was no time to fight the pain. Green turned into the next blow and took it in his stomach, but he grabbed the felt boot and kept hold of it. From close up the boot didn't look so white: it was smeared with mud and spattered with blood. He jerked it towards himself, knocking Ace off his feet.

He let go of the boot so that his fingers could reach Ace's throat, but his adversary rolled aside and dodged out of the way.

They jumped to their feet at the same moment, face to face.

It was bad that his revolver was still in the pocket of his coat. There it was, hanging on the hallstand – a long way away, and it was pointless in any case: he couldn't fire in the room, it would bring everyone in the hotel running.

Julie froze motionless by the wall, with her eyes staring in horror and her mouth open, one hand clutching the bottle of champagne while the fingers of the other automatically tore away the gold foil.

'You bloody bitch,' the bandit said with an angry smile.

'Thought you'd swap your Ace for a spot card, did you? Take a look at him, the ugly freak. He looks like a corpse.'

'You imagined it all, Ace,' Julie babbled in a quavering voice, '– imagined the whole thing. Nothing happened.'

'Don't lie. "Nothing happened"! Ace has the eye of a falcon where treason's concerned – I can sense it straight away. That's why I'm still walking around and not rotting in jail.'

The specialist leaned down and pulled a knife with a long, slim blade out of his boot.

'Now I'm going to carve you up, dead-eyes. Slowly, one little scrap at a time.'

Green wiped his split eyebrow with his sleeve so that the blood wouldn't blind him and held out his bare hands. He'd used his knife on Rahmet. Never mind; he could manage without a knife.

Ace moved closer, taking little steps, easily dodged a right hook and ran his knife across Green's wrist. Red drops began falling to the floor. Julie howled.

'That's for your starters,' Ace promised.

Green said: 'Quiet, Julie. You mustn't scream.'

He tried to catch hold of his opponent by the collar, but again only grabbed empty air and the sharp blade ran through his undershirt and stung his side.

'And that's for the soup.'

With his left hand Ace grabbed a carafe off the table and flung it. To avoid it hitting his head, Green had to duck down, losing sight of the specialist for a moment. The knife immediately took its opportunity, whizzing past right beside his ear, which was suddenly aflame, as if the contact had set it on fire. Green raised his hand – the top of his ear was dangling by a thin strip of skin. He tore it off and threw it into the corner. Something hot streamed down his neck.

'That was the meat course,' Ace explained. 'And now we'll get to the dessert.'

Green had to change his tactics. He retreated to the wall and stood there motionless. He had to ignore the knife. Let it cut. Throw himself towards the blade, seize his opponent's chin with one hand and the top of his head with the other, then twist sharply. Like in 1884, in the fights in the Tyumen transit prison.

But Ace was in no hurry to come at him now. He stopped three steps away, shuffling his fingers, and the knife flickered through them like a glittering snake.

'All right, Julietta, now who do you choose?' he asked derisively. 'Do you want me to leave him for you? Never mind that he's all battered and cut up, you can lick his wounds for him. Or will you go with me? I've got money now, heaps of it. We could leave old Mother Russia and never come back.'

'I choose you, you,' Julie answered immediately, sobbing and rushing towards Ace 'I don't want him. It was just playing a game – seeing if I could do it. Forgive me, Acey, my sweet, you know the way I am. Compared to you he's nothing, just slobbered all over me, nothing interesting at all. Kill him. He's dangerous. He'll set all the revolutionaries on your tail; there'll be nowhere in Europe you can hide.'

The bandit winked at Green.

'Do you hear the smart woman's advice? Naturally, I was going to finish you off anyway. But you can thank Julietta for one thing. You'll go quick. I was going to play with you a bit longer – slit your nose and your eyes . . .'

The specialist didn't finish. The green bottle descended on his head with a crunch and he collapsed at Green's feet.

'Ai! Ai! Ai! Ai!' Julie screeched shrilly, at regular intervals, staring in fright, first at the broken neck of the bottle, then at the man on the floor, then at the blood frothing up as it mingled with the spilled champagne.

Green stepped over the motionless body, took Julie by the shoulders and shook her firmly.

CHAPTER 7

in which the investigation is right back where it started

Erast Petrovich had intended to make a start on the search the very first thing on Tuesday morning, but he failed to make an early start, because his female guest once again spent the night at the outhouse on Malaya Nikitskaya Street.

Esfir turned up without any warning, after midnight, when the State Counsellor was walking around his study, counting his beads. His visitor had a determined air, and she didn't waste any time on conversation – right there in the hallway, without even taking off her sable cloak, she put her arms around Erast Petrovich's neck and gave him a tight hug; and naturally it was quite some time before he was able to concentrate on his deductions again.

In fact, he only managed to get back to work in the morning, when Esfir was still asleep. Fandorin slipped quietly out of bed, sat in an armchair and tried to restore the broken thread of his thought. The results were not very good. His beloved jade beads, which disciplined the workings of his mind with their rigorous, crisp clicking, had been left behind in the study; and walking to and fro, so that the movement of his muscles would stimulate the activity of his brain, was too risky – the slightest sound would wake Esfir. And he could hear Masa snuffling behind the door – the servant was waiting patiently for the moment when he and his master could do their gymnastic exercises.

Difficult circumstances are no hindrance to the superior man in contemplating higher things, the State Counsellor reminded himself, recalling a maxim from the great sage of the Orient. As if she had overheard the phrase 'difficult circumstances', Esfir stuck her bare arm out from under the blanket and ran her hand over the pillow beside her. Finding nobody there, she moaned pitifully, but still unawares, without waking up. Even so, he had to think quickly.

Diana, Fandorin decided – he should start with her. The other lines of enquiry were already taken in any case.

The mysterious female collaborator had links to the Office of Gendarmes and the Okhranka, and the revolutionaries. Very probably she was a traitor to them all. An entirely amoral individual and, moreover, judging from Sverchinsky and Burlyaev's behaviour, not only in a political sense. But then, it seemed, did it not, that in revolutionary circles the view taken of relations between the sexes was more liberal than the general view in society?

Erast Petrovich cast a glance of vague misgiving at the sleeping beauty. The scarlet lips moved, shaping soundless words, the long black eyelashes trembled, the two moist embers framed between them flared up brightly and were not extinguished again. Esfir opened her eyes wide, saw Fandorin and smiled.

'What are you doing?' she asked in a voice hoarse from sleep. 'Come here.'

'I'd like t-to ask you ...' he began, then hesitated and broke off in embarrassment.

Was it fitting to exploit personal relationships to gather information for his investigation?

'Ask.' She yawned, sat up on the bed and stretched sweetly, so that the blanket slipped down and Erast Petrovich had to make a serious effort not to be distracted.

He resolved his moral dilemma as follows.

Of course he should not ask about Diana. Even less should he ask about the revolutionary groups – in any case, Esfir was hardly likely to be involved in any serious anti-government activity. But it was permissible for him to extract information of a quite general, one might say sociological, nature.

'Tell me, Esfir, is it t-true that the women in revolutionary circles take ... an absolutely free view of amorous relationships?'

She burst into laughter, pulling her knees up to her chin and clasping them in her arms. 'I knew it! How predictable and bourgeois you are after all. If a woman hasn't acted out the proper performance of unavailability for you, you're ready to suspect she is debauched and promiscuous. "Oh, sir, I am not that kind of girl! Phoo, how disgusting! No, no, no, only after the wedding!"' she mocked in a repulsive, lisping voice. 'That's how you want us to behave. But of course – the laws of capitalism apply, don't they? If you wish to sell your commodity for a good price, first you have to make it desirable, set the buyer's mouth watering. But I am not a commodity, Your Honour. And you are not a buyer.' Esfir's eyes blazed with righteous indignation and her slim hand sliced through the air menacingly. 'We women of the new age are not ashamed of our nature and we choose for ourselves who to love. There's one girl in our circle. The men all run a mile from her, because the poor thing is so terribly ugly – a real fright, an absolute nightmare. But for her intelligence she gets far more respect than all the great beauties. She says that free love is not lustful sin but the union of two equal beings – naturally, a temporary union, because it is the nature of feelings to be inconstant; you can't incarcerate them for life. And you don't need to be afraid that I'll try to drag you to the altar. I shall drop you soon anyway. You're not my type at all, and in general you're absolutely awful! I want to gorge myself until I've had enough and I'm finally disillusioned with you. Well, what are you gaping at? Come here immediately!'

Masa must have been listening at the door, because at that very moment it opened a little and a round head with narrow eyes was thrust into the room through the crack.

'Goo' morin',' the head said with a joyful, beaming smile.

'Go to hell with your gymnastics!' Esfir exclaimed resolutely, flinging a well-aimed pillow at the head; but Masa bore the blow without flinching.

'Letter from impotan' gen'man,' he declared, holding up a long white envelope.

'Impotan' gen'man' was what the Japanese called the Governor General, so the reason for his intrusion had to be accepted as legitimate. Erast Petrovich opened the envelope and took out a card bearing a gold crest.

Most of the text was printed; only the name and the note at the bottom were written in His Excellency's regular, old-fashioned hand.

My dear Erast Petrovich

On the occasion of Butter Week and the forthcoming festival of Shrovetide, I request your company for pancakes.

The cordial supper in an intimate circle will commence at midnight. Gentlemen invited are requested not to trouble themselves by wearing uniform. Ladies are free to choose a dress at their own discretion.

Vladimir Dolgorukoi

Erast Petrovich you must come. You can tell me how our business is going.

And do bring your new flame – it is an unofficial supper and as an old man I am curious to see her.

'What is it?' Esfir asked, disgruntled, '–a summons from the terrible Tsar? Tie a dog's head to your saddle and ride off to work – severing heads?'

'Not at all,' Fandorin replied. 'It's an invitation to pancakes at the Governor General's residence. Listen.'

He read it out loud, naturally omitting the handwritten note. Fandorin was not at all surprised by how well informed the prince was concerning the private lives of his aides – all the years they had worked together had accustomed him to that.

'You know, we could g-go together if you like,' he said, absolutely certain that the only way Esfir would go to the Governor General's residence for pancakes was wearing shackles and under armed escort.

'What does "an intimate circle" mean?' she asked, wrinkling up her nose squeamishly. 'Is it just the sultan and his viziers and the especially trustworthy eunuchs?'

'Shrovetide pancakes at the prince's house are a tradition,' Fandorin explained. 'It has been going on for more than twenty years. "An intimate circle" means seventy or eighty close officials and honoured citizens with their wives. They spend the whole night sitting there eating, drinking and dancing. Nothing interesting about it. I always leave early.'

'And can I really wear any dress I like?' Esfir asked pensively, not looking at Erast Petrovich, but gazing off somewhere into space.

Having taking his leave of Esfir until the evening, Fandorin tried several times to call the telephone number that Lieutenant Colonel Burlyaev had given to the operator two days before, but there was no reply, and Erast Petrovich began wondering if perhaps he ought to take advantage of the female agent's absence to carry out a secret search of the townhouse on Arbat Street.

He gathered together the necessary assortment of tools and then telephoned again, just to make certain, and the earpiece suddenly responded in the American manner, with a long, drawling whisper: 'Hel-lo?'

Against all his expectations, Diana failed to recall that the State Counsellor had been declared persona non grata and immediately agreed to a meeting.

Nor was Fandorin obliged on this occasion to wait in front of a locked door. After ringing the bell, he pushed on the brass handle and, to his surprise, the door yielded – apparently it had been unlocked in advance.

Erast Petrovich followed the familiar route up the steps into the mezzanine, knocked on the door of the study and entered without waiting for an answer.

Just like the previous time, the thin curtains were tightly drawn and the woman on the divan was wearing a hat with a veil.

The State Counsellor bowed and was about to sit in an armchair, but the woman beckoned him.

'Over here. It's hard to whisper right across the room.'

'Do you not find all these precautions excessive?' Fandorin could not resist asking the question, although he knew it was not a good idea to annoy his hostess. 'It would be quite enough for me not to be able to see your face.'

'No-o,' Diana murmured. 'My sound is a rustle, a whisper, a hiss. My element is shade, darkness, silence. Sit down, sir. We shall make quiet conversation and in the pauses listen to the stillness.'

'As you wish.'

Erast Petrovich seated himself side on to the lady, some slight distance away from her, and tried to make out at least some features of her face through the veil. Alas, the room was too dark for that.

'Are you aware that in progressive young people's circles you are now regarded as an intriguing individual?' the collaborator asked derisively. 'Your intervention in darling Pyotr Ivanovich's operation the day before yesterday has split my revolutionary friends into two camps. Some see you as a state official of a new type, the first herald of forthcoming liberal changes. While others . . .'

'What d-do the others say?'

'The others say that you should be eliminated, because you are more cunning and dangerous than the stupid sleuths from the Okhranka. But don't be alarmed.' Diana touched Erast Petrovich gently on the shoulder. 'You have an intercessor – Firochka Litvinova – and after that evening she has the reputation of a true heroine. Ah, handsome men can always find women to intercede for them.'

There was the sound of muffled, almost soundless laughter, which produced a distinctly unpleasant impression on the State Counsellor.

'Is it true what our people say – that Larionov was executed by the CG?' Diana asked, inclining her head inquisitively. 'It had been rumoured that he was an agent provocateur. In any case, our people no longer mention his name. A taboo – the kind that primitive savages have. Was he really a collaborator?'

Erast did not answer, because something else had occurred to him. Now it was clear why Esfir had never mentioned the deceased engineer.

'Tell me, my lady, do you know a female individual who goes by the alias Needle?'

'Needle? I've never heard it before. What is she like?'

Fandorin repeated what he had heard from Rahmet-Gvidon. 'She looks about thirty. Thin. Tall. Plain . . . I think that's all.'

'Well, we have plenty like that. I might know her by name, but in conspiratorial circles she is known by her alias. My connections are extensive, Monsieur Fandorin, but not deep; they do not reach into the depths of the underground. Who told you about this Needle?'

Again he did not answer. It was time to approach the most important question.

'You are an unusual woman, Diana,' Erast Petrovich began with affected enthusiasm. 'At our last m-meeting you made a quite indelible impression on me, and I have been thinking about you ever since. I think this is the first time I have met a genuine femme fatale who can make respectable grown men lose their heads and neglect their duty.'

'Go on, go on,' whispered the woman with no face and no voice. 'It's a pleasure to listen to such words.'

'I can see that you have driven Burlyaev and Sverchinsky completely insane, and they are very sober and serious gentlemen. They are consumed with burning jealousy for each other. And I am sure that on both sides their suspicions are not unfounded. How elegantly you toy with these two men, who are feared by the whole of Moscow! You are a bold woman. Others only speak of free love, but you preach it with your entire life.'

She laughed in gratification, throwing her head back. 'There is no such thing as love. There is only the human being, living alone and dying alone. There is nothing and nobody who can share that solitude. And it is not possible for anyone to merge completely into anyone else's life. But you can play at someone else's life, taste it. You are an intelligent man, Mr Fandorin, I can be entirely frank with you. You see, by vocation I am an actress. I should be glittering on the stage in the finest theatres, rousing my public to tears and laughter, but . . . the circumstances of life have prevented me from using my talent for its true purpose.'

'Which circumstances?' Erast Petrovich enquired cautiously.

'Do you mean your noble origins? I have heard that you come from good society.'

'Yes, something of the kind,' Diana replied after a pause. 'But I have no regrets. Playing at life is far more interesting than playing on the stage. With stupid young people who have crammed their heads full of pernicious literature, I play one part; with Burlyaev I play another, and with Sverchinsky I play a different one again . . . I am more fortunate than many people, Mr Fandorin. I am never bored.'

'I understand the difference between the roles of a nihilist and a collaborator, but do you really have to behave differently with the gendarme colonel Sverchinsky and the gendarme lieutenant colonel Burlyaev?'

'Oho, you obviously understand nothing at all about the theatre.' She fluttered her hands rapturously. 'The two roles are quite different. Shall I tell you how to be successful with men? Do you think beauty is required? By no means! How can I be beautiful if you cannot even see my face? It is all very simple. You have to understand what a man is like and play a contrasting part. It is like electricity: opposite charges attract. Take Pyotr Ivanovich, now. He is a strong, coarse individual, inclined to direct action and force. With him I am weak, feminine, vulnerable. Add to that professional interest, a whiff of the mystery to which men are so partial – and poor Burlyaev becomes soft putty in my hands.'

Erast Petrovich sensed that he was very close to the goal – he must not make a false step now.

'And Sverchinsky?'

'Oh, he is entirely different. Cunning, cautious, suspicious. With him I am open-hearted, carefree, a little crude. I have already mentioned professional interest and mystery – those are essential components. Would you believe that last week Stanislav Filippovich went down on his knees in front of me and begged me to tell him if I was intimately involved with Burlyaev? I threw him out and told him not to show his face until he was summoned. Not bad for a "collaborator", ah? The top gendarme in the entire province, and I have him dancing like a performing poodle!'

So there he had his first result: Sverchinsky had not been here since last week, and so Diana could not have received any information about Khrapov's arrival from him.

'Brilliant!' the State Counsellor said approvingly. 'So the unfortunate Stanislav Filippovich has b-been in exile for an entire week? Poor fellow! No wonder he's so furious. The field was left open for the Department of Security.'

'Oh no!' the femme fatale gasped, quite overcome by her own quiet laughter. 'That's the whole point! I gave Burlyaev his marching orders for a week too! – so that he would think I had chosen Sverchinsky over him!'

Erast Petrovich knitted his brows and asked: 'And in actual fact?'

'In actual fact ...' The collaborator leaned closer and whispered confidentially. 'In actual fact I had the usual woman's troubles and was in any case obliged to take a break from both my lovers!'

The State Counsellor involuntarily started back, and Diana broke into an even more intense fit of merriment, hissing and whistling in delight at the effect she had produced.

'You are a very sensitive and proper gentleman, you adhere to strict rules, and therefore I try to intrigue you with my cynicism and violations of the conventions,' the frustrated actress blithely confessed. 'However, I am not doing it for any practical purpose, but solely out of my love of art. My woman's problems are over now, but you, Monsieur Fandorin, have no reason to hope for anything. There is no point in your trilling like a nightingale and showering me with compliments. You are simply not my type at all.'

Erast Petrovich got up off the divan, overwhelmed by horror, hurt feelings and disappointment.

The initial feeling was horror: how could this nightmarish creature have imagined that he was attempting to win her favours!

The hurt feelings came with the recollection that this was the second time today a woman had told him he was not her type.

But the strongest feeling, of course, was disappointment: Diana could not have been the channel through which the leak had occurred.

'I assure you, madam, that you are completely m-mistaken as far as I am concerned,' the State Counsellor said coolly and walked towards the door, to the accompaniment of rustling, muffled laughter.

Shortly after four Fandorin drove on to Bolshoi Gnezdikovksy Lane in a morose and depressed state of mind.

The only promising theory left for him to explore had collapsed in a totally ignominious fashion and now nothing remained for him but to play the pitiful role of a sponger. The State Counsellor was not accustomed to feeding on crumbs from others' tables and the anticipation of humiliation had put him in a foul mood; but nonetheless it was absolutely essential for him to obtain some information about the progress of the investigation, for that night he would have to report to the Governor General.

The Department of Security seemed to have been depopulated. There was not a single agent in the duty room on the ground floor – only a police sergeant and a clerk.

Zubtsov was languishing in the reception room upstairs. He was quite delighted to see Erast Petrovich: 'Mr State Counsellor! Do you have anything?'

Fandorin shook his head glumly.

'We haven't come up with anything either,' the young man sighed, casting a despondent sideways glance at the telephone. 'Would you believe it, we've been sitting here all day, glued to the spot, waiting for some word from Gvidon – Mr Pozharsky and myself.'

'He's here?' Erast Petrovich asked in surprise.

'Yes, and he's very calm. I'd go so far as to say he's quite placid – sitting in Pyotr Ivanovich s office reading magazines. The Lieutenant Colonel has gone to the student hostel on Dmitrovka Street to interrogate suspects. Evstratii Pavlovich has taken his wild men and, in his own words, they've "gone off gathering mushrooms and berries". Sverchinsky went to make the rounds of all the turnpikes this morning and for some reason feels it necessary to telephone from every one of them. I don't even inform the prince any more. This evening the indefatigable Stanislav Filippovich is going to check in person on his men's work at the railway stations, and he intends to spend the night at the Nikolaevsky – how's that for professional zeal!' Zubtsov smirked ironically. 'Showing the new boss how energetic he is. Only the prince is no fool; you can't deceive him with sham diligence.'

Recalling the threats that Sverchinsky had made against their visitor from the capital only the day before, Erast Petrovich shook his head: it was quite possible that diligence had nothing at all to do with the matter and the artful gendarme officer had something quite different in mind.

'So there's nothing from Gvidon?'

'Nothing,' Zubtsov sighed. 'Ten minutes ago some man called, but unfortunately I happened to be in the office with the prince. I left the clerk by the telephone. Now I can't get that call out of my mind.'

'Well, send someone to the t-telephone exchange,' Erast Petrovich advised him. 'Get them to identify the number from which the call was made. It's perfectly feasible technically, I've checked. May I go in?' he asked, blushing slightly as he indicated the door of the office.

'Why do you even need to ask?' Zubtsov exclaimed in surprise. 'Of course, go in. I think I really shall send someone to the telephone exchange. We'll find out the address from the number and make cautious enquiries about who the phone belongs to.'

Fandorin knocked and entered the office of the head of the Department of Security.

Pozharsky was sitting beside the lamp in an extremely snug-looking pose, with his feet pulled up on to his leather armchair. In his hand the deputy director of police, aide-de-camp and rising star was holding an open copy of the popular new magazine *The Journal of Foreign Literature*.

'Erast Petrovich!' Gleb Georgievich exclaimed enthusiastically. 'How delightful of you to call in. Please, have a seat.' He put the magazine down and smiled disarmingly.

'Are you angry with me for edging you out of the case? I understand; in your place I would be annoyed too. But it's the Emperor's own order; I am not at liberty to change anything. I only regret that I have been deprived of any access to your analytical talent, about which I have heard so much. I did not dare give you an assignment, since I am not your superior. I must admit, however, that I very much hope you will meet with success in your independent line of inquiry. Well then, do you have a result?'

'What result could I possibly have, when you hold absolutely all the threads in your hands?' Fandorin asked with a shrug of feigned indifference. 'But I believe you have nothing here either?'

The prince declared confidently: 'They're checking Gvidon. That's very good. He has already begun to hate his former comrades – because he has betrayed them. And now he will develop an absolutely passionate hatred for them. I know human nature. Especially the nature of betrayal – I am obliged to understand that by virtue of my profession.'

'Tell me then, is the psychology of betrayal always the same?' the State Counsellor asked, intrigued by the subject despite himself.

'By no means; it is infinitely varied. There is betrayal out of fear, betrayal out of resentment, out of love, out of ambition and a host of different causes, up to and including betrayal out of gratitude.'

'Out of g-gratitude?'

'Yes indeed. Permit me to relate to you a certain incident from my professional experience.' Pozharsky took a slim *papyrosa* out of his cigarette case, lit it and savoured the smoke as he drew it in. 'One of my finest agents was a sweet, pure, unselfish old woman – the very kindest of creatures. She doted on her only son, but in his youthful foolishness the boy got mixed up in a business that smacked of hard labour. She came to me, begging and weeping, told me the entire story of her life. I was younger myself then, and more soft-hearted than I am now – anyway, I took pity on her. Just between the two of us, I even went so far as to commit an official crime: I removed certain documents from the case file. To cut the story short, the boy was released; he got off with a fatherly caution, which, to be quite honest, made not the slightest impression on him. He became involved with revolutionaries again and plunged into a life of dissipation. But then what do you think happened? Inspired by her undying gratitude to me, his mother began diligently providing me with highly valuable information. Her son's comrades had known her for a long time as a hospitable hostess, they felt quite uninhibited by the innocuous old woman's presence and spoke quite openly in her company. She used to make notes of everything on scraps of paper and bring them to me. There was even one report that was written on the back of a recipe. Truly a case of, Do good and ye shall have your reward.'

Erast Petrovich listened to this edifying homily with mounting irritation and then could not help asking: 'Gleb Georgievich, isn't that repugnant? – encouraging a mother to inform on her own son?'

Pozharsky paused before he replied, and when he did, his tone had changed – it was no longer jocular, but serious and rather tired.

Mr Fandorin, you give the impression of being an intelligent, mature individual. Are you really like that pink-cheeked boy-officer who was here yesterday? Do you really not understand that we have no time now for goody-goody sentiment? Do you not see that there is a genuine war going on?'

'I do see. Of course I do,' the State Counsellor said passionately. 'But even in war there are rules. And in war people are usually hanged for employing traitors to spy for them.'

'This is not the kind of war in which any rules apply,' the prince countered with equal conviction. 'It is not two European powers who are fighting here. No, Erast Petrovich, this is the savage, primordial war of order with chaos, the West with the East, Christian chivalry with Mamai's horde. In this war no peace envoys are despatched, no conventions are signed, no one is released on his word of honour. This is a war fought with all the relentless cruelty of Asiatic science; molten lead is poured down men's throats and they are flayed alive, innocents are slaughtered. Did you hear about our agent Shverubovich getting sulphuric acid thrown in his face? Or the murder of General von Heinkel? They blew up the entire house, in which, apart from the General himself – who, as it happens, was a fine blackguard – there happened to be his wife, three children and servants. The only survivor was the youngest daughter; she was thrown from the balcony by the blast. Her back was broken and her leg was crushed, so that it had to be amputated. How do like that for a war?'

'And you, the custodian of society, are prepared to wage war on those kind of term' – to reply with the same methods?' asked Fandorin, stunned.

'What would you have me do – capitulate? Let the frenzied mobs burn houses and toss the best people of Russia on their pitchforks? Let our home-grown Robespierres inundate our cities with blood? Let our Empire become a bogeyman for the rest of humanity and be thrown back three hundred years? Erast Petrovich, I am no lover of high-flown sentiment, but let me tell you that we are only a narrow cordon, holding back the mindless, malevolent elements. Once they break through the cordon, nothing will stop them. There is no one standing behind us. Only ladies in hats, old grannies in mob-caps, young Turgenevian ladies and children in sailor suits – the little, decent world that sprang up in the wild Scythian steppes less than a hundred years ago thanks to the idealism of Emperor Alexander the Blessed.'

The prince broke off his impassioned speech, clearly embarrassed by his own outburst, and suddenly changed the subject. 'And by the way, concerning methods . . . Tell me, my dear Erast Petrovich, why did you plant a hermaphrodite in my bed?'

Fandorin assumed he must have misheard.

'I beg your pardon?'

'Nothing really important, just a charming joke. Yesterday evening, after taking supper in the restaurant, I went back to my room. When I enter it – good Lord, what a surprise! Lying there in my bed is a lovely lady, entirely undressed; I can see her delightful breasts above the top of the blanket. I try to show her out – she does not wish to get up. And a moment later there is a mass invasion: a police officer, constables and the porter shouting in a phoney voice: "This is a respectable establishment!" I can even see a reporter trying to slip in from the corridor, with a photographer in tow. And then things get even more interesting. My visitor jumps up out of bed, and, my sainted fathers, I've never seen the like before in all my life! A complete double set of sexual characteristics. Apparently an individual well known around Moscow, a certain gentleman – or a certain lady – who goes by the name of Coco. Very popular among those gourmands who prefer exotic amusements. An excellent idea, Erast Petrovich, bravo. I never expected it of you. Showing me up in an absurd and indecent light is the best possible way to regain control over the investigation. The sovereign will not tolerate lascivious behaviour from the servants of the throne. Goodbye to my aide-de-camp's monogram and farewell to my career.' Gleb Georgievich assumed an expression of exaggerated admiration. 'A most excellent plan, but I wasn't born yesterday, after all. When necessary I am more than capable of employing tricks of that kind myself, as you have had occasion to see in the case of Rahmet-Gvidon. Life, my dearest Erast Petrovich, has taught me to be cautious. When I leave my room, I always place an invisible mark on the door, and the servants are strictly forbidden to enter in my absence. When I looked at the door, I saw that the hair I left had been broken! The rooms on each side were occupied by my men – I brought them from St Petersburg. So I called them, and I was not alone when I entered the room – they were with me. When your police inspector saw these serious people with revolvers at the ready, he was confused and embarrassed. He grabbed the outlandish creature by the hair and dragged it out of the room, taking the newspaper men away with him as well; but never mind, the porter, a certain Teplugov, was still there and he was absolutely frank with me. He explained who this Coco was, and he told me how the gentlemen from the police had told him to be ready. Just see what enterprising action you have proved capable of, and yet you condemn my methods.'

'I knew nothing about this!' Erast Petrovich exclaimed indignantly, and immediately blushed – he had remembered Sverchinsky muttering something about Coco the day before. So that was what Stanislav Filippovich had had in mind when he was planning to make the official from St Petersburg a general laughing stock.

'I can see you didn't know,' Pozharsky said, nodding. 'Naturally, it's not the way you behave. I just wanted to make sure. In actual fact the responsibility for this trick with Coco lies, of course, with the highly experienced Colonel Sverchinsky. I came to that conclusion this morning, when Sverchinsky started calling me every hour. He was checking to see if I had guessed. Of course it was him, it couldn't be anyone else. Burlyaev lacks the imagination for tricks like that.'

Just at that moment there was a tramping of numerous feet outside the door, and Burlyaev himself – speak of the devil! – came bursting in.

'Disaster, gentlemen,' he gasped. 'I've just been informed that there's been a hold-up – the carriage of the state financial instruments depository. There are dead and wounded. They stole six-hundred-thousand roubles! And they left their sign: CG.'

Dejected confusion – that was the predominant mood at the extraordinary meeting of the leaders of the Office of Gendarmes and the Department of Security that dragged on late into the evening.

Occupying the chair at this doleful council was the Deputy Director of the Police Department, Prince Pozharsky – tousle-haired, pale-faced and angry.

'How wonderfully well you do things here in Moscow,' the man from the capital repeated yet again. 'Every day you despatch state funds for transfer to the most remote regions of the Empire, but you don't even have even any official instructions for the transportation of such immense sums! Who has ever heard of security guards going dashing after some bomber and leaving the money almost completely unprotected? All right, gentlemen, there's no point in repeating myself,' said Pozharsky, gesturing despairingly. 'We have all visited the scene of the crime and seen everything. Let us draw the sad conclusions. Six hundred thousand roubles have migrated to the revolutionary treasury which, by dint of great effort, I had only just emptied. It is terrible to think of all the atrocities the nihilists will commit with that money ... We have three men dead and two wounded, but during the shooting in Somovsky Cul-de-Sac only one man was wounded, and then only slightly. How was it possible not to guess that the shooting was started as a deliberate diversion, while the main action was taking place at the carriage?' the prince asked, growing furious now. 'And again that insolent challenge – the CG's calling card! What a blow to the prestige of the authorities! We underestimated the size of the Combat Group and its daring! There are not four men at all, but at least ten. I shall demand reinforcements from St Petersburg and special powers. And what wonderful execution! They had absolutely precise information about the route of the carriage and the guards! They struck quickly, confidently, mercilessly. They left no witnesses. Another example for our discussion of methods.' Gleb Georgievich glanced at Fandorin, who was sitting in the far corner of Burlyaev's office. 'True, one man – the driver Kulikov – did manage to get away alive. We know from him that the core group consisted of two men. Going by his description, one of them is our beloved Mr Green. The other was called Ace. Now, that seems like a clue! Ah, but no! The body of a man with a fractured skull was discovered at the India Inn. He was dressed exactly like Ace, and Kulikov identified him. Ace is a rather common alias in criminal circles; it signifies "a dare-devil, successful bandit". But most likely this was the legendary St Petersburg hold-up specialist Tikhon Bogoyav-lensky. He is rumoured to have had connections with the nihil-ists. As you are aware, the body has been sent to the capital for identification. But what's the point! Mr Green has snapped that thread in any case. Most convenient, no need to share the money either ...' The prince hooked his fingers together and cracked his knuckles. 'But the robbery is by no means the worst of our troubles. There is an even more distressing development.'

The room was completely silent, for those present could not imagine any misfortune worse than the robbery.

'You know that Titular Counsellor Zubtsov found out who owns the telephone from which some man called shortly before the attack on the carriage. It is in an apartment belonging to the well-known barrister Zimin, on Myasnitskaya Street. Since Zimin is presently involved in a trial in Warsaw – all the newspapers are writing about it – I sent my agents to make discreet enquiries about the gentleman who was too shy to speak with Sergei Vitalievich. The agents saw that there was no light on in the apartment, they opened the door and inside they discovered a body ...'

The new silence that followed was broken by Erast Petrovich, who asked in a quiet voice: 'Could it have been Gvidon?'

'How did you know?' Pozharsky asked, swinging round towards him. 'You couldn't possibly know that!'

'It's very simple,' Fandorin said with a shrug. 'You said that something even more distressing than the theft of six hundred thousand roubles had happened. We all know that in this investigation you had staked your greatest hopes on the agent Gvidon. Nobody else's murder could possibly have upset you so badly.'

The deputy director of police exclaimed irritably:

'Bravo, bravo, Mr State Counsellor. Where were you earlier with your famous deduction? Yes, it was Gvidon. There were clear indications of suicide; he was clutching a dagger bearing the letters CG in his hand, and the stab wound in his heart had been made by the same blade. Apparently I was mistaken in my assessment of this individual's psychological constitution.'

It was evident that Gleb Georgievich found self-castigation difficult, and Fandorin appreciated how much this gesture must have cost him.

'You were not so very mistaken,' he said. 'Obviously Gvidon was about to betray his comrades and he even phoned the

Department, but at the last moment his conscience awoke. It happens sometimes, even with traitors.'

Pozharsky realised that Fandorin was referring him back to their recent conversation and he smiled briefly; but then his face immediately darkened and he turned in annoyance to Lieutenant Colonel Burlyaev.

'Where has that Mylnikov of yours got to? He's our last hope now. Ace is dead, Gvidon is dead. The unidentified man found behind the church wall in Somovsky Cul-de-Sac is dead too, but if we can establish his identity, it might be the start of a new trail.'

'Evstratii Pavlovich has set all the local constables on it,' Burlyaev boomed, 'and his agents are checking the dead man's photograph against all our card files. If he's from Moscow, we're sure to identify him.'

'Allow me to draw your attention to one more thing, Erast Petrovich – in continuation of our discussion,' Pozharsky said, glancing at the State Counsellor. 'The unidentified man had only been wounded in the neck, not fatally. However, his accomplices didn't take him with them; they finished him off with a shot to the temple. That is the way they do things!'

'Or perhaps the wounded man shot himself in order not to be a burden to his comrades?' Fandorin responded.

Gleb Georgievich's only response to such misplaced idealism was to roll his eyes up and back, but Colonel Sverchinsky rose halfway out of his seat and asked: 'Mr Deputy Director, will you order me to head the effort to identify the man? I can line up all the yard-keepers in Moscow. We'll need more men than Mylnikov and his agents for this.'

Several times that evening when Stanislav Filippovich had tried to make useful suggestions, the prince had stubbornly refused to take any notice of him. But this time Pozharsky seemed to explode.

'Why don't you keep quiet!' he shouted. 'Your department is responsible for order in the city! Fine order! What was it you were planning to deal with today? The railway stations? Then go, and keep your eyes open! The bandits are bound to try to ship their loot out of the city, most likely to Petersburg, in order to replenish the party funds. Take care, Sverchinsky; if you bungle this too, I'll see that you pay for everything at once! Go!'

The Colonel, deadly pale, gave Pozharsky a long glance and walked towards the door in silence. His adjutant, Lieutenant Smolyaninov, dashed after him.

Mylnikov came dashing towards them from the reception, looking delighted. 'We've done it!' he shouted from the doorway. 'Identified him! He was on record from last year! He's in the card file. Arsenii Nikolaevich Zimin, the barrister's son! A private house on Myasnitskaya Street!'

In the sudden silence that followed, the puzzled Evstratii Pavlovich's fitful breathing was clearly audible.

Fandorin turned away from Pozharsky, afraid that the prince might read the gloating in his eyes. It was not exactly gloating, but the State Counsellor did experience a certain involuntary sense of satisfaction, of which he immediately felt ashamed.

'Well now,' Pozharsky said in a flat, expressionless voice. 'So this move has led us into a dead end too. Let us congratulate each other, gentlemen. We are right back where we started.'

When he returned home, Erast Petrovich had barely changed his frock coat for a white tie and tails before it was time to go to collect Esfir from the banker Litvinov's house on Tryokhsvyatskaya Street, a building famous throughout Moscow.

This pompous marble palazzo, built only a few years earlier, seemed to have been transported to the quiet, sedate little street directly from Venice, instantly overshadowing the old nobles' mansions with their peeling columns and identical triangular roofs. Even now, in the hour before midnight, the buildings beside it were lost in darkness, but the handsome house was all aglow, glimmering like some fairy-tale palace of ice: the magnificent pediment in the very latest American fashion was illuminated by electric lights.

The State Counsellor had heard about the great wealth of the banker Litvinov, who was one of Russia's most generous benefactors of charity, a patron of Russian artists and zealous donor to the Church, a man whose recent conversion to Christianity had been more than compensated for by his fervent piety. But even so, in Moscow high society the millionaire was regarded with condescending irony. They told a joke about how when Litvinov was awarded a decoration for his assistance to orphans, a star that conferred the status of a noble of the fourth rank, he supposedly began saying to people: 'Please, why struggle to get your tongue round "Avessalom Efraimovich". Just call me "Your Excellency".' Litvinov was accepted in all the best houses of Moscow, but at the same time it was sometimes whispered to the other guests, as if in justification, that 'a baptised Jew is a thief forgiven'.

However, on entering the spacious Carrara marble vestibule, decorated with crystal chandeliers, vast mirrors and monumental canvases showing scenes from Russian history, Erast Petrovich was struck by the thought that if Avessalom Efraimovich's financial affairs continued in the same successful vein, the title of baron was a certainty, and then the ironic whispers would stop, because people who are not simply rich, but super-rich, and also titled, have no nationality.

Despite the late hour, the imperious manservant was dressed in a gold-embroidered camisole and was even wearing a powdered wig. Once Fandorin gave his name, there was no further need to explain the purpose of his visit.

'One moment, sir,' the valet said, bowing ceremoniously, with an air that suggested he had previously served in the palace of some grand prince, if not somewhere even grander. 'The young lady will be down straight away. Perhaps Your Honour would care to wait in the sitting room?'

Erast Petrovich did not care to do so, and the servant hurried up the gleaming, snow-white staircase, while somehow managing to maintain his majestic composure, to the first floor. A minute later a small, nimble gentleman with an extremely expressive face and a neat lick of hair across his balding head came tumbling down in the opposite direction like a rubber ball.

'My God, I'm so terribly, terribly pleased to meet you,' he began when he was only halfway down the stairs. 'I've heard a lot about you, and all of it most flattering. I am extremely glad that Firochka has such reputable acquaintances, you know, it was always those long-haired types in dirty boots with coarse voices ... That's because she was still young, of course. I knew it would pass. Well, actually, I am Litvinov, and you, Mr Fandorin, have no need to introduce yourself; you are a very well-known individual.'

Erast Petrovich was somewhat surprised to see the banker wearing a frock coat and his star in his own home – he was probably going out somewhere too. But certainly not to Dolgorukoi's for pancakes, for that Avessalom Efraimovich would have to wait until his baronial title arrived.

'Such an honour, such an honour for Firochka to be going to an intimate supper at His Excellency's home. I'm very, very glad.' The banker was now very close to his visitor and he extended a white, puffy hand. 'I am exceedingly glad to make your acquaintance. We are at home on Thursdays and would be truly delighted to see you. But never mind our at-homes, simply come at any time that is convenient. My wife and I are doing everything to encourage this acquaintance of our Firochka's.'

The ingenuousness of this final phrase left the State Counsellor feeling somewhat uneasy. He felt even more embarrassed on noticing that the door leading to the inner chambers on the ground floor was ajar and someone was studying him attentively from behind it.

But Esfir was already walking down the stairs, and the way she was dressed immediately made Fandorin forget both the ambiguity of his position and the mysterious spy.

'Papa, why have you pinned on that trinket of yours again!' she exclaimed menacingly. 'Take it off immediately, or he'll think you sleep with it on. I suppose you've already invited him to the at-homes? Don't even think of coming, Erast. That would be just like you. A-ha' – Esfir had noticed the half-open door – 'Mama's peeping. Don't waste your time; I'm not going to marry him!'

It was instantly clear who ruled the roost in these marble halls. The door immediately closed, startled Papa instantly covered his star with his hand and, speaking in a timid voice, asked the question that was also occupying Erast Petrovich: 'Firochka are you sure you can go to His Excellency's gathering dressed like that?'

Mademoiselle Litvinova had covered her short black hair with a gold net, which made it look as if her head was encased in a gleaming helmet; her scarlet tunic, cut in the loose Greek style, narrowed at the waist, where it was belted with a broad brocade girdle, below which it expanded into spacious folds; but the most striking element was the gash that extended down almost as far as her waist – not so much because it was so deep, as because it clearly indicated the absence of any brassiere or corset.

'The invitation said: "Ladies are free to choose a dress at their own discretion,"' said Esfir, glancing at Fandorin in alarm. 'Why – doesn't it suit me, then?'

'It suits you very well,' he replied in the voice of a doomed man, pondering the effect it would produce.

The effect exceeded Erast Petrovich's very worst apprehensions.

The gentlemen came to the Governor General's house for pancakes without their official decorations, but nonetheless in white tie and tails; all the ladies came in dresses in the semi-official bluish-white range. Against this copperplate-engraving background Esfir's outfit blazed like a scarlet rose on the dirty March snow. Another comparison also occurred to Fandorin: a flamingo that had flown into a chicken hutch by mistake.

Since the supper was an informal one, His Excellency had not yet joined his guests, allowing them an opportunity to mingle freely; but the furore created by State Counsellor Fandorin's escort was so great that it was quite impossible to maintain the light conversation customary in such circumstances – there was a hint of scandal in the air, or at least of a savoury incident that would be the talk of Moscow the following day.

The women surveyed the crop-haired damsel's outfit, cut in the latest shameless style that still provoked outrage even in Paris, with their lips pursed fastidiously and a greedy gleam in their eyes. The men, however, as yet uninformed of the approaching revolution in the world of ladies' fashion, stared openly, mesmerised by the free swaying of those two hemispheres barely covered by the extremely fine material. This sight was far more impressive than the accustomed nakedness of ladies' shoulders and backs.

Esfir did not appear to be even slightly embarrassed by the general attention and she examined the people around her with even franker curiosity.

'Who's that?' she asked the State Counsellor in a loud whisper. 'And that buxom one over there – who's she?'

At one point she exclaimed in a loud, clear voice: 'Oh good Lord, what a freak show!'

At first Erast Petrovich bore it manfully. He exchanged polite bows with his acquaintances, pretending not to notice the aim of those numerous glances, some with the naked eye, some assisted by lorgnettes. However, when Frol Grigorievich Vedishchev approached the State Counsellor and whispered: 'He wants to see you,' Fandorin excused himself to Esfir on grounds of urgent business and went dashing off with shameful haste to the inner apartments of the gubernatorial residence, abandoning his companion to the whim of fate. Just as he reached the doors, a pang of conscience made him look back.

Esfir did not seem lost at all, and she was not gazing after the deserter. She was standing facing a bevy of ladies, examining them with calm interest, and the ladies were trying as hard as they could to pretend that they were absorbed in casual conversation. Apparently there was no need to feel concerned for Mademoiselle Litvinova.

Dolgorukoi listened to the report from his Deputy for Special Assignments with undisguised satisfaction, although for the sake of appearances he gasped at the theft of state funds, even though they had, in fact, been destined for despatch to Turkestan.

'They're not having it all their own way,' said Vladimir Andreevich. 'Oh, fine smart fellows they found to put the blame on Dolgorukoi. Now, they can sort it out. So, the smug gentleman from the capital has run straight into a brick wall? Serves him right, serves him right.'

Vedishchev finished attaching the prince's stiff starched collar and cautiously sprinkled His Excellency's wrinkled neck with talc, so that it wouldn't get chafed.

'Frolushka, fix this bit.' The Governor General stood in front of the mirror, turned his head this way and that, and pointed to his crookedly poised chestnut wig. 'Of course, Erast Petrovich, they will never forgive me for Khrapov. I have received a very cold letter from His Majesty, so some day soon I'll be asked to vacate the premises. But I really would like to make that camarilla eat dirt before I go. Stick the solved case under their noses: *There, eat that and remember Dolgorukoi.* Eh, Erast Petrovich?'

The State Counsellor sighed. 'I can't promise, Vladimir Andreevich. My hands are tied. But I will t-try.'

'Yes, I understand . . .'

The prince started towards the doors leading into the hall. 'How are my guests? Are they all here?'

The doors opened as if of their own accord. Dolgorukoi halted on the threshold, to give the assembled public time to notice their host's entrance and prepare themselves accordingly.

The prince glanced round the hall and started in surprise: 'Who's that there in scarlet? The only one standing with her back to me?'

'That is my friend, Esfir Avessalomovna Litvinova,' the State Counsellor replied mournfully. 'You did ask . . .'

Dolgorukoi screwed up his long-sighted eyes and chewed on his lips.

'Frol, my old darling, dash to the banquet hall and change round the cards on the table. Seat the Governor and his wife further away and move Erast Petrovich and his lady friend so that they are on my right.'

'What's that you say – in the kisser?' the Governor General asked incredulously, and suddenly began blinking very fast – he had just noticed the edges of the gash in his neighbour's dress moving apart.

The upper end of the table, where the most eminent of the titled guests were sitting, suddenly went very quiet at the sound of that appalling word.

'Why yes, in the kisser,' Esfir repeated loudly for the deaf old man. 'The director of the school told me: "With that kind of behaviour, Litvinova, I wouldn't keep you here for a whole mountain of Yiddish pieces of silver." So I smacked him in the kisser. What would you have done in my place?'

'Well yes, there really was no other option,' Dolgorukoi admitted and asked curioiusly, 'And what did he do?'

'Nothing. He expelled me in disgrace, and I completed my studies at home.'

Esfir, who was seated between the prince and Erast Petrovich, was managing to do justice to the celebrated pancakes and conduct a lively conversation with the ruler of Moscow at the same time.

There were, in fact, only two people taking part in the conversation: His Excellency and his extravagant guest. No one else within hearing opened their mouth, and the unfortunate State Counsellor had completely turned to stone.

Female sensuality, the workers' question, the harmfulness of underwear, the pale of settlement – these were only some of the subjects that Mademoiselle Litvinova found time to touch on during the first three servings. When she left the table, making sure to inform everyone where she was going, Vladimir Andreevich whispered to Fandorin in absolute delight: '*Elle est ravissante, votre élue.*' And when Esfir came back, she turned to Erast Petrovich to express her approval of the prince: 'Such a nice old man. Why do our people talk so badly about him?'

During the sixth serving of pancakes, after the sturgeon, sterlet pâté and caviar had been replaced by fruit and various types of honey and jam, the duty adjutant appeared at the far end of the banqueting hall. With his aiguillettes jingling, he ran the entire length of the chamber on tiptoe, and his sprint did not pass unnoticed. From the officer's despairing expression it was clear that something quite out of the ordinary had happened. The guests turned round to watch the messenger as he ran past, and only the Governor General, whispering something in Esfir Avessalomovna's ear, remained unaware.

'That tickles,' she said, pulling away from his fluffy dyed moustache, and stared curiously at the adjutant.

'Your Excellency, an emergency,' the captain reported, breathing heavily.

He tried to speak quietly, but in the silence that had descended his words carried a long way.

'Eh? What's that?' asked Dolgorukoi, with a smile still on his face. 'What sort of emergency?'

'We've only just heard. There was an attack on the acting head of the Provincial Office of Gendarmes, Sverchinsky, at the Nikolaevsky Station. The Colonel was killed. His adjutant has been wounded. The attackers escaped. All trains to St Petersburg have been halted.'

CHAPTER 8

'. . . get yourself a pig'

He only slept for two hours that night. It wasn't a matter of the bedbugs or the stuffy atmosphere, or even the throbbing pain – minor difficulties like that simply weren't worthy of his attention. The problem bothering him was something far more vital.

Green lay on his back with his hands under his head, thinking intensely. Emelya and Bullfinch were sleeping beside him on the floor of the cramped little room. The former was tossing and turning restlessly, obviously tormented by little bloodsuckers. The latter was crying out feebly in his sleep. It was amazing he'd managed to fall sleep at all after the events of the previous day.

The unexpected outcome of their collaboration with Ace had required rapid action. First of all Green had brought the hysterically sobbing Julie to her senses, for which he had had to slap her gently across the cheeks. After that she had stopped shaking and done everything he told her to do, but avoided looking at the motionless body and the bright puddle of wine that was rapidly darkening as the blood mingled with it.

Then he had hastily bound up his own wounds. The hardest thing to deal with was his ear, so he simply covered it with a handkerchief and pulled his shop assistant's peaked cap down tight over the top. Julie brought him a jug of water to wash the blood off his face and hands.

Now they could leave.

Green left Julie on guard by the sleigh while he carried the sacks out of the room. This time he couldn't take two at a time – he had to avoid aggravating the wound on his wrist.

He only started wondering where to take the money after the India had been left safely behind.

To take it to their meet, the railway lineman's hut near the Vindava Station, would be dangerous. It was an open spot with no shelter; someone might see them carry in the sacks and suspect they were stolen goods from a freight train.

Go to another hotel? They wouldn't be allowed to take the sacks into a room, and leaving them with anybody for safe keeping would be too risky.

It was Julie who came up with the answer. She seemed to be just sitting there sulking in her ruffled chintzy dress, not asking any questions, not interfering with his thinking.

But then she suddenly said: 'What about the Nikolaevsky Station? My bags are in the left-luggage room. I'll take the suitcases and leave the sacks instead. They're very strict there; no one will go rummaging in them. And the police will never guess the money's right there under their noses.'

'I can't show my face there,' Green explained. 'They've got my description.'

'You don't have to. I'll say I'm a maid, come to collect my mistress's suitcases. I have the ticket. No one will take any notice. You're the driver: you can stay in the sleigh and not go into the station. I'll bring some porters.'

It felt awkward to hear her talking to him in such an intimate tone of voice. But the left-luggage room was a good idea.

From the station they went on to the Hotel Kitezh near Krasnye Vorota Square. It wasn't a first-class place, but it did have a telephone beside the counter, and that was particularly important now.

Green phoned the party courier and asked: 'How are they?'

Needle replied in a voice trembling with excitement: 'Is that you? Thank God! Are you all right? Do you have the goods?'

'Yes. What about the others?'

'They're all well. Arsenii's the only one who fell ill. He had to be left behind.'

'Is he getting treatment?' he asked, frowning.

'No, it was too late.' Needle's voice trembled again.

'Send for my men from Vindava Station. Tell them to come

to the Kitezh Hotel. Bring some medical alcohol, a needle, coarse thread.'

Needle was quick to arrive. She nodded briefly to Julie, barely even giving her a glance, although it was the first time she had seen her. She looked at Green's bandaged head and blood-caked eyebrow and asked: 'Are you seriously wounded?'

'No. Did you bring the things?'

She put a small grip bag on the table. 'This is the alcohol, needle and thread you asked for. And there's gauze, cotton wool, bandages and plaster. I studied to be a nurse. Show me and I'll do everything.'

'That's good. I can fix my side myself. The eyebrow, ear and hand are awkward. The plaster's good. I've got a broken rib; it needs to be held together.'

He stripped to the waist, and Julie gasped pitifully when she saw the bruises and the blood-soaked bandage.

'A knife, not very deep,' Green commented on the wound in his side. 'Nothing crucial damaged. Just needs washing and sewing up.'

'Lie down on the divan,' Needle told him. 'I'll wash my hands.'

Julie sat down beside him. Her doll-like face was contorted in suffering. 'Greeny, my poor darling, does it really hurt a lot?'

'You shouldn't be here,' he said. 'You've done your bit. Let her get on with it. Go.'

Needle cleaned the wound with alcohol, working quickly and deftly. She soaked the coarse thread in alcohol too, and heated the needle in the candle flame. So that she wouldn't tense up, Green tried to make a joke: 'Needle with a needle.'

Obviously it wasn't funny enough – she didn't smile.

She warned him: 'This will hurt. Grit your teeth.'

But Green scarcely even felt the pain – he was well trained, and Needle knew what she was doing.

Green watched closely as she made the rows of fine, neat stitches, first on his side and then on his wrist. He asked: '"Needle" – is this the reason?'

The question came out awkwardly – he felt that himself; but Needle understood.

'No. This is the reason.' She raised her hand rapidly to the tight knot of hair at the back of her head and pulled out a long, sharp hairpin.

'What for?' he asked in surprise. 'To defend yourself?'

She washed his split eyebrow with alcohol and put in two stitches before she answered. 'No, to stab myself if they arrest me. I know the spot – right here.' She pointed to her neck. 'I have claustrophobia. I can't tolerate narrow spaces. I might not be able to stand it in prison; I could break down.' Needle's face flushed red – the confession had obviously not been easy for her to make.

Soon Emelya and Bullfinch arrived.

'Are you wounded?' Bullfinch asked, alarmed.

Emelya looked around, screwing up his eyes, and asked: 'Where's Rahmet?'

Green didn't answer the first question because there was no point. He answered the second one briefly: 'There are three of us now. Tell me everything.'

Bullfinch told the story, with Emelya putting in occasional comments, but Green was hardly even listening. He knew the boy had to get it all out – it was the first time he'd been on a genuine operation. But the details of the gunfight were of no importance; he had something else to think about now.

'... He ran off a bit and then fell. He was hit here.' Bullfinch pointed to a spot just above his collarbone. 'Me and Nail tried to pick him up, but he put the revolver to his temple so quick ... His head jerked to the side, and he fell again. And we all ran for it ...'

'All right,' Green interrupted, deciding that was enough. 'Back to business. The sacks of money are at the station. We took them all right, now we have to get them to Peter. It's hard: police, gendarmes, plain-clothes men. They were only looking for us before; now there's the money too. And it's urgent.'

'I've been thinking,' Needle said rapidly. 'We could send six people, give them a sack each. All six of them couldn't get caught, someone would be bound to get through. I'll arrange it tomorrow. I have five people, I'll be the sixth. It will be easier for me as a woman.'

'Tomorrow it is then,' Emelya drawled. 'So we can sleep on it . . .'

'I can take one too,' Julie piped up. 'Only a sack would look strange with my luggage. I'll put the bundles of money in a suitcase, all right?'

Green took out his watch. Half past eleven. 'No. Tomorrow they'll have everything bottled up so tight, you'll never get through. They'll be searching people's things. Today.'

'Today?' Needle asked incredulously. 'You mean get the money through today?'

'Yes. The night train. At two.'

'But that's absolutely impossible! The police are everywhere already. On my way here I saw them stop several carts. And just imagine what's going on at the station . . .'

Then Green outlined his plan.

The one thing they'd failed to foresee was the station master being so badly shaken by the explosion that he would delay the departure of the St Petersburg train and halt all the traffic on the line. Apart from that, everything had gone absolutely according to plan.

At twenty minutes to two, Green drove Needle and Julie, dressed like a lady and her maid, up to the left-luggage room and waited with the sleigh because there was no way he could show his face in the station.

A porter loaded the sacks on to a trolley and was all set to trundle them off to the train when suddenly the severe, skinny lady started giving her pretty maid a roasting over some hatbox that had been left at home and got so carried away that she completely forgot where she was until the second bell, and then she turned on the porter – why was he dawdling like that and not taking the sacks to the luggage van? Against all Green's expectations, Needle managed the role magnificently.

Emelya and Bullfinch were supposed to make their move exactly when the second bell rang. There had been plenty of time for them to go to Nobel's place and collect a fully primed bomb.

They did it – just as the trolley with the sacks approached the exit to the platform and four men in civilian dress started towards the porter, whom the cantankerous little lady was prodding in the back with her handbag, there was the dull rumble of an explosion from the direction of the platforms, followed by screams and the tinkling of broken glass.

The police agents immediately forgot about the trolley and went rushing towards the thunderous roar, but the lady nudged the dawdling porter to make him turn back immediately. *Never mind what's happened at the station – the train won't wait!*

Green didn't see what happened after that, although he had no reason to doubt that Needle and Julie would reach the carriage safely and the sacks would be deposited in the luggage section. The gendarmes and police agents wouldn't be interested in checking luggage now.

But the minutes passed, and there was still no final bell. At twenty past two Green decided to go and reconnoitre.

Judging from the chaotic flurry of blue greatcoats he could see through the windows of the station, there was no need to worry about being recognised. He had a word with a bewildered attendant and discovered that some officer had blown up a senior police official and fled. That was good. But he also discovered that the line would be closed for the rest of the night. And that meant the most important part of the operation had failed.

He had to wait for almost an hour before Needle and Julie came back with the sacks. Then he left the women and took the money to the secret meet at the Vindava goods sheds.

Emelya told him all the details.

'Before they let me out of the station to the trains, they gave me a thorough frisking. But I was clean, no luggage and a third-class ticket to Peter. They couldn't touch me. I went through to the platform and stood on one side, waiting. Then I saw Bullfinch strolling up. Clutching a huge bunch of flowers, with his fizzog bright red. They didn't even give him a glance. Who'd ever think a cherub like that had a bomb in his bouquet? We went into a huddle in a dark corner. I took the bomb out gently and slipped it in my pocket. The place was crowded, even though it was night. The passenger train from Peter was late and there were people waiting to meet it. And passengers arriving for our two o'clock train. *Just right*, I think. *No one's going to be staring at me.* I keep sneaking a look at the duty office. It has a window overlooking the platform, Greenich. The curtains are wide open, and I can see everything inside. Our guest of honour was sitting at the table, and there was a young officer by the door, yawning. Every now and then someone went in and came out. They weren't sleeping in there, they were working. I stroll past for a closer look and, Holy Mother – I spot the small window at the top is wide open. It must have been really hot in there. And that gave me a real warm feeling too. *Eh, Emelya*, I think to myself, *it's not your turn to die yet. With a stroke of luck like that, you might get away in one piece after all.* Bullfinch is standing facing the window like we agreed – about twenty paces away. I'm huddled down on one side in the shadow. The bell sounds once. Ten minutes left before the train goes, nine, eight. I'm standing there praying to good Saint Nikolai and sinful Old Nick himself that they won't close that window. Jingle-jangle – that's the second bell. It's time. I walk past the window, taking it slow, and just flick the bomb in through the top, like a cat with its paw. It went in real neat, didn't even catch on the frame. After I took another five steps there was an almighty boom! And then all hell broke loose. Men running about blowing whistles and yelling. I heard Bullfinch shout out: "He went that way, towards the tracks! In an officer's coat!" The whole crowd went tramping off in that direction, and we just slipped out quietly through the side door on to the square. Then made a run for it.'

Green listened to what Emelya said, but he was watching Bullfinch. The boy was unusually quiet and downcast. He was sitting on a sack of money with his head propped in his hands, a miserable expression on his face and tears in his eyes.

'Never mind,' Green said to him. 'You did everything right.

It's not your fault it didn't work out. Tomorrow we'll think of something else.'

'I wanted to shout, but I was too late,' Bullfinch sobbed, still looking down at the ground. 'No, that's a lie. I lost my head. I was afraid if I shouted I'd give Emelya away. And the second bell had already rung. But Emelya couldn't see from the side . . .'

'What couldn't I see?' Emelya asked, surprised. 'He couldn't have gone out. When I walked past the window, I squinted sideways – his blue coat was still there.'

'He was there all right, but when you moved on, some people went into the office. A lady – she had a boy with her, a schoolboy. He looked about fifth class.'

'So that's it,' Emelya said with a frown. 'I'm sorry for the boy. But you did right not to shout. I'd have thrown the bomb all the same; it would just have been harder to get away.'

Bullfinch looked up with confusion in his tearful eyes. 'All the same? They had nothing to do with anything.'

'But our two ladies did,' Emelya replied harshly. 'If you and me had dallied, the bloodhounds would have picked them up with the money, and that would have been everything down the drain. And then Arsenii would have died for nothing, and we'd have lost Julie and Needle too, and no one would bother to save our lads in Odessa from the hangman's rope.'

Green walked up to the boy, put one hand on his shoulder awkwardly and tried to explain as clearly as possible something that he had thought about many times.

'You have to understand. We're soldiers. We're at war. There are all sorts of people on the other side. Some of them are kind and good and honest. But they wear a different uniform and that makes them our enemies. It's just like the battle of Borodino – *Tell me, uncle* . . . You remember that bit? When they were shooting at somebody, they didn't think about whether he was good or bad. If he's French, then blaze away. *Moscow's right behind us, isn't it?* But these enemies are worse than the French. We can't pity them. That is, we can and we must, but not now. Later. First we defeat them, then we pity them.' In his mind the words sounded very convincing, but out loud they weren't so persuasive.

Bullfinch flared up. 'I understand about the war. And about our enemies. They hanged my father, they killed my mother. But what have that schoolboy and that lady got to do with it? When soldiers fight, they don't kill civilians, do they?'

'Not deliberately. But once a cannon's fired, who knows where the shell will land? It could be in someone's house. It's bad, it's a shame, but it's war.' Green clenched his fingers into a fist so that his phrases wouldn't come out tight and lumpy – Bullfinch wouldn't understand if they did. 'They don't have pity on our civilians, do they? At least we do it by mistake, not deliberately. You talk about your mother. Why did they lock her up to die in a punishment cell? Because she loved your father. And what do they do to the people every day, year after year, century after century? Rob them, starve them, humiliate them, make them live in filth, like pigs.'

Bullfinch didn't say anything to that, but Green could see the conversation wasn't over. Never mind, there'd be more time for that.

'Sleep,' he said. 'It's been a hard day. And we have to send the money off tomorrow. Otherwise it all really was for nothing.'

'Oho-ho,' Emelya sighed, arranging a sack with a hundred thousand roubles in it under his head. 'The effort we went to getting these damned bits of paper, and now we don't know how to get shut of them. It's just like they say: if you haven't got a care, get yourself a pig.'

He thought for most of the night. He thought in the morning. He just couldn't make it work.

Six sacks was a pretty large load. You couldn't take it out without being noticed, especially after yesterday's events.

What was it Needle had suggested – dividing up the sacks between six couriers? They could do that. But most likely Julie and Needle would slip through all right, and the other four wouldn't. The police agents were most suspicious of young men. They'd lose two-thirds of the money and hand over four comrades as well – that was too high a price to pay for two hundred thousand.

Perhaps they could just send the women with a hundred thousand each, and hold on to the rest of the money for the time being? They could, but that was risky too. There had been too many slip-ups in the last few days. Rahmet had been the worst. He was certain to have given the Okhranka a full description of all the members of the group, and of Needle as well.

Rahmet hadn't known how to find Needle, but he must surely have betrayed the private lecturer with the apartment on Ostozhenka Street. Aronson was another untidy loose end. The Okhranka could find Needle through him.

And then there was Arsenii Zimin. The body in Somovsky Cul-de-Sac would have been identified by now, of course. They were tracing the dead man's contacts and acquaintances, sooner or later they would pick up something.

No, the group had to travel light, with no excess baggage. They had to get rid of the money as soon as possible.

This difficult task was complicated even further by his need to lie down and rest to restore his strength. Green listened closely to his body and concluded that he wasn't fit for full-scale action today. After the brawl with Ace, his body was telling him it needed time to recover, and Green was used to trusting what his body said. He knew it wouldn't make excessive demands, and if it wanted to take a breather, it meant it really needed one. If he took no notice, things would only get worse. But if he accepted his body's demands, it would restore itself quickly. There wouldn't be any need for medicines, just complete rest and self-discipline. Lie without moving a day, or two would be better, and his broken rib would start to knit, the stitched wounds would heal over, the battered muscles would recover their resilience.

Six years earlier, in Vladimir, Green had escaped from a prison convoy by breaking out the bars of the railway-carriage window. Unfortunately, when he jumped down on to the rails, he landed right in front of a sentry and took a lunge from a bayonet under his shoulder blade. As he fled from his pursuers, dodging and swerving across the rails and between the trains, his back was soaked in blood. Eventually he hid in a warehouse, among massive bundles of sheepskins. He couldn't go out – they were searching everywhere for the escaped prisoner. But he couldn't stay there either – they'd started loading the bundles into a train, and there were fewer and fewer of them. He slit one open and clambered inside, in between the smelly, damp skins – they'd obviously been soaked to make them weigh more. So the extra weight of his body wasn't noticed. The loaders grabbed the massive bundle with hooks and dragged it over the boards. The wagon was sealed from the outside and the train set off gently westwards, past the cordon, past the patrols. Why would anyone think of checking a sealed wagon? The train took a long time to reach Moscow: six days. Green assuaged his thirst by sucking on the damp wool, which only dried out very slowly, and he didn't eat at all, because there was nothing to eat. But he didn't grow weak – on the contrary, he grew stronger, since he directed his willpower to patching up his body for twenty-four hours of the day. It turned out that he didn't need food for that. When they unsealed the wagon at the shunting yard in Moscow, Green jumped down on to the ground and walked calmly past the hung-over, indifferent loaders to the exit. No one tried to stop him. When he managed to reach the party's doctor and showed him the wound on his back, the doctor was astonished: the hole had already sealed itself with scar tissue.

This old memory gave him the answer to his problem. Everything would turn out very simple, if only Lobastov agreed.

He had to agree. He already knew that the CG had managed things without his help. He knew about Sverchinsky too. He'd be too wary of the consequences to refuse.

There was another possible consideration, still unverified. Could Timofei Grigorievich Lobastov perhaps be the mysterious letter writer TG? It seemed very probable. He was cunning, cautious and insatiably curious about other people's secrets. He was a far from straightforward man, he was playing his own game, and only he knew what it was.

But if he was TG, he'd be all the more willing to help.

Green woke Emelya quietly, so as not to disturb Bullfinch. Speaking quietly, he explained the assignment to him – briefly, because although Emelya looked like a dumb oaf, he was quick on the uptake.

Emelya got dressed without saying anything, ran his massive fingers through his hair to straighten it and pulled on his peaked cap. No one would give him a second look. An ordinary factory hand – Lobastov had thousands like that at his plant.

He led the horse out of the shed and threw the sacks into the sleigh, casually tossing a piece of sackcloth over them, and set off across the fresh snow of the vacant lot, towards the dark goods sheds.

Now Green had to wait.

He sat motionless by the window, counting the beats of his heart and feeling the needle-pricks as his torn flesh mended, the broken bone knitted and the cells of new skin drew together.

At half past seven the lineman Matvei, the little hut's usual inhabitant, came out into the yard. He had given his only room to his guests and gone to sleep in the hayloft. He was a morose, taciturn man, the kind that Green liked. He hadn't asked a single question. If people had been sent by the party, then they ought to be here. If they didn't explain why, then they weren't supposed to. Matvei scooped up some snow, rubbed his face with it and set off with a waddling stride towards the depot, swinging his knapsack of tools.

Bullfinch woke up shortly after ten.

He didn't leap up, blithe and cheerful, as he usually did, he got up slowly and glanced at Green, but didn't say a single word. He went to get washed.

There was nothing to be done. The boy was gone now, but the Combat Group had a new member. Bullfinch's colour had changed subtly since the previous day: it was no longer a tender peach tone, it was denser and sterner.

By midday the problem had been solved.

Emelya himself had watched as the money was loaded into a wagon full of sacks of dye for Lobastov's factory in St Petersburg and the door was sealed. A small shunting locomotive had tugged the wagon off to Sortirovochnaya Station, where it would be coupled on to a goods train, and at three o'clock that afternoon the train would leave Moscow, moving slowly.

Julie would take care of all the rest.

His heart was pumping regularly, one beat a second. His body was restoring its strength. Everything was all right.

CHAPTER 9

in which a lot is said about the destiny of Russia

Erast Petrovich spent the rest of that sleepless, agitated and confused night at Nikolaevsky Station, trying to piece together a picture of what had happened and pick up the perpetrators' trail. Although there were numerous witnesses, both blue-coated gendarmes and private individuals, they failed to make things any clearer. They all talked about some officer who had supposedly thrown the bomb, but it turned out that no one had actually seen him. The attention of the uniformed and plain-clothes police had naturally been focused on departing passengers, and no one had been watching the windows of the station building. In the presence of dozens of men professionally trained to be observant, someone had blown up their senior commander, and no one had a clue about how it had happened. The sheer ineptitude of the police could only be explained by the incredible daring of the attack.

It was not even clear where the bomb had been thrown from. Most probably from the corridor, because no one had heard the sound of breaking glass before the explosion. And yet a piece of paper with the letters 'CG' on it had been found under the window, on the platform side. Perhaps the device had been thrown in through the small upper window?

Of the four people who were in the duty office at the time of the explosion, Lieutenant Smolyaninov was the only one who had survived, and only because just at that moment he happened to drop his glove on the floor and clamber under the table to get it. The sturdy oak had shielded the adjutant from most of the shrapnel and he had only caught one piece of metal in his arm, but he had proved to be a poor witness. He could not even remember if the small window had been open. Sverchinsky and an unidentified lady had been killed on the spot. A schoolboy had been taken away in an ambulance carriage, but he was unconscious and obviously not destined to live.

At the station Pozharsky was in charge, having been appointed to take over the dead man's position on a temporary basis in a telegram from the Minister. Erast Petrovich felt like an idle onlooker. Many people cast glances of disapproval at his formal tailcoat, so inappropriate for the circumstances.

Shortly after seven in the morning, having realised that he could not clarify anything at the station, the State Counsellor agreed to meet Pozharsky later in the Office of Gendarmes and went home in a state of intense thoughtfulness. His intentions were as follows: to sleep for two hours, then do his gymnastic exercises and clear his head by meditating. Events were developing so rapidly that his rational mind could not keep up with them – the intervention of the soul's deeper powers was required. It has been said: *Among those who run, halt; among those who shout, be silent.*

But his plan was not to be realised.

Quietly opening the door with his key, Erast Petrovich saw Masa sleeping in the hallway, slumped against the wall with his legs folded up under him. That was already unusual in itself. He must have been waiting for his master, wanting to tell him something, but been overcome by fatigue.

Fandorin did not wake his incorrigibly curious valet, in order to avoid unnecessary explanations. Stepping silently, he crept through into the bedroom, and there it became clear what Masa had wanted to warn him about.

Esfir was stretched out across the bed, with her arms thrown up over her head, her little mouth slightly open and her scarlet dress hopelessly creased. She had obviously come straight there from the reception, after Erast Petrovich had excused himself and left for the scene of the tragic event.

Fandorin backed away, intending to retreat into the study, where he could make himself very comfortable in a spacious armchair, but his shoulder brushed against the jamb of the door.

Esfir immediately opened her eyes, sat up on the bed and exclaimed in a clear, ringing voice, as if she hadn't been sleeping at all: 'There you are at last! Well, have you said your tearful goodbye to your gendarme?'

After his difficult and fruitless night, the State Counsellor's nerves were on edge, and his reply was untypically abrupt: 'In order to kill one lieutenant colonel of gendarmes, who will be replaced tomorrow by another, at the same time the revolutionary heroes shattered an entirely innocent woman's head and tore a young boy's legs off. A fiendish abomination – that's what your revolution is.'

'Ah, so the revolution's an abomination?' Esfir jumped to her feet and set her hands on her hips belligerently. 'And your empire – isn't that an abomination? The terrorists spill other people's blood, but they don't spare their own either. They sacrifice their own lives, and therefore they have the right to demand sacrifices from others. They kill a few for the well-being of millions! But the people you serve, those toads with cold, dead blood, smother and trample millions of people for the well-being of a tiny group of parasites!'

'"Smother and trample" – what sort of cheap rhetoric is that?' Fandorin rubbed the bridge of his nose wearily, already regretting his outburst.

'Rhetoric? Rhetoric?' Esfir cried, choking on her indignation. 'Just . . . Just you listen to this.' She picked up a newspaper that was lying on the bed. 'Look, it's the *Moscow Gazette*. I was reading it while I waited for you. In the same edition, on facing pages. First the servile, sickening, pap: "The Moscow Municipal Duma has voted to present a memorial cup from the happy citizens to the aide-de-camp Prince Beloselsky-Belozersky for procuring the Most-Merciful missive from God's Anointed to Muscovites on the occasion of the most devoted address that was presented to His Imperial Majesty in commemoration of the forthcoming tenth anniversary of the present blessed reign . . ." Phoo, it turns your stomach. And here, right beside it, how do you like this: "At long last the Ministry of Education has called for the rigorous observance of the rule forbidding the admission to university of

186

individuals of the Jewish faith who do not possess a permit to reside outside the pale, and in any event for no exceptions to the established percentage norm. The Jews in Russia are the most oppressive heritage left to us by the now defunct Kingdom of Poland. There are four million Jews in the Empire, only four per cent of the population, but the poisonous stench of the vile vapours emanating from this weeping ulcer is choking us ..." Shall I go on? Are you enjoying it? Or how about this? "The measures taken to counter famine in the four districts of the Province of Saratov are not yet producing the desired effect. It is anticipated that during the spring months the affliction will spread to the adjacent provinces. The Most Reverend Aloizii, Archbishop of Saratov and Samara, has given instructions for special services of prayer for the defeat of the scourge to be held in the churches." Services of prayer! And our pancakes don't stick in our throats!'

Erast Petrovich listened with a pained grimace, and was on the point of reminding the denouncer of iniquity that only yesterday she herself had not disdained Dolgorukoi's pancakes, but he didn't, because it was petty, and also because, on the whole, she was right.

But Esfir still didn't calm down, she carried on reading: 'Just you listen, listen: "The patriots of Russia are absolutely outraged by the Latvianisation of the public schools in the Province of Liefland. The children there are now obliged to learn the native dialect, for which purpose the number of classes devoted to Scriptural Studies has been reduced, as these are supposedly not necessary for the non-Orthodox." Or this from Warsaw, from the trial of the cornet Bartashov: "The court declined to hear Pšemyslska's testimony, since she would not agree to speak in Russian, claiming that she did not know it well enough." And that's in a Polish court!'

This final extract reminded Fandorin of one of the investigation's snapped threads – the dead terrorist Arsenii Zimin, whose father was defending the unfortunate cornet in Warsaw. The vexatious memory reduced Erast Petrovich to a state of total wretchedness.

'Yes, there are many scoundrels and fools in the state apparatus,' he said reluctantly.

'All of them, or almost all. And all, or almost all, of the revolutionaries are noble and heroic,' Esfir snapped and asked sarcastically, 'Doesn't that circumstance suggest any idea to you?'

The State Counsellor replied sadly: 'Russia's eternal misfortune. Everything in it is topsy-turvy. Good is defended by fools and scoundrels, evil is served by martyrs and heroes.'

It was evidently just that kind of day – they were talking about Russia in the Office of Gendarmes too.

Pozharsky had occupied the newly vacant office of the deceased Stanislav Filippovich, which had thus naturally become the headquarters of the investigation. Lieutenant Smolyaninov, paler than usual and with one arm in an impressive black sling, was standing in the reception room beside the telephone that never stopped ringing. He smiled at Fandorin over the receiver and pointed to the boss's door as if to say: *Please go through.*

The prince had a visitor sitting in his office – Sergei Vitalievich Zubtsov, who looked very agitated and red in the face.

'A-ha, Erast Petrovich,' said Pozharsky, getting to his feet. 'I can see from the blue circles under your eyes that you didn't get to bed. And here I am, sitting around doing nothing. The police and the gendarmes are prowling the streets, the police agents are snooping around the alleyways and rubbish tips, and I've just settled in here, like some huge spider, to wait until my net twitches. Why don't we wait together? Sergei Vitalievich here has just dropped in and he's propounding some remarkably interesting views on the workers' movement. Carry on, dear fellow. Mr Fandorin will find it interesting too.'

The thin, handsome face of Titular Counsellor Zubtsov blossomed into pink spots, either from pleasure or some other feeling.

'I was saying, Erast Petrovich, that it would be much easier to defeat the revolutionary movement in Russia with reforms, rather than with police methods. In fact, it's probably quite impossible to defeat it with police methods, because violence engenders a violent and even more intransigent response, and it just keeps on building up and up until society explodes. We need to pay some attention to the estate of artisans. Without the support of the workers, the revolutionaries can never achieve anything: our peasant class is too passive and disunited.'

Smolyaninov came in quietly. He sat down at the secretary's table, held down a sheet of paper awkwardly with his bandaged arm and started making a note of something, holding his head on one side, like a schoolboy.

'How can the revolutionaries be deprived of the support of the workers?' the State Counsellor asked, trying to understand the significance of those pink spots.

'Very simply.' Zubtsov was evidently talking about something he had thought through a long time ago, something that had been on his mind, and he was apparently hoping to interest the important visitor from St Petersburg in his ideas. 'If a man has a tolerable life, he won't go to the barricades. If all the artisans lived as they do at Timofei Grigorievich Lobastov's factories – with a nine-hour working day, decent pay, a free hospital and holidays – the Greens of Russia would be left with nothing to do.'

'But how well the workers live depends on the factory owners,' Pozharsky observed, gazing at the young man in amusement. 'You can't just order them to pay a certain amount and set up free hospitals.'

'That is exactly what we, the state, are here for,' said Zubtsov, tossing his head of light-brown hair, '– to give orders. This is an autocratic monarchy, thank God. We need to explain to the richest and most intelligent where their own best interest lies and then act from above: pass a law establishing firm terms for the employment of workers. If you can't observe the law – close down your factory. I assure you that if matters went that way, the Tsar would have no more devoted servants than the workers. It would reinvigorate the entire monarchy!'

Pozharsky screwed up his black eyes. 'Rational. But hard to achieve. His Majesty has firm ideas concerning the good of the Empire and the social order. The sovereign believes that a tsar is a father to his subjects, a general is a father to his soldiers and an employer is a father to his workers. It is not permissible to interfere in the relationship between a father and his sons.'

Zubtsov's voice became soft and cautious – he was evidently approaching the most important point.

'Then, Your Excellency, we ought to demonstrate to the supreme power that the workers are no sons of their employer, but all of them, the factory owners and the factory hands, are equally His Majesty's children. It would be good to seize the initiative without waiting for the revolutionaries finally to organise the artisans into a herd that we cannot control. To intercede for the workers with their masters and occasionally put pressure on the factory owners. Let simple people start getting used to the idea that the state machine protects the workers, not the money bags. We could even help promote the establishment of trade unions, only direct their activities into law-abiding economic channels instead of subversion. And this is the time to do it, Your Excellency, or it will too late.'

'Don't call me "Your Excellency",' Pozharsky said with a smile. 'To my competent subordinates I am Gleb Georgievich, and if we become close, simply Gleb will do. You'll go a long way, Zubtsov. In this country people who can think like true statesmen are worth their weight in gold.'

Sergei Vitalievich flushed, and his pink spots were drowned in a flood of pink.

Looking at him closely, Fandorin asked: 'Did you really come here, to the Office of Gendarmes, in order to share your views on the workers' movement with Gleb Georgievich? – today of all days, with everything that's going on?'

Zubtsov became embarrassed, evidently taken aback by this question.

'Naturally, Sergei Vitalievich did not come here to theorise,' said Pozharsky, looking calmly at the young idealist. 'Or at least, not only to theorise. As I understand it, Mr Zubtsov, you have some important information for me, but first you decided to sound out whether I share your general political idea. I do – wholly and completely. I shall be unstinting in offering you every possible support. As I said, in our administration intelligent people are worth their weight in gold. And now let me hear what you have for me.'

The titular counsellor swallowed and started speaking, but not in the same smooth, easy manner as before. He was very nervous now, and he gestured with his hand to support his points.

'I ... I, gentlemen, I would not like you to consider me a double-dealer and . . . an informer. But this isn't really informing at all . . . Very well, then, an unprincipled careerist . . . It's only out of concern for the good of the cause . . .'

'Erast Petrovich and I have no doubt at all about that,' the prince interrupted impatiently. 'That's enough of the preamble, Zubtsov; get to the point. Is it some intrigue by Burlyaev or Mylnikov?'

'Burlyaev. And not an intrigue. He has planned an operation . . .'

'What operation?' Pozharsky exclaimed loudly, and Fandorin frowned in concern.

'To capture the Combat Group. Wait, I'll start at the beginning. You know that all of Mylnikov's agents were thrown into trailing the revolutionary groups that might provide leads to the CG. My recent reference to the factory owner Lobastov was no accident. According to information received from agents, Timofei Grigorievich flirts with the revolutionaries and sometimes gives them money. A prudent man, backing both sides just in case. Well then. Mylnikov placed him under surveillance along with all the others. This morning the agent Sapryko saw a certain artisan go to Lobastov's office, and for some reason he was shown straight in to see the boss. Timofei Griogorievich treated his visitor with great consideration. He spoke with him about something for a long time, then they both went away somewhere for an entire hour. The mysterious worker bore a very strong resemblance to the terrorist who goes by the alias of Emelya, as described by the agent Gvidon, but Sapryko is an experienced sleuth and he didn't go off half-cocked, he waited for the man at the control post and followed him cautiously. The target checked several times to see if he was being followed, but he didn't spot his tail. He took a cab to the Vindava Station, dodged about between the railway lines there for a little while and eventually disappeared into a lineman's hut. Sapryko remained under cover, summoned the nearest police constable with his whistle, and sent a note to the Department of Security. An hour later our men had the little house completely surrounded. It has been ascertained that the lineman is called Matvei Zhukov and he lives alone, with no family. Emelya did not come out of the hut again, but before reinforcements arrived, Sapryko saw a young man emerge whose appearance matched the description of the terrorist Bullfinch.'

'What about Green?' Pozharsky asked avidly.

'That's the problem: there's no sign of Green. It looks as though he isn't in the hut. That's precisely why Pyotr Ivanovich gave the order to wait. But if Green doesn't show up the operation will start at midnight. The Lieutenant Colonel wanted it to be earlier but Evstratii Pavlovich persuaded him to wait a while, in case some big fish swam in.'

'This is abominable!' the prince exclaimed. 'Stupid! Agent Sapryko is to be congratulated, but your Burlyaev is an idiot! We need to keep them under observation, shadow them! What if they're keeping the money somewhere else? What if Green doesn't show up there at all? The operation can't go ahead – under no circumstances!'

Zubtsov picked up his theme, speaking rapidly: 'Your Excellency, Gleb Georgievich, that's exactly what I told him! That's why I overcame my natural scruples and came here! Pyotr Ivanovich is a man of great determination, but he's too bull-headed, he likes to flail at things with an axe. But this isn't something you can just take a wild swing at, this has to be handled with kid gloves. He's afraid that you'll take all the credit, he wants to distinguish himself in the eyes of St Petersburg, and that's understandable, but he can't be allowed to put everything in jeopardy for the sake of his own ambition! You are my only hope.'

'Smolyaninov, get Gnezdikovsky Lane on the telephone!'

Pozharsky ordered, getting to his feet. 'No, don't. The telephone's no good for this. Erast Petrovich, Sergei Vitalievich. Let's go!'

The official sleigh tore away from the entrance in a shower of powdered snow. Glancing back, Fandorin noticed another, simpler sleigh pull away from the opposite pavement to follow them. There were two men in identical fur caps sitting in it.

'Don't worry, Erast Petrovich.' The prince laughed. 'They're not terrorists – quite the contrary. They're my guardian angels. Take no notice of them, I'm well used to their company. My chief attached them to me after the gentlemen of the Combat Group almost filled me full of holes on Aptekarsky Island.'

Pushing open the door of Burlyaev's office, the deputy director of police declared from the threshold: 'Lieutenant Colonel, I am removing you from command of the Department of Security pending special instructions from the Minister and temporarily placing Titular Counsellor Zubtsov in charge.'

The sudden intrusion caught Burlyaev and Mylnikov sitting at the desk, studying some kind of plan that was laid out on it.

They reacted differently to Pozharsky's forceful declaration: Evstratii Pavlovich took a few soft, cat-like steps backwards and retreated to the wall, but Pyotr Ivanovich simply stood his ground and lowered his head like a bull.

'I'm afraid you can't do that, Mr Colonel,' he growled. 'I believe you have been appointed acting head of the Office of Gendarmes? Well then, act in that capacity, but I am not subordinated to the Office of Gendarmes.'

'You are subordinate to me as deputy director of the Police Department,' the prince reminded him in an ominously low voice.

The Lieutenant Colonel's glaring eyes glinted. 'I see my department has bred a traitor.' He jabbed a finger at Zubtsov, who was standing in the doorway, pale-faced. 'But you won't build a career on my bones, my dear friend Sergei Vitalievich. You've backed the wrong horse this time. Look!' He took a piece of paper out of his pocket and waved it triumphantly through the air. 'It came forty minutes ago. A telegram from the Minister himself. I outlined the situation and requested permission to carry out the operation I had planned to detain the Combat Group. Read what His Excellency writes: "To Lieutenant Colonel Burlyaev of the Special Corps of Gendarmes. Act at your own discretion. Take the blackguards dead or alive. God speed. Khitrovo." So I'm sorry, Your Excellency, this time we shall get by without you. You have already covered yourself in glory for throwing Rahmet away with such outstanding psychological acuity.'

'Pyotr Ivanovich, if we do go head-on, then we will take them dead, not alive,' said Mylnikov, suddenly breaking his silence for the first time. 'These are desperate folk, they'll keep shooting to the last man. But it would be good to take them alive. And I feel sorry for our lads, we'll lose more than one of them too. It's open space all around the hut, wasteland. You can't approach under cover. Perhaps we ought to wait until they come out by themselves?'

Rattled by this blow from the rear, Burlyaev swung round sharply towards his deputy.

'Evstratii Pavlovich, I am not going to change my decision. We'll take everyone who's there. And you don't need to explain to me about the open space, I've been making arrests for years. That's why we're waiting until midnight. Here, on Mariinsky Passage, they put the street lights out at eleven; it will be completely dark then. We'll file out of the goods sheds and approach the house from all sides. I'll go first myself. I'll take Filippov, Guskov and Shiryaev with me, and that – what's his name? – the great beefy fellow, with the sideburns . . . Sonkin. They'll break down the door straight away and go in, and I'll follow them, then another four that you'll choose, only with strong nerves, so they won't get the wind up and shoot us in the back. The others will stay here, around the edge of the yard. And those little darlings won't stand a chance. I'll have them before they know what's hit them.'

Pozharsky maintained a bewildered silence, obviously still stunned by the Minister's treachery, and so it was Erast Petrovich who made the final attempt to get the high-handed lieutenant colonel to see sense.

'You are making a mistake, Pyotr Ivanovich. Listen to Mr Mylnikov. Arrest them when they come out.'

'There are already thirty agents sitting in the warehouses around that piece of waste ground,' said Burlyaev. 'If they try to leave while it's still light, so much the better – they'll fall straight into my hands. But if they stay the night there, I'll come for them myself on the stroke of midnight. And that's my final word.'

CHAPTER 10

A letter for Green

The sun crept slowly across the sky, never rising far above the flat roofs, even at its highest point. Green sat at the window, perfectly still, watching as the lamp of heaven followed its foreshortened winter route. The punctilious disc of light had only a very short distance left to travel to the final point – the dark, monolithic mass of a grain elevator – when a squat figure appeared on the deserted path that led from the railway lines to Mariinsky Passage.

It wasn't such a bad place, even if it was cramped and there were bedbugs, thought Green. This was the first passer-by since midday, he hadn't seen another soul – just the small shunting locomotive darting backwards and forwards, shuffling the wagons about.

The sun was shining from behind the walker, and Green could only see who it was when the man turned towards the hut.

Matvei, his host.

What was he doing here? He'd said he had a shift until eight, but it was only five.

Matvei came in and nodded to Green instead of saying hello. His expression was sullen and preoccupied.

'Here, looks like this is for you . . .'

Green took the crumpled envelope from him. He read the name written on it in block capitals, with purple ink: 'MR GREEN. URGENT'.

He glanced briefly at Matvei. 'Where from?'

'Devil only knows,' said the other man, turning even more gloomy. 'I don't understand it. It turned up in the pocket of my coat. I was at the depot, and they called me into the office. There were lots of folk hanging about; anyone could have stuck it in. What I think is, you need to leave. Where's your third one – the young lad?'

Green tore open the envelope, already knowing what he would see: lines of typewritten words. There they were:

The house is besieged on all sides. The police are not sure that you are inside, and so they are waiting. At exactly midnight the house will be stormed. If you manage to break out, there is a convenient apartment No. 4, Vorontsovo Place.

TG

First he struck a match and set fire to the note and the envelope. As he watched the flame, he counted his pulse.

When his circulation had recovered its normal rhythm, he said: 'Walk slowly, as if you're going back to the depot. Don't look back. The police are all around. If they try to arrest you, let them. Tell them I'm not here, I'll be back before nightfall. They're not likely to arrest you. More likely they'll let you through and put a tail on you. We have to disengage and move out. Tell the comrades I said to move you to illegal work.'

His host really was strong. He stood there for a moment, without asking any questions. Then he opened a trunk and took out a small bundle, thrust it under his sheepskin coat and set off at a stroll back along the path towards Mariinsky Passage.

That was why there weren't any passers-by, Green realised. And the police had plenty of places to deploy their men – all those warehouses on every side. It was a good thing he'd been sitting to one side of the window and the curtain; they were sure to be watching through several pairs of binoculars.

As if to confirm his guess, a bright spark of light glinted in the attic window of the repair workshops. Green had seen other sparks like that earlier, but he hadn't attached any importance to them. A lesson for the future.

It was after five. The goods train with the wagon carrying Lobastov's dyes had already left for Peter. In five minutes Julie would leave on the passenger express. Bullfinch would check to make sure she got away and then come back here. Of course she'd get away – why shouldn't she? She'd overtake the goods train and meet it in Peter tomorrow and collect the sacks. The party would have money. Even if the CG was wiped out tonight, it would have been worth it.

But perhaps it wouldn't be wiped out. That remained to be seen. Forewarned was forearmed.

By the way, how well armed was he?

Green knitted his brows as he recalled that his stock of bombs had been left in the barrister's apartment, and you couldn't fight much of a war with just revolvers. He still had a little of the explosive jelly and some detonators left, but no casings and no filling.

'Emelya!' he called. 'Get your coat on, there's work.'

Emelya raised his small eyes from *The Count of Monte Cristo*, the only book they had found in the house.

'Hang on, eh, Greenich? This is really exciting! I'll just finish the chapter.'

'Later. There'll be time.'

Green explained the situation. 'Go to the shop and buy ten tins of stewed pork, ten tins of tomato paste and three pounds of two-inch screws. Walk calmly; don't look back. They won't touch you. If I'm wrong and they do decide to take you, fire at least one shot so I can prepare.'

He wasn't wrong. Emelya went away and came back with his purchases, and soon Bullfinch arrived too. He said Julie had got away. Good.

Midnight was still a long way off; they'd have time to get everything ready. Green let Emelya read about his count – the great hulk's fingers were too coarse for fine work – and got Bullfinch to help.

The first thing they did was open all twenty tins with a knife and dump the contents in the slop bucket. The meat tins each held a pound; the tomato tins were smaller, only half as wide. Green began with the narrow ones. He filled them halfway up with the explosive mixture – there wasn't enough for more than that, but never mind, even that would be more than adequate. Very carefully he pushed in the little glass tubes of the detonators. The principle was very simple: when the detonator compound and the explosive mixture came together, they produced an explosion of tremendous destructive force. Great care was required. Plenty of comrades had been blown to pieces when they scraped the fragile glass against the metal of the casing.

Bullfinch watched with bated breath.

After he had cautiously pressed the small tube into the jellified mass, Green bent the jutting lid back down and stood the tomato tin in an empty pork tin. The result was almost ideal. He tipped as many screws as would fit into the space between the walls of the two tins. Now all that remained to be done was close the outside lid and the bomb was ready. Any sudden blow would shatter the little tube, the explosion would tear the thin walls of the casing apart, and the screws would be transformed into deadly shrapnel. It had been tested more than once and the results were excellent. There was only one drawback: the range of the shrapnel was up to thirty paces, so you could easily be hurt yourself. But Green had his own ideas about that.

At midnight – that was excellent.

If only they didn't change their minds and start earlier.

'That Villefort's a real louse!' Emelya muttered as he turned a page. 'Just like our court officials.'

They turned out the light at eleven. Let the police think they'd gone to bed.

One by one, opening the door only a narrow crack, they slipped out into the yard and lay down by the low fence.

Their eyes soon adapted to the darkness, and at a quarter to twelve they saw the silent, agile shadows start moving towards the little house across the white wasteland.

The shadows halted in a compact circle, still about ten paces away from the fence. There were so many! But that was no bad thing. The tumult would be all the greater.

The shadows straight ahead, on the path, gathered together

into a large cluster. There was a sound of voices whispering and something jangling.

When the cluster began moving towards the gate in the fence, Green gave the order: 'Now.' He threw one tin at the advancing cluster, then another straight away, and dropped face down into the snow, covering his ears.

The double boom still rattled his eardrums anyway. And there were more booms off to the right and the left: one, two, three, four. Emelya and Bullfinch had thrown their bombs.

Immediately they jumped to their feet and ran straight ahead, while the police were still blinded by the flashes and deafened by the explosions.

As he jumped over the bodies stretched out on the track, Green was surprised to realise that his stitched side and broken rib didn't hurt at all. That was what the body's inner strength could do if you trusted it.

Emelya tramped along heavily beside him. Bullfinch went dashing ahead like a frisky young foal.

By the time shots were fired after them, they had almost reached the sanctuary of the goods sheds.

No point in the police shooting now. It was too late.

The apartment at Vorontsovo Polye turned out to be very comfortable: three rooms, a back entrance, a telephone and even a bathroom with heated water.

Emelya immediately settled down with his book – as if he hadn't heard any explosions, or run across the snowy waste lot with bullets whistling after him, and then dodged for ages through all those dark side streets.

Bullfinch, exhausted, collapsed on the divan and fell asleep.

Green examined the apartment carefully, hoping to discover some thread that might lead him to TG.

He didn't find anything.

The apartment was fully furnished, but there were no signs at all of real life. No portraits or photographs, no knick-knacks, no books.

Obviously, no one lived here.

Then what was the apartment for? Business meetings? Just in case?

But only a very wealthy man could have maintained an apartment like this for business meetings or 'just in case'.

Again everything pointed to Lobastov.

Green found the mystery alarming. Not that he suspected any immediate danger – if this was a trap, why bother to help the group escape from the Okhranka raid? It had been the right thing to disengage in any case.

He telephoned Needle. He didn't explain anything; all he said was that tomorrow he would need a new apartment, and he gave her their address. Needle said she would come in the morning. Her voice sounded troubled, but the clever woman didn't ask any questions.

Now sleep, Green told himself. He settled down in an armchair without getting undressed. He set out his Colt and four remaining bombs on the low table in front of him.

He was tired after all. And his rib wasn't doing as well as he'd thought. That was from running so fast. Surprising the jolting hadn't broken the detonators in the bombs. That would have been stupid.

He closed his eyes and it seemed like only a moment later that he opened them again, but outside the window the sun was shining and the door bell was trilling.

'Who's there?' Emelya's gruff bass asked in the hallway. Green couldn't hear the reply, but the door was opened.

Morning, and not early either, Green realised.

His body had taken what it needed after all – at least ten hours of total rest.

'How are your wounds? What about the money?' Needle asked as she came into the room. Without waiting for an answer, she said: 'I know what happened last night. We have Matvei. All Moscow is buzzing with rumours about the battle of the railway lines. Burlyaev himself was killed, that's absolutely certain. And they say huge numbers of police were killed too. But why I am telling you? – you were there . . .'

Her eyes looked different now, lively and full of light, and it was suddenly clear to him that Needle was no old maid. She was simply a stern, strong-willed woman whose life had been full of trials.

'You're a genuine hero,' she said in a serious, calm voice, as if she were affirming a scientifically proven fact. 'You're all heroes. As good as the People's Will.'

The look she gave him made him feel uncomfortable.

'The wounds don't bother me any more. The money's been sent. It'll be in Peter today,' he said, answering her questions in order. 'I didn't know about Burlyaev, but it's good news. "Huge numbers" is an exaggeration, but we did get a few.'

Now he could get down to business: 'First – another apartment. Second – the explosive has run out. We need to get more. And detonators. Chemical, impact type.'

'They're looking for an apartment. We'll have one by evening. We have detonators, as many as you like. Last month they delivered a whole suitcase of them from St Petersburg. The explosive's not so simple.' She thought for a moment, pursing up her thin, pale lips. 'Unless I go to Aronson ... I keep a watch on his windows; there's no alarm signal. I think I could take the risk. He's a chemist, he must be able to make it. The question is, will he want to? I told you, he's opposed to terror.'

'No need,' said Green, kneading his rib. It didn't hurt any more. 'I'll do it. He can just get us the ingredients. I'll write them down.'

While he was writing, he could feel her steady gaze on him.

'I've only just realised how like him you are ...'

Green broke off in the middle of the long word 'nitroglycerine' and looked up.

No, she wasn't looking at him, but over his head.

'You're dark and he was light. And the face is quite different. But the expression is the same, and that turn of the head ... I used to call him Tyoma, but his party alias was "Conjuror". He used to do wonderful card tricks ... We grew up together. His father was the manager on our Kharkov estate ...'

Green had heard of Conjuror. He had been hanged in Kharkov three years earlier. They said Conjuror had had a fiancée, a count's daughter. Like Sofia Perovskaya. So that was the way of it. There was no point in saying anything, and Needle didn't seem to expect words in any case. She gave a dry little cough to clear her throat and didn't go on. Green easily pieced the rest of the picture together for himself.

'We won't go anywhere,' he said briskly, to help her overcome her moment of weakness. 'We'll wait for you. So, first – an apartment. Second – the chemicals.'

When it was almost evening the door bell rang again. Green sent Emelya and Bullfinch to the back entrance while he went to open the door, holding a bomb in his hand just in case.

There was a white rectangle lying beside the door on the floor of the hallway.

An envelope. Someone had dropped it through the slit in the door.

Green opened the door.

Nobody.

Typed words on the envelope: 'Mr Green. Urgent.'

A rare opportunity. Today at 10 o'clock the leaders of the investigation, Prince Pozharsky and State Counsellor Fandorin, will be alone, without any guards, in the Petrosov Baths, private room No. 6. Strike while the iron is hot.

TG

CHAPTER 11

in which Fandorin learns how to fly

'This unparalleled orgy of terror after so many years of relative calm places our professional reputations and our very careers in jeopardy; however, at the same time, the possibilities that it opens up to us are boundless. If we can get the best of these unprecedentedly audacious criminals, then, Erast Petrovich, we shall be assured of a place of honour in the history of Russian statehood and – what is even more important as far as I am concerned – an enviable position in the Russian state itself. I have no desire to present myself as an idealist, which I am not – not even to the slightest degree. Take a look at that impossibly stupid monument.'

Pozharsky casually swung his cane to indicate the bronze figures of the two heroes who saved the throne of Russia from the Polish invasion. State Counsellor Fandorin, hitherto totally absorbed in their conversation, suddenly noticed that they had already reached Red Square, the left side of which was thickly overgrown with builder's scaffolding – the construction of the Upper Trading Rows was in full swing. Half an hour earlier, when the leaders of the investigation had noticed that they were going over and over a theory that they had already considered (which was hardly surprising after two nights without sleep), Pozharsky had suggested they should continue their discussion as they walked, since the day had turned out quite superb – sunny, with no wind and just the right touch of frost, refreshing and cheerful. They had walked down carefree Tverskaya Street, speaking of vitally important matters and united in their common misfortune and acute peril, while the prince's guardian angels strolled along about ten paces behind, with their hands in their pockets.

'Feast your eyes on that blockhead, my renowned ancestor,' said Gleb Georgievich, jabbing his cane towards the seated statue, 'lolling there and listening, while the man of commerce waves his hands about and trills like a nightingale. Have you ever heard of any other of the princes Pozharsky, apart from my heroic namesake? No? Hardly surprising. They've been squatting on their backsides like that for almost three hundred years, until they've worn out their final pair of pants, and in the meantime Russia has fallen into the hands of the Minins. The name's not important – Morozovs, Khlyudovs, Lobastovs. My grandfather, a Riurikovich, had two serfs and ploughed the earth himself. My father died as a retired second lieutenant. And I, a down-and-out little count, was taken into the Guards, purely because of my euphonious family name. But what good is the Guards to someone with nothing in his pocket but a louse on a lead? Ah, Erast Petrovich, you have no idea what a furore it caused when I applied to be transferred from the Cavalry Guards to serve in the Police Department. My regimental comrades started turning their noses up, the senior officers wanted to disenroll me from the Guards altogether, but they were afraid of provoking the wrath of the Emperor. And what happened? Now my former comrades-in-arms are captains and only one who moved to the army is a lieutenant colonel; but I am already a colonel – and not simply a colonel, but an aide-de-camp. And that, Erast Petrovich, is not just a matter of a monogram and fine appearances – I don't attach much importance to such things. The important thing is breakfast tête-à-tête with His Majesty during my monthly period of duty at the palace. That is something of real value. And another important point is my uniqueness. Never before has an officer serving in the Police Department, while registered with the Guards, been accorded such an honour. The sovereign has almost a hundred aides-de-camp, but I am the only one from the Ministry of the Interior, and that's what I value.'

The prince took Fandorin by the elbow and continued in a confidential tone: 'I'm not telling you all this out of an innocent desire to boast. You probably realised some time ago that I don't have much innocence about me. No, I want to jolt you into action, so that you won't become like that seated idol. You and I, Erast Petrovich, are pillars of the nobility, the very pillars on which the entire Russian Empire rests. I can trace my descent from the Varangians; you are a descendant of the Crusaders. We have ancient bandit blood flowing in our veins, the centuries have made it as rich as old wine. It is thicker than the thin red water of the merchants and the shopkeepers. Our teeth, fists and claws must be stronger than those of the Minins, otherwise the Empire will slip through our fingers, such is the time now approaching. You are intelligent, keen-witted, brave, but you have a certain fastidious, aristocratic torpor about you. If you are walking along and you come across – pardon the expression – a pile of shit, you will glance at it through your lorgnette and walk round it. Other people may step in it, but you will not sully your delicate feelings and white gloves. Forgive me, I am deliberately expressing my thoughts in a crude and offensive manner, because this is a sore point with me, an old *idée fixe* of mine. Just look at the unique position in which you and I find ourselves owing to the whim of fate and the conjunction of circumstances. The head of the Office of Gendarmes has been killed, the head of the Department of Security has been killed. You and I are the only ones left. They could have sent a new top man from the capital to head up the investigation – the director of the Police Department, or even the Minister himself, but those gentlemen are old stagers. They're concerned about their careers, so they preferred to hand over complete authority to me and you. And that's excellent!' Pozharsky gestured energetically. 'You and I no longer have anything to fear or anything to lose, but we could gain a very great deal. The telegram addressed to us from His Imperial Majesty said "unlimited authority". Do you understand what "unlimited" means? It means that for the immediate future, you and I effectively control Moscow and the entire political investigative apparatus of the Empire. So let's not jostle each other's elbows and get in each other's way, as Burlyaev and Sverchinsky used to do. Good Lord, there will be laurels enough for both of us. Let's join forces and combine our efforts.'

Erast Petrovich's response to this prolix and impassioned diatribe was just two words: 'Very well.'

Gleb Georgievich waited to see if anything else would be said and nodded in satisfaction.

'Your opinion of Mylnikov?' he asked, reverting to a brisk, businesslike tone. 'In terms of seniority, he ought to be appointed acting head of the Department of Security, but I would prefer Zubtsov. We can't wait for a new man to get the feel of the job.'

'No, we can't have a new man. And Zubtsov is a competent worker. But what we need now from the Department of Security is not so much analysis as practical investigation, and that is Mylnikov's province. And I wouldn't choose to offend him unnecessarily.'

'But Mylnikov was responsible for planning the failed operation. You know the result: Burlyaev and three agents killed, and another five wounded.'

'Mylnikov was not to blame,' the State Counsellor said with conviction.

Pozharsky gave him a keen look. 'No? Then what do you think was the reason for the failure?'

'Treason,' Fandorin replied briefly. Seeing the other man's eyebrows creep upwards in astonishment, he explained. 'The terrorists knew when the operation would start, and they were ready for it. Someone w-warned them – one of our people. Just as they did in the Khrapov case.'

'That's your theory, and you've kept quiet about it until now?' the prince asked incredulously. 'Well, you really are quite inimitable. I ought to have spoken openly with you sooner. However, this suggestion of yours is too serious altogether. Precisely whom do you suspect?'

'Only a small group of people were privy to the details of the night operation: myself, you, Burlyaev, Mylnikov, Zubtsov. And Lieutenant Smolyaninov could have heard something too.'

Gleb Georgievich snorted indignantly, apparently finding the State Counsellor's suggestion absurd; but nonetheless he started bending down his fingers as he counted.

'Very well, let's try it. With your permission, I'll start with myself. What possible motive is there? Did I sabotage the operation so that the glory for catching the CG would not go to Burlyaev? That seems rather excessive, somehow. Now Mylnikov. Did he want his boss's job? And to get it was he willing to sacrifice three of his best agents, the men he fusses over like old Uncle Chernomor? And it's still not clear if he will actually get the boss's job ... Zubtsov. A rather complex individual, I grant you, and we know how deep still waters run. But why would he wish to destroy Burlyaev? To get rid of a man who fought revolution using the wrong methods? I think that kind of extravagance would be out of character for Sergei Vitalievich. Of course, he does have a revolutionary past. A double agent, like Kletochnikov in the Third Section? Hmm, we'll have to check that ... Who else is there? Ah, the rubicund Smolyaninov. I pass on that; it's altogether too much for my imagination. You know him better. And by the way, how does a young man from a family like that come to be serving in the gendarmes? He doesn't seem to be an ambitious careerist like yours truly. Perhaps there's some reason behind it? Perhaps he is infected with the demonic bacillus of romantic subversion of authority? Or something simpler – a love affair with some nihilist female?'

Having apparently started jokingly, Pozharsky now seemed to be seriously intrigued by Fandorin's hypothesis. He paused and looked at Erast Fandorin with an odd expression, then suddenly said: 'On the subject of love and nihilist femmes fatales ... Could a leak not perhaps occur via your own lovely Judith, who made such a great impression on the good society of Moscow? She has connections in suspicious quarters, does she not? I know only too well how skilful enchanting women are at sucking out your secrets. Could you not possibly have found yourself in the role of Holofernes? Only please answer to the point – no offended pride, no challenges to a duel.'

Fandorin had indeed been about to reply to the prince's monstrous suspicion with sharp words, but the State Counsellor was suddenly struck by an idea that made him forget his affronted sensibilities.

'No, no,' he said quickly, 'that is absolutely impossible. But there is another distinct possibility: Burlyaev could have let something slip to Diana. She was probably involved somehow in the business with Sverchinsky too.'

Fandorin told the prince about the mysterious vamp who had turned the heads of both commanders of Moscow's political investigative agencies.

The theory proved to be remarkably coherent, at least in comparison with the others, but Pozharsky's reaction was sceptical. 'An intriguing speculation, certainly, but it seems to me, Erast Petrovich, that you are narrowing down the list of suspects too far. Undoubtedly, there is treachery here. We have to review the entire line of the investigation from that perspective. But the traitor could have been any pawn, any of the agents and police officers used in the cordon, and that is eighty men. Not to mention several dozen cabbies who were mobilised to transport Burlyaev's *Grande Armée*.'

'No police agent, let alone a cabby, could have been privy to the details,' Fandorin objected. 'And it would have been difficult for any rank-and-file participant to get away from his post. No, Gleb Georgievich, this is no pawn. Especially if we recall the circumstances of General Khrapov's murder.'

'I agree, your theory is more elegant and literary,' the prince said with a smile, 'and even more probable. But we have agreed to work in harness together, so this time why don't you be the shaft horse, and I'll gallop on in the traces. Right, we have two lines to follow up: the double agent Diana or one of the small fry. We'll investigate both. Do you choose Diana?'

'Yes.'

'Excellent. And I'll deal with the minnows. Will today be enough time for you? Time is precious.'

Erast Petrovich nodded confidently.

'And for me, although I have a laborious task, probing and checking such a huge number of men. But never mind, I'll manage. Now let's agree on our rendezvous.' Pozharsky thought for a long time. 'Since we have no confidence in our own men, let's meet outside official premises, in a place where no one will be eavesdropping or peeping. And not a word about this meeting to anyone, all right? I tell you what – let's meet in the baths, in a private room. We shall conceal absolutely nothing from each other.' Gleb Georgievich laughed. 'Here in Moscow the Petrosov Bathhouse is very good, and it is conveniently located. I shall tell my *bashi-bazouks* to book, let's say, room number six.'

'No one must mean no one,' said Erast Petrovich, shaking his head. 'Give your bodyguards the day off, to maintain the integrity of the search. And don't say a word to them about our meeting. I'll go to Petrosov's and book room number six myself. We'll meet alone, discuss our conclusions and draw up a plan of further action.'

'At ten?'

'At t-ten.'

'Well then,' Gleb Georgievich said jocularly, 'the place of the assignation is set. And so is the time. Forward, the aristocrats! Time to roll our sleeves up.'

Opened only recently close to Rozhdestvenka Street, the Petrosov Bathhouse had already become one of the showplaces of Moscow. Only a few years earlier, this site had been occupied by a single-storey log building where you could be washed for fifteen kopecks, have blood let, cupping glasses applied and calluses removed. Respectable society never called into this filthy, odorous barn, preferring to wash itself in Khludov's establishment at the Central Baths. However, when a new owner, a man of business acumen on a truly European scale, acquired the bathhouse, he totally transformed Petrosov's in line with the very latest word in international technology. He erected a veritable stone palace with caryatids and telamons, set a fountain burbling in the small inner courtyard, faced the walls with marble and hung mirrors all over them, set out soft divans, and the former fifteen-kopeck establishment was transformed into a shrine to luxury that even the pampered Roman Emperor Heliogabal would not have scorned. No trace was left of the 'commoners' section'; there were only 'merchants' sections' and 'nobles' sections' for both sexes.

After he and Pozharsky parted to go about their separate business, Fandorin made his way to the 'nobles' section'.

At that time in the morning there were no customers in the baths yet, and the obliging supervisor took his promising client on a tour of the private rooms.

The nobles' section was arranged as follows: at the centre, a common hall with an immense marble pool, surrounded by Doric columns; around the pool, a gallery on to which the doors of the six private rooms opened. However, the main entrances to the rooms were not from the common hall; they lay on the other side, from the broad corridor that ran round the building. The exacting civil servant inspected the rooms. He didn't look too closely at the silver washtubs and the gilded taps, but he tugged insistently at the bolts on the doors leading to the pool hall and strolled right round the external corridor. To the right it could be followed to the women's half of the baths; to the left it led to the service stairs. From that side there was no way out to the street, which for some reason seemed to please Fandorin particularly.

The State Counsellor did not act entirely as he and Gleb Georgievich had agreed. Or rather, he did more than they had agreed: not only did he book room number six for that evening, he booked all the other five rooms as well, leaving only the common hall for any other customers.

But that was only the first strange thing that Fandorin did.

The second was that the State Counsellor did not really take a very thorough approach to his main task for the day – the meeting with Diana; one might even say that he rolled his sleeves back down. After telephoning the collaborator from the vestibule of the bathhouse and arranging to meet her straightaway, Erast Petrovich immediately set off for the inconspicuous townhouse on Arbat Street.

In the familiar twilit room, with its scent of musk and dust from the permanently closed curtains, the visitor was greeted rather differently from the previous occasion and the occasion before that. No sooner did Fandorin step across the threshold of the quiet study than a slim shadow darted impetuously across the room towards him in a rustle of silk, pliable arms embraced him round the shoulders and a face concealed by a veil was pressed against his chest.

'My God, my God, how happy I am to see you,' a faltering voice murmured. 'I'm so afraid! I behaved so stupidly the last time – forgive me, in the name of all that's holy. You must pardon the self-assurance of a woman who had become too enamoured of the role of a breaker of hearts. The signs of attention with which Stanislav Filippovich and Pyotr Ivanovich showered me completely turned my head . . . Poor, poor Pierre and Stanislas! How could I ever imagine . . .' The whisper became a sob, and a perfectly genuine tear fell on the State Counsellor's shirt, then a second, and then more.

However, Erast Petrovich had no thought of exploiting this psychologically advantageous moment in the interests of the investigation. Gently moving aside the weeping collaborator, he walked into the room and sat down, not on the divan, as he had on the previous occasion, but in an armchair beside the writing desk, on which he could make out the dull gleam of the nickel-plated keys of a typewriter.

Diana was not at all disconcerted by her visitor's restraint. The slim, shapely figure followed Fandorin, halted for a moment in front of the armchair, then suddenly folded in half – and the eccentric lady plumped down on to her knees, raising her clasped hands in supplication.

'Oh, do not be so cold and cruel!' It was astonishing that the whisper in no way restricted the dramatic modulation of her voice – she had obviously been very well trained. 'You cannot imagine how much I have suffered. I have been left completely alone, with no protector, no patron. Believe me, I can be useful and . . . grateful. Do not go. Stay here with me for a little longer! Console me, dry my tears. I can sense a calm, confident strength in you. Only you can restore me to life. With Burlyaev and Sverchinsky I was the mistress, but with you I can be the slave! I will fulfil your every desire!'

'R-really?' Fandorin asked, looking down on the dark figure. 'Then first of all remove your veil and turn on the light.'

'No, anything but that!' Diana cried, leaping to her feet and shrinking away. 'Any other desire, anything at all, but not that.'

The State Counsellor sat there without speaking, even looking off to one side, which was not very considerate.

'Will you stay?' the femme fatale gasped pitifully, pressing her hands to her breast.

'Unfortunately I cannot. A matter of official duty. I can see that you are in an emotional state, and I do not have the time for a long conversation.'

'Then come this evening,' the voice rustled alluringly. 'I shall be waiting for you.'

'I cannot come this evening either,' Fandorin replied and explained in a confidential tone. 'So that you will not take my refusal as an affront, let me explain what I shall be doing. I have an appointment of a quite different kind, far less romantic. At ten o'clock I am meeting Prince Pozharsky, the Deputy Director of the Police Department. And, just imagine, at the Petrosov Bathhouse. Amusing, isn't it? The price of secrecy. But it does guarantee the absolute confidentiality of our tête-à-tête. Room number one, the very best in the whole nobles' section. There, my lady, see in what exotic circumstances the leaders of the investigation are obliged to meet.'

'Then for the time being, just this . . .' She took one quick step forward, raised her veil slightly and pressed her moist lips against his cheek.

Erast Petrovich shuddered at this touch, gave the collaborator a look of consternation that was almost fright, bowed and walked out.

After that the State Counsellor's behaviour became queerer still.

From Arbat Street he called into the Office of Gendarmes, without any apparent purpose in mind. He drank a cup of coffee with Smolyaninov, who had finally been reduced to the role of telephone operator, for the current state of affairs in the large building on Nikitskaya Street was extremely strange: all the various subsections and services were operating in emergency mode, although in effect there was no one actually in charge.

The temporary boss, Prince Pozharsky, was not sitting at his desk, and if he did drop in, it was only briefly – to listen to a report from the adjutant, to leave some instructions – and then he set out once more for parts unknown.

They remembered the deceased Stanislav Filippovich, spoke about the Lieutenant's wounded arm and the audacity of the terrorists. The Lieutenant was of the opinion that a demonstration of chivalry was called for.

'If I were in Mr Pozharsky's place,' he said fervently, 'I wouldn't send spies and provocateurs to this Green, I would print an appeal in the newspapers: "Stop hunting down us servants of the throne. Stop shooting at us from round corners and throwing bombs that kill innocent people. I am not hiding from you. If you, my dear sir, truly believe that you are right and wish to sacrifice yourself for the good of humankind, then let us meet in an honest duel, for it is also my sacred belief that I am right and I will gladly give my life for Russia. So let us stop spilling Russian blood. Let God or – if you are an atheist – Fate or Destiny decide which of us is right." I'm certain that Green would agree to such terms.'

The State Counsellor listened to the young man's reasoning and asked with a serious expression: 'And what if Green k-kills the prince? Then what?'

'What do you mean?' Smolyaninov exclaimed, wincing in pain as he attempted to wave his wounded arm through the air. 'Are there more terrorists or defenders of order in Russia? If Pozharsky were to be killed in the duel, then of course Green would have to be allowed to go free – that's a simple matter of honour. But the next day you would challenge him. And if your luck failed, then others would be found.' The young officer blushed. 'And the revolutionaries would be left with no way out. It would be impossible for them to refuse the challenge, because they would lose their reputation as bold, self-sacrificing heroes in the eyes of society. And soon there would be no terrorists left: all the fanatics would have died in duels, and the others would have been forced to abandon violence.'

'This is the second time just recently that I have had occasion to hear an original idea for the elimination of terrorism. And I'm not sure which of them I prefer,' Fandorin said as he stood up. 'I have enjoyed talking with you, but I must go now. I shall relay your idea to Gleb Georgievich this evening.' He glanced at the empty reception room and lowered his voice. 'For your ears only, in the strictest secrecy: at ten o'clock this evening the prince and I are having a tête-à-tête at which our entire plan of future action will be determined – at the Petrosov Bathhouse, in the nobles' section.'

'Why the bathhouse?' the Lieutenant asked, fluttering his silky eyelashes in astonishment.

'For the sake of secrecy. There are private rooms there, no uninvited guests. We have booked the finest room specially – number two. I shall definitely suggest that Pozharsky try the challenge via the newspapers. But, I repeat again, not a word to anyone about our meeting.'

From the Office, Fandorin went to the Department on Gnez-dikovsky Lane, where the role of the connecting link between all the various groups of agents was being played by Titular Counsellor Zubtsov, with whom Erast Petrovich drank not coffee but tea. They spoke of the deceased Pyotr Ivanovich, a hot-tempered individual of coarse sensibilities, but honest and sincerely devoted to the cause. They complained about the irreparable damage done to the old capital city's reputation in the eyes of the sovereign by the recent sad events.

'I'll tell you what I can't understand,' Sergei Vitalievich said cautiously. 'The entire investigative machine is working at full capacity, the men get no sleep at night, they're dead on their feet. We're trailing Lobastov, everyone who's unreliable, suspicious or even slightly dubious, reading their post, eavesdropping, peeping and prying. This is all essential routine activity, of course, but somehow we're not following a single line of inquiry. Naturally, my rank doesn't permit me to intrude into the area of higher tactics – that's your area of competence and Gleb Georgievich's, but even so, if I had some idea at least of the main direction of inquiry, then for my part, within the limits of the abilities I have been granted, I could perhaps also be of some use . . .'

'Yes, yes,' said Fandorin, nodding. 'Please don't think that the prince and I are concealing anything from you. We both sincerely hold you in the highest regard, and we will immediately involve you in the analytical work, as soon as certain circumstances have been clarified. As a token of my t-trust, I can tell you, in the very strictest confidence, that at ten o'clock this evening Gleb Georgievich and I are having a private meeting at an agreed rendezvous, where we shall determine the very line of which you spoke. The meeting will be confidential, but you will be informed immediately of the outcome. The reason for the secrecy is that' – the State Counsellor leaned forwards slightly – 'there is a traitor among our men and we do not yet know who exactly it is. Today, though, that might well become clear.'

'A traitor?' Zubtsov exclaimed. 'Here in the Okhranka?'

'Sh-sh,' said the State Counsellor, putting one finger to his lips. 'Who he is and where exactly he works is what the prince and I shall determine today, after we exchange the information we shall have collected. That is why we have arranged to meet so mysteriously in room number three of the nobles' section in the Petrosov Baths, believe it or not.' Erast Petrovich smiled cheerfully and took a sip of cold tea. 'By the way, where is Evstratii Pavlovich?'

The conversation that Fandorin held with Evstratii Pavlovich Mylnikov, whom the State Counsellor tracked down at the temporary observation post he had set up in a dusty attic close to the Lobastov plant, was in part similar to those that had preceded it, and in part different from them, for in addition to the deceased Pyotr Ivanovich, they also discussed the unsuccessful nocturnal operation, the perfidious millionaire and the question of a gratuity for the families of the agents who had been killed. However, the conversation concluded in exactly the same manner: the State Counsellor told the other man the precise time and place of his meeting with the Deputy Director of Police. Only this time he gave a different room number: number four.

And after his visit to the observation post Fandorin did not go on to do anything else at all. He took a cab home, and on the way he whistled an aria from *Geisha*, a very rare event for Erast Petrovich and a sign of quite uncommon optimism.

In the outhouse on Malaya Nikitskaya Street, Fandorin and his servant held a long, circumstantial conversation in Japanese. In fact Erast Petrovich did most of the talking and Masa listened, constantly repeating: 'Hai, hai.'

In the course of the conversation the State Counsellor drew on a sheet of paper a diagram that looked like this:

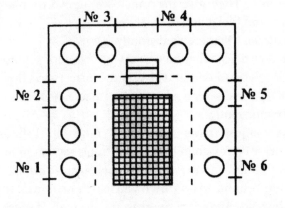

Then he replied to a few questions and went off, serenely calm, to sleep, although it was only shortly after two in the afternoon, and nothing of importance had been achieved.

He slept for a long time, until six o'clock. When he arose, he dined with a good appetite, did a little gymnastics and dressed in a light English sports outfit that did not restrict his movements: a short checked jacket, a close-fitting silk waistcoat, narrow trousers with foot straps.

But that was not the end of Erast Petrovich's toilette: he thrust a small stiletto in a light sheath of oiled paper under the elastic suspender of his right sock; he thrust a Velodog – a miniature pistol invented for bicyclists who are pestered by stray dogs – into a holster on his back, and put his main weapon – a seven-round Herstahl-Baillard, the latest invention from the master-gunsmiths of Liège – into another holster, designed for wearing under the arm.

Fandorin's servant tried to attach to his belt a most sinister-looking steel chain with two heavy spheres attached to it, but the State Counsellor resolutely rejected this unconventional weapon, since the spheres clanged against each other as he walked, and that attracted attention.

'Don't try to do anything yourself,' Erast Petrovich told his faithful helper, not for the first time, as he put on his cloth-covered fur coat in the hallway. 'Just remember which room they go into. Then give the knock we agreed on the door of room six, and I'll let you in. *Vakatta?*'*

'*Vakattemas,*' Masa replied stoutly. '*De mo—*'†

He didn't finish what he was saying, because someone rang the door bell repeatedly and insistently: once, twice, three times.

'That's your new concubine,' the valet sighed. 'No one else rings so impatiently.'

'Have you just arrived, or are you going out?' Esfir asked on seeing Erast Petrovich in his coat, with his top hat in his hands. She hugged him and pressed her cheek against his lips. 'You're going out. Your nose is warm. If you had just come in, your nose would be cold. And for some reason you smell of musk. When will you be back? I'll wait; I've missed you terribly.'

'Esfir, I asked you to telephone,' Fandorin said, disconcerted. 'I really am going out; I don't know yet when I'll be back. And Masa will be going out soon.'

'I can't stand the telephone,' the black-eyed beauty snapped. 'It's so dead, somehow. And where are you off to?'

'It's a piece of important b-business,' Erast Petrovich replied evasively; then, yielding to a sudden, unaccountable impulse, he added quickly, 'I'm meeting Prince Pozharsky at the Petrosov Baths. In the nobles' section . . . room five.'

The State Counsellor's face instantly flushed a deep red and his long eyelashes fluttered guiltily.

'That is, not number f-five, but number six. A slip of the tongue . . .'

---

* 'You understand?'
† 'I understand . . . But—'

'My God, what do I care which room you're meeting that villain in? Fine company you've chosen for yourself! In the bathhouse – that's simply charming!' Esfir exclaimed with an angry laugh. 'Male entertainment – I've heard a great deal about that. I expect you'll call in a few girls too. Goodbye, Your Honour; you'll never see me again!' And before Fandorin even had time to open his mouth, the door slammed shut with a deafening thud. There was the sound of heels stamping across the porch, and then snow crunching under running feet.

'Not a woman, but the eruption of Mount Fuji in the fifth year of the age of the Eternal Treasure,' Masa exclaimed admiringly. 'So, master, you say I should not take any weapons? Not even my very smallest knife, that can be hidden so conveniently in my loincloth?'

There would have been nowhere to hide the knife in any case, because no one wore a loincloth in the common hall with the pool. The men were completely naked and, to Masa's taste, extremely ugly – as hairy as monkeys and with excessively long arms and legs. One of them was particularly unpleasant to look at, with thick red fur on his stomach and chest. Several times Masa surveyed his own smooth body, so beautifully rounded at the sides. If the learned English sage Tiaruridszu Daruin was right, and man really was descended from a monkey, then the Japanese had progressed much further along that path than the red-hairs.

Masa did not like it in the bathhouse at all. The water was not hot enough, the awkward stone steps gleamed too brightly, and the wait was dragging on for too long altogether.

In addition to the valet, there were nine other men splashing in the pool. It was hard to say how many of them were bandits. There was one he had no doubt about – sullen, with black hair, a big nose like a Japanese water sprite's and a lean, muscular torso – he had fresh red scars on his side and his chest, and the top of his left ear had been sliced off. Masa's experienced eye had immediately spotted the traces left by glancing blows from a sharp blade. Obviously a yakuza, except that he had no beautiful

219

coloured tattoos. Masa tried to stay as close as possible to this suspicious character. But there were several other bathers who looked entirely peaceable. For instance, the thin, white-skinned youth sitting on the edge not far away. He was toying distractedly with a chain attached to the bronze railing that ran all the way round the pool. The railing was there for people to hold on to, and Masa couldn't understand why they had hooked an iron chain on to it with that ring. But he didn't rack his brains over it, because he had more important business.

There were six doors leading out on to the gallery located behind the columns, just as the diagram had indicated. His master should be behind the last door on the right. The bandits wouldn't try to get in there. They would break down one of the first four doors. He just had to remember which one it was and then run to his master. Nothing could be simpler.

But how would the bandits manage without weapons? Red-hairs didn't know how to kill people with their bare hands; they had to have steel. Where would they get a pistol or a knife in a bathhouse?

'Now,' the man with the scars said unexpectedly.

The shouting and splashing instantly stopped. Four hands grabbed Masa's wonderful sides tightly from behind and pushed him towards the edge, and before the valet could gather his wits, the nice-looking youth had pulled the chain out of the water. At the other end of the chain, there was another iron ring, which was instantly clicked shut around Masa's wrist.

'Gently now, sir,' the youth said. 'Stay here quietly and nothing bad will happen to you.'

'I say, come now, gentlemen; what kind of trick is this?' a voice shouted in outrage. Masa turned round and saw three other men, obviously chance visitors, who had also been chained to the railing in the same way as himself. All the other bathers – six young men, including their leader with the big nose – quickly clambered out of the pool.

That very moment, another two came running in through the doors leading to the changing rooms. They were fully dressed, and both of them were carrying tall heaps of clothes in their hands.

The naked bandits quickly dressed, paying no attention to the outraged shouts of the chained men.

Masa tugged on his chain, but it held firm. It was a pair of genuine handcuffs, the kind used for restraining arrested criminals – why hadn't he guessed sooner? The bandits had come earlier, attached one end of the handcuffs to the rail, dropped the other into the water and then waited for the appointed hour. Their crafty, dishonest trick had deprived Masa of the chance to fulfil his duty. Now the bandits would break into one of the doors, see there was no one there, and start checking all the others, and there was no way he could warn his master.

It was pointless to shout. Firstly, in the gleaming marble hall any howl would shatter into a myriad worthless echoes, mingling with the splashing of the water and the rumbling voices of the bathers. Of course, Masa could shout very, very loud, and perhaps his master would hear his voice through the closed door; but his master would not flee to save himself, he would come hurrying to his aid. And he must not allow that to happen, no matter what!

The conclusion?

Wait until the bandits broke into one of the doors, and then yell with all the power his lungs could muster.

Meanwhile the bandits had put their clothes on, and out of nowhere revolvers had appeared in their hands. *Eight men with revolvers – that is too many*, thought Masa. *If only they had no revolvers, just knives, that would be all right.* The two of them could have managed. But this was really bad: the master was alone, there were eight of them, and with guns.

The yakuza chief cocked his revolver and said: 'Pozharsky's tricky. No dawdling, fire immediately. Emelya, Nail, you get the door.'

The two largest bandits went dashing up the marble steps with the others hanging back a little behind them.

They're giving the first two space to run at the door and break it down, Masa guessed, wondering which way they would turn – to the left, towards the first three rooms, or to the right?

They turned to the right. So they had to be going to room number four.

But the bandits who had been allocated the role of battering ram went straight past door number four without giving it a glance. They didn't stop at door number five either.

Even though Masa was standing up to his chest in hot water, he felt a sudden chill of horror.

'*Dann-a-a-a! Kio tsuke-e-e!*'*

Erast Petrovich reached the main entrance of the Petrosov Baths at precisely ten.

'The gentleman's waiting for you in room six,' the attendant announced with a bow. 'No one has arrived in the other five rooms yet.'

'They will,' the State Counsellor replied. 'L-Later on.'

He walked along the wide corridor, up to the *piano nobile*, along another corridor, round a corner. On his right was the entrance to the ladies' section, on the left the private rooms began, with the service staircase beyond them. Before he entered the room, Fandorin surveyed the location once again and was satisfied. If they needed to withdraw in haste, it was very convenient: one provided covering fire while the other ran to the corner. Then the roles were reversed. Short sprints: the risk of taking a bullet was minimal. And things would probably not get as far as shooting.

'Are there many visitors in the l-ladies' section at about this time?' he asked his guide, just in case.

The man smiled in a most polite manner, with just the slightest hint of playfulness.

'Plenty as yet, but there won't be any more coming in. It's a bit late already for the fair sex.'

'Is this their way in and their way out?' Fandorin asked in alarm.

* 'Master! Beware!'

'Certainly not, sir. The way out's on the other side. Specially arranged. A woman, Your Worship, doesn't take kindly to being observed after the bathhouse, with a towel over her hair. Instead of going out through the main door, they prefer to duck into the sleigh, and adieu!'

Erast Petrovich gave the man a coin and went into his room.

'As a young rake awaits his ardent tryst, so have I waited all the day for when . . . something or other . . . in my secret basement!' Pozharsky greeted him boisterously. The naked prince was sitting in an armchair with a cigar clenched in his teeth.

Standing on the table in front of him were a bottle of Cachet Blanc, two glasses and a bowl of fruit, with a newspaper lying open beside them.

'Champagne?' Fandorin asked, raising one eyebrow slightly. 'Do we have some cause for celebration?'

'I do,' Gleb Georgievich replied mysteriously. 'But let's start at the beginning and not get ahead of ourselves. Get your clothes off and take a dip' – he pointed to the small pool in the floor – 'and afterwards we'll have a talk. How about you – have you brought any booty?'

Erast Petrovich glanced at the locked door that led into the common hall and replied evasively: 'I shall have some s-soon.'

Pozharsky gave him a curious glance and wound a napkin round the bottle. 'Well, why are you standing there like a buyer at a slave market? Get undressed.'

It had not been Erast Petrovich's intention to get undressed, since his plan envisaged the likelihood of a hasty retreat, but to parade fully clothed in front of a completely naked man seemed stupid and improper. What if the trick completely failed to work? Should he just carry on standing there in his jacket? Fortunately, his comfortable and simple sports costume could be donned in mere seconds – after all he could ignore the leotard, the waist-coat, the cuffs and the collar.

'What's this – are you shy?' The prince laughed. 'That's not at all like you.'

The State Counsellor pulled off his clothes and put them on

the divan, placing both revolvers and the stiletto on top of them as if it were an afterthought.

Pozharsky whistled: 'A serious arsenal. I'm a great respecter of prudence. I'm exactly the same. Will you show me your toys later? And I'll show you mine. But business first. Jump in, jump in. One thing is no obstacle to the other.'

Erast Petrovich glanced round at the door again and jumped into the pool, but he didn't splash around in the water for long; instead, he climbed out straight away.

'You're a genuine Antinous,' said the prince, surveying Fandorin's physique appreciatively. 'This is a fine outlandish setting we have for an operational conference. To work?'

'To work.'

The State Counsellor sat down in an armchair and lit up a cigar himself, but he kept his leg muscles tensed, ready to leap up just as soon as Masa knocked on the door.

'How was Diana?' Pozharsky asked with a strangely jovial smile. 'Did she confess her sins?'

Fandorin thought the intonation of the question sounded strange, and he paused before replying.

'Allow me t-to inform you of my conclusions a little later. I have serious grounds to hope that the m-main culprit will be exposed today.'

However, these words failed to produce the anticipated effect on the other man.

'But I know how to find our elusive CG,' the prince parried, 'and very soon now I shall snap it up.'

Erast Petrovich felt himself turning pale. If Pozharsky was telling the truth, it meant that he had found a shorter and more effective way to solve this complex puzzle.

Suppressing his wounded *amour propre*, Fandorin said: 'C-Congratulations, that is a great success. But how—'

He didn't finish, because at that moment there was a loud shout outside the door. He couldn't make out the words, but there could be no doubt that it was Masa shouting. And that could only mean one thing: the plan had failed, and failed in some extremely unpleasant way.

Erast Petrovich leapt to his feet, about to make a dash for his clothes, but suddenly there was a deafening crash as the door leading to the pool was torn off its hinges by a powerful blow.

Two men came hurtling through into the room, with an entire mob pressing in behind them. Fandorin didn't need a time-and-motion study to realise he would never reach his clothes or his weapons. He could only hope there would be enough time to leap out into the corridor.

Pozharsky pulled a small double-barrelled pistol out from under the newspaper and fired twice. The leading attacker threw his arms up and ran on for a few more steps from sheer inertia, collapsing face down in the pool, and the prince flung away his discharged weapon and dashed after Fandorin with astounding agility.

They flew through the doorway simultaneously, bumping their naked shoulders together. Wood dust showered down on to Erast Petrovich's head as a bullet slammed into the lintel of the door, and the next moment the two leaders of the investigation tumbled out into the corridor. Without even looking round, Pozharsky set off to the right. There was no point in running in the same direction: the initial battle plan with alternating short sprints under covering fire had been rendered meaningless by the lack of any weapons.

The State Counsellor dashed to the left, towards the service stairway, although he had no idea where it led to.

As he grabbed hold of the banister with one hand, crumbs of stone spurted from the wall. Fandorin glanced back briefly, saw three men running after him and sprinted upwards – he had spotted a grille across the steps leading down.

He covered one flight in huge bounds, three steps at a time – a padlocked door. Another two flights – another lock.

He could hear the clatter of hasty footsteps below him.

There was only one more flight now – and there was the dark form of a door on the upper landing.

It was locked! A curved rod of iron, a padlock.

Erast Petrovich grabbed hold of the metal rod and, following the precepts of the teaching of spiritual power, imagined that it was paper. He jerked the feeble rod towards himself, and the lock suddenly flew off to one side, clanging down the stone steps.

There was no time to celebrate. Fandorin ran into a dark room with a low, slanting ceiling. Through the little windows he could see sloping roof tiles glinting dully in the moonlight.

Another door, but with no lock, and flimsy. One kick was enough.

The Deputy for Special Assignments ran out on to the roof, and for a moment the icy wind took his breath away. But the cold was not the worst thing. A rapid glance around was enough for him to realise that he had absolutely nowhere left to go.

Fandorin dashed to one edge of the roof and saw a brightly lit street with people and carriages far below.

He rushed to the opposite side. Down below he saw a snow-covered yard.

There was no time left for further exploration. Three shadows detached themselves from the attic superstructure and slowly moved towards the doomed man standing frozen on the edge of the precipice.

'You're a fast runner, Mr State Counsellor,' one of them said when they were still some distance away. Fandorin could not make out his face. 'Let's see if you can fly too.'

Erast Petrovich turned his back to the shadows, because it was painful and senseless to look at them. He glanced down.

Fly?

The highest level of mastery in the clan of the Stealthy Ones, who had taught Fandorin the art of controlling his spirit and his body, was the trick known as 'The Flight of the Hawk'. Erast Petrovich had often perused drawings in old manuscripts, which depicted the technique of this incredible trick in great detail. When the kingdoms of the land of the Root of the Sun fought an internecine war lasting many centuries, the Stealthy Ones were regarded as spies nonpareil. It was nothing to them to scramble up sheer walls, infiltrate a besieged fortress and discover all the secrets of the defence. It was far more difficult, however, to get away with the information gathered. The spies did not always have time to lower a rope ladder, or even a silken cord. It was for this that the Flight of the Hawk had been invented.

The instruction of the teaching was: 'Jump without pushing off, smoothly, so that the gap between you and the wall is two foot lengths, no more and no less. Hold your body perfectly straight. Count to five, then kick your heels hard against the wall, turn over in the air and land, not forgetting to offer a prayer to the Buddha Amida.'

It was said that the masters of olden times could perform the Flight of the Hawk from a wall as high as a hundred *siaku*, that is fifteen *sazhens*, but Erast Petrovich did not believe that. With a count of only five, the body would drop no more than five or six *sazhens*. The somersault that followed would, of course, soften the impact, but even so it could hardly be possible to survive if you jumped from a height of more than seven or eight *sazhens*, and to survive at all you would have to be blessed with incredible agility and the special favour of the Buddha Amida.

However, this was not an appropriate moment for scepticism. The leisurely footfalls behind him were drawing closer – the nihilist gentlemen had no more reason to hurry now.

How many *siakus* was this? The State Counsellor tried to work it out. No more than fifty. Absolute child's play for a medieval Japanese spy.

Fixing firmly in his mind that he had to jump without pushing off, he drew himself erect and took a step into empty space.

Erast Fandorin found the sensation of flight repugnant. His stomach attempted to leap out through his throat, and his lungs froze, unable to breathe either in or out; but all that was of no consequence. The important thing was to count.

At 'five' Fandorin kicked back as hard as he could with both feet, felt the scorching contact with a hard surface and performed the relatively simple manoeuvre of 'The Attacking Snake', known in the European circus as a double somersault.

In his mind Fandorin had just enough time to recite 'Namu Amida Butsu'* before he stopped seeing or hearing anything.

Later his senses reawoke, but not all of them. It was very cold, there was nothing to breathe and he still couldn't see anything. For a moment Erast Petrovich was afraid that because of his prayer he had been consigned to the Buddhist Hell of Ice, where it is always cold and dark. But it was hardly likely that anyone in the Hell of Ice would know Russian, and that was definitely the language he could hear being spoken by those voices somewhere up in the heavens.

'Schwartz, where is he? He disappeared into thin air.'

'There he is!' cried another voice, very young and clear. 'Lying in a snowdrift! He just flew a long way out.'

It was only then that Fandorin, stunned by his fall, realised that he had not died and not gone blind, but was lying face down in a deep snowdrift. His eyes, his mouth and even his nose were packed with snow, and that was why it was dark and he couldn't breathe.

'Let's go,' someone up above him decided. 'If he's not dead, he must have broken every bone in his body.'

And the heavens fell silent.

He certainly hadn't broken all his bones – the State Counsellor realised that when he managed to get up on all fours, and then stand erect. Perhaps the art of the Stealthy Ones had saved him, or perhaps the Buddha Amida, but most likely it had been the opportunely located snowdrift.

He staggered across the yard, through the passage, and out into Zvonarny Lane – straight into the arms of a police constable.

'Oh Lordy Lord, people have completely taken leave of their senses,' the constable gasped at the sight of a naked man caked in snow. 'Shooting off guns with no rhyme or reason and bathing in the buff in snowdrifts! Right then, my good sir, it's a night in the station for you.'

* 'I praise the Buddha Amida'

Erast Petrovich staggered on a little further, clutching at the lapels of the coarse greatcoat rimed with frost, and began slowly sinking to the ground.

CHAPTER 12

Giraffes

There were problems with the move to a new apartment – the police spies were running such a fine-toothed comb through the whole of Moscow that it was too dangerous to turn to sympathisers for help. There was no way of telling which of them was under surveillance,

They decided to stay at Vorontsovo Polye, especially in view of one consideration: If TG was so well informed about the gendarmes' plans, why make his relationship with the group any more complicated than it was? Whoever the mysterious correspondent might be, and whatever goals he was pursuing, he was clearly an ally, and a truly invaluable one.

The previous day's operation at the Petrosov Baths could hardly have gone worse. First, they had lost Nail, killed outright by a bullet from the deputy director of police. That preternaturally evasive gentleman had got away again, even though Green himself had led the pursuit; and the job with State Counsellor Fandorin had been botched too. Emelya, Schwartz and Nobel should have gone down into the yard and finished him off. The deep snow could have cushioned his fall. It was quite possible that the Governor General's deputy had got away with minor injuries like broken legs and ruptured kidneys.

The evening before, when the Combat Group, its numbers enlarged by the Muscovites who had passed the test of the expropriation, was preparing for the operation at the Petrosov Baths, Needle had brought the chemicals and the detonators from Aronson. So today Green had set up a laboratory in the study and started work on augmenting his arsenal. He made a burner for heating the paraffin out of a kerosene lamp and adapted a coffee-grinder for grinding up the picronitric acid, while the place of a retort was taken by an olive-oil jar, and a samovar made a tolerable still. Bullfinch made the casings and filled them with screws.

The others took it easy. Emelya was still reading his *Count of Monte Cristo* and only looked into the study occasionally to share his feelings about what he had read. The novices – Marat, Beaver, Schwartz and Nobel – had nothing to offer in any case. They settled down to a game of cards in the kitchen. Although they were only playing for finger-flicks to the forehead, the game was heated and noisy, with plenty of laughter and shouting. That was all right. They were only young lads, high-spirited – let them have a bit of fun.

Putting together the explosive mixture was painstaking work; it took many hours and required total concentration. One slip of the hand and the entire apartment would be blown sky-high, taking the attic and the roof with it.

Some time after two in the morning, when the process was only half-completed, the telephone rang.

Green picked up the earpiece and waited to see who would speak.

Needle.

'The private lecturer has fallen ill,' she said in a worried voice. 'It's very strange. When I got back from your apartment I took a look at his windows through my binoculars, just to check – in case his generosity with the chemicals might not have gone unnoticed. I saw the curtains were closed.' She suddenly broke off, perturbed by his silence. 'Hello, is that you, Mr Sievers?'

'Yes,' he replied calmly, remembering that closed curtains meant 'disaster'. 'This morning? Why didn't you let me know?'

'What for? If he's been taken, there's nothing we can do to help. We'd only make things worse.'

'Then why now?'

'Five minutes ago one of the curtains was opened!' Needle exclaimed. 'I immediately phoned the Ostozhenka Street apartment and asked for Professor Brandt, as agreed. Aronson said: "I'm afraid you have the wrong number." Then he said it again, as if he was asking me to hurry. His voice sounded pitiful, it was trembling.'

The code phrase meant that Needle should come to the apartment alone – Green remembered that. What could have happened to Aronson?

'I'll go,' he said, 'and check.'

'No, you mustn't. It's too risky. And why should you? He can't be in serious danger, and we have to take care of you. I'm going to Ostozhenka Street, and then I'll come to your apartment.'

'All right.'

He went back to his improvised laboratory, but a mounting sense of alarm prevented him from concentrating on the job at hand.

A strange business: first the signal for disaster, and then suddenly an urgent summons. He shouldn't have sent Needle. It was a mistake.

'I'm going out,' he told Bullfinch, and stood up. 'Something I have to do. Emelya's in charge. Don't touch the mixture.'

'Can I go with you?' Bullfinch asked eagerly. 'Emelya's reading, the others are playing cards, what am I going to do? I've done all the tins. I'm bored.'

Green thought for a moment and decided: Why not? If anything went wrong, at least he could warn their comrades.

'If you like. Let's go.'

From the street everything looked clear.

First they drove past in a cab and examined the windows. Nothing suspicious. One curtain closed.

Then they separated and walked along Ostozhenka Street. No idly loitering yard-keepers, no sharp-eyed vendors of spiced honey punch, no one casually strolling by.

The building was definitely not under surveillance.

Somewhat reassured, Green sent Bullfinch to the barber's directly opposite Aronson's entrance – to have the fluff on his cheeks shaved. He told him to sit by the window there and keep an eye on the alarm signal. If the second curtain was opened, he should go up. If nothing happened to the curtains for more than ten minutes, it meant there was an ambush in the apartment and he should leave immediately.

There was a brass plate on the door:

PRIVATE LECTURER SEMYON LVOVICH ARONSON

He stopped beside it and listened for a long time, because there were very strange sounds coming from the apartment: long low howls, as if someone had locked a dog inside. Once there was a very brief, piercing shriek – hard to interpret: it was as if someone had tried to yell at the top of his voice but choked.

People didn't choke on screams for no reason, and Aronson didn't have a dog, so Green took out his revolver and rang the bell. He looked around, weighing up his position: thick walls, solidly built. A shot there on the stairs would be heard, of course, but a shot inside probably wouldn't.

Rapid footsteps in the corridor. Two men.

The chain jangled, the door opened slightly, and Green struck out with his gun butt, straight between a pair of moist, gleaming eyes.

He shoved the door as hard as he could, jumped over the fallen man (all he noticed was a white shirt with the sleeves rolled up) and saw another man who had staggered back in surprise. He grabbed this man by the throat to stop him shouting and slammed his head against the wall. Then he supported the limp body and let it slide slowly to the floor.

A familiar face: he'd seen that curled moustache and that camlet jacket before somewhere.

'What's happening?' a voice asked from somewhere further inside the apartment. 'Have you got him? Bring him here!'

'Yes, sir!' Green bellowed and ran along the corridor towards the voice – straight ahead and to the right, into the drawing room.

He recognised the third man's pink face and white hair immediately, and at the same time recalled the first two: Staff Captain Seidlitz, the head of General Khrapov's guard, and two of his men. He'd seen them in the carriage at Klin.

The room was full of things that required examination, but there was no time for that now, because when he saw the stranger with a revolver in his hand, the gendarme (not in uniform this time – he was wearing a sandy-coloured three-piece suit) bared his teeth in a scowl and reached under his jacket. Green fired one shot, aiming at the head to finish the job, but his aim was poor. Seidlitz clutched at his throat where the bullet had torn it open, made a gurgling sound and sat down on the floor. His whitish eyes glared balefully at Green. He had recognised him.

Green didn't want to fire again. Why take the risk? He stepped towards the wounded man and smashed in his temple with the butt of his revolver.

Only then did Green allow himself to glance at Aronson and Needle. She was tied to a chair. Her dress was torn across her chest, and he could see the white skin and the shadowy cleavage. There was a gag in her mouth, her lips were split and she had a bruise that was turning blue under her eye. The private lecturer seemed to be in a very bad way. He was sitting at the table with his head lowered on to his arms, swaying rhythmically, howling quietly and insistently.

'One moment,' said Green, and ran back into the corridor. The stunned agents might come round at any moment.

First he finished off the one who was lying motionless on his back. Then he turned to the other, who was slumped against the wall, batting his eyelids senselessly. A swing of the arm, a crunch of bone. It was done.

He ran back to the room and pulled back the curtain to signal to Bullfinch and let in more light.

He didn't touch Aronson – it was obvious he wouldn't get any sense out of him.

He untied Needle and took the gag out of her mouth; carefully dabbed her bleeding lips with his handkerchief.

'Forgive me.' That was the first thing she said. 'Forgive me. I almost got you killed. I always thought I'd never let myself be taken alive, but when they grabbed my elbows and dragged me in here, I simply froze. And I could have done it, when they put me in the chair. I could have pulled out the needle and stuck it in my throat. I've imagined how it would be a thousand times. But I didn't ...' She suddenly started sobbing and a tear rolled down across her bruised cheekbone.

'It doesn't matter,' Green reassured her. 'Even if you had done it, I'd still have come anyway. So it's all right.'

His explanation failed to console Needle; on the contrary, it only upset her more. Tears started streaming from both her eyes.

'Would you really have come?' she said, asking a question that made no sense.

Green didn't even bother to answer it. 'What is all this?' he asked. 'What's wrong with Aronson?'

Needle tried to pull herself together. 'That's the head of Khrapov's guard. I didn't realise at first; I thought he was from the Okhranka. But they don't act like this. He's some kind of madman. They've been here since yesterday evening. They were talking; I heard them. The white-haired one wanted to find you. He's scoured the whole of Moscow.' Her voice was firmer now; her eyes were still wet, but the tears had stopped flowing. 'Aronson's apartment was under secret surveillance by the Okhranka for days. Obviously since the business with Rahmet. And he' – she nodded again towards the dead staff captain – 'bribed the police agent who was in charge of the observation.'

'Seidlitz,' Green explained. 'His name's Seidlitz.'

'The police agent?' Needle asked, astonished. 'How do you know?'

'No, that one,' he said with a sharp nod, annoyed with himself at having wasted time on an irrelevant detail. 'Go on.'

'Yesterday the agent told Seidlitz that I'd been here to see Aronson and left with some kind of bundle. An agent tried to follow me, but he failed. I didn't see the tail, but just in case I turned into a tricky little passage on Prechistenka Street. A habit.'

Green nodded, because he had the same kind of habits himself.

'When the agent told Seidlitz, he suddenly turned up here with two of his men and they tortured Aronson all night long.

He held out until the morning, and then broke down. I don't know what they did to him, but you can see for yourself . . . He just sits there like that. Rocking to and fro, howling . . .'

Bullfinch came running in from the corridor. White-faced and wide-eyed. 'The door's open!' he shouted. 'There are bodies!' Then he saw what was in the drawing room, and fell silent.

'Close the door,' said Green. 'Drag those two in here.'

He turned back to Needle. 'What did they want?'

'From me? They wanted me to say where you were. Seidlitz only asked questions and swore; it was that one, with his sleeves rolled up, who beat me.' (Bullfinch, deadly pale, was just dragging the agent in the white shirt across the parquet floor.) 'Seidlitz asked and I didn't answer; then that one beat me and held my mouth shut, so that I couldn't scream.' She put her hand to her cheekbone and frowned.

'Don't touch,' said Green. 'I'll do it. But him first.'

He went across to the deranged private lecturer and touched him on the shoulder.

Aronson straightened up with a sickening howl and shrank back against the armrest of his chair. The swollen, unrecognisable face gazed at Green with a single, wildly goggling eye. There was a gaping crimson hole where the other eye should have been.

'A-a-a,' Aronson sobbed. 'It's you. Then you have to kill me. Because I'm a traitor. And because I can't go on living any more anyway.' The private lecturer's words were hard to understand, because his mouth was full of short, pointed stumps instead of teeth.

'At first they just beat me. Then they hung me upside down. Then they drowned me. It all happened in the bathroom, there . . .' He pointed towards the corridor with a trembling finger.

Green saw that Aronson's shirt was streaked with dried blood. There were spots on his fingers too, even on his trousers.

'They're totally insane. They don't understand what they're doing. I could have stood anything – prison and hard labour, honestly.' The private lecturer grabbed hold of Green's hand.

'But I can't go on without my eyes! I've always been afraid of going blind, ever since I was a child! You can't even imagine . . .' He started shaking all over, swaying and whimpering again. Green had to shake him by the shoulders.

The private lecturer came to his senses and started lisping again: 'The albino said – it was morning, and I'd thought the night would never end – he said: "Where's Needle? I'm only going to ask you again twice. After the first time, I'll burn out your left eye with acid, and after the second time, I'll burn out your right eye. The same as your people did to Shverubovich." I didn't say anything. Then . . .' A dull sob erupted from deep in Aronson's chest. 'And then he asked the second time and I told him everything. I couldn't stand any more! When she telephoned, I could have warned her, but I didn't care any longer . . .'

He grabbed hold of Green with his other hand as well and implored him in a frantic whisper: 'What you have to do is shoot me. I know that's nothing for you. I'm finished now in any case. A broken man, with only one eye, and after this' – he jerked his chin towards the dead bodies – 'I'm a dead man. They'll never forgive, and your people won't either.'

Green freed his hands and said severely: 'If you want to shoot yourself, go ahead. Take Seidlitz's revolver over there. But it's stupid. And there's nothing to forgive. Everyone has his limits. And you can be useful to the cause even with one eye. Even with no eyes at all.'

'I probably wouldn't have held out either,' said Needle. 'It's just that they hadn't really tortured me yet.'

'You'd have held out.' Green turned away from both of them to give Bullfinch his instructions. 'Take him to the hospital. He's a chemist. An explosion in his private laboratory. Then leave immediately.'

'What about this?' Bullfinch pointed to the bodies.

'I'll handle it.'

When the two of them were left on their own, he started tending her face.

He brought a bottle of alcohol and some cotton wool from

the bathroom (it was bad in there – blood everywhere and pools of vomit). He washed the grazes and gently brushed ointment on the bruise.

Needle sat there with her head thrown back and her eyes closed. When Green gently parted her lips with his fingers, she submissively opened her mouth. He carefully touched her teeth, so white and even. One right incisor wobbled, but not much. It would set back in.

Green had to unfasten her torn dress even further. He saw a blue spot below her collarbone and pressed gently on the fine, tender skin over the bone. Not broken.

Needle suddenly opened her eyes. As she looked up at him her gaze was confused, even frightened. Green felt his throat tighten, and he forgot to remove his hand from her exposed breast.

'You're scratched,' Needle said in a quiet voice.

He involuntarily put his hand over his scratched cheek, a reminder of the stupid failure at the baths.

'And I'm all battered and beaten. I look horrible, don't I?' I'm plain enough anyway. Why are you looking at me like that?'

Green blinked guiltily, but he didn't look away. She didn't look plain to him at all now, although the blue patch on her cheekbone was growing more distinct by the moment. He couldn't believe he had thought this face was lifeless and withered. It was full of life and feeling, and he had been wrong about Needle's colour: it wasn't a cold grey; it was warm, with a hint of turquoise. Her eyes turned out to be turquoise too, and they had the frightening ability to look deep into Green's soul and draw the long-forgotten, irrevocably faded azure back up to the surface.

The fingers that were still pressed against her skin suddenly felt hot. Green tried to pull them away, but he couldn't. And then Needle put her hand over his. The contact made both of them tremble.

'It's impossible . . . I swore to myself . . . It's absolutely point-less . . . It will pass in a moment, just a moment . . .' she mur-mured incoherently.

'Yes, it's pointless. Absolutely,' he agreed fervently.

He leaned down impulsively, pressed his lips against her swollen ones, and felt the taste of blood on his tongue . . .

Before they left, Green paused in the doorway so that he would never forget the strange place where this thing he was afraid to name had happened.

An overturned armchair. The rolled-up edge of a carpet. Three bloody bodies. A harsh smell of kerosene and a very faint odour of gunpowder.

Needle said something unexpected. Something that made Green shudder.

'If there's a child . . . what will it be like after *this*?'

Green lit the match and threw it on the floor. The dancing flame traced a bright blue trail across the drawing room.

Night. Quiet.

Apart from Emelya, rustling the pages of his book in the study, everyone was sleeping.

In the bedroom Green sat beside the bed, looking at Needle. She was breathing regularly, occasionally smiling at something in her sleep. He couldn't leave her – she was holding on tight to his hand.

He sat there like that for an hour and ten minutes. Four thousand, two hundred and seventeen beats of his heart.

After what had happened, Needle couldn't be allowed to go home, and so Green had brought her to the secret apartment. She hadn't said a word all evening, hadn't joined in the conversations, just smiled a gentle smile he had never seen before. Before that day he had never seen her smile at all.

Then they had started getting ready for bed. The lads had settled down on the floor in the drawing room, giving up the bedroom to the woman. Green had said he was going to finish preparing the explosive mixture.

He went in to see Needle. She took hold of his hand and lay there, looking at him, for a long time. They didn't say anything.

When she did speak it was brief, something unexpected again: 'We're like a pair of giraffes.' And she laughed quietly.

'Why giraffes?' he asked, frowning because he didn't understand.

'When I was little I saw a picture in a book: two giraffes; gangling and clumsy; standing there with their necks twined together, the ungainly creatures, looking as if they didn't know what to do next.'

Needle closed her eyes and fell asleep, and Green thought about what she had said. When her fingers finally trembled and released their grip, he cautiously got to his feet and walked out of the bedroom. He really did have to finish making the explosive jelly.

As he stepped out into the corridor, he happened to glance in the direction of the hallway and froze on the spot.

Another white rectangle. Lying below the slit in the door.

A letter:

You botched it. You let them both get away. But you have a chance to redeem your error. Pozharsky and Fandorin are having another secret meeting tomorrow. In Briusov Square, at nine in the morning.

TG

Green caught himself smiling. Even more astonishing was the thought that had just come to him.

God did exist after all. His name was TG, he was an ally of the revolution and he had a Remington No. 5 typewriter.

Wasn't that what they called a 'joke'?

Something was changing, in him and in the world around him. For the better or for the worse – he couldn't tell.

CHAPTER 13

in which something appropriately unlucky happens

When he came round and saw a white open space with a bright yellow sphere at its centre, Erast Petrovich did not immediately realise that he was looking at a ceiling and the globe of an electric light. He turned his head a little (it transpired that his head was lying on a pillow, and he himself was lying in a bed) and his gaze encountered a gentleman who was sitting beside him and observing him very keenly. The man seemed vaguely familiar, but the State Counsellor could not immediately recall where he had seen him, especially since the man's appearance was entirely uninteresting: small facial features, a neat parting, an unpretentious grey jacket.

I ought to ask where I am, why I'm lying down and what the time is, Erast Petrovich thought; but before he could say anything the man in the grey jacket got up and walked out quickly through the door.

He would have to try to find the answers himself.

He started with the most important question: why was he in bed?

Was he wounded? Ill?

Erast Petrovich moved his arms and legs, paying close attention to his body's reaction, but failed to discover anything alarming, except for a certain reluctance in his joints, such as there might be after heavy physical work or a concussion.

Immediately he remembered: the baths, the jump from the roof, the police constable.

Obviously, his conscious mind had spontaneously switched off and he had been plunged into the deep sleep that his spirit and its corporeal shell required in order to recover from the shock.

The swoon could hardly have lasted more than a few hours. The electric light and the drawn curtains indicated that the night was not yet over. But he still had to determine precisely where they had brought the naked man who had fainted in that chilly side street.

To all appearances, this was a bedroom, only not in a private home but in an expensive hotel. Fandorin was led to this conclusion by the monogram adorning the carafe, glass and ashtray standing on the elegant bedside table.

Erast Petrovich picked up the glass to take a closer look at the monogram: the letter 'L' under a crown. The symbol of the Loskutnaya Hotel.

That finally made everything clear: this was Pozharsky's room.

It also revealed the identity of the unremarkable gentleman: he was one of the 'guardian angels' who had been striding along behind Gleb Georgievich during their recent conversation.

The questions now answered were replaced by a new one: what had happened to the prince? Was he alive?

The answer came immediately – the door swung open and the deputy director of police himself rushed into the room, not only alive, but apparently quite unharmed.

'Well, at last!' he exclaimed in sincere delight. 'The doctor assured me that there was nothing broken and your faint was the result of nervous shock. He promised that you would soon recover consciousness, but you stubbornly refused to come round – it was quite impossible to rouse you. I'd begun to think you were going to turn into a genuine sleeping beauty and ruin my entire plan. You have been reclining at your leisure for a whole day and night! I never thought you had such delicate nerves.'

So this was the next night. Following the Flight of the Hawk Erast Petrovich's spirit and corporeal shell had required more than twenty-four hours of rest.

'I have some questions,' the State Counsellor hissed inaudibly.

He cleared his throat and said it again, in a voice that was hoarse but intelligible. 'I have some questions. Before we were interrupted, you said that you had picked up the Combat Group's trail. How did you manage that? That is one. What measures have you taken while I was sleeping? That is two. What is this plan of which you speak? That is three. How did you manage to escape? That is four.'

'I escaped in an original manner, which I omitted to describe in my report to our supreme ruler. By the way' – Pozharsky raised one finger significantly – 'there has been a fundamental change in our status. Following yesterday's attempt on our lives, we are now obliged to inform His Imperial Highness's chancellery directly of the progress of the investigation. Ah, look who I'm telling! A man like you, so far removed – *as yet* – from the exalted empyrean of St Petersburg, is quite incapable of appreciating the significance of this event.'

'I take your word for it. Then what was this manner? You were undressed and unarmed, as I was. You ran to the right, in the direction of the main entrance, but you wouldn't have had time to reach it; the terrorists would have filled your back full of holes.'

'Of course. And therefore I did not run towards the main entrance,' Gleb Georgievich said with a shrug. 'Naturally, I ducked into the ladies' section. I managed to skip through the changing room and the soaping room, although my indecent state provoked a great hullabaloo. But the fully clothed gentlemen who were chasing after me were less fortunate. The entire wrath of humanity's lovelier half was unleashed on their heads. I believe my pursuers were given a taste of boiling water, and sharp nails, and fierce jabs. In any case, there was no longer anyone pursuing me along the alley, although the promenading public did pay my modest person certain signs of attention. Fortunately, I did not have to run far to reach the police station, otherwise I should have been transformed into a snowman. The most difficult thing was persuading the officer in charge that I was the deputy director of police. But how did you manage to get out? – I've been racking my brains over that; I've combed every nook and cranny at Petrosov's, but I still can't understand it. The only place you can reach by the stairway that you ran up is the roof!'

'I was simply lucky,' Erast Petrovich replied evasively, and shuddered at the memory of that step into the empty void. He had to admit that the cunning Petersburgian had found a simpler and more ingenious way out of their difficulty.

Pozharsky opened the wardrobe and started throwing clothes on to the bed.

'Choose whatever fits you. And in the meantime, tell me this. Back there in room number six, you said that you were expecting the answer to the riddle very shortly. Does that mean you had anticipated the possibility of an attack? And was it supposed to tell you who the traitor is?'

Fandorin paused before he nodded.

'And who exactly was it?'

The prince looked searchingly at the State Counsellor, who had suddenly gone very pale.

'You have still not answered all of my questions,' Fandorin said eventually.

'Very well, then.' Pozharsky sat down on a chair and crossed his legs. 'I'll start from the very beginning. Naturally, you were right about the double agent, I realised that immediately. And, like yourself, I had only one suspect: our mysterious Diana.'

'B-But then why—'

Pozharsky raised his hand to indicate that he had anticipated the question and was about to answer it.

'So that you would not be concerned about any rivalry from my side. I confess, Erast Petrovich, that I am something of a moral freethinker. But then, you've known that for a long time already. Did you really think that I would go chasing around like a little puppy-dog, asking all the police agents and cab drivers idiotic questions? No, I inconspicuously installed myself in your wake, and you led me to the modest little townhouse on Arbat Street where our Medusa has her lodging. And don't go raising your eyebrows so indignantly! Of course, what I did was improper, but you know, your behaviour was not exactly comradely, was it? – telling me about Diana, but keeping the address secret? Is that what "working together" means?'

Fandorin decided it would be pointless to take offence. Firstly, this descendant of the Varangians had absolutely no concept of what conscience was. And secondly, it was his own fault – he ought to be more observant.

'I gave you the right of the first night,' the prince said with a mischievous smile. 'You, however, did not linger for long in the delightful rose's abode. But when you left the said abode you had such a satisfied look that I felt quite wickedly envious. Could Fandorin really have gutted her already, I wondered, as quickly as that? But no, from the way the enchantress behaved, I realised that you had come away with nothing.'

'You spoke with her?' asked the State Counsellor, astonished.

Pozharsky laughed, apparently deriving genuine pleasure from this conversation.

'Not only spoke – Good Lord, his eyebrows have shot up again! You have a reputation as Moscow's leading Don Juan, and yet you don't understand women at all. Our poor Diana had been orphaned; she suddenly felt abandoned and unwanted. She used to have such distinguished, influential suitors hovering around her, but now she was just an ordinary collaborator, except that she had taken her dangerous game too far. Did she not try to make you her new protector? There, I can see from your blush that she did. I am not so conceited as to imagine that she fell in love with me at first glance. But you spurned the poor woman, and I did not. For which I was rewarded in full measure. Ladies, Erast Petrovich, are at the same time far more complicated and far simpler than we think.'

'Then Diana was the traitor?' Fandorin gasped. 'It's not possible!'

'She was, she was, my dear chap. In psychological terms it is very easy to explain, especially now, when all the circumstances have become clear. She imagined that she was Circe, the sovereign mistress of all men. It was exceedingly flattering to her vanity that she could toy just as she chose with the fate of such dread organisations, and the very Empire itself. I believe that gave Diana quite as much erotic pleasure as her amorous adventures did. Or, rather, they complemented each other.'

'But how did you manage to make her c-confess?' asked Erast Petrovich, still stunned.

'I told you: women are constituted far more simply than Messrs Turgenev and Dostoevsky would have us believe. Forgive my vulgar boasting, but in the hierarchy of love, I am not a mere aide-de-camp, but a field marshal at least. I know how to drive a woman insane, especially if she is greedy for sensual pleasure. At first I employed all my talents to transform Mademoiselle Diana into a melting ice cream, then I was suddenly transformed from syrup into steel. I adduced the facts in my possession and frightened her a little, but most effective of all was the sunlight. I drew back the curtains and her strength was drained completely, like a vampire's.'

'B-But why? Did you see her face? And who was she?'

'Oho, you'll find that very interesting,' said the prince, laughing at something or other. 'You'll realise straightaway what all the mystery was about. But we'll come back to that later. Well then, it turned out that Diana was getting secret information from Burlyaev and Sverchinsky and transmitting it to the terrorists in the Combat Group by means of notes. She signed her notes "TG", which means Terpsichore the Goddess, who, as you no doubt remember, lived with the other Muses on Mount Helicon. Quite an original touch of humour, don't you think?' Pozharsky sighed. 'It was only afterwards that I realised why she launched into her confessions so readily. She knew about our meeting at the baths and was certain that neither you nor I would emerge from it alive. She calculated that I would want to use her to catch the terrorists. And she was right. An artful creature, I grant her that. No doubt she had a good laugh at my air of triumph as well.'

'So you told her that you and I would be in room number six?' Erast Petrovich asked, his face brightening.

But the bright little ray of hope was immediately extinguished.

'That's just the point: I didn't. I didn't tell Diana anything about that at all. But she did know about our meeting, there's no doubt at all about it. Later that night, when I went back to Diana's, ablaze with the thirst for vengeance, she gaped at me as if I had risen from hell. That was when I realised. She knew, the vile beast, she knew. But this time I acted more cleverly and left one of my men to watch her. While one was here, on guard duty with you, the other was watching Diana. But really, how *did* she find out about room number six?' Pozharsky asked, returning to the unpleasant subject. 'You didn't tell anyone in the Department or the Office, did you? She must have someone else, apart from Burlyaev and Sverchinsky.'

'No, I didn't t-tell anyone in the Department or the Office about room number six,' Fandorin replied, choosing his words carefully.

The prince inclined his head to one side: his straw-coloured hair and his coal-back eyes made him look like a performing poodle.

'Well, well. And now for my plan, in which you have been given absolutely the most pivotal part to play. Thanks to the insidious Diana, we know where the Combat Group is hiding. In fact the apartment belongs to Diana, but our collaborator has not lived there for a long time. She finds life more interesting beneath an official roof.'

'You know where the CG is hiding?' Erast Petrovich froze with his arm halfway into the sleeve of a blue frock coat that appeared to be cut to his size. 'And you haven't detained them yet?'

'Do I look to you like that idiot Burlyaev, God rest his soul?' the prince asked with a reproachful shake of his head. 'There are seven of them, all armed to the teeth. It would be another battle of Borodino; we'd have to rebuild Moscow again afterwards, like they did in the twelfth century. No, Erast Petrovich. We'll take them nice and neatly, and choose a time and place that suit us.'

Having finished dressing, Fandorin sat down on the bed, facing the enterprising deputy director of police, and prepared to listen.

'This evening, about three hours ago, another note was left

at our partisans' apartment. What it said was: "You botched it. You let them both get away. But you have a chance to redeem your error. Pozharsky and Fandorin are having another secret meeting tomorrow. In Briusov Square, at nine in the morning." After the miraculous agility that you and I demonstrated at the baths, Mr Green will throw his entire army against us, we need have no doubt about that. Do you know Briusov Square, with the public park?'

'Yes. An excellent place f-for an ambush,' the State Counsellor admitted. 'In the morning it is empty; no innocent bystanders will be hurt. Blank walls on three sides. The marksmen can be positioned on the roofs.'

'And on the battlements of the St Simeon Monastery – the archimandriite has already given his blessing for such a godly cause. As soon as they enter the square, we seal off the street too. We'll manage without any gendarmes. At dawn the Flying Squad arrives from St Petersburg, I've summoned them. They're genuine Mamelukes, the cream of the Police Department, the best of the best. Not a single terrorist will get away; we'll wipe them out to the last man.'

Erast Petrovich frowned: 'Without even t-trying to arrest them?'

'Are you joking? We have to fire without warning, in salvoes. Shoot them all, like mad dogs. Otherwise we'll lose some of our men.'

'It's our men's job to risk their lives,' the State Counsellor declared obstinately. 'And it's illegal to carry through an operation like this without giving them a chance to lay down their arms.'

'Damn you, then we'll give them a chance. Only you must realise that the risk to you will be greater as a result.' Pozharsky smiled mischievously and explained: 'Under the plan of action you, my dearest Erast Petrovich, have been awarded the honourable role of the live bait. You will sit on a bench, supposedly waiting for me. Let the CG start to nibble and move in a bit closer to you. They won't kill you before I put in an appearance. After all – pardon my lack of modesty – for them the deputy director of police is a daintier morsel than a Moscow functionary, even if he does deal with special assignments. But I shall not present myself to their gaze until the trap has snapped shut. I shall observe all the requirements of the law. Of course, they won't even think of surrendering, but my announcement will be the signal for you to jump up and take shelter.'

'T-Take shelter? Where?' asked Fandorin, screwing up his blue eyes. He had found Gleb Georgievich's plan excellent in absolutely every respect, except one: for a certain State Counsellor the road from the park in Briusov Square would lead directly to the cemetery.

'Did you think I'd decided to leave you there, facing a hail of bullets?' Pozharsky asked in an offended tone. 'All the preparations have already been made; they couldn't possibly be improved upon. You sit on the third bench from the entrance to the square. To the right of it is a snowdrift. And under the snow is a pit. In fact, it's the beginning of a trench that leads back all the way to the street. They're going to lay sewer pipes in it. I ordered the trench to be covered over with boards and then piled over with snow, it's invisible now. But there's only thin plywood under the snowdrift beside the bench. As soon as I appear in the square, you jump straight into the snow and astound the watching terrorists by disappearing through the ground. Then you make your way along the trench under the battlefield to the street and climb out, without a scratch. How's that for a plan?' the prince asked proudly, and then suddenly became concerned. 'Or perhaps you're not well after all? Or you don't wish to expose yourself to such a risk. If you are afraid, then speak out. No need to put on a brave face.'

'It's a good p-plan. And the risk is quite moderate.'

Fandorin was in the grip of a feeling stronger than fear. The imminent operation, the risk, the shooting – they were all trifles in comparison with the weight that had suddenly come crashing down on Erast Petrovich: the terrorists had burst into room number six, not any other, and there could be only one explanation ...

'I have a suggestion,' said the prince, pulling his watch out of his waistcoat pocket by the chain. The hour is already late, but I assume you have slept your fill, and I can never get to sleep before a serious operation. Nerves. Why don't we pay a visit to our lovely little recluse? I'll show her to you in the light. I can promise you will find the effect most impressive.'

The State Counsellor gritted his teeth. These final words, which seemed to him to be spoken in a deliberately casual manner, had finally torn the veil away from poor Erast Petrovich's eyes.

Oh God! How could You be so cruel?

That was the reason for the darkness and the veil, the reason for the whispering!

And Pozharsky's behaviour finally made sense. Why would such an ambitious man have waited until his colleague finally came round? He could have invented a different plan of operations, without involving the Moscow functionary at all. Then he would not have had to share the glory. But apparently he would not have to anyway. The last thing Fandorin would be interested in was glory.

Pozharsky was not merely a careerist. Success in his job was not enough for him: he needed the feeling of victory over everything and everyone. He always had to be the first. And now he had an excellent opportunity to trample down and destroy a man whom he was bound to see as a serious rival.

And there was nothing with which Fandorin could reproach the prince – except perhaps excessive cruelty; but that was an intrinsic feature of his character.

The doomed State Counsellor got to his feet, ready to drain the cup of humiliation to the dregs.

'Very well, let's go.'

The door of the Arbat Street townhouse opened as they approached. A quiet gentleman, who looked very much like the one who had been sitting by the bed, bowed briefly and announced: 'She's in the study. I locked the door. I took her to the water closet once. She asked for water twice. That's all.'

'I see, Korzhikov. You can go back to the hotel. Catch up on

your sleep. His Excellency and I will manage on our own here.'
And he winked conspiratorially at Erast Petrovich, provoking in
him a fleeting but very powerful desire to take the scoffer's neck
in both hands and snap the vertebrae that link together body
and soul.

'Now, I shall introduce you anew to the celebrated breaker
of men's hearts, actress of unsurpassed talent and mysterious
beauty.' Pozharsky laughed malevolently as he set off up the
stairs first.

He unlocked the familiar door, stepped inside and turned the
lever of the gas bracket. The room was flooded with gently
flickering light.

'Well, mademoiselle, why don't you turn round?' Gleb
Georgievich asked derisively, addressing an individual whom
Fandorin, still in the corridor, could not see.

'What!' the prince suddenly roared. 'Korzhikov, you dolt, I'll
see you in court for this!'

He darted into the room and from the doorway the State
Counsellor saw a slim female figure standing motionless, facing
the window. The woman's head was inclined melancholically to
one side, and the figure only appeared motionless at first glance.
A second glance revealed that it was swaying slightly from side
to side, and the feet were not quite touching the floor.

'Esfir . . .' Erast Petrovich whispered, overcome. 'Oh God . . .'

The prince took a knife out of his pocket, slashed the rope,
and the body slumped to the floor, flapping its arms with the
inanimate grace of a rag doll and banging its forehead against
the parquet floor before becoming truly motionless.

'Ah, damn.' Pozharsky squatted down and clicked his tongue
in annoyance. 'She had outlived her usefulness, but even so it's
a pity. She was a quite remarkable character. And I wanted to
give you a little treat . . . Well, now's there's nothing to be done,
you'll see this beauty already withered and faded.'

He took the dead woman by the shoulders and turned her on
to her back.

Erast Petrovich involuntarily squeezed his eyes shut, but then,
ashamed of his own weakness, he forced himself to open them.

The sudden shock of what he saw made him squeeze them shut again. And then he began fluttering his eyelashes in consternation.

Fandorin had never seen the woman lying on the floor before – once seen, a face like that could never be forgotten. One half of it was perfectly normal and even rather pretty in a way, but the features of the other half were flattened and squashed, so that the slit of the eye was set almost vertically, and the cheek bone overlapped the ear.

Pozharsky laughed, very pleased with the effect produced.

'Lovely, isn't she, the she-devil? A birth trauma. The obstetrician grabbed her clumsily with the forceps. Now do you understand Mademoiselle Diana's reason for behaving the way she did? What else could she feel for the men who recoiled from her in horror in the light of day? What else but hate? That's why she liked to live in this enchanted castle, this realm of gloom and silence. Here she was not an unfortunate freak, but the most radiant beauty that any man's imagination could possibly conjure up. Brrrr!' Gleb Georgievich shuddered as he looked at that terrible mask and complained. 'It's all very well for you, but when I think that I spent half of yesterday gratifying a monster like that, it gives me the shivers.'

Erast Petrovich stood there in state of total emotional numbness, still stunned by the shock, but he already knew that the first emotion he would feel as soon as his heart recovered slightly would be acute shame.

'But then, it's quite possible that in hell, where the newly departed has undoubtedly gone, it is precisely her kind that are regarded as the foremost beauties,' the prince remarked philosophically. 'Anyway, our plan remains in force, Erast Petrovich. Don't forget: the snowdrift is on the right.'

CHAPTER 14

The pit

Pozharsky was late.

Six minutes past nine. Green put his watch back in the pocket of his greatcoat. His Colt was in there too, and his fingers folded firmly round the comfortably fluted butt.

The revolution wasn't in such a bad way after all, if the top brass of the criminal investigation authorities were obliged to meet like conspirators, in secret from their own subordinates. The enemy's camp had been plunged into alarm and uncertainty; everyone there was afraid of his own shadow; they didn't trust anyone. And they were right not to.

Or did they have their suspicions about TG?

It was all very simple. No cause could ever triumph if its supporters were more concerned for their own well-being than anything else. That was why the victory of the revolution was inevitable.

Only you won't live to see it, Green reminded himself, in order to drive that azure blue back deep inside, the azure that had been struggling so hard to rise to the surface after what had happened yesterday. *You are a match, and you've already been burning for longer than usual. And you yourself excluded the joys of life from your own existence.*

State Counsellor Fandorin was sitting on the next bench, tapping one glove on his knee in his boredom, gazing at the jackdaws hopping about in the branches of an old oak tree.

This handsome, foppishly dressed man was about to die. And it would be impossible ever to find out what he had been thinking about during the final minutes of his life.

Green shuddered at this unexpected thought. *When you're*

training your sights on the enemy, you mustn't think about his mother and his children, he thought, reminding himself of what he had told Bullfinch many times. Once a man had put on the enemy's uniform, he was no longer a civilian, but a soldier.

The greatcoat that Green was wearing was thick, made of good cloth. Nobel had brought it from home – his father was a retired general. Needle had glued on Green's grey moustache and sideburns – an excellent disguise.

There was Bullfinch walking along the path of the park, dressed as a grammar-school boy. He was supposed to have checked the street to make sure everything was clear. As he walked past, he nodded lightly and then sat down on the bench beside Fandorin. He scooped up some fresh snow and crammed it into his mouth. He was nervous.

Nobel and Schwartz were scraping down the avenue with spades. Emelya was standing on the other side of the railings, pretending to be a police constable. Marat and Beaver, dressed in artisans' kaftans and felt boots, were playing at stick-knife right beside the entrance to the park. Pozharsky and Fandorin had chosen an excellent time for their talk: no strollers, not even any chance passers-by.

'You can go whistle for your three kopecks! That for your money,' Marat shouted, cocking a snook and jumping to one side. And he set off along the avenue, whistling, casually sticking his hands in his pockets as he went.

That was the signal; it meant Pozharsky had shown up.

Beaver went rushing at Marat: 'What d'you think you're playing at?' he shouted (Beaver was a fine, calm young lad, an ex-student). 'Come on, pay up!' And behind him the long-awaited deputy director of police appeared. Wearing a Guards greatcoat, a white royal-retinue cap, with a sabre. A fine conspirator.

Pozharsky stopped at the entrance to the square, planted his bright, gleaming boots in a wide stance, grasped his sword belt in picturesque fashion and shouted: 'Nihilist gentlemen! You are completely surrounded! I recommend you to surrender!' And that very second he ducked nimbly behind the fence and disappeared behind the snow-covered bushes.

Green glanced round at Fandorin, but the State Counsellor, suddenly roused from his reverie, also displayed remarkable agility. He grabbed Bullfinch by the collar and pulled him close, and then for some strange reason plunged into the tall snowdrift on the right of his bench.

Suddenly there was a tremendous rumbling and crashing from all sides, as if someone were ripping the very world in half.

Green saw Marat throw up his hands and jerk violently, as if he had been struck hard in the back. He saw Beaver firing from under his elbow, aiming somewhere upwards and off to one side.

He grabbed the Colt out of his pocket and went dashing to help Bullfinch. A bullet knocked his hat off his head and grazed his temple. Green swayed, lost his balance and collapsed into the snowdrift on the left of the next bench.

What happened next was quite incredible.

The snowdrift proved to be much deeper than he could have imagined from its appearance. There was a loud crack from somewhere, for a moment everything went dark, and then he landed hard on some solid surface. An avalanche of white immediately collapsed on him, and Green began floundering about in it, completely unable to understand what was happening.

When he somehow managed to get to his feet, he saw that he was standing in a deep pit, buried up to his chest in snow. He could see the sky, the clouds, the branches of the trees. The shooting was even louder now, and he could almost make out the individual shots, snatched up and amplified by the echo.

Up above there was a battle going on, and here was he, the man of steel, sheltering in a trench!

Green jumped up and his fingers touched the edge of the pit, but there was nothing to grab hold of. Then he discovered that he had lost his revolver in the fall, and searching for it in the snowy mush looked as if it would be long job, perhaps even a hopeless one.

Never mind, if only he could just clamber out somehow.

He started furiously tamping down the snow – with his hands, his feet, even his buttocks. And then suddenly the firing stopped.

The silence made Green afraid for the first time in many long years. He'd thought he would never again feel that chilly, heart-stopping sensation.

Was it really all over? So quickly?

He climbed on to the hard-tamped snow and stuck his head up out of the pit, but immediately squatted back down again. There was a line of men in civilian clothes walking towards the railings, holding smoking carbines and revolvers in their hands.

You couldn't even shoot yourself without a gun. Just sit there, like a wolf who's fallen into a trap, and wait for them to drag you out by the scruff of the neck.

He squatted down and began fumbling about feverishly in the snow. If he could only find it, if he could only find it. Just at that moment Green could not imagine any greater happiness.

Hopeless. The revolver was probably somewhere right at the very bottom.

Swinging round, Green suddenly saw a black hole that led off somewhere to one side. Without even pausing for thought, he stepped into it and realised it was an underground passage: narrow, a little higher than the height of a man, smelling of frozen earth.

He had no time to feel surprise.

He ran into the darkness, with his shoulders bumping against the walls of the passage.

Quite soon, after about fifty strides, he saw a glimmer of light up ahead. Moving faster, he suddenly found himself in an open trench. It was screened off with planks, and up above it on the stone wall of a building there was a sign: 'Möbius and Sons. Colonial Goods'.

Then Green remembered: in the side street that led to the square, there had been some kind of trench, with a hastily cobbled together wooden fence along its edges. That was where he was.

He clambered out of the trench. The side street was empty, but he could hear the sound of many voices from the square.

He pressed himself against the wall of the building and peeped round the corner.

The men in civilian clothes were dragging bodies on to the

avenue of the park. Green saw two agents dragging along a policeman, and didn't immediately realise who it was, because the skirts of the dead man's greatcoat had turned up to conceal his face. A thick book in a familiar binding fell out from behind his lapel: *The Count of Monte Cristo*. Emelya had brought it with him to the operation – he'd been afraid they might not be going back to the apartment and he wouldn't find out if the count ever took his revenge on the traitors or not.

'What is all this, eh?' a frightened voice asked behind Green.

It was a yard-keeper, sticking his head out from a gateway. Wearing an apron, and his metal badge. He looked at the man covered in snow and explained guiltily: 'I'm just staying put, not sticking my head out, like we were told. Who was that you got, eh? Khitrovka gangsters? Bombers?'

'Bombers,' Green replied, and set off along the street at a fast walk.

It was still very early.

'We're leaving,' he said to Needle when she opened the door. 'Quick.'

She turned pale, but didn't ask any questions, just dashed to put her shoes on.

Green took two revolvers, cartridges, the jar of explosive mixture and several detonators. The finished casings had to be left behind.

Not until they were down in the street and safely round the corner did it finally become clear that the apartment was not surrounded. The police had obviously been certain that the Combat Group would come to the trap and decided to avoid external surveillance, in order not to give themselves away by accident.

'Where to?' Green asked. 'Not to a hotel. They'll be looking.'

Needle hesitated and then said: 'To my house. Only . . . Never mind, you'll see for yourself.'

She told the cab driver to take them to Count Dobrinsky's house on Prechistenka Street.

On the way, Green told her in a low voice what had happened

at Briusov Square. Needle's face never quivered, but the tears streamed down her cheeks one after another.

The sleigh stopped in front of a large, old pair of cast-iron gates embellished with a crown. Through the railings Green could see a yard and a large three-storey palace that had probably once been gorgeous and magnificent, but now its paint had flaked off and it was clearly abandoned.

'Nobody lives there; the doors are boarded up,' Needle explained, as if she were making excuses. 'When my father died, I let all the servants go. But I can't sell it. My father entailed the house to my son. If I have one. And if I don't, when I die it goes to the Council of the Order of St George ...'

So what they said about Conjuror's fiancée was true: she was a count's daughter, Green thought absent-mindedly, his mind gradually stealing up on the most important question.

Needle led him past the locked gates and along the railings to a little annexe with a mezzanine, one wing of which reached right out to the street.

'The family doctor used to live here,' said Needle. 'Now I do. Alone.' But he was no longer listening.

He followed her through some room without even bothering to look around him. He sat down in an armchair.

'What do we do now?' Needle asked.

'I have to think for a while,' Green replied in a steady voice.

'Can I sit beside you? I won't bother you ...'

But she did bother him. Her gentle, turquoise gaze would not allow his mind to organise itself; all sorts of peripheral and entirely unnecessary thoughts crowded into his head. With an effort of will, Green forced himself not to stray from a straight line and concentrate on the essential task. The essential task was called TG. And apart from Green there was no one to solve it.

What did he have to work on?

Only his own well-trained memory. That was where he should look.

TG had sent eight letters altogether.

The first had been about Bogdanov, the Governor of Ekaterinburg. It had arrived soon after the unsuccessful attempt on Khrapov's life, on 23 September last year. Appeared out of nowhere on the dining table of the clandestine apartment on Fontanka Street. Written on an Underwood typewriter.

The second had been about general of gendarmes Selivanov. It had simply turned up in the pocket of Green's coat in December last year. At a party 'wedding'. The typewriter was an Underwood again.

The third had been about Pozharsky and the unnamed 'important agent', who had turned out to be Stasov, a member of the Central Committee in exile. It had been found on the floor in the clandestine apartment on Vasilievsky Island in St Petersburg on 15 January. The same typewriter.

The fourth had been about Khrapov. At the Kolpino dacha. Emelya had picked up the note that was wrapped round a stone, lying under the open window. That was on 16 February. TG had used an Underwood again.

So, the first four letters had been received in St Petersburg, and almost five months had passed between the first and the last. But in Moscow TG's pace had been feverish – four letters in four days.

The fifth had been about Rahmet, and it had said Sverchinsky would be at the Nikolaevsky Station that night. It came on Tuesday the nineteenth. Once again, just as at the 'wedding', in some mysterious manner it had appeared in the pocket of his coat while it was hanging up. The typewriter had changed; this time it was a Remington No. 5. The Underwood had evidently been left behind in Peter.

The sixth had been about the police blockade at the railway goods sheds and the new apartment. That was on Wednesday the twentieth. The letter was brought by Matvei, who found it in the pocket of his sheepskin coat. It was typed on a Remington.

The seventh had been about the Petrosov Baths. Dropped through the door on 21 February. The Remington again.

The last one, the eighth, luring them into the trap, had arrived in the same way. That was yesterday, Friday. The typewriter was a Remington.

What followed from all this?

Why had TG first provided invaluable help, and then betrayed him?

For the same reason as others turned traitor: he had been arrested and broken. Or he had been discovered and deliberately fed false information. Never mind, that was irrelevant.

The important question was: who was he?

In four cases out of eight TG or his intermediary had been in Green's immediate vicinity. In the other four, for some reason he hadn't wanted to come close to Green, or hadn't been able to, and he had acted, not from the inside, but from the outside: through an open window, through the door, through Matvei. Well, the situation at Kolpino was clear enough: after the January expropriation Green had put the group in quarantine and they had stayed at the dacha without going anywhere or seeing anyone.

But in Moscow TG had only had direct access to Green on one occasion, 19 February, when Ace gave his briefing before the attack on the state currency-shipping carriage. After that for some reason TG no longer had direct access. What had happened between Tuesday and Wednesday?

Green jerked upright in his chair, suddenly struck by the arithmetical simplicity of the solution. Why hadn't he thought of it before! Because there simply hadn't been that genuine, absolute necessity that lends such a wonderfully keen edge to the workings of thought.

'What is it?' Needle asked in fright. 'Are you feeling unwell?'

Without answering, he grabbed a pencil and a sheet of paper from the table. He paused for about a minute, then quickly dashed off a few lines and wrote an address at the top.

'This is for the telegraph office. The extra urgent rate.'

CHAPTER 15

in which Fandorin learns to be flexible

Green was not as Erast Petrovich had imagined him to be. The State Counsellor could not see anything fiendish or especially bloodthirsty about the man sitting on the next bench. A severe face, its features stamped in metal, a face that was hard to imagine smiling. And quite young still, despite the clumsy masquerade with that grey moustache and those sideburns.

Apart from Fandorin himself and the terrorists, Briusov Square seemed to be completely empty. Pozharsky had chosen an excellent spot for the operation. There was a policeman, undoubtedly someone in disguise, strolling along on the other side of the railings. Two young yard-keepers with unnaturally long beards and remarkably cultured expressions on their faces were clumsily scraping away snow with plywood spades. A little further away another two young lads were playing stick-knife, but they didn't really seem very interested in the game – they kept looking round far too often.

It was after nine already, but Pozharsky was taking his time. He was obviously waiting for the youngest of the terrorists, the one playing the part of a grammar-school boy, to come back.

And there he was now. He whistled as he walked across the avenue, sat down only an arm's length away from Erast Petrovich, right beside the snowdrift with the pit, and greedily thrust a handful of snow into his mouth. *Would you believe it*, the State Counsellor thought, *no more than a child, and already a seasoned killer!* Unlike the fake general, the 'schoolboy' looked perfectly convincing. He must be Bullfinch.

Pozharsky appeared, and the stick-knife players began drifting towards the centre of the park. Erast Petrovich focused his inner energies for action.

The prince shouted his offer for the nihilists to surrender and Fandorin sprang nimbly to his feet, effortlessly grabbed the 'schoolboy' by the collar of his coat and dragged him down into the refuge of the snowdrift. It was too soon for the boy to die.

The snow received the State Counsellor softly, but did not admit him very far – barely much more than an *arshin*, in fact. Bullfinch fell on top of him and began floundering about, but it was not easy to break free of Erast Petrovich's strong hands.

Shots thundered out from every side. Fandorin knew that the marksmen of the Flying Squad, reinforced by Mylnikov's agents, were firing from the monastery walls and the surrounding roofs, and they would not cease firing as long as there was anything left alive and moving in the square.

Where was the pit that had been promised?

Erast Petrovich applied gentle pressure to one of the young terrorist's nerve points to stop him kicking and struggling, then struck the ground with his fist – once, twice, three times. If it had been plywood there, under the snow, it would have yielded and sprung back, but no, the solid ground remained solid.

The 'schoolboy' no longer attempted to break free, but from time to time he jerked, as if stung by an electric shock, although there was no real reason why he should – Fandorin had not pressed the nerve point hard, only just enough for ten minutes of total calm.

Several times bullets slammed into the snow, too close for comfort, with a furious hissing sound. Erast Petrovich hammered ever more furiously on the unyielding plywood and even tried to bounce up and down on it, as far as that was possible in a lying position, with a load to support. The pit stubbornly refused to open up. Either the plywood had hardened to oak overnight, or something else had gone wrong.

Meanwhile the shooting had started to thin out and soon it died away completely.

He heard voices in the avenue: 'This one's a goner. A regular tea-strainer.'

'This one too. Just look at the way his face is all twisted and torn, unidentifiable.'

To climb out of the snowdrift would have been imprudent – they would have put a dozen bullets in him instantly – and so Erast Petrovich called out without getting up: 'Gentlemen, I am Fandorin, do not shoot!'

And only then, having set aside the peacefully sleeping Bull-finch, did he stand up, thinking that he probably looked like a snowman.

The park was full of men in civilian clothes. There must have been fifty of them at least, and he could see more outside the railings.

'Wiped out the lot, Your Honour,' said one of the 'flyers', who had a youthful air despite his grey moustache. 'No one left to arrest.'

'There is one still alive,' Erast Petrovich replied, dusting himself off. 'T-Take him and lay him out on a bench.'

The agents took hold of the 'schoolboy', but dropped him again immediately. The snow on his coat was stained red with blood in several places, and there was a black hole in his forehead, just below the hair line. It was clear now what had made the poor boy twitch so violently.

Erast Petrovich gazed in bewilderment at the lifeless body that had shielded him from the bullets, and failed to notice Pozharsky swooping down on him from behind.

'Alive? Thank God!' Pozharsky shouted, putting his arms round Fandorin's shoulders. 'I'd given up hope! Now for God's sake tell me what on earth made you jump into the snowdrift on the left? I told you a hundred times: jump into the one on the right, on the right! It's an absolute miracle you weren't hit!'

'That is the snowdrift on the right, there!' the State Counsellor exclaimed indignantly, recalling his vain attempts to jump up and down in a lying position. 'And that's the one I j-jumped into!'

The prince began batting his eyelids, his gaze shifted from Fandorin to the bench, to the snowdrift, then back to Fandorin, and he started chuckling uncertainly.

'Why yes, of course. I never sat on the bench, I only looked at it from here. Here I am, and there's the snowdrift, on the right of the bench. But if you sit down, then of course it's on your left ... Oh, it's too much! Two wise men ... two great strategists ...'

And the deputy director of police folded over in a paroxysm of irresistible, choking laughter – no doubt the result, in part at least, of nervous strain.

Erast Petrovich smiled, because Gleb Georgievich's laughter was infectious, but his gaze was caught once again by the slim figure in the school coat and he suddenly became serious.

'Where's G-Green?' he asked. 'He was sitting right there, dressed up as a retired general.'

'There isn't one like that, Your Honour,' the man with the grey moustache said with a frown, turning towards the bodies laid out along the avenue. 'One, two, three, four, five, and the schoolboy makes six. No more. Ah, damnation, where's number seven? There were seven of them!'

The prince was no longer laughing. He looked around despairingly, gritted his teeth and groaned. 'He got away! Got away through the trench. So much for our victory. And in my mind I'd already composed the report: "No losses. Combat Group completely annihilated".'

He grabbed hold of Fandorin's arm and squeezed it tight. 'Disaster, Erast Petrovich, disaster. We're left holding the lizard's tail, but the lizard has fled. And it will grow a new tail – it wouldn't be the first time.'

'What are we g-going to do?' asked the State Counsellor, his anxious blue eyes gazing into the prince's equally anxious black ones.

'*You* are not going to do anything,' Gleb Georgievich replied listlessly. His triumphant air was gone; he seemed somehow faded and very tired now. 'You go and light a candle in a church, because today the Lord has granted you a miracle, and then rest. I'm no good for anything much at the moment, and you're even worse. The only hope is that our agents will pick him up somewhere. He won't go back to the apartment, of course – he's no fool. We'll have everyone who's red, pink, or even light magenta under secret surveillance. All the hotels too. But I'm going back to mine, to sleep. If anything comes up, they'll wake me, and I'll let you know. Only it's not very likely . . .' He gestured hopelessly. 'We'll start scheming again tomorrow morning. But for today, that's it: *je passe.*'

Erast Petrovich did not go to light a candle in a church, because that was superstition, nor did he feel that he had any right to rest. Duty required that he take himself off to the Governor General's residence: for various reasons beyond his control, it was four days since he had last shown his face there, and he needed to present a detailed report on progress made in the search and the investigation.

However, it was unthinkable to appear in His Excellency's residence smothered in snow, with a torn collar and a crumpled top hat, so first he had to go back home, but only for half an hour at the most. At a quarter past eleven Fandorin entered His Excellency's reception room, wearing a fresh frock coat and an immaculate shirt with a white tie.

There was no one in the spacious room apart from the prince's secretary, and the State Counsellor was on the point of following his usual habit and entering unannounced when Innokentii Andreevich cleared his throat in an emphatically discreet manner and warned him: 'Erast Petrovich, His Excellency has a lady visitor.'

Fandorin leaned down over the table and wrote a note on a piece of paper:

Vladimir Andreevich, I am ready to report on today's operation and all the events that preceded it.

E.F.

'Please g-give him this immediately,' he said to the bespectacled pen-pusher, who bowed as he took the note and slipped in through the door of the study.

Fandorin took up a position right in front of the door, certain that he would be admitted immediately, but the secretary slipped back out and returned to his seat without saying a word to him.

'Did Vladimir Andreevich read it?' the State Counsellor enquired in annoyance.

'That I don't know, although I did whisper to His Excellency that the note was from you.'

Erast Petrovich nodded and began striding impatiently across the carpet – once, twice. The door remained closed.

'Who is it in there with him?' Fandorin asked, unable to contain himself.

'A lady. Young and very beautiful,' said Innokentii Andreevich, gladly setting aside his pen and seeming quite intrigued himself. 'I don't know her name, she went through without being announced; Frol Grigorievich showed her in.'

'So Vedishchev is in there too?'

The secretary did not have to answer, because the tall white doors opened with a quiet creak and Vedishschev himself came out into the reception room.

'Frol Vedishchev, I have urgent business for His Excellency, business of extreme importance!' Fandorin declared irritably. Prince Dogorukoi's valet responded in mysterious fashion: first he put one finger to his lips and then, using the same finger, he beckoned to Erast Petrovich to follow him, and hobbled off nimbly along the corridor in his low felt boots.

The State Counsellor shrugged and followed the old man, thinking to himself: *Perhaps they are right in St Petersburg when they complain that the Moscow administration is turning senile in its old age.*

Vedishchev opened five doors one after another and made several turns to the right and the left, until he finally emerged into a narrow little corridor, which Fandorin knew connected the Governor General's study with the inner apartments.

Here Frol Grigorievich stopped, put his finger to his lips once again and gave a low door a gentle push. It opened slightly without making a sound, and Fandorin discovered that the narrow crack allowed him an excellent view of everything that was happening in the room.

Dolgorukoi was seated with his back towards Erast Petrovich, and sitting in front of him, quite remarkably close, was a lady. Strictly speaking, there was no distance between them at all – the female visitor had her face buried in His Excellency's chest, and from behind the shoulder, with its gold epaulette, all that could be seen was the top of her head. The only sound breaking the silence was a miserable sobbing, mingled with equally pitiful sniffing.

Fandorin glanced round at Vedishchev in puzzlement, and the valet suddenly did something very odd: he winked at the State Counsellor with his wrinkled eye. Totally bewildered now, Erast Petrovich took another look through the narrow crack of the door. He saw the prince raise his hand and gingerly stroke the crying woman's black hair.

'Come now, my darling, that's enough,' His Excellency said affectionately. 'You were right to come to this old man and unburden your soul. And right to have a little cry too. I'll tell you what to do about him. Put him out of your heart completely. He's no match for you. Or anyone else, for that matter. You're a forthright girl, passionate – you don't know how to live by halves. But he – although I truly am very fond of him – he is not really alive somehow, as if he had been touched by hoar frost. Or sprinkled with ashes. You'll never thaw him out or bring him to life. Many have tried already. Take my advice, don't throw your heart away on him. Find yourself someone young and uncomplicated, straightforward. There's more happiness with someone like that. Believe what an old man tells you.'

Erast Petrovich listened to what the prince was saying, and his finely formed eyebrows shifted uncertainly towards the bridge of his nose.

'I don't want anyone straightforward,' the dark-haired visitor said in a tearful voice that was perfectly recognisable despite its distinct nasal twang. 'You don't understand anything; he's more alive than anyone I know. Only I'm afraid he doesn't know how to love. And I'm afraid all the time that he'll be killed . . .'

Fandorin listened to no more after that.

'Why did you bring me here?' he whispered furiously to Frol Grigorievich and walked rapidly out of the corridor.

Back in the reception room, the State Counsellor leaned so hard on his pen that the ink spattered across the paper as he wrote the Governor General a new note, substantially different from the previous one in both tone and content.

But before he could hand it to the secretary, the white door swung open and he heard Dolgorukoi's voice: 'Go, and God be with you. And remember my advice.'

'Good morning, Esfir Avessalomovna,' the State Counsellor said, bowing to the young beauty who had emerged from the study.

She measured him with a scornful glance. It was impossible even to imagine that this haughty creature had just been sobbing and sniffing like a primary-school girl cheated of her ice cream. Except perhaps for the fact that her eyes, still moist with tears, were gleaming more brightly than usual. The Queen of Sheba swept on and away without favouring Erast Petrovich with a reply.

'Ah,' Vladimir Andreevich sighed. 'If only I were sixty again . . . Come in, come in, my dear fellow. I'm sorry for making you wait.'

By tacit agreement, they did not mention the recent female visitor, but moved straight on to business.

'Circumstances have developed in such a way as to prevent me from coming to report to Your Excellency any sooner,' Fandorin began in an official tone of voice, but the Governor General took him by the elbow, sat him down in the armchair facing his own and said good-naturedly: 'I know everything. Frol has his well-wishers in the Department of Security and other places. I have received regular reports on your adventures. And I am also fully informed about today's battle. I received a communiqué from Collegiate Assessor Mylnikov, with all the details. A fine fellow, Evstratii Pavlovich – very keen to fill the vacancy left by Burlyaev. And why not? – I could have a little word with the Minister. I have already sent His Majesty an urgent despatch about today's heroic feats – a little sooner than that prince of yours. The most important thing in these cases is who submits his report first. I painted your valorous deed in the most glowing colours.'

'For which I am m-most humbly grateful,' Erast Petrovich replied, somewhat confused. 'However, I really have nothing very much to boast of. The most important c-criminal escaped.'

'He escaped, but six were neutralised. That's a great achievement, my dear fellow. It's a long time now since the police have had such a great success. And the victory was won here in Moscow, even if help was brought in from the capital. The sovereign will understand from my despatch that six terrorists were killed owing to your efforts, and the escape of the seventh was Pozharsky's blunder. I know how to compose despatches. I've been sailing the inky oceans for nigh on half a century now. Worry not, God is good. Perhaps they will realise up there' – the prince's wrinkled finger was jabbed upwards towards the ceiling in appeal to either the sovereign or the Lord – 'that it is too soon to throw Dolgorukoi out on the rubbish heap. Just let them try. And I also mentioned your long-delayed appointment as head police-master in my despatch. We'll see who comes out of this best . . .'

Erast Petrovich emerged from the Governor General's palace in a pensive state of mind. As he pulled on his gloves, he halted beside an advertising column and for no particular reason read an announcement set in huge type:

A Miracle of American Technology!

Edison's latest phonograph is to be demonstrated at the Polytechnical Museum. Mr Repman, head of the department of applied physics, will personally conduct an experiment in the recording of sound, for which he will perform an aria from 'A Life for the Tsar', Entrance fee 15 kopecks. The number of tickets is limited.

A snowball struck Erast Petrovich in the back. The State Counsellor swung round in amazement and saw a light two-seater sleigh standing beside the pavement. There was a black-eyed young lady in a sable coat sitting on the velvet seat, leaning against its curved back.

'Get in,' said the young lady. 'Let's go.'

'Been to tell tales to the boss, have we, Mademoiselle Litvinova?' Fandorin enquired with all the venom that he could muster.

'Erast, you're a fool,' she declared peremptorily. 'Shut up, or we'll quarrel again.'

'But what about His Excellency's advice?'

Esfir sighed. 'It's good advice. I'll definitely act on it. But not now. Later.'

Before he entered the large house on Tverskoi Boulevard that was known to everyone in Moscow, Fandorin halted, overwhelmed by his conflicting feelings. So now here it was, the appointment that had been spoken about for so long, in which Erast Petrovich had already ceased to believe. It had finally come to pass.

Half an hour earlier a courier had arrived at the outhouse on Malaya Nikitskaya Street, bowed to the State Counsellor, who had come to the door in his dressing gown, and informed him that he was expected immediately at the head police-master's residence. The invitation could mean only one thing: the Governor General's despatch of the previous day to the supreme ruler had produced an effect, and more quickly than anticipated.

Fandorin had tried to make as little noise as possible as he performed his morning ablutions, put on his uniform, complete with medals, and buckled on his sword – the occasion called for formality – and then, with a glance at the closed door of the bedroom, he had tiptoed out into the hallway.

In career terms, promotion to the position of the second most important individual in the old capital meant elevation to almost empyrean heights: quite certainly a general's rank, immense power, an enviable salary and – most important of all – a certain path to even more vertiginous heights in the future. However, this path was strewn with briars as well as roses, and in Fandorin's eyes the prickliest briar of all was the total loss of privacy. The head police-master was required to live in his official residence, which was grand, showy and uncomfortable – and also directly connected to the secretariat building; to participate as one of the central figures in numerous mandatory official functions (for instance, the gala opening of the Society for the Sponsorship of Public Sobriety was planned for the Week of the Adoration of the Cross, under the patronage of the city's foremost custodian of the law); and finally, to set the citizens of Moscow an example of moral living which, in view of his present personal circumstances, Erast Petrovich felt was a goal that would be hard to achieve.

All this meant that Erast Petrovich was obliged to summon up his courage before stepping across the threshold of his new residence and his new life. As usual, there was consolation to be found in a saying of the Wisest of All Sages: 'The superior man knows where his duty lies and does not attempt to shirk it.'

To shirk it was impossible, to draw things out was stupid, and so Erast Petrovich heaved a sigh and crossed that fatal boundary line marking the final countdown to his new career. He nodded to the saluting gendarme, cast a lingering glance around the familiar, elegant vestibule and shrugged off his fur coat into the arms of the doorman. The Governor General's sleigh should arrive any moment now. Vladimir Andreevich would show his protégé into the office and ceremonially present him with a seal, a medal on a chain and a symbolic key to the city – the formal attributes of the head police-master's authority.

'How touching of you to come in full uniform, and with all your medals,' a cheerful voice declared behind him. 'So you know already? And I wanted to surprise you.'

Pozharsky was standing on a short flight of four marble steps, dressed in a style that was far from formal – a morning coat and checked trousers – but with his lips set in a very broad smile.

'I accept your congratulations with gratitude,' he said with a humorous bow, 'although such solemnity is really rather excessive. Come into the office. I have something to show you.'

Erast Petrovich did not give himself away by so much as a single gesture, but when he happened to catch a glimpse in the mirror of the brilliant gleam of his medals and the gold embroidery on his uniform, he blushed painfully at his ignominious error. The Wisest of the Wise came to his assistance: 'When the world appears completely black, the superior man seeks for a small white speck in it.' The State Counsellor made an effort and the white speck was immediately found: at least now he would not be required to preside over public sobriety.

Without saying a word, Erast Petrovich followed Pozharsky into the head police-master's office and halted in the doorway, wondering where to sit – the divan and the armchairs were covered with dust sheets.

'I haven't had a chance to settle in yet. Here, let's use this,' said Pozharsky, pulling the white sheet off the divan. 'I received the telegram informing me of my appointment at dawn. But for you that's not the most important thing. This is ... a text for the newspapers, forwarded from St Petersburg. Intended for publication on the twenty-seventh. Dolgorukoi has already been sent the imperial edict. Read it.'

Erast Petrovich picked up the telegraph form with the official stamp 'Top Secret' and ran his eyes down the long column of paper ribbons glued closely together.

Today, on the supremely festive occasion of His Majesty the Sovereign Emperor's birthday, Moscow has been blessed as never before by the Tsar's beneficent favour: the Autocratic Ruler of Russia has placed the first capital city of His Empire in the direct charge of His Most August Brother, the Grand Duke Simeon Alexandrovich, by appointing His Highness as Governor General of Moscow.

There is profound historical significance in this appointment. Moscow enters once again into direct communion with the Most August House of the Russian Tsars. The centuries-old spiritual link between the leader of the Russian people and the ancient capital of Russia today assumes that external, palpable form which is of such profound importance for the clear national awareness of all the people.

Today the Sovereign Emperor has deemed it a boon to exalt even further Moscow's significance as a national palladium by appearing as His representative there none other than His Own Most August Brother.

Muscovites will never forget the easy accessibility for which Prince Vladimir Andreevich was so noted, the cordial consideration that he extended to all those who turned for him to help, the energy with which . . .

'Have you read the bit about easy accessibility?' asked Pozharsky, evidently impatient to proceed with the conversation. 'You don't need to read any more; there's a lot, but it's all froth. So there you are, Erast Petrovich: your patron's finished. And now the time has come for the two of us finally to clarify our relationship. From now on Moscow changes, and it will never again be the same as it was under your amiable Dolgorukoi. Genuine authority is being established in the city, firm power, without any of that "easy accessibility". Your boss failed to understand the true nature of power, he failed to distinguish between its sacred and practical functions, with the result that your city became bogged down in its old patriarchal habits and was making no progress at all towards the new century approaching.'

The prince spoke seriously, with energy and conviction. This was probably what he was really like, when he wasn't playing the hypocrite or being cunning.

'Sacred authority will be represented in Moscow by His Highness, my patron, whose interests I have actually represented here from the very beginning. I can now speak about that openly, without dissimulation. The Grand Duke is a man of a somewhat dreamy cast of mind, with rather distinctive tastes, about which you have no doubt already heard.'

Erast Petrovich recalled what people used to say about Simeon Alexandrovich: that he liked to surround himself with handsome young adjutants; but it was not clear if that was what Pozharsky had in mind.

'But then, that's not so very important. The fundamental point is that His Highness is not going to interfere in any business apart from the public gala parade variety – that is, he will not bedim the mystical halo of authority with "easy accessibility" and "cordial consideration". The practical power, the real power over this city of a million people, will go to Moscow's head police-master, and from today onwards, that happens to be me. I know that you will never stoop to writing underhand denunciations and whispering in ears, and therefore I think it possible to be absolute frank with you.' Gleb Georgievich glanced at Fandorin's medals and gave a little frown.

'I get rather carried away sometimes, and I think I have offended you. You and I have become involved in a stupid kind of puerile rivalry, and I was simply unable to deny myself the pleasure of having a little joke with you. The joke turned sour. I beg your pardon yet again. I knew about the despatch that your patron sent yesterday, in which he requested the sovereign to confirm your appointment as head police-master. Dolgorukoi's secretary, the quiet and inoffensive Innokentii Andreevich, spotted which way the wind was blowing a long time ago, and he has been of quite invaluable assistance to our party. Did you really think that I went back to the hotel to sleep after Briusov Square?'

'I never even g-gave it a thought,' Erast Petrovich said coldly, breaking his silence for the first time.

'You *are* offended,' Pozharsky declared. 'Well, I'm sorry, I'm sorry. Ah, forget about these foolish pranks. We're talking about your future here. I have had the opportunity to appreciate your exceptional qualities. You possess a keen intellect, firm resolve, courage, and also something that I value most of all in you: a talent for emerging from the flames without even singeing your wings. I'm a lucky man myself and I can recognise those who are favoured by fortune. Why don't we check to see whose luck is the stronger, yours or mine?'

He suddenly pulled a small pack of cards out of his pocket and held it out to the State Counsellor.

'Guess if the card on the top is red or black.'

'Very well, but put the p-pack on the table,' Erast Petrovich said with a shrug. 'Being too trusting in this game once nearly cost me my life.'

The prince was not offended in the least; in fact he laughed approvingly.

'Quite right. Luck is a lady; she should not be coralled into a corner. Well then?'

'Black,' Fandorin declared without even a moment's thought.

Pozharsky pondered for a moment and said: 'I agree.'

The top card proved to be the seven of spades.

'The next card is also black.'

'I agree.'

It was the three of clubs.

'Black again,' Erast Petrovich said patiently, as if he were playing a boring, infantile game with a little child.

'Unlikely that there would be three in a row ... No, I think red,' the prince declared – and turned over the queen of clubs.

'As I suspected,' Gleb Georgievich sighed. 'You are one of fortune's true darlings. I should have been sorry to lose such an ally. You know, from the very beginning I saw you as someone who was useful, but also dangerous. But now I no longer regard you as dangerous. For all your brilliant qualities, you have one immense shortcoming. You completely lack flexibility, you cannot alter your colour and shape to suit the circumstances. You are incapable of turning aside from the road already mapped out on to a roundabout side track. And so you won't be biding your time to stab me in the back – that is an art that you, of course, will never master, which suits me perfectly. And as for flexibility, there is a lot I could teach you about that. I propose an alliance. Together we could move mountains. It's not a matter of any specific position for you just yet – we can agree that later. What I need at present is your agreement in principle.'

The State Counsellor gave no reply, and Pozharsky continued, smiling disarmingly: 'Very well, let us take our time. For the time being let us simply get to know each better. I'll teach you how to be flexible, and you'll teach me to guess the colour of cards. Is it a deal?'

Fandorin thought for a moment and nodded.

'Excellent. Then I propose that from now on we should address each other informally and this evening we can seal the concordance by drinking to *Brüderschaft*,' the prince said, beaming. 'How about it? "Gleb and Erast"?'

'"Erast and Gleb",' Erast Petrovich agreed.

'My friends actually call me Glebchik,' the new head policemaster said with a smile, holding out his hand. 'Well then, Erast, until this evening. I have to go out shortly on important business.'

Fandorin stood up and shook the outstretched hand, but seemed in no hurry to leave.

'But what about the search for Green? Are we not going to d-do anything about it? As I recall, Gleb,' said the State Counsellor, uttering the unaccustomed form of address with some effort, 'you said that we were going to "start scheming again".'

'Don't you worry about that,' Pozharsky replied, smiling like Vasilisa the Wise telling the young Tsarevich Ivan that tomorrow is a new day. 'The meeting for which I am departing in such haste will help me close the case of the Combat Group once and for all.'

Crushed by this final blow, Fandorin said no more, but merely nodded dejectedly in farewell and walked out of the office.

He walked down the stairs with the same crestfallen stride, crossed the vestibule slowly, threw his fur coat across his shoulders and went out on to the boulevard, swinging his top hat melancholically.

However, no sooner had Erast Fandorin moved a little distance away from the yellow building with the white columns than his bearing underwent a quite dramatic change. He suddenly ran out into the roadway and waved his hand to stop the first cab that came along.

'Where to, Your Excellency?' the grey-bearded cabby cried smartly in a Vladimir accent when he spotted the glittering cross of a medal under the open fur coat. 'We'll get you there quick as a flash!'

But the important gent didn't get in; instead he took a look at the sturdy, shaggy-haired horse and kicked the sleigh's runner with the toe of his boot.

'So how much is a rig like this nowadays?'

The cabby wasn't surprised, because this wasn't his first year driving a cab in Moscow and he'd seen all sorts of cranks in his time. In fact those cranks were the best tippers.

'Oh, nigh on five hundred,' he boasted, naturally stretching the truth a bit to make the figure sound respectable.

And then the gent did something really queer. He took a gold watch on a gold chain out of his pocket and said: 'This diamond Breguette is worth at least a thousand roubles. Take it, and give me the sleigh and the horse.'

The cabby's jaw dropped and his eyes went blank. He gazed spellbound at the bright specks of sunlight dancing on the gold.

'Make your mind up quickly,' the crazy general shouted, 'or I'll st-stop someone else.'

The cabby snatched the watch and stuffed it into his cheek, but the chain wouldn't fit, so it was left dangling down across his beard. He got out of the sleigh, dropped his whip, slapped the sorrel mare on the rump in farewell and legged it.

'Stop!' the weird gent shouted after him – he must have changed his mind. 'Come back!'

The cabby plodded miserably back towards the sleigh, but he didn't take the booty out of his cheek yet; he was still hoping.

'M-m-ma-m, mimim, mamimi mummi mumi mamokumi,' he mooed reproachfully, which meant: 'Shame on a gent like you for playing tricks like that, you should have given me a tip for vodka too.'

'L-Let's swap clothes,' the crackpot said. 'Your sheepskin coat and mittens for my heavy coat. And take your cap off too.'

The gent pulled on the sheepskin coat and tugged the flaps of the sheepskin cap down over his ears. He tossed the cabby his cloth-covered beaver-fur coat and plonked the suede top hat down on his head. And then he yelled: 'That's it, now clear out!'

The cabby picked up the skirts of the heavy coat that was too long for him and set off across the boulevard, tramping heavily in his patched felt boots, with the chain of the gold watch dangling beside his ear.

Fandorin got into the sleigh, clicked his tongue to the horse to reassure it, and started waiting.

About five minutes later a closed sleigh drove up to the door of the head police-master's house. Pozharsky came out of the building carrying a bouquet of tea roses and ducked into the closed sleigh. It set off immediately. Another sleigh carrying two gentlemen who were already familiar to Erast Petrovich set off in pursuit.

After waiting for a little while, the State Counsellor gave a wild bandit whistle and whooped: 'Giddup, lazybones! Get moving!'

The sorrel mare shook its combed mane, jangled its sleigh bell and set off at a fast trot.

It turned out that they were going to the Nikolaevsky Station.

There Pozharsky jumped out of the carriage, tidied his bouquet and ran lightly up the station steps, two at a time. The 'guardian angels' followed him, keeping their customary distance.

Then the sham cabby got out of his own sleigh. As if he were simply strolling about aimlessly, he walked close to the covered carriage, dropped his mitten and bent down to pick it up, but didn't straighten up again immediately. He glanced around slyly and suddenly smashed the mounting of the suspension with an immensely powerful blow of his fist, delivered with such lightning speed that it was almost impossible to see. The sleigh shuddered and sagged slightly to one side. The alarmed driver hung down from his box to look, but saw nothing suspicious, because Fandorin had already straightened up and was looking the other way.

After that, while he sat in his sleigh, he refused several fares from the St Petersburg train, one of which was actually highly advantageous: to Sokolniki for a rouble and twenty-five kopecks.

Pozharsky returned with company: an extremely attractive young lady. She was burying her face in the roses and laughing happily. And the prince was not his usual self: his face was positively glowing with carefree merriment.

The lovely lady put her free hand round his shoulders and kissed him on the lips so passionately that Gleb Georgievich's pine-marten cap slipped over to one side of his head.

Fandorin could not help shaking his head in amazement at the surprises thrown up by human nature. Who would ever have thought that the ambitious predator from St Petersburg was capable of such romantic behaviour? But what had all this to do with the Combat Group?

As soon as the prince seated his companion in the carriage, it heeled over decisively to the right, making quite clear that there was no chance of travelling any further in it.

Erast Fandorin pulled his cap further down over his eyes, turned up his collar, cracked his whip smartly and drove straight up to the scene of the mishap.

'Here's a fine light Vladimir sleigh for you!' the State Counsellor yelled in a high falsetto that had nothing in common with his normal voice. 'Get in, Your Honour, I'll take you and the mamselle wherever you like, and I won't ask a lot: just a roople, and a half a roople, and a quarter roople for tea and sugar!'

Pozharsky glanced at this dashing fellow, then at the lopsided carriage and said: 'You can take the lady to Lubyanskaya Square. And I', he said, addressing the new arrival herself, 'will ride to Tverskoi Boulevard with my sworn protectors. I'll be waiting for news.'

As she got into the sleigh and covered her knees with the bearskin rug, the beautiful woman said in French: 'Only I beg you, darling, no police tricks, no shadowing. He's certain to sense it.'

'Don't insult me, Julie,' Pozharsky replied in the same language. 'I don't believe I have ever let you down.'

Erast Petrovich tugged on the reins and set the horse moving along Kalanchovka Street in the direction of Sadovo-Spasskaya Street.

To all appearances the young lady was in a very good mood: first she purred some song without any words, then she started singing in a low voice about a red *sarafan*. She had a wonderfully melodic voice.

'Lubyanka, lady,' Fandorin announced. 'Where to now?'

She turned her head this way and that and muttered peevishly to herself: 'How unbearable he is, always playing the conspirator. 'I tell you what: drive me round in circles.'

The State Counsellor chortled and set off along the edge of the square, driving round the ice-covered fountain and the cab stand.

On the fourth circuit a man in a black coat bounded off the pavement and jumped lightly into the sleigh.

'I'll give you a jump, you bandit!' the 'cabby' roared, raising his whip to lash at the impertinent prankster.

But this proved to be no ordinary passenger; he was very special: Mr Green in person. Only this time he'd glued on a light-coloured moustache and put on a pair of spectacles.

'He's a friend of mine,' the beautiful lady explained. 'The one I was expecting. Where are we going, Greeny?'

The new passenger gave the order: 'Drive across Theatre Lane. Then I'll tell you where next.'

'What's happened?' the songstress asked. 'What does "important business" mean? I dropped everything and here I am, just like magic. Perhaps you were simply missing me?' she asked, with a hint of cunning in her voice.

'I'll tell you when we get there,' the special passenger said, clearly not in the mood for conversation.

After that they drove in silence.

The passengers got out on Prechistenka Street, beside the estate of the counts Dobrinsky, but instead of going in through the gates, they walked up on to the porch of a wing of the main palace building.

Erast Petrovich, who had got down to tighten his horse's girth, saw a young woman open the door: a pale, severe face and smooth hair drawn back into a tight bun.

Following that, State Counsellor Fandorin acted rapidly and without hesitating for even a moment, as if he were not following instinct but carrying through a clear, carefully worked-out plan.

First he drove on for another five hundred paces, then tied the reins to a bollard beside the road, threw the sheepskin coat and cap into the sleigh, thrust his sword under the seat and walked back to the railings of the estate. There were hardly any people in the street, but he waited until it was completely empty before clambering nimbly up the railings and jumping down to the ground on the inside.

He ran quickly across the yard to the wing and found himself under a window with its small upper frame conveniently standing open. Erast Petrovich stood quite still for a moment, listening. Then without any obvious effort he clambered up on to the window sill, squeezed himself up tight and wriggled through the small aperture of the open window in a truly virtuoso feat of gutta-percha flexibility.

The hardest thing of all was to lower himself on to the floor without making any noise, but the State Counsellor managed even that. He found himself in a kitchen that was small but very tidy and wonderfully well heated. Here he had to listen carefully again, because he could hear voices from somewhere deeper inside the wing. Once he had determined which direction the sound was coming from, Erast Petrovich took his Herstahl-Baillard out of its holster and set off soundlessly along the corridor.

For the second time that day Erast Petrovich found himself spying and eavesdropping on someone through a half-open door, but this time he felt no embarrassment or pangs of conscience – only the excitement of the hunt and a thrill of joyful anticipation. His dear friend Gleb's luck could not last for ever, and he could learn more from Fandorin than how to guess the colour of cards.

There were three people in the room. The woman with the smooth hair whom he had seen at the front door was sitting at a table, sideways on to the door of the room, and performing strange manipulations: scooping a grey, jelly-like mass out of a jar with a small spoon and transferring it very carefully, a few drops at a time, to a narrow tin like the ones in which they sold olive essence or tomato paste. There were more tins standing there, both narrow ones and ordinary, half-pound ones. *She's making bombs*, the State Counsellor realised, his joy dimming a little. He had to put the Herstahl away – the woman only had to start in fright or surprise, and the entire wing of the house would be reduced to rubble. The female bomb-maker was not involved in the conversation being conducted by the other two.

'You're simply insane,' the woman who had come on the train said in dismay. 'Working in the underground has given you a persecution complex. You never used to be like that. If you can even suspect me . . .'

It was said in such a sincere and convincing tone that if Erast Petrovich had not seen the young lady in Pozharsky's company with his own eyes, he would certainly have believed her. The dark-haired man with the immobile features stamped in metal had not been present at the meeting at the station, and yet there was a note of unshakeable certainty in his voice.

'I don't suspect. I know. You left the notes. Only I didn't know if something went wrong or it was a deliberate provocation. Now I can see it was deliberate. Two questions. The first is: who? The second . . .' The terrorist leader hesitated. 'Why, Julie? Why? . . . All right, you needn't answer the second one. But you must answer the first. Otherwise I'll kill you. Right now. If you say, I won't kill you. Party court.'

It was quite clear that this was no idle threat. Erast Petrovich opened the door a little wider and saw that Pozharsky's collaborator was staring in horror at a dagger clutched in the terrorist's hand.

'Could you kill me?' – the double agent's voice trembled pitifully – 'after what happened between us? Surely you haven't forgotten?'

There was a faint tinkle of glass from the direction of the woman making the bombs. Turning his head slightly, Erast Petrovich saw that she had turned pale and was biting her lip.

Green, on the contrary, had turned red, but his voice was as steely as ever.

'Who?' he repeated. 'But tell the truth . . . No? Then . . . He grabbed the beauty's neck tightly with his left hand and drew back the right one to strike.

'Pozharsky,' she said quickly. 'Pozharsky, the deputy director of the Police Department, and now the head police-master of Moscow. Don't kill me, Green. You promised!'

The stern-faced man appeared shaken by her confession, but he put his knife away.

'Why him?' he asked. 'I don't understand. Yesterday I understand, but before then?'

'Don't ask me about that,' Julie said with a shrug.

Having realised that her life was not in immediate danger, she calmed down quite remarkably quickly and even started tidying her hair.

'I'm not interested in your games of cops and robbers. All you boys ever want to do is chase around after each other, fire your pop-guns and throw bombs. Women have more serious concerns.'

'And what are your concerns?' Green asked, giving her an intense, perplexed look. 'What is the most important thing in your life?'

'You have to ask? Love, of course. There is nothing more important. You men are monsters because you don't understand that.'

'All for love?' Russia's most dangerous terrorist asked slowly. 'Bullfinch, Emelya, the others – for love?'

Julie wrinkled up her sweet nose. 'For what else? My Gleb's a monster too, the same as you, although he plays for the cops, not the robbers. I did what he asked me to. If we women love, we do it with all our heart, and then we stop at nothing. Not even if the whole world goes to hell.'

'I'll check that now,' Green said and suddenly took his dagger out again.

'What are you doing?' the collaborator squealed, recoiling. 'I confessed! What else do you need to check?'

'Who you love more – him or yourself.'

The terrorist took a step towards her and she backed away towards the wall, throwing her hands up.

'Now you're going to telephone your protector and tell him to come here. Alone. Yes or no?'

'No!' Julie shouted, sliding along the wall. 'Not for anything!' She reached the corner and shrank back into it.

Green moved close without speaking, holding his dagger at the ready.

'Yes,' she said in a weak voice. 'Yes, yes, all right . . . Just put that away.'

Green turned to the seated woman, who was carrying on with her dangerous work as steadily as ever, and told her: 'Needle, find out what the head police-master's number is, will you?'

The woman with the strange alias – the courier that Rahmet-Gvidon had talked about – put down an unfinished bomb and stood up.

Erast Petrovich took heart and readied himself for action. Let Needle get at least ten steps away from that deadly table; then push the door open and cover the distance to Green in three – no four – bounds, stun him with a kick to the back of the head or, if he managed to turn round, to the chin, swing round to Needle and cut off her path to the table. Not easy, but feasible.

'Forty-four twenty-two,' Julie sobbed. 'I remember it, it's an easy number.'

And so, unfortunately, Needle stayed beside her bombs.

Fandorin could not see the telephone apparatus, but it was obviously there in the room, because Green put his dagger away again and pointed off somewhere to one side with his hand: 'Tell him to come. Say it's very urgent. Give me away and I'll kill you.'

'I'll kill you, I'll kill you.' Julie laughed. 'Oh Greeny, what a bore you are. You could at least get furious, shout and stamp your feet.'

What rapid transitions from fear to despair to insolence, the State Counsellor thought. *A rare bird indeed.*

And he proved to have underestimated her audacity.

'So you're sweet on her, are you?' she asked, nodding at Needle. 'You make a funny couple. I'd like to see you two getting lovey-dovey. It must be like metal clanking against metal. The love of two ironclads.'

Aware as he was of the loose morals typical of nihilist circles, the State Counsellor was not at all surprised by this declaration, but Needle suddenly became extremely animated – it was a good thing that she was standing up and not sitting over her bombs.

'What do you know about love?' she shouted in a ringing voice. 'One moment of our love is worth more than all your amorous adventures taken together!'

The beauty seemed to have her reply ready, but Green took her firmly by the shoulder and shoved her towards the invisible telephone: 'Get on with it!'

After that Julie was outside Fandorin's field of view, but he could hear her voice very distinctly.

'Central exchange? Young lady, forty-four, twenty-two,' the voice said without a trace of expression, and a second later it spoke again in a different tone, with overbearing insistence. 'Who? Duty Adjutant Keller? Listen, Keller, I have to speak to Gleb Georgievich immediately. Very urgent ... Julie, that's enough. He'll understand ... Ah, is he? ... Yes, definitely.' The receiver jangled against the cradle.

'He's not there yet. The adjutant said he's expected in a quarter of an hour at most. What shall I do?'

'Ring again in a quarter of an hour,' said Green.

Erast Petrovich backed silently away from the door and left the house quickly – following the same route by which he had entered.

The sorrel mare was still there, but someone had appropriated the sheepskin coat and cap – the temptation must have been too much.

Members of the public taking their Sunday stroll along Prechistenky Boulevard were able to observe the interesting spectacle of a cab sleigh hurtling along the road with a respectable-looking gentleman, dressed in full uniform complete with medals, standing erect in it, whistling wildly and lashing on the plain-looking, shaggy sorrel mare with his whip.

★

He was only just in time. He ran into Pozharsky in the doorway of the head police-master's residence. The prince was agitated, clearly in a hurry, and not pleased by this unexpected encounter. He flung out a few words without even breaking his stride: 'Later, Erast, later. The crucial moment is at hand!'

However, the State Counsellor grasped his superior's sleeve in fingers of steel and pulled the prince towards him.

'For you, Mr Pozharsky, the crucial moment has already arrived. Why don't we go to the office?'

His attitude and tone of voice produced the required impression. Gleb Georgievich gave Fandorin a curious glance.

'What's this then – are we back on formal terms, Erast? That gleam in your eyes suggests you must have discovered something interesting. Very well, let's go. But for no more than five minutes. I have pressing matters to deal with.'

The prince's entire demeanour made it clear that he had no time for long explanations, and he did not take a seat, nor did he offer Fandorin one, although the covers had already been removed from the furniture in the office. But then, Erast Petrovich had no intention of sitting down, since he was in belligerent mood.

'You are a provocateur, a double agent and a state criminal,' he said in a cold fury, skipping through his consonants with no trace of a stammer. 'It was you, not Diana, and you communicated with the terrorists of the Combat Group by means of letters. You were responsible for Khrapov's death, you informed the terrorists about the Petrosov Baths, and you deliberately misinformed me about the snowdrift. You wanted to get rid of me. You are a traitor! Shall I present my evidence?'

Gleb Georgievich continued to regard the State Counsellor with the same expression of curiosity, taking his time before replying.

'I don't think there's any need,' he said after a long moment's thought. 'I believe that you do have evidence, and I have no time for wrangling. Naturally, I'm very curious about how you found out, but you can tell me about that some time later. Well, so be it, I extend the length of our conversation from five minutes to ten, but that's the most I can do. So get straight to the point. All right, I am a provocateur, a double agent and a traitor. I arranged Khrapov's assassination and a number of other remarkable stunts, up to and including a couple of attempts on my own life. Now what? What do you want?'

Erast Petrovich was taken aback, since he had been prepared for long and stubborn denials, and therefore the question that he had intended to ask at the very end had a rather pathetic ring as he stammered it out.

'B-But why? What d-did you want to achieve with all this scheming?'

Pozharsky began speaking with grating confidence: 'I am the man who can save Russia – because I am intelligent, bold and do not suffer from mushy sentiment. My enemies are numerous and powerful: on one side the fanatics of revolt, and on the other the stupid, fossilised swines in generals' uniforms. For a long time I had no connections, no protection. I would have fought my way to the top in any case, but too late: time is passing and Russia has very little of it left. That was why I had to hurry. The Combat Group is my adopted child. I nurtured that organisation, made its name and created its reputation. It has already given me everything it could, and now the time has come to put a full stop at the end of this story. Today I shall eliminate Green. The fame that I created for that uncompromising gentleman will help me rise a few steps higher and bring me closer to my ultimate goal. That's the gist of it, brief and unadorned. Is that enough?'

'And you did all this for the salvation of Russia?' Fandorin asked, but his sarcasm was lost on the prince.

'Yes. And naturally for myself too. I make no distinction between myself and Russia. After all, Russia was founded a thousand years ago by one of my ancestors, and three hundred years ago another assisted in her revival.' Pozharsky thrust his hands into the pockets of his coat and swayed back on his heels. 'And don't think, Erast, that I am afraid of your revelations. What can you do? You have no one in St Petersburg. Your protector in Moscow has been overthrown. No one will believe you, no one will even hear what you say. You can't possibly have anything more than circumstantial evidence and assumptions. Will you go to the newspapers? They won't print it. This is not Europe, thank God. You know' – Gleb Georgievich lowered his voice confidentially – 'I have a revolver in my pocket and it is aimed at your stomach. I could shoot you. Right now, here in this office. I would proclaim that you were an agent for the terrorists, that you are linked with them through your little Jewish girl and you tried to kill me. In the present circumstances I should easily get away with it, I'd even get a medal. But I am opposed to unnecessary extravagance. There is no need to kill you, because you really are no danger to me. Choose, Erast: either play with me, by my rules, or make yourself look like a fool. Actually, there is a third way, which is probably more to your taste. Say nothing and retire quietly. You will at least retain the dignity that is so dear to you. So what is your choice? Play the game, play the fool or keep quiet?'

The State Counsellor turned pale, his eyebrows shifted up and down and his thin moustache twitched. The prince followed this internal struggle with a rather scornful expression, waiting calmly for its outcome.

'Well?'

'All right,' Erast Petrovich said quietly. 'Since it is what you wish, I shall k-keep quiet . . .'

'Well, that's excellent.' The triumphant prince smiled and glanced at his watch. 'We didn't need ten minutes after all; five was enough. But do think about playing the game. Don't bury your talent in the ground, like the lazy, scheming servant described by Saint Matthew.'

So saying, the head police-master strode towards the door.

Fandorin gave a sudden start and opened his mouth to stop him, but instead of a loud call, all that emerged from his lips were four barely audible words: ' "Eradicating evil with evil . . ." '

CHAPTER 16

The flash

Green would have to leave immediately after Pozharsky's execution. He had already decided how: by cab to Bogorodsky, get hold of some skis and cut across Losinoostrovsky Forest, bypassing the turnpikes, to Yaroslavl Highway. If he could just get out of Moscow, after that it was easy.

He regretted the wasted work. The bombs would have to be left behind again: the jar of explosive mixture was still half full, the tins were standing there, equipped with detonators and charged with shrapnel but not yet closed. They would only be an unnecessary burden.

His travelling bag contained nothing but the bare essentials: false documents, underwear, a spare revolver.

Needle was looking out of the window at the boarded-up palace. In a few minutes she would be leaving the house where she had grown up. Probably leaving it for ever.

Before she phoned the head police-master for a second time, Julie looked into his eyes and asked: 'Green, do you promise not to kill me?'

'If he comes.'

She crossed herself and called the exchange. 'Hello, Central? Forty-four twenty-two.'

This time Pozharsky was there.

'Gleb,' Julie said to him in a voice trembling with excitement. 'Darling, come here quickly, quickly. I only have one little moment, no time to explain. Prechistenka Street, the Dobrinsky estate, the wing with a mezzanine – you'll see it. Only come alone, you must be alone. I'll open the door for you. You simply can't imagine what I've got here. You'll kiss my pretty little hands. That's all, no more, I can't say any more!' And she cut off the phone.

'He'll come,' she said confidently. 'He's bound to come running. I know him.' She took hold of Green's hand and said imploringly: 'Greeny, you promised. What are you going to do with me?'

'A promise is a promise,' he said, freeing his hands in disgust. 'You'll see him die. Then I'll let you go. Let the party decide. You know the sentence. They'll declare you an outlaw. Everyone who sees you is obliged to kill you, like vermin. Run to the end of the world, hide away in a deep hole.'

'Never mind,' said Julie, shrugging frivolously. 'There are men everywhere. I'll get by; I've always dreamed of seeing the New World.'

Perfectly calm now, she shifted her gaze from Green to Needle and sighed in sympathy. 'Ah, you poor, poor things. Give up all this damned nonsense. She loves you, I can see that. And you love her. You could just live and be grateful for such happiness. Stop all this killing. You'll never build anything good on it anyway.'

Green didn't answer, because he was thinking of what he was about to do, and because discussion was pointless. But Needle, examining the double traitor with contemptuous incomprehension, was unable to restrain herself: 'Don't you say anything else about love. I haven't made you any promises. I might shoot you.'

Julie wasn't frightened in the slightest, especially since Needle's hands were empty.

'Do you despise me because I didn't want to die for Gleb? You're wrong. I didn't betray my love – I listened to my heart. If it had told me, "Die," I would have died. But it said: "You can survive even without Gleb." I can pretend to any one else, but not to myself.'

'Your heart could never have said anything else,' Needle declared with loathing in her voice, and after that Green stopped listening.

He went out into the corridor and stood beside the kitchen

window to keep an eye on the street. Pozharsky should turn up any moment now. Justice would be done, his comrades would be avenged: Bullfinch, Emelya, Beaver, Marat, Nobel, Schwartz. And Nail as well.

His eye suddenly spotted something strange: the print of a sole on the window sill, directly under the small open frame. There was some disquieting meaning in this sign, but Green had no time to think about it – the door bell rang.

Julie went to open the door. Green stood behind it with his Colt at the ready.

'Don't try anything,' he whispered.

'Oh, shut up,' she said dismissively, then drew back the bolt and spoke to someone invisible. 'Gleb, darling, come in, I'm alone.'

The man who came into the hallway was wearing a dark-grey coat and a pine-marten cap. He didn't notice Green and stood with his back to him. Julie gave Pozharsky a quick kiss on the ear and the cheek and winked at Green over his shoulder.

'Come on, I'll show you.'

She took the head police-master by the hand and pulled him after her into the room. Green followed them silently.

'Who's this?' Pozharsky asked when he saw Needle. 'Just a moment, don't introduce yourself, I'll get it . . . Ah, I've guessed! What a pleasant surprise. What does this mean, Julie? Have you managed to incline Mademoiselle Needle to the side of law and order? Clever girl. But where is the idol of my heart, the valorous knight of the revolution, Mr Green?'

At this point Green stuck a gun barrel between his shoulder blades. 'I'm here. Keep your hands where I can see them. Over to the wall, turn to face me slowly.'

Pozharsky held his hands out to the sides, level with his shoulders, took ten steps forward and turned round. His face was tense, his brows were knitted sternly.

'A trap,' he said. 'It's my own fault. I thought you loved me, Julie. I was wrong. Well, everyone makes some mistakes.'

'What does TG mean?' Green asked, keeping his finger on the trigger.

The head police-master laughed quietly. 'So that's it. I was wondering why Mr Green didn't simply put a bullet in the back of my head. Well, well, a few aspects of humanity are not alien to you after all? Curious, are we? All right then. For the sake of our old friendship, I'll answer all your questions. At least that way I'll keep breathing for another couple of minutes. I'm very pleased to meet my long-time correspondent face to face at last. You're exactly as I imagined you. So ask whatever you like, please don't be bashful.'

'TG,' Green repeated.

'Nonsense, a joke. It stands for "*tertius gaudens*", a Latin phrase meaning "the joyful third party". The police kill you, you kill the people who stand in my way, I watch your fun and games and rejoice. I think it's rather witty.'

'Stand in your way? Why? Governor Bogdanov, General Selivanov, the traitor Stasov . . .'

'Don't bother, I remember them all very well,' Pozharsky interrupted. 'Bogdanov? That was not so much business, more a personal matter. I needed to do a favour for the deputy director of the Department, my predecessor in that post. He was involved in a long-standing affair with the Governor of Ekaterinburg's wife and he dreamed of her being widowed. His dreams were entirely platonic, but one day a rather incautious little note that His Excellency had written to his passion happened to come into my possession: "How I wish the terrorists would reach your better half soon. I would gladly help them." I simply had to make use of it. After you shot Bogdanov so heroically, I had a confidential talk with the enamoured dreamer, and the position of deputy director became vacant. Lieutenant General Selivanov? Oh, that was quite different. He was a man of very keen intellect, pursuing the same goals as I was, but he was already several steps ahead of me. He was getting in my light and that's a risky thing to do. I am tremendously grateful to you for Selivanov. When you despatched him to the realm of Hades, the throne's most promising defender became your devoted servant. Next, I think, came the Aptekarsky Island incident, the attack on me and the collaborator Stasov? There was a double goal involved that time: firstly, to enhance my professional reputation. If the CG was hunting me, it meant the group appreciated my professional qualities. And secondly, Stasov had outlived his usefulness and asked to be set free. Of course, I could have let him go, but I decided it would be more useful for him to die. Once again it would mean more prestige for our Combat Group.'

Green's face contorted as if he were struggling to suppress pain, and Pozharsky laughed in satisfaction.

'Now for your most important achievement, the murder of Khrapov. You must admit that I handed you a wonderful little idea, without forcing it on you at all. And for my part I admit that you managed the business brilliantly. The ruthless execution of a heartless satrap, whose very worst atrocity was that he could not stand the sight of me and did absolutely everything he could to hinder my career . . . Here in Moscow you caused me no end of trouble, but eventually everything could not possibly have turned out better. Even your little trick with the expropriation came in useful. Thanks to our feather-brained friend Julie, I found out who the new party treasurer was, and very soon I was ready to take back the state treasury's money. That would have been an especially impressive thing to do in my new post as Moscow's head police-master: Look, I may not be in the capital, but I sit high and see far! What a shame. Clearly it was not meant to be,' Pozharsky said with a fatalistic sigh. 'But you must at least appreciate the elegance of the conception . . . What else was there? Colonel Sverchinsky? A scoundrel, an odious trickster. You helped me get even with him for a certain vile joke. Burlyaev? I helped you out there, just as I did with Rahmet. The last thing I needed was for my beloved brainchild, the CG, to be neutralised by the head of the Moscow Okhranka. That wouldn't have been fair. The person who plants the seed should reap the harvest. So well done for finishing off Burlyaev! His department came under my total control. Only you messed things up with Fandorin, and he kept on getting under my feet in a most annoying manner. But I don't blame you for Fandorin, he's a special case . . . Well, and then the time came to round off our epic adventure together. Alas, all good things come to an end. I thought out the operation down to the finest detail, but chance intervened. Annoying. I was just beginning to gather speed; a little bit longer, and it would have been impossible to stop me ... Destiny.'

Julie sobbed.

'Never mind,' the head police-master told her with a smile. 'I bear no grudge against you, only destiny. You made me feel happy and light-hearted, and as for betraying me, well, there was evidently nothing that could have been done about that.'

Incredibly enough, there were tears streaming down Julie's face. Green had never seen this carefree, frivolous woman cry before. But there was no sense in continuing the conversation. Everything had been explained already. Not even during the pogrom had Green ever felt so miserable as he did during these few minutes that had cancelled out the entire meaning of a long, hard struggle full of sacrifices. How would he carry on living? – that was the question he had to think about, and he knew it would not be easy to find an answer. But one thing was absolutely clear: this smiling man must die.

Green aimed the gun barrel at the manipulator's forehead.

'Hey, my dear chap!' Pozharsky exclaimed, throwing up one hand. 'What's the hurry? We were having such a wonderful chat. Don't you want to hear about Julie and our love? I assure you it is far more absorbing than any novel.'

Green shook his head and cocked the hammer: 'It's not important.'

'Gleb! No-o-o-o!' Julie screamed. She pounced on Green like a cat and hung on his arm. Her grip was surprisingly strong and her sharp teeth sank into the wrist of the hand holding the Colt.

Green shifted the revolver to his left hand, but it was too late: Pozharksy put his hand in his pocket and fired through the flap of his coat.

I'm hit, thought Green as his back struck the wall and he slid towards the floor. He tried to raise the hand holding the revolver, but it wouldn't obey him.

Julie sent the Colt flying with a kick of her shoe.

'Bravo, little girl,' said Pozharsky. 'You're simply wonderful. I dragged things out for about as long as I could, but it still wasn't long enough. I told my men to wait for exactly ten minutes and then break in. He would have finished me by then.'

Something was roaring and howling in Green's ears and the room was swaying, first to the right, then to the left. He couldn't understand how the two men who came running in from the corridor managed to stay on their feet.

'You heard the shot?' the head police-master asked. 'Well done. I've downed this one, he's dying. The woman's for you; she's the famous Needle. She can't be left alive; she heard too much.'

The light began to dim. Pozharsky's face must not be the last thing he saw as his life drained away. Green ran his fading gaze round the room, searching for Needle. She was standing with her hands clasped together and looking at him without speaking, but he couldn't make out the expression in her eyes.

What was that glint between her fingers, that slim, bright thing?

A detonator – it's a detonator, Green realised.

Needle turned towards the vessel with the explosive mixture and snapped the narrow glass tube over it.

Life ended just as it was supposed to – in an instant flash of flame.

Epilogue

At the Kutafya Tower he had to let the cabby go and continue on foot. The new order of things was not yet obvious in the city, but here in the Kremlin things were no longer what they used to be: everything disciplined and carefully tended, patrols everywhere, and not a day that passed without the ice and snow being scraped off the cobblestones – you couldn't get through on a sleigh. Supreme authority had set up its home here now – the new master of the old capital had decided it was beneath him to live in the Governor General's residence and moved into the Maly Nikolaevsky Palace behind the tall red-brick walls.

Erast Petrovich walked uphill across the Trinity Bridge, one hand holding down his sword, the other clutching his cocked hat. Today was a most solemn day: the officials of Moscow were being presented to His Imperial Highness.

The old prince, Vladimir Andreevich Dolgorukoi, had departed to live out his remaining years in the odious leisure of Nice, and fundamental changes were afoot in the lives of his former subordinates – some would be elevated, some would be transferred to new positions, some would be retired altogether. An experienced man immediately took note of the time of day appointed for his reception or his department's. The earlier it was, the more alarming the implications. Everyone knows that a new broom sweeps briskly at first and its first priority is to be strict. There is a double purpose here: on the one hand, to instil the appropriate fear and trepidation in others, and on the other hand, to commence with punishments and conclude with favours. And again, it had been well known for a long time that the worst jobs – the district councils, the land-use committee, the orphans' trusteeship and all sorts of insignificant departments – were usually disposed of first of all, while the truly important positions were left until last.

Both of these signs indicated that State Counsellor Fandorin was an important individual, marked out for special attention. He had been invited to present himself to the clear gaze of the grand duke's eyes last of all, at half past five in the afternoon, even later than the commander of the military district and the top gendarme officers. This distinction, however, could signify absolutely anything, in either a flattering or an alarming sense, and therefore Erast Petrovich had not indulged in empty surmise but decided to entrust himself entirely to destiny. It has been said: 'The superior man meets wrath and favour with equal dignity.'

Beside the walls of the Chudov Monastery, the State Counsellor ran into Lieutenant Smolyaninov, also in dress uniform and looking even more flushed than usual.

'Good afternoon, Erast Petrovich!' he exclaimed. 'On the way to your reception? He's seeing you very late. You must be due for promotion.'

Fandorin shrugged and asked politely: 'Have your people already been received? What happened?'

'There are changes at the Okhranka. Mylnikov has been kept in his old position, and Zubtsov has been appointed head of department. And still only a titular counsellor – how do you like that? They're sending us someone from St Petersburg for the Office of Gendarmes. But it's all the same to me. I'm putting in an application, Erast Petrovich. Moving from the Corps of Gendarmes to the Dragoons. I've finally made up my mind.'

Erast Petrovich was not at all surprised, but he asked anyway: 'Why so?'

'I didn't like the way His Highness spoke about the tasks of the state police,' the Lieutenant declared ardently '"You", he said, "must inspire the inhabitants with the fear and awe of authority. Your task is to spot the weeds in good time and eradicate them up without mercy, in order to educate and encourage the others." He said the man in the street should be petrified by the very sight of a blue uniform. That we have to strengthen the foundations of the Russian state, otherwise nihilism and permissiveness will finally erode it completely.'

'Perhaps that's right?' Fandorin put in cautiously.

'Very possibly. Only I don't want anyone to be petrified at the very sight of me!' Smolyaninov tugged testily at his sabre knot. 'I was taught that we must eradicate lawlessness and protect the weak, that the Corps of Gendarmes is the spotless handkerchief with which the supreme power wipes away the tears of the suffering!'

The State Counsellor shook his head in sympathy: 'You'll f-find it hard in the army. You know yourself what the officers think of gendarmes.'

'Never mind,' the rosy-cheeked gendarme replied with a stubborn shake of his head. 'At first, of course, they'll turn their noses up, but then they'll see that I'm not any sort of police sneak. I'll fit in somehow.'

'I don't doubt it.'

After taking his leave of the obdurate adjutant, Erast Petrovich lengthened his stride, because there were only ten minutes left to his appointed time.

The audience did not take place in the study but in the formal drawing room – evidently so that those being presented would appreciate the great significance of the moment. At precisely half past five two solemn footmen with long ringlets opened the double doors and a butler with a gilded mace went in first and announced in a thunderous voice: 'His Honour State Counsellor Fandorin.'

Erast Petrovich bowed respectfully from the doorway and only then took the liberty of examining the most august member of the royal household. Simeon Alexandrovich was strikingly unlike his bullish brother. Gaunt and clean-limbed, with a long, haughty face, a sharp little beard and pomaded hair, he looked more like some Hapsburg prince from the times of Velasquez.

'Hello, Fandorin,' His Highness said. 'Approach.'

Although he knew perfectly well that with members of the

royal family this informal manner of address was a mark of goodwill, Erast Petrovich frowned. He approached the grand duke and shook his white, pampered hand.

'So this is what you look like,' said Simeon Alexandrovich, surveying the imposing official with approving curiosity. 'In his reports Pozharsky recommended you in the most flattering terms. What a tragedy that he was killed. Such an extremely talented man, absolutely devoted to me and the throne.'

The Governor General crossed himself, but Fandorin did not follow his example.

'Your Imperial Highness, I am obliged to inform you of certain f-facts concerning Prince Pozharsky's activies in connection with the Combat Group. I drew up a report for the Minister of the Interior, in which I set forth in the greatest possible detail everything that—'

'I read it,' Simeon Alexandrovich interrupted. 'The Minister felt it appropriate to forward your report to me as Governor General of Moscow. I annotated it: "Absolute nonsense and moreover dangerous". But I knew the late Pozharsky very well, and so I checked every word you wrote. Of course, it was all quite right. You are perceptive and adroit. Pozharsky was not mistaken about you; he was an excellent judge of people. But you should not have written that report. There might have been some point if your rival were still alive. But where's the thrill of the hunt in flogging a dead lion?'

'Your Highness, that was not why my n-note was written. I wished to draw the attention of the supreme authorities to the methods of the s-secret state police . . .' Erast Petrovich protested in dismay, but the grand duke halted him with a condescending gesture.

'Let me say that I am not at all angry with Gleb for his little pranks. In their own way they are actually quite witty. And in general I allow a great deal of leeway to those who are sincerely devoted to me,' His Highness said with special emphasis. 'As you will have the opportunity to learn for yourself. As for your report, I tore it up and consigned it to oblivion. None of it ever happened. The prestige of the authorities takes priority over everything else, including the truth – a point that you still have to master. But I appreciated the meticulous quality of your work. I need helpers like Pozharsky and you – intelligent, energetic, enterprising, willing to stop at nothing. A place at my side has become vacant, and I want you to fill it.'

The State Counsellor was so shaken by the phrase 'little pranks' that he had lost the power of speech. His Highness, however, interpreted his silence in a different sense and smiled understandingly.

'You wish to know what exactly I am offering you? Don't worry, you will not be out of pocket. Tomorrow I shall sign the decree appointing you head police-master and that, if I am not mistaken, is a salary of twelve thousand plus an expense account of fourteen thousand, plus a coach and team of horses and a state residence. And, in addition, the special funds that you can dispose of at your own discretion. The position corresponds to the fourth class of the state service, so you will shortly receive the rank of general. And I shall obtain the title of chamberlain for you without delay, in time for Easter. Well then? As our Moscow merchants say, is it a deal?' The grand duke's lips extended into a broad smile and once again he offered the functionary his hand.

However, the most august palm was left suspended in mid-air.

'I am afraid, Your Highness, that I have decided to leave the state service,' Erast Petrovich said in a clear, confident voice, appearing to look His Imperial Highness full in the face, but somehow at the same time looking straight through him. 'Private life is more to my liking.'

And without waiting for the audience to end, he set off towards the door.

Read on for an excerpt from Boris Akunin's
new novel *The Coronation*.

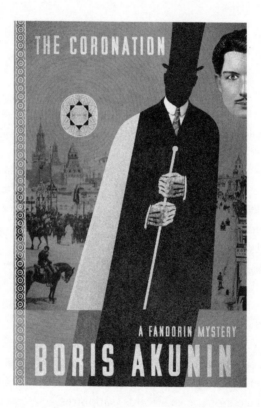

Available in hardcover and ebook.

20 May

He died in front of my very eyes, this strange and disagreeable gentleman.

It all happened so quickly, so very quickly.

The very instant the shots roared out, he was flung back against the cable.

He dropped his little revolver, clutched at the shaky handrail and froze on the spot, with his head thrown back. I caught a momentary glimpse of a white face, bisected by a black strip of moustache, before it disappeared behind the black mantle.

'Erast Petrovich!' I shouted, calling him by his given name and patronymic for the first time.

Or did I only mean to shout?

The precarious decking swayed beneath his feet. His head suddenly bobbed forward as if from a powerful jolt, his body began slumping, chest forward, over the cable, then swung round grotesquely – and the next instant it was already hurtling down, down, down.

The precious casket fell from my hands, struck a rock and split open. There was a flash of blinding sparks from the multi-coloured facets of the diamonds, sapphires and emeralds, but I did not even glance at these incalculable riches as they scattered into the grass.

From the ravine there came the soft crunch of an impact, and I gasped. The black bundle went tumbling down the steep slope, gathering speed along the way and only ceasing its nauseous whirling motion at the very edge of the stream. It dropped one lifeless hand into the water and lay there, face down in the gravel.

I had not liked this man. Perhaps I had even hated him. In any case, I had wanted him to disappear from our lives once and for all. But I had not wished for his death.

His trade was risk, he toyed with danger constantly, but somehow I had never thought he could be killed. He had seemed immortal to me.

I do not know how long I stood there like that, gazing stiffly down. It cannot have been very long. But time seemed to rupture, to split apart, and I fell into the rent – back into the old, serene life that had ended abruptly exactly two weeks earlier.

Yes, that was a Monday too, the sixth of May.

6 May

We arrived in the ancient capital of the Russian state in the morning. Owing to the imminent coronation festivities, the Nikolai I Station was congested with traffic and our train was sent off via a transfer line to the Brest Station, which seemed to me a rather ill-judged decision, to say the least, on the part of the local authorities. I can only assume that a certain coolness in relations between His Highness Georgii Alexandrovich and His Highness Simeon Alexandrovich, the governor-general of Moscow, must have played some part in it. I can think of no other way to explain the humiliating half-hour wait on the points at the marshalling yard and the subsequent diversion of our special express train from the main station to a secondary one.

And we were not met on the platform by Simeon Alexandrovich himself, as protocol, tradition, family connection and, ultimately, simple respect for an elder brother should have required, but only by a member of the reception committee, a minister of the imperial court who, incidentally, immediately departed for the Nikolai I station to receive the Prince of Prussia. But since when has the heir to the Prussian throne been accorded more attention in Moscow than the uncle of His Majesty, the admiral-general of the Russian fleet and the second most senior of the grand dukes of the imperial family? Georgii Alexandrovich did not show it, but I think he felt no less indignant than I did at such a clear affront.

It was a good thing at least that Her Highness, the Grand

Duchess Ekaterina Ioannovna, had stayed in St Petersburg – she is so zealous about the subtle points of ritual and maintaining the dignity of the royal family. The epidemic of measles that had laid low the four middle sons – Alexei Georgievich, Sergei Georgievich, Dmitry Georgievich and Konstantin Georgievich – prevented Her Highness, an exemplary and loving mother, from taking part in the coronation, the supreme event in the life of the state and the imperial family. There were, it is true, venomous tongues who claimed that Her Highness's absence at the celebrations in Moscow was to be explained less by maternal love than by a reluctance to play the part of a mere extra at the triumph of the young tsarina. There was also mention of last year's incident at the Christmas Ball, when the new empress suggested that the ladies of the royal family should establish a handicraft society, and that each of the grand duchesses should knit a warm cap for the little orphans at the Mariinsky Orphanage. Perhaps Ekaterina Ioannovna's reaction to this proposal was a little too severe. It is even quite possible that since then relations between Her Highness and Her Majesty had not been entirely good. However, no provocation was intended by My Lady's not coming to the coronation, I can vouch for that. Whatever Ekaterina Ioannovna's feelings towards Her Majesty may be, under no circumstances would she ever presume to neglect her dynastic duty without a very serious reason. Her Highness's sons really were ill.

That was sad of course but, as the common people say, every cloud has a silver lining, for the entire grand ducal court remained behind in St Petersburg with her, which significantly simplified the highly complex task facing me in connection with the temporary removal to the old capital. The court ladies were very upset that they would not see the festivities in Moscow and expressed their discontent – naturally, without transgressing the bounds of etiquette – but Ekaterina Ioannovna remained adamant: according to ceremonial procedure, a lesser court must remain where the majority of members of the grand ducal family are located, and the majority of the Georgieviches, as our branch of the imperial house is unofficially known, had stayed in St Petersburg.

Four members of the family made the journey to the coronation: Georgii Alexandrovich himself, his eldest and youngest sons and his only daughter, Xenia Georgievna.

As I have already said, I was only too pleased by the absence of the ladies and gentlemen of the court. The court steward, Prince Metitsky, and the manager of the court office, Privy Counsellor von Born, would only have hindered me in doing my job by sticking their noses into matters entirely beyond their comprehension. A good butler does not need nannies and overseers to help him cope with his responsibilities. And as for the ladies-in-waiting and maids of honour, I simply would not have known where to accommodate them, so wretchedly inadequate was the residence allocated by the coronation committee to the Green Court – as our household is known, from the colour of the grand duchess's train. However, we will come to the matter of the residence later.

The removal from St Petersburg went smoothly. The train consisted of three carriages: the members of the royal family travelled in the first, the servants in the second, and all the necessary utensils and the luggage were transported in the third, so that I was constantly obliged to move from one carriage to another.

Immediately after our departure, His Highness Georgii Alexandrovich sat down to drink cognac with His Highness Pavel Georgievich and Gentleman of the Bedchamber Endlung. His Highness was pleased to drink eleven glasses, after which he felt tired and rested all the way to Moscow. Before he fell asleep, when he was already in his 'cabin', as he referred to his compartment, His Highness told me a little about a voyage to Sweden that had taken place twenty years earlier and made a great impression on him. The fact is, although Georgii Alexandrovich holds the rank of admiral-general, he has only ever been to sea on one occasion. The memories that he retains of this journey are most unpleasant, and he frequently refers to the French minister Colbert, who never sailed on a ship and yet transformed his country into a great maritime power. I have heard the story about the Swedish voyage many times, quite often enough to know it off by heart. The most dangerous part in it is the description of the storm off the coast of Gotland. Following the words 'And then the captain yells out, "All hands to the pumps"', His Highness is wont to roll his eyes up and swing his fist down hard onto the table. The same thing happened on this occasion, but there was no damage to the tablecloth and the tableware, since I had taken the timely measure of holding down the carafe and the glass.

When His Highness was quite worn out and began to lose the power of speech, I gave the sign to his valet to undress him and put him to bed, while I went to call on Pavel Georgievich and Lieutenant Endlung. As young men in the very pink of health, they were much less tired after the cognac. You might say, in fact, that they were not tired at all, so it was necessary to keep an eye on them, especially bearing in mind the particular temperament of the gentleman of the bedchamber.

Oh my, that Endlung! I ought not to say so, but Ekaterina Ioannovna made a great mistake when she decided that this gentleman was a worthy mentor for her eldest son. The lieutenant, of course, is a handsome brute, with a clear gaze, a fresh complexion, a neat parting in his golden hair and an almost childishly pink bloom to his cheeks – a perfect angel. Respectful and fawning with older ladies, he can listen with an air of the greatest interest to talk of the preacher Ioann Kronshtatsky or a greyhound's distemper. Yes, it is hardly surprising that Ekaterina Ioannovna's heart warmed to Endlung. Such an agreeable and – most important – serious young man, nothing like those good-for-nothing cadets from the Naval Corps or those scapegraces from the Guards

Company. A fine mentor she found for Pavel Georgievich's guardian on his first long voyage! A guardian of whom I have seen more than enough.

In the very first port, Varna, Endlung dolled himself up like a peacock in a white suit with a scarlet waistcoat, a cravat studded with stars and a massive Panama hat, and set out for a house of ill-repute, taking His Highness, still a boy at the time, along with him. I tried to intervene, but the lieutenant told me, 'I promised Ekaterina Ioannovna that I would not take my eyes off His Highness. Where I go, he goes.'

I said to him, 'No, Lieutenant, Her Highness said, where *he* goes, *you* must go!' But Endlung said, 'That, Afanasii Stepanovich, is hair-splitting. The important thing is that we shall be as inseparable as the Ajaxes.' And so he dragged the young midshipman round every den of iniquity as far as Gibraltar. But from Gibraltar back to Kronstadt both the lieutenant and midshipman behaved very quietly and didn't even go ashore, although they went running to the doctor four times a day for irrigation treatments. What kind of mentor is that? His Highness has changed in the company of this Endlung – he is quite a different person. I have even hinted this to Georgii Alexandrovich, but he simply brushed it off, saying, 'Never mind, that kind of experience can only be good for my Pauly, and Endlung may be a bit of a booby, but he is a good, open-hearted comrade; he won't cause any serious harm.' But in my view this is letting the goat into the garden, to use an expression from the common folk. I can see right through that Endlung – of course I can, since he is so very open. Thanks to his friendship with Pavel Georgievich, he has even been awarded a monogram for his shoulder straps, and now he has been made a gentleman of the bedchamber, which is quite unheard of – such an honourable title for a mere lieutenant!

Left alone together, the two young men had started a game of bezique for forfeits. When I glanced into the compartment, Pavel Georgievich called to me: 'Sit down, Afanasii. Have a game of American roulette with us. If you lose, I'll make you shave off those damn precious sideburns of yours.'

I thanked him and refused, saying that I was extremely busy, although I didn't have anything in particular to do. That would have been the last straw, to play His Highness at American roulette. And Pavel Georgievich knew himself that I would make a hopeless partner in the game – he was simply joking. In recent months he has developed a dismaying habit of bantering with me, and all thanks to Endlung – this is his influence. Endlung himself, it is true, has recently stopped taunting me, but Pavel Georgievich persists in the habit. Never mind. His Highness may do as he pleases; I have no complaints.

For example, just now he told me with an absolutely straight face: 'You know, Afanasii, that phenomenal growth on your face is provoking the envy of certain highly influential individuals. For instance, the day before yesterday at the ball, when you were standing by the door, looking so grand with your gold-plated mace and sideburns jutting out on both sides, all the ladies had eyes for no one but you, and no one even glanced at cousin Nicky, even though he is the emperor. You really, really must shave them off, or at the very least trim them.'

In actual fact, my 'phenomenal growth' is a perfectly ordinary full moustache with sideburns – sumptuous perhaps but by no means excessive, and at all events maintained in perfectly decent order. My father wore the same whiskers, and my grandfather before him, so I had no intention of either shaving them or trimming them.

'Skip it, Pauly,' Endlung intervened on my behalf. 'Stop tormenting Afanasii Stepanovich. Come on, play. It's your turn.'

I can see that I shall have to explain the relationship between the lieutenant and myself. There is a story to it.

On the very first day of the voyage on the corvette *Mstislav,* immediately after we left Sebastopol, Endlung ambushed me on deck, put his hand on my shoulder, looked at me with his eyes totally blank after all the wine he had drunk at the send-off party and said: 'Well, Afon, my little flunkey soul, those mops of yours are looking a bit wild. Is it the breeze that has swept them out like that? (My sideburns had indeed been tousled somewhat by the fresh sea wind – later I would be obliged to shorten them a little for the duration of the voyage.) Will you do something for me, as a personal favour? Run round to that skinflint of a steward and say that His Highness orders him to send a bottle of rum – to help prevent seasickness.'

All the time we were travelling to Sebastopol in the train, Endlung had teased me and mocked me in the presence of His Highness, but I had tolerated it, waiting for an opportunity to clarify matters face to face. Now the opportunity had presented itself.

I delicately removed the lieutenant's hand (at that time he was not yet a gentleman of the bedchamber) with my finger and thumb and said politely: 'Mr Endlung, if you have been visited by the fancy to define my soul, then it would be more accurate to refer to it, not as the soul of a "flunkey", but that of a "housemaster", since for long and irreproachable service at His Highness's court I have been awarded that title, which is a rank of the ninth level, corresponding to that of titular counsellor, staff captain in the army or *lieutenant* in the fleet.' (I deliberately emphasised the latter title.)

Endlung exclaimed: 'Lieutenants don't wait on tables!'

And I said to him: 'One *waits* on tables in restaurants, sir, but in the royal family one *serves*, each performing his duty as honourably as he can.'

After that incident Endlung became as smooth as silk with me: he spoke politely, told no more jokes at my expense, addressed me by my name and patronymic and always spoke politely.

I must say that for a man in my position the question of degrees of politeness is particularly complicated, since we court servants have a quite distinctive status. It is hard to explain why it is insulting to be called by your first name by some people, and insulting to be addressed formally by others. But the latter are the only people that I can serve, if you take my meaning.

Let me try to explain. I can only tolerate being called by my first name by individuals of the royal family. Indeed, I do not tolerate it, but regard it as a privilege and a special distinction. I would simply be mortified if Georgii Alexandrovich, Her Highness or one of their children, even the very youngest, suddenly addressed me formally by my first name and patronymic. Two years ago I had a disagreement with Ekaterina Ioannovna concerning a maid who was unjustly accused of frivolous behaviour. I demonstrated firmness and stood my ground, and the grand duchess took offence and addressed me in strictly formal terms for an entire week. I suffered greatly, lost weight and could not sleep at night. And then we clarified matters. With her typical magnanimity, Ekaterina Ioannovna acknowledged her error. I also apologised and was allowed to kiss her hand, and she kissed me on the forehead.

But I digress.

The card players were being served by the junior footman Lipps, a novice whom I had brought with me especially to get a good look at him and see what he was worth. He had previously served at the Estonian estate of Count Beckendorf and had been recommended to me by His Excellency's house steward, an old acquaintance of mine. He seems like quite an efficient young lad and doesn't talk a lot, but it takes a while to recognise a good servant, unlike a bad one. In a new post everyone makes a great effort to do his best; you have to wait six months or a year, or even two, to know for certain. I observed how Lipps poured coffee, how deftly he changed a soiled napkin, how he stood in his position – that is very, very important. He stood correctly, without shifting from one foot to the other or turning his head. I decided he could probably be allowed to serve guests at small receptions.

The game was proceeding normally. First Endlung lost, and Pavel Georgievich rode along the corridor on his back. Then

Fortune turned her face away from His Highness and the lieutenant demanded that the grand duke must run to the lavatory, completely undressed, and bring back a glass of water.

While Pavel Georgievich was giggling and taking his clothes off, I quietly slipped out through the door, called the valet, told him that none of the servants must look into the grand duke's saloon and took a cape from the duty compartment. When His Highness skipped out into the corridor, peering around and covering himself with his hand, I tried to throw this long item of clothing over him, but Pavel Georgievich indignantly refused, saying that a promise is a promise, and he ran to the lavatory and then back again, laughing very much all the time.

It was a good thing that Madamoiselle Declique did not glance out to see what all the laughter was about. Fortunately, despite the late hour, His Highness Mikhail Georgievich had not gone to bed yet – he was pleased to jump up and down on a chair and then swung on a curtain for a long time. The youngest of the grand dukes is usually asleep at half past eight, but this time Mademoiselle had felt it possible to indulge him, saying that His Highness was too excited by the journey and would not fall asleep anyway.

In our Green Court the children are not raised strictly, unlike in the Blue Court of the Kirilloviches, where they maintain the family traditions of the Emperor Nikolai Pavlovich. There boys are raised like soldiers: from the age of seven they learn campaign discipline, are toughened by sluicing with cold water and put to sleep in folding camp beds. But Georgii Alexandrovich is regarded as a liberal in the imperial family. He raises his sons leniently in the French manner and, in the opinion of his relatives, he has completely spoiled his only daughter, his favourite.

Her Highness, thank God, did not come out of her compartment either and did not witness Pavel Georgievich's prank. Ever since St Petersburg she had locked herself away with a book, and I even know which one it was: *The Kreutzer Sonata*, a work by Count Tolstoy. I have read it, in case there might be talk about it among us butlers, simply in order not to appear a complete dunce. In my opinion it makes extremely boring reading and is quite inappropriate for a nineteen-year-old girl, especially a grand princess. In St Petersburg Ekaterina Ioannovna would never have allowed her daughter to read such smut and I can only think that the novel was smuggled into the baggage. The lady-in-waiting Baroness Stroganova must have provided it; it could not have been anyone else.

The two sailors did not quieten down until it was almost morning, following which even I allowed myself the luxury of dozing for a while because, to be quite honest, I was really rather tired after all the bustle and commotion before we left, and I anticipated that the first day in Moscow would not be easy.